The Martyrdom of Madeline

by

Robert Williams Buchanan

The Martyrdom of Madeline
by Robert Williams Buchanan

ISBN: 978-93-63055-73-5

Published by

DOUBLE 9 BOOKS

2/13-B, Ansari Road
Daryaganj, New Delhi – 110002
info@double9books.com
www.double9books.com
Tel. 011-40042856

ABOUT THE AUTHOR

Robert Williams Buchanan was a Scottish poet, novelist, and dramatist. He was the son of Robert Buchanan (1813-1866), an Owenite speaker and journalist, and was born in Caverswall, Staffordshire, England. Buchanan senior, a native of Ayr, Scotland, resided in Manchester for a few years before moving to Glasgow, where Buchanan junior attended high school and university, where he studied alongside poet David Gray. His essay on Gray, originally published in the Cornhill Magazine, recounts their close connection and their travel to London in 1860 in search of renown. His friend, Scottish-American poet James Mackintosh Kennedy, stated in Scottish and American Poems that "Robert Buchanan, the well-known British poet and most genial and variously gifted man, visited America in 1884-85."He penned two poems about Buchanan, "Lament" for his leaving and "Robert Buchanan" after his death. Kennedy's son, born in 1885, was called Robert Buchanan Kennedy. Buchanan's first published works were collections of poetry produced while he was still living in Glasgow. He appears to have renounced them later in life, as they do not appear in any bibliographic references. His first book, Poems and Love Lyrics, was most likely published in 1857, despite being undated. It was reviewed at the Athenaeum in December 1857.

CONTENTS

PROLOGUE IN THE NIGHT

As the two women gazed at one another under the lamplight, one standing and looking down, the other sitting and looking up, you would have said they might have been twin sisters—they looked so wonderfully alike. Both were fair, with pale forget-me-not eyes, and skins delicately clear; both were tall and slight. Nor was there any very noticeable difference in the dress they wore. She who stood erect, with the rain beating down upon her head, wore only, besides her bonnet and dress of black stuff, a shawl wrapt tightly around her; the shawl was rich and valuable, but looked common enough in the dim light. She who sat, with her elbow on her knees and her chin resting in her open palms, wore a shawl too, and a plain stuff dress, sodden with the rain; her bonnet had fallen back, soaking and unheeded, on her shoulders, just held by the sodden strings.

A close observer, however, would have perceived a world of difference between these two women. The woman standing had the fierce, pained, impatient manner of a wild animal; every look, every gesture was self-contained, determined, yet full of overmastering anxiety, The woman sitting was a crushed, gin-sodden, passionless, powerless waif, with only the courage of a hunted pariah dog, to snap, and crawl uselessly away.

Both were very young, neither being more than twenty-one or twenty-two years of age.

'That way!—over the Bridge!' said the woman sitting, in a husky voice; then she added, as the other seemed about to pass on, 'Stop though! what are you going to stand?'

The other turned quickly, and again looked down with her large eager eyes.

'What do you want?—Money?' The voice was deep and clear, though it trembled a little.

'Yes, I'm as thirsty as a fish. Lend me a shilling, and I'll pay you back some night when I'm in luck. Only a shilling! that won't break you!'

'If I give you the money, what will you do with it?'

'Drink it,' was the curt reply.

Something in the answer had a curious effect on the hearer. She stooped softly down and looked earnestly in the other woman's face.

'You'll know me again when you see me?' 'Do you mind telling me your name?'

'Ellen,—never mind what else. Nell for snort.

'Where do you live?'

'Anywhere.'

'How old are you?'

'Lord knows. Twenty or thereabouts. Are you going to keep on questioning all the blessed night? I want something to drink.'

The girl who stood bent over the sitting girl and placed something in her hand. She uttered a suppressed cry.

'Gold! Why, you've given me a sovereign! What for?'

'I have only another, or I would give you more. I am sorry for you. Good night!'

'Stop! don't go. Let me have another look at you.'

'Well?'

'What a fool I was! Why you're *a lady!*'

It was the other's turn to laugh now—a low, bitter laugh.

'And you've got on a real Injy shawl—let me feel it! And there's a pair of gold bracelets on your wrists! Well, I'm——!!'

This with a prolonged half whistle, expressive of utter surprise. Then she continued—

'I don't know who you are, or where you're a-going, but the streets ain't safe for the likes of *you*. You'd best go home, my lady!'

'I have no home.'

'What!'

'What home I had I have left, never to go back. I am leaving London.'

'Where are you going?'

'Anywhere.' After a moment's pause she pointed across the river and over the house-tops, and added, 'Out there.'

'Friends there, I suppose?'

'No friends.'

'And not much coin. Ah, well, you've them swell bracelets; and the shawl, too, is worth money.'

It was very strange—innocent as the remark seemed, it appeared to make the tall figure of the listener tremble with agitation, perhaps with anger. With a quick impetuous movement she drew off her bracelets and threw them into the girl's lap.

'Take them—I don't want them! And the shawl too—take it, and give me yours.'

'No, you're joking!'

'Quick!'

In a moment the change was effected; and the women now stood erect and face to face. The commoner and more outcast creature seemed utterly stupefied by what had taken place. Suddenly the other seized both her hands, and said quickly—

'The river—is it there?'

A light seemed suddenly to flash in upon the outcast's bewildered brain.

'You're not a-going to drown yourself? No!' 'I don't know—perhaps!'

This with a peculiar smile.

'It's no use; there's too many eyes a-watching. I tried it myself once, slap off the Embankment, but I was fished out like a wet rag. Don't you be such a fool! You're a lady, and you had best go home.'

Without replying, the lady began to move rapidly away. Seized by a peculiar impulse, the outcast cried after her—'Come back—take your things—it's a shame for me to have them. Take them back.'

'No; keep them. Good-bye. May I kiss you?' 'If you like,' was the stupefied reply.

The lips of the two women met, their breaths mingled for a moment. Then, while the one stood petrified, staring in utter astonishment, the other flitted rapidly and silently away.

CHAPTER I
A DANCING LESSON UNDER DIFFICULTIES

Twelve years before the occurrence of the incident described in my prologue, a curious group was assembled in a quiet corner of Grayfleet Churchyard. Gray fleet is a damp, aguish, lonely, desolate village, on the verge of the great Essex marshes; and its old church, like a skull with two empty, lifeless eyes, gazes with two dreary windows right down on the marshes, towards that low-lying mist where they mingle with the sea.

The group of which I have spoken consisted of some six girls and one little boy. The girls were of divers ages, from six to sixteen, and all were more or less smartly dressed in holiday clothes, for it was a Good Friday. They stood in a ring round a flat tombstone, grey with age, and green with slime of moss. On this tombstone a fair little girl of eight, with dishevelled hair and flushed cheeks, was practising the first steps of a dance. Her instructress was the eldest of the party, a pale, red-haired wench of sixteen, who watched her with keenly critical eyes, and at times stepped forward, took her place on the tombstone, and showed her how to use her feet.

First position—heel and toe—cut and shuffle.

'Lookee here, Mawther!' cried one of the girls to a passer by. 'Come and see Polly Lowther teaching Mark Peartree's girl to dance.'

¯Another girl came running into the churchyard, and joined the group.

'That's the style!' exclaimed Polly Lowther, as the red-haired girl was called. 'You'll soon learn, if you only try. Look at me, Madlin. Watch my feet.'

First position—heel and toe—cut and shuffle.

The girls clapped their hands enthusiastically, and the little boy, who was sitting astride on a green grave, grinned approval.

Fired by the applause bestowed on her teacher, the little fair girl— 'Madlin,' as the others called her—began wildly practising the steps.

First position—heel and toe—cut and shuffle.

Suddenly there was a rush, a cry. The troop of girls scattered on every side and disappeared: the little boy cried and ran. Only 'Madlin' remained, so absorbed for the time being in her dancing that for a moment she did not notice that she was left alone, and that a tall figure in black, with white neckcloth, stood frowning at her.

The next moment she was conscious of her predicament. Flushed and panting, she stood and gazed, and recognised to her horror the Rector of the parish.

She gave one glance around, to see if she was quite abandoned, and then, seeing no trace of her companions, she curtsied timidly, and stood her ground.

'Little girl,' said the Rector, in a terrible voice, 'I don't know you—what is your name?'

She hung her head awkwardly, and made no reply.

'Do you hear me? What is your name?'

The little girl raised her head, looked straight at the Rector, and answered in a clear voice—

'If you please, sir, I'm Madlin—Mark Peartree's girl.'

The Rector's brows came down still more.

'Mark Peartree; I think I know the man—he lives down at the ferry, and sails in a barge. Is he your father?'

The girl, who had a common straw hat swinging by the ribbon in her mouth, gnawed the ribbon, and replied shortly—

'No, he ain't.'

'What is he, then?' asked the Rector. 'Some relation?'

'No,' was the immediate reply. 'I call him uncle, but he isn't a *real* uncle, nor Uncle Luke neither. I'm a foundling—Aunt Jane found me, out *there!*'

And with a back sweep of her hand, the little girl indicated the great marshes, steaming and reddening in the setting sun.

'And whoever you are, are you not aware,' said the Rector, improving the occasion, 'that you are a very wicked little girl? Upon this holy day of all days in the year I find you practising a vicious pastime here, in God's own acre! On a tombstone! Little girl, do you know that there is a dead fellow-creature lying under you, and that you are profaning his place of rest?'

The girl gave a start and a scared look downward, as if half expecting the dead man to arise and confront her; then half unconsciously she edged off the tombstone and stood ankle deep in the long churchyard grass.

'I am afraid,' said the Rector, shaking his forefinger at her. 'I am really very much afraid that you have been very badly brought up. Tell me, have you ever heard the word of God? Do you ever go to church?'

The answer was at any rate prompt and explicit.

'No—never.'

'Ah, I thought so. A sad case. And your father—I mean your adopted father—is he not ashamed of himself to bring you up in ignorance and sin?'

This was touching rather a dangerous chord. The little girl flushed, panted, opened her large blue eyes full on the minister and exclaimed—

'Uncle Mark isn't ashamed of himself, no more is Uncle Luke! They go to their meeting, and I go too. They're United Brethren, and when I grow up, *I'm* to be a Brethren too!9

'Brethren!'

This was said in a tone which clearly implied that their cup of moral delinquency, in the Rector's eyes, was now full and overflowing. The good pastor could have endured a family which repudiated Christianity altogether, but any form of Dissent was worse even than the rankest blasphemy. It is doubtful what turn the interview would have taken, but just at this moment an unexpected diversion took place. A thin shrill voice, doubtless appertaining to one of the little girl's late companions, suddenly pealed out, from some mysterious corner where its owner lay hidden—

'Look out, Madlin! Here's your Uncle Luke a-comin'!'

Madeline looked startled; then, strange to say, her face grew quite bright and eager. The Rector seemed perplexed, and uncertain what to say next. Just then the gate of the churchyard opened, and a little man, with very short legs and a very large head, looked in, and seeing Madeline, quietly entered.

'Uncle! Uncle Luke!'

The little man nodded his head and smiled. Then, seeing the Rector, he took off his hat and grinned.

It was a peculiarity of the little man that he expressed all thoughts and moods by means of a rather mindless smile, sometimes broadening into a grin. For the rest, he had large watery eyes and a large mouth, and his general appearance was homely and awkward in the extreme.

By this time Madeline was at his side, holding his hand and looking up into his face.

The Rector strode across the churchyard.

'I have just been warning this child against dancing upon the tombstones. I have told her that she is a very wicked child, and she has informed me that her relations belong to some Methodist persuasion. Be that as it may, you will doubtless agree with me that her conduct to-day has been extremely sacrilegious.'

The little man, still holding his hat in his hand, looked at the Rector, then looked at Madeline, then smiled imbecilely, then, feeling the smile out of place, tried to frown, but only succeeded in distorting his good-humoured countenance into a confirmed grin. Then suddenly darting his mouth down to the little girl's ear, he hoarsely whispered—

'What is it, Madlin? What's the matter?'

'Polly Lowther was teaching me to cut and shuffle,' said the girl out loud, fixing her eyes in a fearless way on the Rector; 'and Parson came out and found us, and all the others ran away. I know dancing's wicked, because Uncle Mark says so, but I couldn't help it, and Parson says Uncle Mark ought to be ashamed of himself, and I told Parson it isn't *true!*'

This explanation seemed to confuse the little man still more. He scratched his head and peeped at the Rector with a grin.

'Dancing's downright wicked,' he said, 'no doubt o' that.'

'It is no laughing matter,' cried the Rector, indignantly, irritated at the unaccountable expression on the little man's face. 'Be good enough to leave the precincts of the church. The child is a bad child, and has been badly trained. There, there, hold your tongue—I desire no further explanations; only remember this, if that child desecrates the churchyard again, I shall resort to severer measures.'

So saying he waved the pair from the churchyard, shut the gate sharply upon them, and stalked away to the Rectory, with a bosom full of holy emotion and Christian wrath.

The little man stood for some minutes in the open road, dazed, gaping, and looking at the tall retreating figure. Then he quietly put on his hat, and, conscious of the little hand within his own, looked down at his companion, at a loss what to say or do. At last he cut the Gordian knot of his perplexity by grinning from ear to ear.

'Parson be in a powerful rage,' he said; 'but dancing be downright wicked, that's a fact;' and he added, with a perplexed look, as if communing with his own thoughts, 'What shall I say to your Uncle Mark?'

Madeline seemed to muse for some moments, then, as if struck by a sudden inspiration, she exclaimed—

'Come along, Uncle Luke—let's go home.'

The little man laughed contentedly, as if finding in the proposition a solution of all his difficulty; and the little legs began to move. Hand in hand, the two hurried down the descent leading from the church to the outskirts of the village. As they went along, Madeline peeped up quietly from time to time at her companion, as if trying to read his thoughts; then, squeezing his hand tight, she said in a coaxing voice—

'Uncle Luke!'

'Yes, Madlin.'

'You won't tell Uncle Mark about my dancing.'

'I don't know—dancing be downright wicked.'

'I couldn't help it. Polly Lowther offered to teach me, and all the other girls can dance a bit. And if you won't say a word to Uncle Mark, I'll let you cut up my new money-box that Uncle Mark gave me, and find out what's inside.'

Unaccountable as it may seem, this extraordinary proposition seemed to find peculiar favour in Uncle Luke's eyes. His large eyes twinkled, and his mouth broadened from ear to ear, but he pretended to shake his head from side to side in solemn deprecation of the bribe. Madeline watched him keenly, and just as he seemed wavering, she lifted his great brown hand to her mouth, and gave it a passionate kiss. This seemed to unsettle Uncle Luke altogether, and he murmured eagerly—

'All right, Madlin, I shan't tell.'

And Madeline knew well that a promise of this sort from Uncle Luke was as good as an oath from any other man. They quickened their pace, but she continued to play with and fondle his hand, and now and then to hold it to her lips. Confidence of this sort was what the little man loved best of all things in the world, and the smile upon his face grew broad and bright with intelligent content.

CHAPTER II
'UNCLE' LUKE AND 'UNCLE' MARK

While the setting sun gleamed on Grayfleet, its grim church, and its cluster of red-tiled dwellings, Uncle Luke took a footpath leading across the marshes. All around them the landscape was flat and level, with little or no vegetation; for over the dark low levels the sea had crawled, and would crawl again. Here and there hovered a seagull, tempted in from the distant salt water, and searching the marsh for plunder; and once, as they passed a shallow pool, blood-red in the light, a heron rose with a harsh cry and flapped slowly away.

A walk of half a mile across the marsh brought them to the river side, and within view of a sort of pendant to the upper village, in the shape of a row of tiny red-tiled cottages on the very bank. Here there was a ferry-house, with a licence 'to sell ale and tobacco.'

As they turned into the river path, the ferry-boat was crossing leisurely, with a freight of country girls on their way home from Grayfleet.

Uncle Luke trotted cheerfully along, still holding Madeline by the hand. Her eyes were now on the shining river and the drifting ferry-boat, and she had almost forgotten her scene with the Rector.

They were a curious pair. The girl was a slender slight thing, wild as some wayside weed. Her form was curiously light and graceful; her face, with its large passionate eyes, very wistful and sad. The common cotton frock and coarse country shoes and stockings became her well, though her limbs were somewhat long and shapeless as yet. And if the girl was not a little fairylike, Uncle Luke would certainly have passed well for a Gnome, or say rather, one of those quaint Trolls whose task it was, according to Scandinavian legend, to work busily in the bowels of the earth.

All the week long Uncle Luke *did* work, on the black river barge of which he was mate and his brother captain. From Monday to Saturday his figure was clad in blue jersey, red cap, and rough tarpaulin trousers, and he helped to work the barge on its short journeys up and down the crowded river. But on the present occasion, it being a holiday, his attire was radiant—a high chimney pot hat, very broad at the brim, and large enough to descend to his ears, a blue pilot coat, a white waistcoat, and a coloured cotton shirt, blue navy trousers, and lace-up boots. For Uncle Luke loved splendour, and nothing suited him better than to shine glorious in the eyes of his neighbours; though Uncle Mark, who was his elder brother, and strictly pious, disapproved of all these vanities of apparel.

It may be admitted, without further preamble, that Uncle Luke, though able-bodied, was mentally deficient; indeed, in the estimation of many sober and wiser people, a simple fool, or, in the local parlance, little better than a natural. Yet his shortcomings were by no means upon the surface, and it would have taken a very wise man to understand them at a glance. He was harmless, industrious, and in some respects particularly shrewd. He knew how many pence make a shilling, and how many shillings a pound, as well as most men, and he had a sharp intuitive perception of human character. With all this he was simple beyond measure, and his reasoning faculties were absolutely infinitesimal.

Great as was his good nature, he strongly resented any imputation on his sagacity. His brother Mark had secured him work at a very low wage, on the understanding that he was weak and easily tired; and there on the barge, under his brother's eye, he laboured cheerfully, save when some one was cruel enough to take advantage of his weakness or to deride his infirmity. At such times, he was subject to wild fits of passion. When these were over, he would creep into the cabin, cry like a child, and perhaps take to his hammock for days.

But to-day he looked happy enough, partly on account of his lucky escape from the Rector, and partly because Madeline had promised him the unparalleled treat of cutting open her bright new money-box.

This was a kind of temptation he never could resist. Had he possessed a watch, he would have taken it to pieces to examine the works; and he had been languishing with curiosity for days, puzzling his head, as many a child has done, to know what was inside the money-box labelled 'Savings' Bank,' with its front pointed like a town hall, and a slit in its top for the reception of vagrant pence.

Having come in sight of the ferry, the two walked on quickly. The sun blazed down on them with golden splendour, and from beneath their feet the dust arose in a cloud. Neither spoke; Madeline continued to impress an occasional kiss on the hand which she still held fondly in hers—and to each of these exhibitions of feeling her companion replied by a broad grin. Suddenly, however, he gave a start and, looking down at his flushed and dusty companion, said quickly—

'I say, Madlin, you'd best put on your Sunday hat. There be Uncle Mark at the garden gate!'

Without a word, Madeline obeyed. She took the hat, which for coolness and comfort she had swung on her arm, and tied it carefully on her head. Then regaining possession of her uncle's hand, she walked decorously up to one of the little green cottage gates, on the other side of which stood, indeed, her Uncle Mark.

Though Luke and Mark were brothers, they were as unlike one another as two men could possibly be. Mark Peartree stood six feet in his shoes; he was very thin, and he stooped slightly at the shoulders. His hair was grey, his face red as a Ripston pippin, but his cheeks were sunken, perhaps from the loss of many teeth.

The cottage was one of a row of red brick, with creepers crawling over the front, a small plot of garden facing the river, enclosed by green wooden railings and a green wooden gate. Upon one of the gates now leaned Uncle Mark, clad, too, in his Sunday best, but much less gaudily than Luke, and looking down the road with impatience marked on every lineament of his face.

'Here you be at last,' he said, when the vagrant pair came up. 'Why, mate alive, can't you be home at meal times? Mother's in a powerful rage. Brother Brown be coming this afternoon, and he'll be here afore we can get our wittles done!'

At this speech the smile faded from Luke's face; but, before he could utter a word in reply, another voice, evidently that of a female, chimed in from the cottage—

'I'm sure, father, it be like you to be asking Brother Brown and the Brethren here of a Good Friday, as if we didn't get enough of them every day i' the year. However, coming they be, but we shan't get the dinner over any the quicker with you standing racketing there!'

The speaker stood in the doorway, the red brick and the green creepers framing her as she stood. A comfortable looking woman, dressed in a clean cotton gown, with a coarse white apron tied round her waist. She was short and stout, with a brown good-humoured face and glossy black hair. She wore a cap the long ends of which were thrown over her shoulders and pinned behind, as if for freedom; her sleeves were rolled up nearly to the elbow, and her hands and arms were mottled brown and red with constant work in soap and water.

At sight of this figure, no other indeed than Mrs. Mark Peartree, or, as Madeline called her, 'Aunt Jane,' the good-humoured grin again took possession of Uncle Luke's face. Passing through the little gate he made for the door and at once entered the house, while Madeline transferred her attentions to Uncle Mark.

'It wasn't any fault o' Uncle Luke's,' she said, looking up into the weather-beaten face, 'indeed, Uncle Mark, 'twas all on account o' *me* that he was so long—I was up there with Polly Lowther, looking at the graves.'

In her eagerness to excuse her favourite, Madeline might have revealed the dreaded secret of the dance, but Uncle Mark, who had his own reasons for wishing to get the dinner quickly disposed of, patted her hand and said—

'All right, Madlin, my lass;' and, taking her small hot hand in his big horny first, led her into the house.

It was a very small house. A long narrow passage led from the front door to the back, and midway in the passage was a flight of narrow carpetless stairs. On the right opened out two rooms—a kitchen, and a parlour, as it was called. During the week, while the men were at work on the river, the parlour was carefully closed up. No fire was ever lit in it—it was dark, well polished, and genteel, with a bit of drugget for a carpet, a china shepherd and shepherdess, and several shells on the mantelpiece, and on the walls two highly illuminated pictures, one representing the Prodigal Son, the other Susannah and the Elders. But in the centre of the mantelpiece stood the crowning glory of the apartment—a small 'weather-cottage' made of wood, formed in the shape of a roofed shed, and containing two figures, one of 'Darby' and another of 'Joan,' standing on either side of a piece of wood, suspended in the centre by a quicksilver pole. When the weather was fine, Joan swung out, with her basket on her arm, as if going to market, and left Darby under cover; when it was wet, Joan retreated, and Darby emerged to brave the elements like a man. This weather-cottage was a miracle of art in Madeline's eyes, and was regarded with no little reverence by all the members of the house. Indeed, the parlour altogether was a sanctuary, full of a pious clamminess and darkness, and even Mrs. Peartree never entered it without a certain awe, tempered with a sense of increased respectability. From week's end to week's end they remained in the red-tiled kitchen, while on Sunday evening, and indeed on every festive occasion like the present, the parlour was thrown open for the family use.

CHAPTER III
EASTER SOLEMNITIES OF THE BRETHREN

It was in the paven kitchen, however, that the party now assembled, and taking their seats round the square deal table, which was spread with a clean table-cloth, began at once upon the dinner—a boiled leg of pork and potatoes.

With her little feet swinging to and fro, and her large blue wistful eyes roving wistfully about the room, Madeline sat and ate up her portion contentedly. The sun streaming through the back window caressed her bright cheek and dusty hair, and made her think of the glad light which had touched her only a short time ago, while she had been learning to dance upon the tombs. Suddenly a strange thought seemed to strike her.

'Uncle Mark,' she said, while Uncle Luke dropped his knife and fork in wonder, 'can dead folk *feel?*'

'No, my lass,' returned Uncle Mark, with some little surprise in his mild blue eyes. 'Dead men is dead as nails is—they can't feel nothing. What put that into your head?'

But Madeline did not answer; a sense of great satisfaction had stolen over her at this brief assurance, and, with a glance of meaning at Uncle Luke, she said to herself that, for once in his life, the parson had been wrong.

Dinner being over, there was a general movement, and a great awe came over the family as the door of communication between the kitchen and parlour was thrown open, and the latter was seen in all its sepulchral splendour. Uncles Mark and Luke passed reverently in, and closed the door; but soon Madeline was made straight and clean, and sent in after them, while Aunt Jane, who seemed seized with unaccountable irritability, remained to tidy up the kitchen.

Once in the parlour, Madeline crept up to the window, and gazed with wistful dreamy eyes across the little garden on the great still river, which crept past flashing and darkening in the sun. Uncle Mark, seated on a very shiny and sticky horsehair sofa, was deep in the pages of the family Bible, while Uncle Luke, with a face as grave as a judge, was repeating in an undertone the words of an Easter hymn. All was quiet and still in the sepulchral chamber; but through the closed door they could distinctly hear the rattling of dishes, the clangour of pots and pans, from the kitchen. Presently this rattling and clangour became positively furious, and simultaneously a loud rat-a-tat was heard at the front door. Finally, to the same noisy accompaniment, the room door was opened, and a number of visitors came in one by one.

They consisted of a tall thin man, dressed in glossy black, with a long thin face, broad protruding forehead, and a bald head; followed by several very rough-looking figures in high hats and rude Sunday suits. Each as he entered doffed his hat, with a nod of solemn greeting to Uncles Mark and Luke. The tall man paused in the centre of the room and breathed heavily, while Uncle Mark rose to receive him. He was evidently expected.

The tall man in black, a retired tradesman, known in the neighbourhood as 'Brother Brown,' was the leader of the sect known as the 'United Brethren,' of which Uncles Mark and Luke were lowly members. He was a person of some importance and some property, but, having no wider field in which to practise his feats of piety, he was content every Sunday to visit the row of cottages, and, gathering his satellites together in one house or another, discourse to them on the lights and shadows of another world.

After the keen glance into the room, Brother Brown gave his whole hand to Uncle Mark, and the tips of his fingers to Uncle Luke, nodded grimly to Madeline, and sinking on the sofa, covered his face with large red hands, and sank into deep silence. This manoeuvre was followed by all the others present except Madeline. Each covered his face with his hand, and took a gentle header, so to speak, into himself. If we may continue the metaphor, all remained under water for many minutes. The effect was awe-inspiring.

At last Brother Brown uncovered his face and came up refreshed; the other men emerged one by one.

'Brother Peartree,' he said, addressing Uncle Mark, 'are we all here?'

'Yes, sir,' answered Uncle Mark, while his blue eyes wandered over the group. 'Here be Brother Strangeways, Brother Smith, Brother Hornblower, Brother Billy Horn-blower, Brother Luke Peartree, and myself. Not to speak of little Madlin—she axed to come in, and a child can't begin too early.'

Brother Brown coughed heavily and looked at the kitchen door, through which came at intervals a dull clangour as of pots and pans.

'Then I suppose,' he said, 'Sister Peartree is still obdurate. Will she not join our little gathering, and listen for once to the words of healing?'

Uncle Mark looked very red and uncomfortable, and jerked his thumb awkwardly towards the door.

'Never mind the missus to-day, Brother Brown—she's had a heap o' worrit during the week, and the fact is, she ain't just tidy enough to come into the best parlour.'

Brother Brown's heavy brow darkened.

'"Six days shalt thou labour,"' he said. 'Well, brother, you are the head of your own house, and I leave our unregenerate sister to you. Let us pray.'

Thereupon all, including Madeline, knelt down, while Brother Brown exercised his spirit in a long prayer, with variations and expressions of sympathy in the form of low groans and ejaculations from his companions— who had all again (to resume a former metaphor) retired under water. Emerging once more, and receiving a signal from Brother Brown, Brother Billy Hornblower, an overgrown young bargee of twenty, began a homely hymn, in which all the others gruffly joined.

> Pilot the boat to the City of Jesus,
> Up with the tide, though there's danger afloat*
> Far up the stream lies the City of Jesus,
> Dark is the night, but we'll pilot the boat.
> > Chorus.
> Pilot the boat, mates! pilot the boat!
> Hark, the wind rises—there's danger afloat—
> Courage! for up to the City of Jesus,
> Steadily, safely, we'll pilot the boat.
> See, mates, the lights of the City of Jesus,
> Steer for them lights, thro' the dangers afloat—
> Up to the wharves of the City of Jesus,
> Ere the tide turns, we must pilot the boat.
> > Chorus.
> Pilot the boat, mates! pilot the boat!
> Hark, the wind rises—there's danger afloat—
> Courage! and up to the City of Jesus,
> Steadily, safely, we'll pilot the boat.

As the music grew louder, the clatter in the kitchen increased, to the obvious dissatisfaction of Brother Mark. The hymn ceased, and Brother Brown delivered a short sermon, founded on the text, 'Those that go down to the sea in ships,' which was felt to be especially suitable to those who went down the river in barges.

After this, Brother Mark rose, and in a few brief words, interspersed freely with Scriptural quotations, addressed the Brethren, taking for his theme the sacred character of the day, and greatly troubling the soul of little Madeline by gloomy references to dead sinners in their graves.

After a short address to the same effect from Brother Strangeways, a waterside worthy with a very weatherbeaten face and a very weather wise sort of oratory, and another hymn from Brother Billy Hornblower, the service was concluded.

Then, as a concluding solemnity, all shook hands, and the conversation suddenly grew secular.

'Going down with the tide i' the morning, mate?' asked Brother Strangeways. 'It be high water at four, and we be loaded since day afore yesterday.'

'Where for, mate?' asked Uncle Mark.

'Down right away Southam,' was the reply.

'Well, mate, *I* be anchored at home with the old woman till Monday, and then I goes up with first flood to Crewsham Basin.'

'Lime?' asked Brother Strangeways, sententiously.

'Lime it is,' answered Brother Mark, and forthwith the talk became professional.

In the meantime, Brother Brown had drawn from his pocket several loose leaves or tracts, a species of torpedo which he was in the habit of dropping surreptitiously wherever he went, for the confusion of recalcitrant and unrepentant sinners. Selecting three of these, each of which had special reference to the forlorn spiritual condition of a person of the other sex, he proceeded to pin them on the parlour walls—one over the Shepherdess on the mantelpiece, a second under the picture of the Prodigal Son, a third under that of Susannah and the Elders. When this was done he shook hands with Uncle Mark, nodded to Uncle Luke, and passed out of the house; the other men, each with a 'Good night, mate,' for each of the two Pear-trees, immediately followed, solemnly, in single file.

No sooner had the street door closed than Mrs. Pear-tree, with the sleeves of her gown tucked up to the elbow, entered the precincts of the chamber. Scorn was in every lineament of her countenance, but directly her eyes fell on the parlour walls, the scorn deepened to wrath.

'Brother Brown's been at them walls again,' she cried. I wonder at *you,* Mark Peartree, to sit still and see him do it. Tracts agin your own wedded wife, stuck on the walls of her own best parlour—oh, I'd "tract" him!'

As she spoke, she made a dash at each of the papers in succession, and tore them angrily away.

'My lass,' said Uncle Mark, gruffly, 'read'em—they're left for your convarsion.'

'Stuff and rubbish!'

'Salvation ain't rubbish, mother, and this here earth's a wale. A wale it is! And let me tell you, tho' you are my missus, it don't become you to put Brother Brown so much about. Why, while we was a-singing, I heard you clattering the dishes like a barge a-heaving anchor, and I see Brother Brown looking at the door out of the corner of his eyes. No, my lass, it don't become you, and it ain't settin' a good example to little Madlin, who may be a wessel herself by and by.'

'Never, if I can help it,' answered the woman. 'We've wessels enough in *our* family, what with you and Uncle Luke. Look at the mark o' the dirty muddy feet on the clean carpet. I wish you'd meet outside, or in some other house but mine.'

'And I wish *you'd* join us—it'd do you a power of good.'

Mrs. Peartree's only answer was to toss her head and walk back into the kitchen. Uncle Luke followed very crestfallen and pitiful at the domestic disagreement; while Uncle Mark remained in the parlour, and showed the pictures in Foxe's 'Book of Martyrs'—a precious tome of tremendous antiquity—to Madeline. The child shuddered as she saw on every page flame consuming those who testified to the truth in evil times.

'Uncle Mark,' she said, 'do they ever burn people *now?*'

'Not in this here world, my lass; only in t'other. And even then only the wery bad ones—them as hates their neighbours, and can come to no manner o' good *without* burning!'

Madeline did not answer, but she thought of Aunt Jane, who was the very essence of gentleness and good nature, but who was made utterly unregenerate by the intensity of her hate for Brother Brown.

CHAPTER IV
UNCLE MARK PARTS WITH THE OLD BARGE

When Madeline slipped from her bed on the Tuesday after Easter Monday, drew aside the chintz curtains from her little window and looked forth, she was astonished to see that the sunshine of the preceding days had been followed by a drizzling rain. The river looked black and very solemn as it slipped between its sedgy banks; the marshes, turning a white face to the sullen sky, looked dreary enough as they drank in the falling rain, and the red tiles on the houses of Grayfleet were redder than ever with the ceaseless washing of the showers.

She had slept heavily, but had not yet wholly recovered from the depression caused by the preaching of the past few days, and of so many hours spent in the sanctuary of the best room.

She dressed hastily, ran down stairs, and peeped into the parlour at the 'weather cottage.' Alas! Joan was under shelter, and Darby was outside. So it was to be a wet day indeed!

The house was very quiet. The front door stood open and a clammy breeze swept into the passage and kissed her cheeks. The parlour had been cleared out an hour before by Aunt Jane's industrious hands, and was carefully prepared for next Sunday. But a clear fire burned in the kitchen, casting its light on the bright paven floor, and upon the buxom figure of Aunt Jane herself, who stood by the table preparing breakfast.

'Eh, bless the child, how you did make me jump!' she exclaimed, as Madeline put her* head in at the door.

'Come, lass, and get your breakfast; 'tis near time you were starting for school.'

After bestowing a hearty kiss on Mrs. Peartree's sunburnt cheek, Madeline took her seat at the table; then suddenly looking round she asked:—

'Why, Aunt Jane, where be Uncle Luke?'

'Gone away two hours or more wi' Uncle Mark; they sailed up wi' the tide an hour afore thou was out o' thy bed!'

'Gone to London without *me!*' cried Madeline, her large eyes filling with tears. 'Uncle Luke did promise to take me with him this time!'

'There, there, ha' done wi' your crying, like a good lass!' said Aunt Jane, soothingly. Your Uncle Luke he did want to take ye, but I would have none on't this woyage. A pretty like morning to take you from your bed!—why the rain was falling and the wind blowing enough to give you your death. But if you are a good lass and learn your lessons well you shall go next time. They'll bring down the barge to-morrow, and likely they'll be for taking her back o' Thursday. Then you shall go.'

With this assurance Madeline was fain to content herself. She had been on the barge once or twice when it had lain in Gray fleet basin, opposite the ferry; she had seen it spread out its great red wings and glide along the track of the river—until it looked like a great black swan—passing silently between the marshes, and fading behind the grey mist which for ever hung about them like a cloud; and her childish imaginations had often conjured up pictures of the strange scenes towards which the great black swan was drifting. London was to her the great world, the mysterious city, so different to the dark slimy river and low-lying marshes of Grayfleet. Ever since she could remember, this magic word 'London' had been the one which had ever urged her on to good deeds, the final goal to which all her virtuous deeds were to lead. Whenever she was bad, Aunt Jane never forgot to repeat the awful words—

'There, Madlin, if you can't be a better lass, you shall never go to London with me and Uncle Mark.'

And when she had been unusually good she never failed to hear the timeworn promise—

'You've been downright good! You shall go to London with me, and see the great waxwork wi' the kings and queens, and the Sleepin' Beauty as large as life.'

When this magical visit was to be paid seemed somewhat indefinite. That Aunt Jane was strongly opposed to what she called 'gadding about,' may be gathered from the fact that during the six-and-twenty years of her married life she had spent only two days out of her own home. But Madeline had been content to hope and wait on—and dream over the many things she would do when at length the happy day did come. Just before Easter, however, she went half wild with ecstasy—for Uncle Luke in the exuberance of his gratitude to her for not laughing at him when his curiosity induced him to cut open a cheap concertina, 'to see where the music came from,' promised to take her immediately on to the barge and show her himself the wonderful sights of the great City.

It was a great blow to Madeline to learn that her uncles had departed to the magical place without her, but by the time she had finished her breakfast the sadness caused by the disappointment had worn away. She bestowed another impulsive kiss on Aunt Jane's brown cheek, and taking her books under her arm, trotted off gleefully through the rain towards the great red-brick public school where most of her days were spent.

She was wonderfully light-hearted all day, and when evening came she firmly refused Polly Lowther's invitation to take another dancing lesson, and trotted home to keep Aunt Jane company. She found the kitchen neat and clean as usual, with plates sparkling on the dresser, dishes smiling from the walls, and Mrs. Peartree sitting in their midst with a skein of worsted round her neck, and her busy fingers darning Uncle Mark's guernsey. When Madeline came she laid her work aside and got the tea. The two sat down together.

'Madlin, what in the world be you a-laughing at?' asked Aunt Jane presently, astonished at the continual outbursts and half-smothered laughter of the child.

But for the life of her Madeline would not tell—she only knew that she felt within her a strange hysterical sort of joy which would not be suppressed. Everything made her laugh; the gleaming dishes, the glancing firelight, the cat purring on the hearth, Aunt Jane's sunburnt face, and even her looks of astonishment and frowns of reproach.

Mrs. Peartree looked distressed; for she was superstitious.

'As sure as you're alive, Madlin,' she cried reprovingly, 'that laugh o' yourn means no good. I mind the day my poor brother Jim were drowned dead—I was laughing like a mad thing afore I got the news. Them as laughs i' the morning will cry before night, I'm thinking.'

At this solemn warning Madeline's hilarity received a sudden check, only to burst out again with renewed vehemence.

''Tis not on account of bad news, Aunt Jane!' she said, ''tis because I'm soon going with Uncle Mark to London!'

But Aunt Jane was not to be convinced. She gravely shook her head, and a few hours later when she put the child to bed she said:—

'There, Madlin, try to go to sleep, do, and give o'er that giggling—'tain't nature for a child to laugh so—and 'twill take all the sleep from my eyes wi' thinkin' o' my poor dear brother that's gone to heaven.'

Madeline promised implicit obedience, and nestled her dark little head into the snowy pillow. When she found herself alone, she slipped from her bed, drew aside the window curtain and looked out, half expecting to see the great black barge sail, like a spectre, through the hazy mist of rain. But no such vision appeared—the faint ray of the young moon showed her the silently sleeping river, through the silvery threads of rain which still fell from the ever-darkening sky.

'Uncle Mark, Uncle Luke!' exclaimed Madeline, clapping her hands, 'make haste and come home, and I'll try not to laugh any more.'

At that moment the barge, with Uncles Mark and Luke on board, was gliding slowly up the river, ten miles away. The wind had been fair all day and the barge had made good speed, but as night came on and the rain fell faster, the breeze completely died.

The barge lay heavily on the shining river, with the great red sail flapping listlessly above and black shadows all around. They had hoisted the side-lights, and now and then through the impenetrable blackness a faint light answered them—this was the only indication of human life which came to them at all.

Uncle Luke was at the helm, peering with his small keen grey eyes into the blackness; and Uncle Mark was below, eating his supper. Presently the latter passed his red night-capped head out of the hatchway, and gave a sharp glance around him; then his whole long body emerged, and he strolled to Luke's side.

'Well, mate,' he said, 'there don't seem much wind, and I'm a-feared there ain't much a-coming; suppose you go and turn in?'

But Uncle Luke shook his head decidedly.

'No, no, Mark!' he answered; 'reckon *you're* more knocked up nor what I be. Just you turn in for a bit while 'tis calm—and when the wind comes I'll sing out.'

After a little more discussion as to which should get the first spell of sleep, Uncle Mark descended to the cabin and Luke was left alone.

It was very dreary above, very dark and wet; but Uncle Luke, who was generally in a happy state of mind, seemed quite contented. He grasped the tiller firmly in his hard, horny hand, and fixed his eyes with wonderful keenness upon the moving lights around him.

There was scarcely any wind at all now, and the barge lay like a log; but ever and anon she was lifted up as on a bosom in gentle breathing, while the great sail flapped listlessly above, and the side-lights shone out like glimmering stars in the darkness, and flashed their brightness at the sky which loomed so darkly overhead.

An hour or so passed thus, and then the rain gradually ceased to fall, the black in the sky began to float gently on before a cold, light wind, which bellied out the sail, swung the heavy boom over the side, and made the barge glide softly on.

Uncle Luke, holding the tiller more firmly, rapped sharply on the deck with his hob-nailed shoes, and in a very short space of time Uncle Mark emerged, fresh and active, from the cabin hatchway.

'Ah, we shall get a goodish bit o' wind before morning, mate,' he said as he took possession of the tiller; 'get the sheets clear, Luke, we mustn't lose much time i' working round;—remember the old barge ain't been over spry sin' she got water-logged, and there be goodish bit o' traffic here.'

Uncle Luke trotted aft obediently, and now that Mark had relieved him of all responsibility, he turned his mind again to solve the great problem which had been worrying him ever since he left home—whether he should take Madeline a present from the great City, or allow her to buy it for herself when she got there.

While he was speculating thus, his eyes were dreamily surveying the scene around him, and his hands were busy hauling in the sheets, for the breeze was coming more and more ahead, and less upon the quarter.

As the night passed off and day began to dawn, the breeze grew fresher and fresher, until it spread quite fiercely over the surface of the water, driving it up into little crisp wavelets fringed with foam.

The thick black clouds had drifted westwards, and left the east a mass of scarlet and grey. The landscape was still dim, as with distance, and the light was of that palpitating silvern kind which is neither daylight nor moonlight.

They had left the low-lying marshes of Essex far behind them, and already they could see dimly in the distance, like a cloud brooding over a mountain peak, the smoke which for ever rises above the great City.

The river now seemed alive with traffic, barges beating onwards, laden almost to the water's edge—others running down—steam tugs and ocean steamers, blackening the air with smoke—all twining in and out, passing and repassing, in a bewildering maze.

Uncle Mark still grasped the tiller, and though he performed his task with skill, it was a difficult job. The bends of the river were innumerable; often the wind came dead ahead; the barge was an unwieldy sailer at all times, and now she was overloaded into the bargain. Once or twice Uncle Mark, miscalculating her power of 'coming about,' had brought her into danger, and had a narrow escape from collision. Then the river grew clearer and the wind came straight on the quarter. She scudded onward merrily, and the water all round her was white with foam.

'Look out, Mark, look out!' cried Uncle Luke presently, and Uncle Mark, stooping to look under the red mainsail, saw that a steam-tug was swiftly steaming down on their course.

'She's straight ahead. Ain't ye goin' to keep away?' screamed Uncle Luke, for the whistling of the wind was deafening.

Mark noted the speed of the barge, then measured the distance between the two.

'All right, mate,' he shouted, 'we'll clear.'

The barge sped on, the tug advanced quickly, Uncle Mark watched, carelessly at first, then anxiously. The tug was woefully near; by swerving slightly from her course she could have passed by the barge's stern—by keeping steadily on she seemed likely to cut it through the middle. Uncle Mark concluded that the tug would clear him; the tug calculated that the barge must 'keep away;' and she came straight on.

A collision seemed unavoidable, when Uncle Mark screamed:—

'Haul in the main sheet!' and, with a cry, he put down the helm.

He had jibbed her as the only chance of escape. The barge swept round before the shrieking wind with her bowsprit within a few inches of the tug's side, quivering through and through as she heeled over, with a thunder crash, almost wrenching out the mast. Then there was a crash, like the bursting of a cannon, a great splash in the water—a shout from the tug.

Uncle Luke, who had been thrown flat on his face, scrambled to his feet to find the tiller abandoned, the great boom in two, the mast bending like a reed, and Uncle Mark—gone!

Abandoned by the helmsman, the barge swept round into the wind, with her great sails flapping uselessly, and her whole fabric like a drifting wreck.

Confused by the accident and the thunderous sound of shrouds and sails, Uncle Luke, who could not at any time get his ideas to work quickly, gazed about him for a few moments in horrified despair—then he saw that the tug, having reversed her engines, was close upon the barge, and that a boat which she had put out was rowing swiftly towards a figure which was floating, apparently lifeless, on the waves—the figure of Uncle Mark. Dead? It seemed so—the body was moveless, the face livid, and it floated without a struggle.

Suddenly Uncle Luke became aware that the deck of the barge was withdrawing itself from his feet. The shaking of the mast had wrenched open the timbers—the water was pouring in like a torrent, the barge was rapidly sinking. He leapt into the punt which floated behind, cut the painter with his knife, and, utterly unmindful of the barge, pulled rapidly to the spot where they were rescuing Uncle Mark.

They had got him into the boat by this time, and he lay in the stern motionless, his cheeks ashen grey, his lips bloody, his eyes half closed.

With a wild cry like that of a child, Luke leapt into the boat, abandoning his own, seized the cold wet hand, smoothed back the dripping hair, and began to cry and moan.

'Mark, mate, open your eyes,' he cried. 'What ails you?—don't you know Luke—your brother Luke?'

But Mark answered neither by sign nor word—a splinter of the boom had struck him senseless, and almost killed him at a blow.

'We'd best take him aboard,' said one of the men; 'see, the barge is sinking fast.'

As he spoke the barge settled down and disappeared, leaving only the point of her topmast visible above the waves. But poor Luke thought nothing of the vessel; his thoughts were full of the injured man.

'Where do ye live, mate?' asked one of the sailors from the tug.

'At Grayfleet, master,' answered Luke, sobbing, and still chafing the cold limp hand. 'And oh, mates, do take him aboard, and get him home quick, and then mayhap he won't die.'

The men agreed to take the two men on board, especially as their course lay past Grayfleet. Nevertheless, as they looked on the face of Uncle Mark, they firmly believed it to be the face of a corpse. But after they had got him aboard the tug, stripped him of his wet clothes, and administered some restoratives, he heaved a little sigh, and opened his eyes.

'Luke, mate,' he said, recognising his brother, 'try and say a prayer for me. I doubt I'm a dead man!'

CHAPTER V
UNCLE MARK SAILS UP THE SHINING RIVER

All that night Madeline, sleeping peacefully, had been dreaming happy dreams. Her little feet had been pattering through the busy streets of the Golden City; her wondering eyes had been feasted with all the gay sights, her ears with all the gay sounds, which the wondrous ways afford. When she awoke in the morning, she was a little disappointed, and a good deal astonished, to find herself in her little room at home.

It was broad daylight, and Madeline thought it must be late; Mrs. Peartree stood at the window, gazing dreamily forth. Madeline lay for a time and watched her; then she said suddenly:—

'What are you looking at, Aunt Jane?'

At the sound of the voice the woman turned, and bent to impress her usual kiss on the flushed little cheek on the pillow.

'Get up, Madlin,' she said, ''tis close on eight o'clock, and you'll be late for school again.'

'What were you looking at?' reiterated Madeline, after returning the caress.

'Nought, lass, nought—'twas only one of them little steam tugs that stopped off the ferry and sent a boat ashore—but now the boat has gone back again, and the tug has steamed away.'

'What did it stop for?' asked Madeline, rising on her pillow.

'Bless the lass, how can I tell? for nought that consarns *us*, be sure. There, get up quick, and I'll cut the bread and butter.'

So saying, she departed, and Madeline, slipping from the bed, began to dress herself. She had pretty nearly completed her task, and had her arms raised, and her frock suspended above her head, when the sound of voices reached her from below.

She listened, and recognised the tones of Uncle Luke. Her heart bounded, her cheek flushed, a minute afterwards she flew down the stairs, thrusting her arms into the wrong sleeves, and alighted, radiant, panting, and half-dressed, on the kitchen floor.

It was Uncle Luke sure enough, but how strange he looked! His weather-beaten cheeks were ghastly—his nervous fingers worked at a big hole in his guernsey, he stared about him in perplexed silence, but when Madeline entered he quietly sat down and burst into tears.

'It warn't no fault o' mine, mother,' he sobbed; 'don't think it! He went on hisself, he jibbed the old barge hisself, and that's how it all came about.'

Mrs. Peartree looked aghast, and her cheeks gradually grew pale too.

'Mercy onus, Luke, can you not speak?' said she, irritably. 'What's happened to Mark? Is he hurted?—is he—killed?'

As she spoke she grew sick at heart with apprehension, and turning at a heavy sound of footsteps came face to face with her husband. He lay upon a stretcher covered with rugs and blankets, and carried by one or two of the Brethren who used to meet in the parlour on Good Friday. His face was deathly pale, but his eyes wandered restlessly about, and when they lighted on his wife's face they gleamed with recognition. He smiled faintly, and stretched towards her a trembling hand.

'Don't 'ee cry, mother,' he said, seeing that her lips trembled and her eyes grew dim; then, seeing Madeline in the background ready to spring upon him, he added feebly, 'Don't come a-nigh me, little Madlin—I'm a'most worn out.'

Mrs. Peartree was a woman of strong emotions, but she had a wonderful power of self-control. She resolutely choked back the rising desire to scream and fall into hysterics—and laying her brown hand on her husband's cold wet brow, said quietly but firmly:—

'Why, Mark, Mark—what's to do? I never thought to see my man brought back to me like this.'

Then motioning Madeline to keep back, she had Uncle Mark carried into the bright warm kitchen, where the breakfast was set, and, bringing in the horsehair sofa from the parlour, drew it up beside the fire, and had him placed thereon.

She had need of her resolution, for all poor Uncle Luke could do in this time of trouble was to sit in a corner and cry like a child, asserting, with strange vehemence, that he had no hand in the disaster, while Madeline, as if for sympathy, sat by his side and cried too.

The movement and excitement seemed to have completely overpowered Uncle Mark; no sooner did he get upon the couch than he sank back with his eyes closed, and seemed to breathe his last.

Meantime one of the Brethren had run off for the doctor, while another held a glass containing a little whisky, and Mrs. Peartree, taking the drooping head under her arm, poured between the livid lips a few drops of the spirit. At this he seemed to revive a little—he opened his eyes, again recognised his wife, and fixed his gaze on hers.

In a few minutes the messenger returned, flushed and panting from his run. The doctor wasn't at home, he said; he had gone to visit a patient several miles away; when he returned they would send him on.

Uncle Mark listened, smiling faintly, then he said:—

'Ah, I don't want ne'er a doctor, mate. I've got my physic at last, Lord knows.'

'Mark, Mark, don't 'ee talk so,' said Mrs. Peartree, almost breaking down.

But Uncle Mark smiled faintly again, and reached forth his trembling hand towards her.

'Mother,' he said, "'tain't no use denying of it, I'm agoing away. That there spar did the job for me—but nobody's to blame for it, only me;' then, as his wandering gaze fell upon his brother, who sat sobbing in a corner, he asked suddenly:—

'Luke, mate, what's come o' th' old barge?'

'She be clean sunk, mate,' returned Luke, dashing away the tears with the back of his rough, weatherbeaten hand. 'She be sunk out there in the river, up to Southam Beacon.'

'She was a good wessel,' said Mark, faintly; 'many's the year we sailed her, you and me. And she be sunk at last!'

'O, mate,' cried Uncle Luke, piteously, 'don't take on about that. We'll get her up again, but if you go and die we shall all be adrift together—little Madlin, and mother, and me, and all our hearts'll be broke.'

Uncle Mark did not reply; he lay back with closed eyes, his breathing was laboured, and the hand which lay in his wife's turned cold as stone.

For a moment Mrs. Peartree's heart sank in dread, for she thought that he was dying, but she neither spoke nor moved; she only clasped the hand a little tighter in her own, and let the scalding tears run down her cheeks.

It was a sorrowful group, and the warmth and comfort of the surroundings seemed to make the sorrow of parting more keen. There was a death-like silence in the room, the ticking of the old Dutch clock in the corner rang out bell-like and clear, and between the ticks came the stifled sobs of Madeline and Uncle Luke. The kettle was singing on the hob, the cat purring on the hearth, and the sun-rays creeping in through the window touched the bowed heads of those about the sofa, and laid a soft caressing hand on the child's trembling form.

Presently Uncle Mark opened his eyes, and rousing himself suddenly, gazed wildly about him.

'Luke, mate,' he said, 'that warn't right about the old barge. No, no, she bean't sunk. Why look, there she be a-sailing up to the bridge—only her sails be white—so white—and there be a chap in white at the helm. What's that noise? It be like a steamboat's whistle i' the fog. Oh, if my head warn't so dazed-like I could hear it—but I be kind o' stupid to-night. Give me a light; it's black dark.'

'Uncle Mark, it's morning,' said Madeline, creeping to his side. 'Dear, dear Uncle Mark, can't you see the sun?'

But Uncle Mark did not seem to hear the child's voice. His eyes were fixed on vacancy, or, rather, on some vision unbeheld of eyes.

'Look out there ahead,' he said faintly. 'There be a white barge coming down with the wind on her quarter, and the waters all black beneath her. Look, there be folk in white standing on her deck and singing. Hark! that be Brother Billy Hornblower's voice, sure—ly?'

Brother Hornblower, who indeed stood near, turned pale at the mention of his name.

'He think's it's me a-singing,' he observed, brushing his sleeve across his eyes; and he added, bending gently over Uncle Mark, 'Will I sing a bit of a hymn, Brother Peartree?9

'Aye, aye,' murmured Uncle Mark, closing his eyes.

Whereupon Brother Hornblower, clasping his hands before him and looking on vacancy, commenced to sing in his own peculiar style part of a hymn which was very popular with the Brethren of the river:

> Up the shining river,
> Sailing with the tide,
> Jesus is my pilot,
> Jesus is my guide.
> Steer the wessel, Jesus,

Steer it night and day,
To the Golden City
Far, far away.

See how hard 'tis blowing,
Th're'll be win; to-night—
Tremble not, my brothers,
He will steer us right.
Steer the wessel, Jesus,
Steer it night and day.
To the Golden City
Far, far away.

While the hymn lasted, Uncle Mark remained lying in his wife's arms as if asleep—he remained so for some time after the hymn was done. The kettle went on singing, the cat went on purring, and the clock seemed to tick with more bell-like clearness than before. When he again opened his eyes the old wandering look had passed away.

'Do you know me, Mark, dear?' asked his wife.

'Aye, mother—I know ye all. There be Luke—there be little Madlin—and that be Brother Billy Hornblower—I've been a-dreaming that he was a-singing to me.'

'And so I were, Brother Peartree,' exclaimed the musician softly.

'Was ye now?9 said Uncle Mark, smiling gently. 'Well, mate, I take that as wery kind.'

He closed his eyes again. Brother Hornblower turned his simple face to Mrs. Peartree and whispered:—

'There be another werse, Sister Peartree—shall I sing it? He seems to feel it kind o' soothin', and,' he added eagerly, 'them's blessed words.'

Mrs. Peartree nodded; she could not speak, for her tears choked her; and the thin but musical voice piped again:

Who's afraid when Jesus
Like an angel stands,
Holding sheet and tiller
In His holy hands?
Steer the wessel, Jesus,
Steer it night and day,
To the Golden City
Far, far away.

When the hymn ended this time, Uncle Mark opened his eyes, turned a radiant face to the singer—then he turned to his wife.

'Up the shininsr river,' he said. 'Aye, there I be agoing straight away. Kiss me, mother, and let little Madlin kiss me too—I be goin' to Jesus- -up the shining river to Jesus, mates. It be all for the best—if it weren't for you three I shouldn't mind goin'.'

'Oh Mark, Mark,' sobbed his wife, now fairly breaking down.

'Mother, don't 'ee take on—there be one at the helm as'll look arter you, and Luke, and little Madlin too. He's taking me away, the old barge be sunk, and I be going up the river, mates—up the shining ri— — —'

He was silent, and they thought he had passed away. Those were the last words which Uncle Mark spoke on earth, but he did not die at once. He lay on the sofa for several hours, breathing heavily, like one in a troubled sleep; the time dragged wearily on, the day brightened, then faded, and as the last rays of the setting sun fell across the floor, Uncle Mark heaved his last sigh. He passed away like one in sleep, lying in his wife's arms, and not for several minutes after his last breath was taken did they know that he was dead.

CHAPTER VI
MADELINE IS ABOUT TO REALISE HER DREAM

For several days Uncle Mark lay solemnly silent in the front parlour. An inquest was held over him, and a careful inquiry made into the manner of his death, the jury bringing in a verdict to the effect that the people in the tug were in no respect to blame, and that the fatal result was entirely 'accidental.'

At last, amid general grief, Uncle Mark was carried to his last home.

The Brethren, with solemn faces, bore him to his grave; and when the simple service was over, one of them stood forward, and, with tears in his eyes, chanted forth the words of the simple hymn which he had sung to Brother Mark as he passed away.

Up to this Mrs. Peartree, who stood with the men at the grave, had borne her burthen well, but no sooner did she hear the hymn which had ceased, as it were, with her husband's dying breath, than she wailed and broke down. For a time all the bitterness of that sudden parting came back upon her; she clasped the hand of little Madeline, who stood by her, and burst into passionate tears.

But she could not indulge her stormy grief for long; troubles and necessities clamoured like wolves around her, and turned her soul sick with a new fear. Now that her strong husband was gone, the whole weight of their little household was upon her; and no sooner was he in his grave than she had to speculate upon the future. The verdict of the jury destroyed all chance of receiving any compensation from the owners of the tug, and indeed Mrs. Peartree never dreamed of putting in any claim. Her husband's earnings had been small, but she had managed to save a little, enough to keep her for a week or so—'to turn herself round,' as she expressed it— while she decided what was best to be done.

That Luke Peartree was thrown upon her hands she knew from the moment of her husband's death. As we have said, he was generally regarded as a kind of natural; and everybody knew that had it not been for his brother he would never have got work at all. Mark Peartree had been a skilful bargeman, and in order to secure his services the barge owners had been quite willing that he should sail with his brother as mate. Consequently, Mrs. Pear-tree knew that it was quite useless for him to seek for work alone. For a time she was at her wits' end to know what to do with him.

Suddenly she remembered that he had a cousin across the river in Kent who might be willing to give him work on a riverside farm.

She wrote, and got for answer that Joss Peartree wanted an odd hand, and would be glad, for kinship's sake, to take on 'Cousin Luke.'

Luke cried like a child when the news was told him, and Mrs. Peartree cried a bit too. It was like another death, this thought of parting with simple Luke, but what was she to do? She could not keep him; it was as much as she could do to keep herself—and the only prospect she saw of doing this was to go out as a monthly nurse, a post for which she was specially suited. Meantime her little store of money was rapidly diminishing, and each coin that was taken out warned her that her household must break up soon.

After she had cried silently for a time, she resolutely dried her eyes, and set about comforting Uncle Luke. She promised that if he would only try to be happy she would try to visit him once or twice a year—and after she had earned a little, she would try to rent a small room in Gray-fleet, and make it a home where Luke could come and stop again with her. This assurance comforted Luke a good deal; at the same time it made him more keenly alive to what was taking place, and he asked, suddenly—

'Be you a-going to give up the house then, mother?'

'Ay, Luke—where be my means to keep it on?'

'And to sell the bit o' furniture?'

'Yes, mate.'

'Then what'll become o' little Madlin?'

Mrs. Peartree glanced uneasily at the child, who was seated on a footstool by her side; then motioning Luke to be silent, she said hurriedly—

'Oh, I'll look after Madlin, never fear.'

But a day or so later, when Madeline was gone to school, Mrs. Peartree went on with the subject as if it had never been stopped.

'I've been thinking about Madlin, Luke, and I've decided to send her away too.'

'What! part wi' Madlin?' cried Luke, aghast, and for a moment it seemed to him that Mrs. Peartree was growing very hard-hearted, but when he looked up he saw that her eyes were dim with tears.

'Ay, mate, part wi' our Madlin,' she said, sorrowfully. 'It a'most broke my heart when I thought on't first, but I'm past that now. 'Twill be for the child's good too. If she stopped wi' us, she'd get but a poor bringing-up at best, bless her; but if she goes to *him* he'll make a lady on her.'

'Him, mother?'

'Mr. White, that first brought her to us, and pays to this day for her keep. He's not her father, nor yet much kin of hers at all; but for all that he's a good gentleman, and will do his duty by her. We'll try him, anyways. If he takes her it will be a sore day for me, but a lucky chance for little Madlin.'

Uncle Luke listened quietly, and soon endorsed Aunt Jane's opinion, that the very best they could do for Madeline was to take her up to London and hand her over to the care of her natural guardian—the benevolent-looking gentleman who left her at the cottage when an infant, and had contributed to her maintenance ever since.

'Don't let her know nothing about it, Luke,' added Mrs. Peartree, 'or Lord only knows what she would do. After she's growed up, bless her, she'd thank us for doin' it, even if we could help it, which we can't.'

This piece of logic pleased Uncle Luke unmeasurably, and he went to bed tolerably contented with Aunt Jane's mode of working, and quite convinced that she was doing everything for the best.

The succeeding days were very sad ones in the cottage, and though Madeline was almost overwhelmed with her grief for Uncle Mark, she could not help wandering at the strange conduct of those whom he had left behind. If she happened to come within arm's length of Aunt Jane she was certain to be caught up and kissed; if Uncle Luke's eye fell upon her, he burst into tears; at meal times she had three times too much food crammed upon her plate; if she approached the fire, her chair was drawn so close as to almost scorch her. But the crowning point came when she was told one morning that she was to go to London, for a day's 'outing' with Uncle Luke.

It was decided that Luke should take her. 'He had seen a good deal of the city,' Mrs. Peartree said, 'and would do the errand better than she.' Luke was quite contented, so it was settled forthwith.

Despite her bereavement, Madeline could not help feeling glad at the thought of realising her dream at last. Childish griefs are not very enduring, and at another time a visit to London would have sent her mad with joy. But her pleasure was considerably damped when she saw Aunt Jane cry so, and Uncle Luke look so very sad.

'Madlin, darlin',' cried Mrs. Peartree, embracing her for the twentieth time, 'you're a-going to see kind friends up in London; and maybe, if you're a good girl, they'll ask you to stay a bit, and see the wax-work, and all the fine sights. And if you stay, don't forget your Aunt Jane that brung you up, and loves you so dear—God bless'ee, Madlin! God bless'ee, and make a lady of ye—my own little darling gel!'

Quite bewildered, the child suffered herself to be led away by Uncle Luke.

After ferrying across the river and walking a mile, they reached the railway station.

When she got into the train her contentment in a measure returned. She nestled up to Uncle Luke's side, stealing her little hand into his, and looked with rapture at the fields gliding past her so rapidly—at the river with its shining bends. As she went on her wonder deepened, and her excitement grew—for she passed little towns, then big stations covered with shining pictures, like palaces—until at length when she felt deep in Dreamland, they glided under a great arch of glass, and Uncle Luke, exclaiming 'Here we be,' rose up and prepared to alight from the train.

CHAPTER VII
INTRODUCES A DISTINGUISHED
LITERARY BOHEMIAN

Still lost in wonder, Madeline alighted from the train, and, clutching Uncle Luke's hand, moved along with the crowd that was surging out of the station.

Once outside, amidst the din of rattling cabs and excited passengers, Uncle Luke seemed perplexed what to do next. He took off his high hat, and scratched his head; and this appeared to remind him that he had a paper carefully tucked into the hat's lining. So he searched for and found the paper, on which was written, in a round, clear hand—

Marmaduke White, Esq.,

The Den,

Willowtree Road,

St. John's Wood.

In his perplexity he turned to a policeman, and, with his usual grin, showed him the paper. The policeman, who happened to be good-natured, informed him that he must walk across London Bridge, and make the best of his way to the Bank, where he would get an omnibus which would take him straight to his destination.

'When you get to the Bank, look for a "City Hatlas"—you'll see "City Hatlas" written on the outside. You can't go wrong.5

Thus instructed, Uncle Luke toddled off as fast as his legs could carry him, and was swept along with the traffic that sets all day from London Bridge Station over the great Bridge. Madeline clung to him in amazement and terror, with her great wistful eyes wide in wonder.

As they passed over the bridge and saw the river gleaming, she uttered a cry, and would have stopped to gaze, but her Uncle pulled her along, being far too excited for explanation or conversation.

In due time they reached the Bank; and now a fresh perplexity occurred, for the little man had quite forgotten the policeman's directions. Madeline, however, remembered, and spying an omnibus labelled 'City Atlas' hurried him towards it.

He showed his paper to the conductor.

'All right,' said that worthy; 'jump in.'

And soon they were well afloat in the great stream of London, with the waters roaring and mingling and crying around them. Madeline gazed out, and her wonder deepened as she saw the great shining shops, and the innumerable horses and vehicles, and the people ever coming and going, like waves of a sea. She thought it beautiful, a kind of terrible Fairyland, and it would have given her perfect pleasure if her heart had not been so full of a great grief. For the time being, indeed, she almost forgot her childish trouble in the strange new sense of a vast and troubled world, of whose mysterious motions she had never dreamed.

It was a long ride, but it seemed only to occupy a few minutes. Uncle Luke was silent, crushed by his sorrow and by the situation; he held her hand tight, and fixed his poor sad eyes on vacancy, seeing and hearing nothing, only conscious that he had a task to perform, and determined, though his heart should break, that he would perform it to the end.

At last they left the long thoroughfares behind and came out into a region comparatively green and countrified, with villas of all tastes and sizes ranged on either side of the road. Here the omnibus stopped, and the conductor told Uncle Luke to alight, announcing that they were at the corner of Willowtree Road, and that the address written on the paper must be close by. So Uncle Luke alighted with Madeline, paid their fare, and stood hesitating, while the omnibus rolled away.

Willowtree Road consisted, from end to end, of detached and semi-detached villas, only variegated at two of the corners by public-houses. It was very quiet and suburban, and as all the trees in the gardens were already green, and many of them in flower, it looked quite rural and bright.

Paper in hand Uncle Luke trotted up and down for some time, in a vain search for the house he sought. The road was quite deserted, and there was no one whom he could consult. At last he came against a telegraph boy, sauntering along and whistling in the leisurely manner of those swift Mercuries of the period.

'I've just come from there,' said Mercury, after inspecting the paper. 'You see that house with the verander? Well, you don't go up the front steps, but walk round to the side, and you'll see a bell marked "Stoodio"; ring that, and ask for Mr. White.'

Thus directed, Uncle Luke approached the house, a small, semi-detached villa, and passing round, as directed, to the side, discovered with some little difficulty the bell in question. Without any hesitation, he rang. Scarcely had he done so, when the door opened as it were of its own accord, and he found himself in a dilapidated garden, face to face with a small building which looked like a diminutive Methodist chapel. Approaching the door of this edifice, he was about to knock, when his eyes fell upon a paper pasted upon it. On this paper was printed rather than written these words—

Mr. White out of town. Back this day week.

With Madeline's aid Uncle Luke spelt out the inscription, and it filled him with complete consternation. There being no date to the announcement, 'this day week' was curiously indefinite, particularly as the paper showed signs of having been there for a considerable time already. While he stood gaping and scratching his head the studio door suddenly opened, and a very small boy with a very old face, clad in a very dirty page's uniform, made his appearance.

'Well, what is it' cried this worthy, snappishly.

'Who do you want?'

Uncle Luke took off his hat respectfully, and handed over the paper. Strange to say, the boy would not deign to inspect it.

'If it's the milk bill, you're to call again next week. If it's a summons, nobody ain't at home. Which of the gents is it for?'

'I'm a-looking for Master White,' said Uncle Luke, timidly, 'and if you please——'

'But he don't please,' answered the boy, with a fierce sense of grievance. 'He ain't at home. Didn't you see the paper on that there door?'

At this juncture another head appeared in the background, and a pair of human eyes seemed rapidly to inspect the intruders. Then a voice said—

'It's all right, Judas. Let 'em come in.'

Thus instructed, the page threw open the door, and Uncle Luke entered, with Madeline clinging to him. Their astonishment was considerable when they found themselves in a large apartment, lighted by glass windows from above, and full of all the paraphernalia of an artist's workshop—several easels, two or three lay figures, paintings in various states of completion. In one corner stood a stove, on the top of which was a loaf of brown bread and a tin coffee pot, and close to the stove was a perfect hecatomb of egg-shells. Indeed, what with general dust and debris of all kinds, the entire 'studio' seemed sadly in need of cleaning out.

Fronting them as they entered was the only tenant of the apartment—a young man with a very light moustache, a watery blue eye, and a large amount of unkempt flaxen hair. He grasped a palette in one hand, a paint brush in the other, and in his mouth he held a black meerschaum pipe.

'Is it anything I can do for you?' he said, with a rather vacant smile. 'I'm Mr. Cheveley.'

'I want to see Master White,' said Uncle Luke in a faltering voice. 'I've come all the way from the country, all along o' Madlin, here. Haven't I, Madlin? If so be he's away, can't some one fetch him, and tell him Luke Peartree wants him, and that Uncle Mark's dead, and that poor Aunt Jane's a widder, and that things has all gone contrary, and all our hearts is broke?'

Tears rose in Uncle Luke's eyes, and he stood choking, while Madeline clung to him and began crying too. The young man looked at them in astonishment for some minutes; then, struck by an idea, he walked rapidly to an inner door and cried loudly—

'Here, White.'

A sleepy voice answered from within—

'What's the matter?'

'Some one to see you—come, get up!'

The answer seemed a combination of strong expressions, combined with inarticulate groans. After listening for a moment, Cheveley turned to Uncle Luke—

'Here, I say!' he said, with the vacant helpless manner peculiar to him. 'He's writing in bed, and he won't rise. You'd better go in and explain your own business. The little girl can wait here.'

Not without some little fear and trembling, Uncle Luke released Madeline's hand, and moved with timid steps into the inner room. It was a very small chamber, furnished as a bedroom; that is to say, it contained an iron bedstead, a washstand, a table, and other conveniences. A chest of drawers gaping open was covered with articles of attire in most admired disorder, and other articles were hung on the walls or scattered about the room.

Perched up on the bed, with an embroidered smoking-cap on his head, was a gentleman in gold spectacles. He was writing rapidly with a pencil in a large manuscript book, and he scarcely looked up as Uncle Luke entered. But when Uncle Luke, whose heart was full and overflowed at the sight of one whom he believed to be a friend of the family, trotted over to the bedside and took his hand, crying like a child, he dropped his notebook and seemed aghast. Then, recognising his visitor, he questioned him, and soon knew the whole sad story—of Uncle Mark's accidental death, of the break-up of the little home, of the despair of the family, and their conviction that they could no longer do their duty by Madeline.

'And Madlin's here,' cried Uncle Luke. 'I brung her, but, Lord, she don't guess *why* I brung her; she thinks she's a-going back. Oh, Mr. White, be a father to her! She ain't got ne'er another, now her Uncle Mark's dead.' Mr. White wiped his spectacles, and seemed utterly stupefied; at last he nodded, as if he had made up his mind.

'Give me those trousers,' he said, 'I'll get up.'

In another minute he had slipped into an old pair of tweed trousers, a pair of very dirty fancy slippers, and an old dressing-gown. Thus attired he even looked less engaging than when composing in bed. His hands were greatly in need of soap, his whiskers were ragged and ornamented with fragments of yolk of egg, and his face, which was otherwise kindly and good-humoured, looked parboiled. Seizing a brush, he went through the formality of brushing the very minute bunches of hair which ornamented his bald head, and then, after a momentary struggle with his whiskers, led the way into the 'studio.' Here they found Madeline in high delight, for Cheveley, seizing a piece of charcoal, had dashed off a rough likeness of her on a canvas which stood vacant. The wild locks, the great wistful eyes, the delicate mouth, were happily caught, and for the moment the child forgot all her troubles.

'Look, Uncle Luke,' she cried, running to him and pointing out the likeness. 'It's me.'

Uncle Luke, still pale and trembling with his great grief, grinned from ear to ear, and gazed upon the artist in pathetic admiration. Meantime White stood blinking benignly through his spectacles; at last Madeline caught his look, and returned it with no little astonishment.

'This is Madlin,' said Uncle Luke, gently.

Thus introduced, Madeline dropped her eyes timidly, and gave a country curtsey, as she had been accustomed to do to the magnates of the village.

CHAPTER VIII
UNCLE LUKE IS BROKEN-HEARTED

It appeared on explanation that the notice on the outside door of the 'studio' was a common ruse of Mr. Marmaduke White whenever he desired perfect solitude, and when the visits of even friends and acquaintances, not to speak of ambassadors from certain adamantine creditors, would be considered irksome.

Although White dwelt in a studio, he was not an artist—not, that is to say, an artist by profession, though he could paint a little, and had a very pretty feeling for colour. By profession he was a man of letters; by special taste and habit, a writer for the theatre. Some of his less ambitious plays had been acted with no little *éclat*, and everybody had thriven through them except the author. Others had failed, and these failures constituted his glory. They were really productions of considerable literary merit. In literary circles White was spoken of as a man of genius whose mission it was to revive 'the poetical drama,' but who had fallen on dark days, when the Muses, having discarded classic drapery altogether, had taken to fleshings and the *can-can*.

He was a gentle creature, with as soft a heart as ever throbbed in human bosom, and as little power of managing his worldly affairs as of creating a profitable taste for dramas in 'five acts and in blank verse.' He lived in a studio, with one artist or another for a companion, not because the place was necessary for his vocation, but because he was naturally a Bohemian, and a studio was a thoroughly Bohemian sort of abode. He was forty years of age, unmarried, and unlikely to marry. The number of his follies could only have been measured by the number of his good deeds, and those were legion. To see him was to like him; to know him was to love him well.

For years past he had paid a small stipend—not much, but a sharp pinch sometimes to him—for the maintenance of Madeline. The way in which he had contracted this responsibility was characteristic, and may at once be explained. A friend of his who was a 'genius'—that is to say, an individual who promised prodigies, and on the strength of his promises, which were never fulfilled, discarded all conventional morality and lived the life of a shabby Don Juan—had become entangled with a country girl. Dying penitent, as well as penniless, he confided to White, who watched by his sick bed like a woman, that he had betrayed the girl, and that she had given birth to a child, then about one year old. White promised that he would seek both mother and child, and help them if possible. So after putting his poor friend into the ground, and moving heaven and earth to get a few tender things about him inserted in the newspapers, White betook himself to the lonely seaside village where the widow dwelt. He found a comely but ignorant girl in a state of comparative destitution, and, to make matters worse, in the last stage of consumption, brought on by exposure and neglect, In the course of the interviews which ensued, he learned such things of his dead friend's treacherous and selfish conduct as would have shaken his faith in genius altogether had he been less simple-hearted. A little later the girl died in his arms, giving him her last blessing and consigning her little daughter to his care.

After considerable reflection, he decided that the best course he could adopt with the little one was to find some good motherly soul, in the mother's sphere of life, who would rear her kindly. During an artistic excursion to Grayfleet he discovered Mrs. Peartree, and, after certain pecuniary preliminaries were arranged, committed the child to her care. What had been originally only a temporary arrangement presently became fixed and habitual. Years passed away. Madeline remained with the Peartrees, who were childless. White, in a very irregular manner, sent them small sums from time to time; but it had never occurred to him to take any more serious responsibility in the matter. He meant the girl to grow up happy in the sphere to which her mother belonged. Though he had beheld her once or twice in infancy, he had for years afterwards seen nothing of her, only hearing of her existence through correspondence from time to time.

When, therefore, Uncle Luke turned up in St. John's Wood, with Madeline under his charge, and explained that sad events had broken up the little home and left Madeline helpless on their hands, White was staggered. It was clear that the Peartrees thought him her natural guardian, and could not comprehend that he stood in no closer relationship to her than they did themselves.

He looked at Madeline, and was astonished to see her so fair and elf-like, with a touch in her eyes of his poor dead friend, the literary Bohemian. Somehow or other he had always pictured her as a fat little country cherub, with very hard cheeks, a pug nose, and ugly feet. As she gazed at him with her great blue eyes, he felt troubled more and more.

'You don't remember poor Fred Hazelmere?' he said to Cheveley. 'No, he was gone before your time. But you've read his "Ballads of Bohemia" — by Jove, sir, some of them are worthy of the "Buch der Lieder."' And he added in a whisper, 'That's his child.'

He had led Cheveley aside, and was conversing with him apart, while Madeline and Uncle Luke sat waiting in the centre of the studio. 'Look at her face,' he proceeded. 'Never saw such a likeness in my life — it quite turns me over. She looks a wild little thing, don't she? The man with her is a sort of natural. It was absurd to think of sending her to me, for what on earth can I do with her? *I'm* not her father, after all. Upon my soul, I'm in a dilemma. I must persuade him to take her back.'

But when White took Uncle Luke aside and tried to explain matters to him, the little man only began to cry. The home was broken up, he said; Aunt Jane's only means of subsistence was to go out as a monthly nurse; and he himself was going to join a distant relation on the coast of Kent.

'It ain't that we want to lose her,' he asseverated; 'but oh, Master White, there be no home for Madlin now. Our hearts be broke, sir, to part wi' her; but we know you're next door to her father, and a gentleman born.

She'll be a heap better off here than ever she was along of us.'

'Here?' gasped the dramatist.

'She's your'n, sir, more than our'n, bless her heart. We couldn't feed her no more, let alone clothe her, now Mark's gone to glory; but you're a gentleman born, and can bring her up well-nigh like a lady. I brung her, Master White,' he continued, reverting to his first fear; 'but I dustn't let her know I'm a-going to leave her — I dustn't, indeed. She thinks she's a-going back with me.'

'But I can't take her!' exclaimed White. 'This is no place for a child, and even if it were she needs a woman's care. I really can't think of it; the very idea's absurd.'

Uncle Luke looked astonished. In his simple judgment, the power of a 'gentleman born,' like Mr. White, was unlimited, and he could not fathom the significance of his refusal.

'She's that good,' he explained gently, 'that she'd be no manner o' trouble to any, 'cept when she's in her tantrums, and they're gone as soon as come. And she's clever, Master White. I've heerd schoolmaster say that she can spell like a good 'un, and her writin's as clear as print. I see her write out the Lord's Prayer on a piece of paper, and she guv it to her Uncle Mark, and if he'd ha' lived, he was a-going to get it framed like a pictur' and hung up on the cabin of the barge.'

This special pleading had little or no effect on White. He was puzzling his brain what to do. Once or twice he thought of repudiating the responsibility altogether, but he was far too good-natured for that. Then he suggested that Luke should take the child back and leave him to think it over, but he soon discovered that such a delay was impracticable.

'Mother said,' explained Uncle Luke, firmly (his sister-in-law, it will be remembered, had always been addressed as 'mother' by her husband, and by all the house)—'mother said I was to leave her along o' you, cause you was her best friend; and mother said you'd never grudge her the wittles what she eat, for you were a gentleman born. Them were her own words. You'd never grudge her the wittles what she eat, for you was a gentleman born.'

'How old is she?' asked White, desperately, not that he had any special reason for asking, but because, in his perplexity, he hardly knew what to say.

Uncle Luke cocked his eye, calculating, and after due deliberation replied—

'Mother says it be just eight year come Whit-Monday since you brung her to us. She remembers the year well, mother does, 'cause 'twas the year when her cousin Jim he was drowned off Woolwich Pier, after he had deserted and was running away for his precious life; and they held a 'quest upon him, and said he was drownded accidental, and had hisself to blame.'

'Between eight and nine years old,' muttered White, pursuing his own feeble reflections. 'Is there no place where she could be put? No person who, for a small consideration, would take her in?'

Uncle Luke shook his head dolefully. He had never questioned for a moment but that White would give the child a welcome, and he was quite incapable of conceiving the manifold objections there might be to her immediate adoption.

Things were at this juncture when Madame de Bemy, who occupied the adjoining house, and from whom White rented the studio, came in smiling. She was a stout little old lady, with a very profound respect for her tenant, who had been useful to her in many ways, as indeed he was almost invariably to everybody with whom he came in close contact. To his surprise she cut the Gordian knot by offering to take care of the child on White's behalf.

All this time Madeline had been listening with growing suspicion. At last the whole truth dawned upon her, and she burst into lamentation. Clinging to Uncle Luke, she cried that she would never leave him, and that she would return to Grayfleet in his company.

It was an exciting scene, over which we have no intention to linger.

Uncle Luke did not depart that night. They made him up a bed in the corner of the studio, where he lay awake till morning, weeping and wondering, but still firm in his desire to see Madeline made into a little lady. The child herself was taken care of by Madame de Berny. But she would not depart from the studio until Uncle Luke had avowed positively that he would be there, waiting for her, in the morning. His simple promise satisfied her, for never in all her life had she known him to break his word.

CHAPTER IX
MADELINE FINDS NEW FRIENDS

The next day Uncle Luke went away.

Words would fail us to describe the parting. The little man wept like a child, and Madeline threw herself, again and again, into his arms, in a perfect frenzy of passion. It was terrible to see so fierce a storm shaking the fragile form of so young a child. Madame de Berny led her, sobbing, into the house, and tried in vain to give her consolation; but for hours upon hours she wept wildly, and her little heart seemed broken.

Poor Marmaduke White was utterly at a loss how to act; but he had resolved, come what might, to accept his burthen and bear it as well as he could. Every look, every gesture of the child, especially during her fierce access of sorrow, reminded him more and more of his dead friend. Her weird and elf-like beauty, moreover, appealed to his strong artistic sense. Yes, he would do what he could for her, and trust to that Providence which feeds the literary raven to find him ways and means.

During his perplexity he found an excellent adviser in Madame de Berny. The good woman, who had a large heart for children, entered cordially into his wishes, and at the end of a long consultation readily undertook the charge of Madeline for the time being. She had plenty of leisure on her hands, the Chevalier de Berny, her husband, a professor of music, being from home, teaching, all day, while her only daughter, an actress at the Pall Mall Theatre, was engaged every evening, and nearly every day, in the pursuit of the business and the pleasures of her profession.

So it was speedily settled, and Madeline was soon installed, as an informal boarder, in the De Berny household, having a little room upstairs next to the gorgeous chamber occupied by Mademoiselle Mathilde.

The grief of childhood heals quickly, and with childhood's inquisitiveness Madeline was soon busy observing the manners and customs of her new friends. Though her heart was still wild and weary, and though every night she sobbed as she thought of her happy home at Grayfleet, hers was too quick and keen a nature to be quite deadened by its sorrow.

And Madame de Berny was very kind; even Aunt Jane could not have been kinder. As to the Chevalier, who came in late at night and departed very early in the morning, she found him a fat, fretful, overworked, but naturally good-hearted little Frenchman, who spent the whole of his one leisure day, Sunday, in smoking a big pipe and reading the French journals. But the queen of the dwelling was Mathilde, a tall, thin blonde, with golden hair, very fine eyes, and a very hard mouth. She dressed very loudly and used a great deal of paint and powder; her whole style, indeed, was 'fast,' and, though she was a Frenchman's daughter, her conversation and all her ideas were vulgarly suggestive of Cockaigne.

Her character, however, was unimpeachable; she was far too calculating and worldly wise to commit herself in any way. Her parents adored her. She had the best room in the house, a little study also where she conned her parts, and these were as the sanctuary of a saint. The Chevalier was firmly convinced that she was only prevented by the malice and wickedness of the world from becoming recognised as a great actress.

'My daughter is too good,' he would say to his friends; 'it is her virtue which keeps her back. If she vere like de rest of de vomen on your stage, it would be different—ah ciel, yes I De managers are in a conspiracy to give her bad parts and to break her leetel heart.'

And Mathilde herself was of the same opinion. Her face was quite worn and haggard with brooding over her professional wrongs, her heart torn daily by the success of her rivals and the real or fancied neglect of the public. Once or twice a week she had violent fits of hysteria, during which she would think and talk of suicide. Recovering from these, she would eat a hearty dinner and drink large quantities of bottled stout—to which she was very partial, chiefly because it was said to be fattening, and her enemies in the stalls considered her too lean.

In the eyes of Madeline, who had hitherto only known the coarse beauties of Grayfleet, Mathilde was a vision of loveliness. The child loved colour and splendour and beauty, and Mathilde seemed to represent all these. The actress's bedroom, too, was like a palace of enchantment, with its delicate rose-coloured curtains, its white French bed and bedding, its bright carpet, and its delicious perfumes.

Mathilde was not particularly fond of children, but homage from any one pleased her, and thus it happened that Madeline became a constant visitor in the sanctuary. When, one day, Mathilde opened her wardrobe and showed all her magnificent costumes, both those she used in private life and those she reserved for the theatre, the bliss of the sight was almost too much to bear. It was like a glimpse of heaven itself!

So the weeks passed away, and the new strange life was growing gradually familiar. The thought of the little Grayfleet home was still bright in the child's mind, and every night she said a prayer that Uncle Luke had taught her, and every night she cried when she went over the beloved names, but her spirit was kindled into a new kind of feverish activity, such as she had never been conscious of before.

In the course of her daily visits to the studio, where even the misanthropic Judas, as he had been profanely christened on account of his forbidding aspect, now gave her a welcome, she saw many things which awakened her wonder. Her previous ideas of Art had been chiefly connected with house-decoration and sign-painting, and she marvelled much at the creations on canvas of young Mr. Cheveley. For White she soon contracted a passionate affection, which deepened into idolatry when the good-natured Bohemian began, in his idle moments, to teach her to draw.

The quickness with which she learned the rudiments of this accomplishment reminded White that her general education was being neglected altogether.

'My dear,' he said to her one afternoon, 4I think I shall have to send you to school.'

She was standing at his side, looking over his shoulder, as he 'touched up' for her a picture of a house which reeled to one side like the leaning tower at Pisa, a tree or two like inverted mops, and a very shabby-looking bridge.

She looked at him right in the eyes, which was her custom.

'I hate school,' she said emphatically.

'So did I at your age, and the child who doesn't always comes to be hung. But I really think you'd pay for a little schooling. You write a shocking hand, to begin with.'

'Uncle Luke said it was *beau*tiful writing, and as clear as print.'

'Humph! well, you see, he looked at it from a different point of view. I don't question its legibility, which after all is the first thing to be aimed at, but it wants style. Then, your grammar is more shady than befits the protégée of a master-stylist, like myself.'

'What's grammar?' asked Madeline, swinging her right foot irritably. 'Nouns, verbs, "I am," "thou art," and all that? I hate 'em all.'

White laid down the drawing on which he had been busy, and took her by the two hands.

'You hate a good many things,' he said mildly. 'Pray, what do you particularly like?'

'I like drawing. I like to hear Mamzelle singing the pretty songs, and trying on her new dresses. I like dancing, too, and music, and all that. And I like to be here with *you*. I like you better than Mr. Cheveley. If I was big enough I'd *marry* you, and then you could take me to the theayter, where Mamzelle goes.'

'Pronounce it theatre,' said White, while his eyes opened in amused wonder. 'So you are beginning to think of marrying already, are you? Precocious child! And you'd marry *me*, would you? Why, I'm old enough to be your father, and by the time you are a young woman I shall be quite on the shelf.'

Madeline surveyed him for some moments critically; then she threw her arms round his neck and kissed him impulsively.

'When I marry you, Mr. White,' she said, 'I'll buy you a nice wig, and then, you see, no one will know!'

'A wig—the gods forbid!'

'A beautiful *black*, like the Chevalier wears. I know it's a wig, because he takes it off and puts on a nightcap when he goes to bed.'

White threw back his head and laughed heartily; then forcing a serious look into his face, he said—

'Don't let us wander from the subject; I began by saying that you must go to school.'

Madeline's face darkened, and her lips pouted.

'I shan't,' she said.

'Come, come, Madeline! Don't you care to learn?'

'No.'

'Nevertheless, learning is a physic which you will be compelled to take. You mustn't grow up a little ignoramus. English grammar, geography, and—yes, by Jove—you shall learn French and music.'

'French!' she cried, with a sudden sparkle in her eyes. 'Like Mamzelle talks sometimes to her pa?'

'Exactly.'

'And music! I love music! And then I shall understand every word they say, and play like Mamzelle on the piano. Oh, Mr. White, do let me go to school and learn French and music!'

All. opposition being thus speedily withdrawn, White determined that Madeline should go to school forthwith. In his customary fashion, therefore, he dismissed the subject from his mind; and it is a question how soon he would have practically carried out the scheme if Madeline herself had not worried him every day with the question, 'Oh, Mr. White, when am I to go to school and learn French and music?' But after a consultation with the Chevalier, a school was found in the neighbourhood—which he himself attended two or three times a week—and after a slight discussion over terms, which were specially reduced in her case, Madeline was sent there as a day scholar.

Once or twice since her translation to London, Madeline had heard from her foster-mother, who was then going from house to house as a monthly nurse. Mrs. Peartree could not write herself, but she sent by deputy many fond and loving messages, which Madeline answered with letters a thousand times more passionate. Since the day of their parting, however, she had heard nothing from Uncle Luke.

But some few weeks after she went to school there arrived a letter for her bearing the post-mark of a small town in Essex. Opening it eagerly, she read as follows:—

Mi dere Madlin,—This comes from uncle Luke, hopping you are quite wel and a good gel which it leaves me at present. I be ni art-broke far away from you and mother working on the river down alonger mi cussin Joss don't kry cos I brung you to London but be a good gel and give my umble respecs to Mister wite mi dere Madlin mi dere Madlin there be no bargis in thes parts and neer a brethren but aples be pourful big and I wish you see the aple-tree in cussin Joss his garding with luv & kisses & hopping you are a good gel & my humble respecks to mister wito good bi at present I am ever fecksonit uncle luke peartree.

P.S. Be a good gel & don't kri cos I brung you.

Many and many a burning kiss did Madeline press on this simple epistle. She wetted it with her most tender tears, and placed it beneath her pillow at night, and carried it about all day in her bosom, to be kissed and kissed yet again. With a certain intuitive shame, she did not show it to any member of the De Berny family, whose fault was a snobbishness characteristic of shabby gentility, but she fearlessly confided in Mr. White and let him read it through. He was touched by its simple affection, penetrating through the rude orthography to the staunch and loving soul of the writer; and he encouraged the girl to talk to him of Uncle Luke and all her lowly friends.

'Those who did not know him,' he thought, as he listened to her eager words and watched her flushed face, 'called poor Fred callous. It's a lie! He had a noble heart, and so, thank God, has his little child!'

CHAPTER X
A TELEGRAPHIC THUNDERBOLT

But only a few days later, as White sat alone in the studio working at the scenario of a new play, the door was thrown open and in rushed Madeline. Her hair was dishevelled, her dress disordered, her whole face distorted with passion. Before he had time to speak she threw herself on a sofa and burst into an agony of tears.

'Madeline!' he cried, bending over her, 'what is the matter? Why are you not at school?'

For a time there was no answer, but at last, between the sobs, the girl spoke—

'Oh! take me home; let me go back to Grayfleet!'

White took her hand softly, and spoke to her soothingly, but his gentleness only made her worse. At last he yielded to his irritation and insisted on an explanation.

Drying her eyes she sat up and looked at him, and he was startled by the white determination in her delicate face.

'Why are you not at school?' he repeated.

'Because I've left, and I'll never go back to school again.'

'Madeline!'

'It's true, and I want to go home, I won't stay here, and I won't go back to school.'

'But what has happened?7

Madeline gave a wild hysterical laugh, and her face assumed an expression of exultation.

'I struck her in the face, Mr. White, and I pulled down her hair, and when she saw I was angry she was frightened and screamed. If I had been stronger, I would have killed her—I would! I would!'

Completely perplexed by this enigmatical tirade, White quietly took his hat and walked off to the young ladies' seminary, which was only a few streets away. Arrived there, he found everything in commotion and the lady superintendent highly indignant.

It appeared, on explanation, that Madeline, for some reason unexplained, had, during the midday play hour, made a savage attack upon a young lady of sixteen, a parlour boarder excellently connected; had sprung upon her with fury, scratched her face, and had clung to her until torn away by force. The superintendent's mind was made up: Madeline must not return to the school.

'She is a very violent child. I have again and again had to rebuke her for fits of passion. I have now discovered, moreover, that her connections are not what I should wish in members of my seminary. Miss de Castro, whom she assaulted, is a sweet girl, incapable of provocation. Her papa is in the India Office. She is niece of Sir Michael de Castro, late Governor of Chickerabad, and I cannot have her assaulted by a common child.'

White stared silently at the lady, and without a word strode back to the studio. There, with a severity unusual to him, he demanded a full explanation. He thus learned that the *fons et origo* of all the mischief was Uncle Luke's letter. By some accident it had fallen from Madeline's bosom and been picked up by Miss de Castro. That 'sweet girl' had read it through to a group of the elder pupils, doing full justice to the orthography, and mimicking, as far as she could imagine them, the living manners of the writer. In the midst of her amusement, Madeline had appeared and demanded her property, which Miss de Castro immediately thrust behind her back, while she indulged in a series of witticisms at the expense of Madeline and all her relations, especially the country correspondent. This was enough. Almost before she herself knew it Madeline was at her throat, and in a white heat of passion. The sweet girl screamed. Madeline was torn away and thrust violently out of the school-yard gate, but not before she had recovered her uncle's letter and thrust it into her bosom. Then she had flown home.

White was greatly perplexed how to act. In his secret heart he sided with the child, and cursed the cruelty of ignorance and caste; but he nevertheless perceived that fits of passion and violence were not to be encouraged. So he frowned terribly, and read Madeline a long and stern lecture on the wickedness of giving up to wrath.

She heard him out with great attention, and with her great eyes fixed pathetically on his. At the conclusion of the harangue, she took out Uncle Luke's letter and quietly kissed it—then smiled faintly through her tears at the thought of her wrongs. It was clear that she was quite impenitent.

Madeline did not go back to school. For some months she remained at home with the De Bernys; White, in his indolent way, postponing the question of where she was to go next.

He was a good deal occupied at this time with the adaptation of a new play which was being acted with great success at the Porte St. Martin, and, as it was necessary to see the play represented by the French actors, he spent some weeks in Paris. He discovered that by carefully lopping the leading idea, making the chief female virtuous instead of vicious, altering the scenes, and turning the moral upside down, he could make the great drama pure enough for the sight of the British playgoer. His English manager approved, sent him a small cheque on account, and begged him 'to do the trick' as quickly as possible.

At this period, therefore, Madeline was thrown more and more into the society of Mademoiselle Mathilde. That vision of loveliness found the child useful, sent her on endless errands, made of her a sort of companion in miniature, and extempore lady's maid. Madeline was only too delighted to serve and worship, and great was her joy when any of the cast-off splendour fell to her share. One evening Madame de Berny took her to the theatre, on the occasion of her daughter's 'benefit.' There was a serio-comedy in which Mathilde played the leading part, and a burlesque to follow, in which (for that occasion only, for she generally despised burlesque) she enacted a fairy prince. Madeline was entranced; the spell of the footlights came upon her once and for ever.

That night, after they had returned home, and the Vision had supped well on oysters and bottled stout, Madeline proffered a request which had lately become a very common one with her,

'Oh, Mamzelle, let me brush your hair!'

Mathilde took a sleepy sensuous pleasure in that part of her toilette, and would sit by the hour together under the soothing manipulation of the brush. So she let down her golden locks, and placed herself, with her eyes half closed, before the mirror, while Madeline began her task, prattling between whiles of the theatre, of all the wonders she had seen, and of the longing that would possess her until she saw them again.

'I used to feel like you once,' yawned Mathilde, 'when I was a dear little thing, with my hair growing down to my waist, and little satin shoes on my feet, and Pa used to take me to the pantomimes. Ah, dear, that's over and done. I hate the theatre.'

'You hate it, Mamzelle?'

'Yes, and sometimes I hate Pa for ever letting me go nigh to it. I suppose it all comes of Ma marrying a Frenchman; for Pa used to teach me to say those long speeches in rhyme out of the French plays, and then I got a taste for recitation. But I hate French now, and I hate the theatre. It's nothing but worry and vexation. There was only five pounds ten in the stalls to-night besides the tickets Pa and Ma sold, and the dress circle was not half full. Did you notice a dark fat man in a private box, who threw a bouquet to Miss Harlington?'

'Do you mean a gentleman with a hook nose, Mamzelle, and his fingers all over big rings?'

'Yes. Well, that was Isaacs, proprietor of the "Evening Scrutator." A nasty beast, always smelling of cigars and rum-and-water. He hates me because I keep myself respectable, and he never suffers any one of his critics to say a good word about me.'

'Who are *they*, Mamzelle?'

'The critics? Tomfools who write in the papers, and don't know good acting from bad, and if they did daren't say so. Why, they praise Miss Harlington—who played "Princess Pretty pet" in the burlesque!'

'Oh, yes,' cried Madeline, in rapture. 'Her in the pink dress with the spangles and the flowers in her hair. Oh, wasn't she lovely, Mamzelle?'

Mathilde tossed her head under the brush, and flushed With virtuous contempt.

'A bandy-legged thing with a voice like a goat. Did you hear the creature sing? I wonder they don't hiss her off the stage. But the men run after her, and she's kept by an earl; and there she is every day in her victoria, driving in the Row among real ladies, while I must go down to rehearsal in the bus. It's disgusting—that's what it is. Do take care. Madeline—you're brushing it all the wrong way.'

She added as an afterthought, less in real consideration for her hearer than as a parade of her own wrongs—

'Never you be an actress, child. Sweep a crossing first, or serve behind a counter, or do anything dreadful. The stage isn't fit for any decent person, and so I've told Pa and Ma a thousand times.'

From this and from many other similar conversations, and from several subsequent visits to the theatre, both before and behind the scenes, Madeline began to acquire a precocious insight into some of the mysteries of life in London. She was clever and quick, and soon understood as much as was comprehensible to so pure a child. Mathilde de Berny, like many of her class, talked freely about things which might well have been nameless, and never seemed to reflect that the listener was so young. Fortunately, Madeline's perfect innocence and simplicity, combined with her real strength of character, kept her pure from taint; but by slow degrees the glory was beginning to depart from the great world of which she knew so little.

Not at all too soon White saw that Madeline was in danger of degeneration. He was a shrewd fellow, and understood that Mathilde de Berny, though a perfectly virtuous young woman, was not really the best companion she could have found. It irritated him too, at last, to see the child sinking into a mere appendage of the actress and general drudge of the house.

'I must get her away,' he said to himself, 'before they spoil her altogether. They neglect her and impose upon her, and teach her things she ought not to know. I don't want Fred's child to grow into a little slattern, with the education, and perhaps the moral instinct, of a ballet-girl. They make a small parasite of her, and she goes errands; they've even got in the habit of sending her for the beer. I'll put a stop to it at once.'

The only way of putting a stop to it was to send Madeline to a boarding-school; and this he ultimately determined to do. He had begun to feel quite a paternal interest in her, and he was more and more struck by her physical beauty and strong natural affection.

After seeking about for some time, and studying the advertising columns of the daily newspapers, he discovered a quiet school at Merton, in Surrey, under the superintendence of a very superior French lady. Hither it was arranged that Madeline should go.

So, after a fond parting with White, Madeline repaired to the seminary at Merton.

For a long time after her departure White was melancholy.

He missed her bright face and her loving ways; and so, in a less degree, did his companion of the studio. But White was a busy man, part of a busy world, and he had no time to be heartbroken about a little girl. Every month or so he received a formal account of her doings, signed by the superintendent, and still oftener a very effusive and loving letter from Madeline herself. She appeared to have become resigned very rapidly to the new conditions of her life; to be sanguine and full of promise; and the official notes of her educational progress were flattering in the extreme.

At this point, our business with Madeline's childhood ceases. We take the dramatist's licence, and at one leap pass over a period of several years.

The school was in connection with a similar one in Normandy, and the pupils had the advantage of being transferred, at a certain stage of their progress, and at little additional expense, to the French establishment. The superintendent was a sensible woman, and so White told her the whole story.

It was presently decided that it would be for Madeline's advantage to go to France for a year, without seeing anything of White or any of her new friends. She was still only a very rough diamond, and needed very considerable polishing to make her approach perfection. A long period spent in pleasant discipline, and with only the most refined surroundings, was absolutely essential to her moral development. So at least thought the lady superintendent; and White agreed.

On receiving the information that she was to be again transplanted, Madeline was in high grief and dudgeon, for she had been thoroughly happy with the De Bernys, and desired no better than to become again a kind of Cinderella to the fair Mathilde.

During her residence at Merton Marmaduke White has been fairly well satisfied with his ward. Beyond complaints of certain erratic habits, and of her general disposition to act from passionate impulse, he had heard little to her detriment, much to her credit.

He had seen her from time to time, and she had spent many of her holidays at Willowtree Road.

From the tone of her letters, and from her words when they met, he gathered that she was happy. She had gained the wish of her heart; had learnt 'French and music,' as well as the other elegances which constitute a good education.

So Madeline was sent to Normandy, with a contingent of young girls from the school at Merton.

One day, when nearly eighteen months had elapsed since their last meeting, White received a photograph from France. It represented a fair maiden, with great wistful eyes, and a face of singular beauty.

At first he scarcely knew it; then he turned it over, and read in a bold handwriting:—

Madeline Hasleere, taken at Rouen on her 17th birthday.

'Little Madeline!' he exclaimed. 'Why, she looks quite a woman!'

About a week after this event, Judas (now grown into a disjointed being of seventeen or eighteen) entered with a telegram. White opened it, and saw with astonishment that it was from Madame Brock, the lady superintendent of the school at Merton.

Then he read as follows:—

Please come down at once. I have had terrible news from Millefleurs.

Your ward, Madeline Haslemere, has run away. I fear it is an elopement.

CHAPTER XI
THE HAWK AND THE DOVE

The scene of our story changes for a time from smoky London to a lonely road close to the sea-coast of Normandy. It is the sunset of a rainy day, a fierce red light beats down on the yellow colza fields, sprinkled with great bells of crimson poppy; on the deep, wind-swept patches of yellow wheat; on the little villages embowered in foliage, each with its old-fashioned auberge and its glittering spire.

An open post-chaise, drawn by a pair of heavy horses, is flying seaward, towards the marine town of Fécamp. Side by side within it sit two figures, a very young lady, wrapped in a fur-lined silk cloak, and a tall, haggard-looking man of thirty, with very long hair and a jet-black moustache.

Every now and again the man leans forward and urges on the driver, then, after a quick glance on the road, which winds far away behind them, he sinks back upon his seat.

They halt and change horses in a quaint little village, where old women and maidens ply their antique spinning-wheels at the cottage doors, and blue-bloused loungers puff their *sous* cigars on wooden forms before the auberge. They do not alight, but the gentleman brings the lady a tiny glass of the liqueur called 'Bénédictin,' and some wine biscuits. She sips the liqueur and breaks a biscuit, while the loungers in blue blouses look on in admiration.

The young lady is very pale, and looks so young that the loungers whisper wonderingly at each other. Now and then her lip quivers, and her eyes fill with tears. The gentleman with her watches her anxiously, trying to anticipate every look and wish, but she scarcely looks at him—her thoughts are far away.

'How far to Fécamp?' the gentleman asks of the ostler, as he slips the *pour-boire* into his hand; and when he finds that it is still many kilometres away, and that it is impossible to reach it in less than three or four hours, he mutters an imprecation.

There is a quick, cat-like look in his eyes, as he converses with the world at large; but when he turns to his companion the look is exchanged for one of touching humility and sweetness.

They are ready to start again, the driver is in his place, when the young lady springs up and cries in French, 'Arrêtez!' The gentleman, who is again seated by her side, looks at her in astonishment, 'Madeline! *mon ange!*'

She answers him in English.

'It is not too late—let us turn and go back. I am sorry now I came away. Monsieur Belleisle, I *insist* on turning back.'

'*Mais non!*'

'Madame Collemache will forgive me—I will go upon my knees and ask her—Madame is a good woman. Oh, why did you ask me to do anything so foolish? Look how these people are staring! Turn back at once!'

But, at a sign from the gentleman, the driver has started off, and they are soon leaving the village at full gallop. To comfort her, Monsieur slips his hand round her waist. He is not prepared for the result, which came in the shape of a sharp slap in the face from the little gloved hand.

'How dare you? I will not be pulled about, and I will go back to Madame. If you are a gentleman you will take me back at once.'

Monsieur rubs his cheek and tries to smile, but there is an angry light in his eyes nevertheless.

'You are cruel, and I—ah, how I love you! Have you not promised to be my little wife? Mine own Madeline!'

He is about to embrace her again, but the look in her face deters him.

'I was angry with Madame because I thought her cruel and unjust. She made me mad, and so I listened to you. Drive me back, Monsieur, and I will like you very much. I will take all the blame upon myself—only drive me back.'

'Do not speak so,' is the reply. 'We love each other—we will be happy— ah, so happy—-with one another. Madeline! my bride!'

'I have changed my mind. I will not marry you, Monsieur Belleisle!'

'*Ah ciel*, you do not mean what you say!'

'I do mean it. Why should I marry you? I do not like you. I shall hate you soon.'

'It is too late to say that.'

'But it is true.'

'Ah, I will not beliefe it! You are triste—the journey make you triste and fatiguée—to-morrow you will smile again upon your own Auguste.'

'Pray don't talk nonsense,' answered the young lady. 'I liked you very well when you gave me my lessons, and last night in my anger, in my wickedness, I thought I would come with you, because I wished to be revenged on Madame and Mademoiselle Blanche. But now I have repented, Monsieur. I was a little fool, and I will beg their pardon. They have been very kind to me. I was ungrateful. I will return.'

All this in an impetuous stream, half soliloquy, half entreaty. In her passion and excitement the girl looks very lovely, and the Frenchman gazes at her in growing admiration. Then a thought seems to strike him, and he looks at her slyly and smiles.

'Why are you laughing, Monsieur?' she cries.

'I was thinking, *mignonne*, how ridiculous you would look if you returned. Ah, Dieu, how they would *laugh!*' This is a move in the right direction. The young lady cannot bear ridicule, and she frowns at the very thought of it. For some minutes she seems plunged in bitter reflection; then she speaks again.

'No, I am not afraid,' she cries; 'I do not fear any but Madame, and when I have apologised she will take my part. Oh, why did I come with you? why did I think of running away?'

'Because you love me, *mon ange!*'

'Love you, Monsieur Belleisle? I like you better than Herr Bunsen, because he is always cross and stupid and you are good-tempered. And I thought you handsome. Well, I did not know my mind. I will not marry you—the thought is ridiculous. You are thirty years old, and I do not like Frenchmen.'

Despite her protestations, the post-chaise still continues its wild career. It is dark at last, and the darkness is deepened by long avenues of spectral fir-trees which line the road on either side. A diligence passes swiftly by, with murmur of voices and jingling of bells.

As night comes on the girl grows frightened, shrinks away from her companion, and sobs bitterly. He tries to comfort her with embraces and loving words, but she avoids his touch, and rejects all his consolations.

If there were enough light to show his face, it would reveal an aspect almost Mephisthophelean in its cat-like expression. His long fingers close and unclose nervously; he would like to use force, but he lacks the courage.

At last he wins her to comparative quiescence by proving to her that return is impossible before the morrow, and by promising that when the morrow comes he will, if she still wishes it, see her safely back to school. With this poor comfort she is obliged to be content; for the house she left at daybreak lies thirty miles behind, and it would be useless to turn thither now.

Presently the lights of a town gleam before them, and, after rattling through some dark suburbs, they draw up before the threshold of an inn—the *Lion d'Or*. It is a large dreary place, with little or no custom. A ghostly waiter shows them to a great *salle à manger*, which is totally deserted.

'While dinner is preparing, perhaps Madame would like to make her toilette?'

He lays emphasis on the 'Madame'; and then demands, respectfully, how many chambers will be required.

Madeline does not hear, but her companion explains that two chambers will be wanted—one for the young lady, one for himself. The waiter bows and withdraws. An elderly chambermaid soon appears, and shows Madeline up to a great bedroom, grim and lonely as an empty barn, with one little chilly bed in the corner. There are no curtains to the window, and the moonlight is creeping in with a ghastly gleam.

Left alone, Madeline resigns herself to remorse and despair, and sobs as if her heart would break. An hour passes thus. Then the chambermaid appears with the intimation that Monsieur is waiting dinner, and is impatient. After a moment's hesitation Madeline descends.

They are alone in the *salle à manger*, and the first course is served, when there enters a muscular young man in a shooting coat, a shirt very loose about the collar, and a loose necktie. 'Englishman' is written in every lineament of his brown, sun-tanned countenance. In the manner of many of his nation, he scowls at his fellow-guests, and then, without a word, falls upon the soup.

Dish after dish goes from Madeline untasted. She breaks a little bread, that is all, and drinks a little Bordeaux and water. Her face is white as death, and all the tremendousness of the situation is full upon her.

Monsieur Belleisle, for his part, feeds ravenously, and drinks more than one bottle of light wine. He is agitated, but preserves his composure. In his heart he curses the unwelcome third party present; he burns for a *tête-à-tête*.

Third party proceeds leisurely with his dinner, only addressing the waiter in monosyllables. He is a man of thirty, of splendid physique and perfect health. He seems to see and hear nothing, but all the time his eyes and ears are wide open. He starts when the young lady—whom he has been watching quietly—speaks in the English tongue.

'The chambermaid says there is a train from this place to Rouen. It leaves at daybreak, Monsieur Belleisle.'

'We will talk of that to-morrow,' murmurs the Frenchman, with his mouth full.

'That will be too late. I will leave by the first train, and get a cab from Rouen to Millefleurs. I will explain all—they may punish me as they please—I do not care.'

'*Diable*, and what will then become of me?'

'I don't know—I suppose you will lose your situation, but you will soon get another.'

Monsieur sinks his voice and whispers—

'Another *wife*, mignonne? Ah non! If you abandon me I shall blow out my brains;' then, still in a low voice, inaudible to the other person in the room, he continues, 'But you are mad, my Madeline, to think of going back.

Hélas, it is too late; you *must* marry me now, or do you know what they will say? They will say that your character is gone, that you are *méchante*, and then no one will marry you to be put to shame. Yes, it is too late. You should have thought of this before to-morrow. You must become Madame my wife, or you will not be able to face the world.'

If the speaker were an individual of any insight, or the least sensitiveness, he would get uncomfortable under the calm unconscious wonder of the eyes which regard him. His threat, for his words amount to a threat, is completely vain. The girl looks at him quietly, and for some minutes makes no reply whatever.

Encouraged by this silence, he pours out a low stream of endearing epithets, cursing all the time the third party whose presence compels him to sink his voice to a whisper.

At that juncture, however, the third party rises, and walks quietly from the room. Monsieur Belleisle jumps up, closes the door, and turns to Madeline with extended aims, repeating in a louder voice his volley of endearments.

'Do not talk nonsense, Monsieur,' is the girl's reply. 'I am not an angel; I am more like a devil, Mademoiselle Collemache has often said. Do not come near me—I will not be embraced. I tell you I will not marry you. Even if I liked you well enough, and I don't, it would be too absurd.'

'Absurd!' echoed the Frenchman, with indignation.

'Yes. I am a great deal too young. It was wicked of you, Monsieur, to tempt me—to come upon me when I was in a passion, and persuade me to elope.'

'But I love you—ah Dieu, how much!'

'Don't speak of it, Monsieur. Let me go back to Madame in peace, and implore her forgiveness—I will do so—on my knees if she wishes it. I deserve whipping—no punishment is too bad for me—I am so wicked.'

'Madeline,' says the Frenchman, yielding at last to the growing fury within him, 'let us finish this folly. I will not lose you so—no, a hundred times no. I tell you there is no escape—you will marry me to-morrow; you will, you must. If you do not, if you refuse, take care.' And his eyes roll with a look of significance, which she does not understand.

'Take care of what, Monsieur?'

'Of the world—of me. Voilà! If you do not marry me, you will never marry another man! You do not know me—I am desperate. I will follow you up and down the world—I will say such things, ah, Dieu, what will I not say?—until at last you go upon your bended knees and beg me to make you my wife.'

As he speaks his face is livid with fury, and he seems positively transformed. The girl looks at him in supreme astonishment and growing dislike; then she gives a little forced laugh.

'Do not lose your temper, Monsieur. One would think you were giving a French lesson to one of the little girls.'

'I will give you such a lesson,' he exclaims, 'as you will remember. I am not a common man, and I will not be so befooled—no, no! You treat all love as nothing—at my devotion you laugh—you are cruel, but *I* can be cruel too.—Ah, now, I do not mean that! I love you too well. You promised to marry me, and you will marry me, *n'est-ce pas*, my Madeline?'

He starts and tries to compose his features, for that moment the obnoxious third party re-enters the room, and, taking a chair, proceeds, with an air of great carelessness, to read a journal.

After an awkward suspense of some minutes, Belleisle, in his turn, leaves the apartment, not without glancing significantly at the stranger, and expressively putting his finger to his lips to enjoin silence.

Scarcely has he vanished when the third party rises, looks at Madeline, and, walking quietly over to her, says in English—

'Pardon me, but is that gentleman your husband?'

CHAPTER XII
CAGED

Thus abruptly interrogated, Madeline goes red as crimson, and trembles violently. Then by a mighty effort she recovers herself, conquers the violent trembling of her hands, and raises her head.

He repeats the question; whereupon Madeline turns her head coldly away.

The movement is abrupt enough to send her *vis-à-vis* straight from the room, but, curiously enough, he lingers. Madeline does not look at him, but she feels that he is examining her—his eyes search her face, her figure, her hands. With an impulsive movement she turns slightly, interlaces her fingers, so as to hide from his searching gaze the third finger of her left hand; then gives one quick glance at his face.

'I do not know you, monsieur!'

'No, *Madame.*' He lays unusual stress upon the title. 'But the fact of your having used the English language must pass as my excuse for having addressed you at all. Can I be of any service to you?'

He asks the question slowly, but without a moment's hesitation Madeline replies—

'No, no.'

The answer, which is more like a pitiful appeal than a cold dismissal, holds the man to his place.

'I have arranged to leave here by the night train,' he says; 'but if I can be of the very slightest assistance to you, pray do not hesitate to say so. If you wish it, I will remain at hand!'

Again Madeline's cheeks burn with a humiliating sense of shame. Perhaps that is the reason she carries her head so haughtily and infuses such a harshness into the tone of her voice.

'There is no need for you to stay; you cannot be of any use to me; but I thank you for the offer, sir. Goodnight.'

And with a bow she brings the interview to a decided close, and walks to the other end of the room. For a moment or two the Englishman lingers. Although he stands at a distance, and with his face turned another way, Madeline can feel that he is watching her. At last, with a cold 'Good-night, Madame,' he leaves the room.

She has turned to answer his 'Good-night,' and now her eyes are fixed upon the door. The flush upon her cheek burns more brightly than ever, and her hands have begun to tremble again; she bites her quivering lip and walks impetuously up and down the room.

'I treated him shockingly,' she says to herself, 'but what else could I do? Humiliate myself before him—confess that I had run away from school, and that now, like a naughty child, I wanted to be punished and then forgiven? If he had been an old man I might have done so. If he had been the least homely and comfortable-looking I might have done so—but he was so handsome and so proud-looking—and so young.'

Presently she adds:—

'I wonder what M'sieur Belleisle is doing? Perhaps I had better ring for the waiter, and make arrangements for leaving by the morning train.'

She crosses the room, lays her hand upon the bell, is about to ring, when Monsieur Belleisle, who has noiselessly entered the room, quietly takes her hand.

At the first touch of his cold fingers Madeline's face again flushes crimson, and she draws her hand away.

Madeline cannot see his face—his head is hung too much forward, but his body bends in all humility before her.

'My Madeline is cruel,' he says in a strangely insinuating tone, 'but I confess to myself that she is right. I confess I have been to blame, but I am an honourable man, and I will make all amends.'

'By marrying me, I suppose you mean, M'sieur?'

The Frenchman smiles.

'That is what I would wish to do, but since it is not *your* wish, I will talk about it no more. I will do what you desire, Mam'selle!'

'You know what I wish. It is to return to Madame Collemache!'

The Frenchman shrugs his shoulders and spreads out both his hands.

'Even so,' he says; 'but you know, Mam'selle, you cannot leave till daybreak, for you have troubled yourself to enquire. Well, in order to screen yourself from *scandal*'—he lays peculiar stress on the word—'I will introduce you to a lady who I know will be philanthropist enough to give you the shelter of her presence to-night, and take you back to Madame Collemache on the morrow.'

His manner is obsequious—far too obsequious to be genuine—but this Madeline does not observe. She only feels a soft sense of relief steal over her, and in her gratitude she impulsively takes the Frenchman's hand.

'You are too good, M'sieur,' she says, 'and I shall never rest until I have repaid you. I will intercede with Madame Collemache—I will write to Mr. White, my guardian—I will get you your reward!'

The Frenchman bows still lower.

'My Madeline will not trouble herself so much on my account,' he says. 'I have won a leetle of Madeline's esteem—and so I have my reward. And now I have a leetle favour to ask for in return.'

Madeline's face falls, and though he does not appear to be looking at her he notices it in a moment.

'Do not be afraid,' he continues, reassuringly, but keeping at a respectful distance from her. 'My request is for your good. It is this—that you promise me to remain quietly here for an hour or two; say nothing to any one, and not to make arrangements about the journey to-morrow: all that shall be done for you. At the end of two hours, say, I will return. I will bring with me the respectable lady I have mentioned—and then, with my Madeline's permission, I will make my adieux.'

'Make your adieux?—ah, M'sieur, I am so sorry for you——'

'Do not talk of me! I shall find another appointment. You will give the promise which I ask of you?'

'Yes.'

He takes her hand, bends over it, and kisses it—and leaves the girl alone.

For a time Madeline stands quite still, stupefied by the very intensity of her relief. She rests her elbow on the mantelpiece, drops her cheeks upon her hands, and fixes her eyes upon the windows, as if to watch the slowly gathering gloom. She feels no self-pity; on the events which will probably transpire on the morrow her imagination refuses to dwell; she can think only of M'sieur Belleisle—of his goodness, his self-sacrifice, his devotion. During the whole time of their acquaintance Madeline has never thought so highly of her tutor as she does at this moment—when she is preparing, as she thinks, to plunge him into ruin.

Her meditations having reached this point are interrupted. The door of the *salle à manger* opens, and the Englishman re-enters the room. He is dressed for travelling; he looks around as if searching for something, then he paused before the girl.

'I am just on the point of starting.' he says abruptly; and Madeline, after puzzling her brain for a suitable reply, says—

'It is a fine night for travelling—I wish you a pleasant journey, M'sieur.'

He pauses, and for a moment there is blank silence; then he returned to the old question—

'You are sure,' he says, 'quite sure, that I can do nothing for you?'

And Madeline, feeling that since her last interview with Monsieur Belleisle her mantle of shame has fallen from her, gives such a decided negative that her companion goes.

How dark it is growing! and, with the coming on of night, how the girl's spirits sink! She lights the gas, and looks at her watch. Half an hour only has passed since Monsieur Belleisle left her; some time, must yet elapse before he returns. Meanwhile, what can she do to make the time hang less heavily on her hands? She resolves to write letters, and, having got the waiter to supply her with pens, ink, and paper, sits down to concoct an epistle to Mr. White.

Madeline is impulsive, and the impulse of gratitude is just now strongly upon her. Her letter to White, after giving a short account of her elopement, is filled with the most pronounced eulogiums upon Monsieur Belleisle— his goodness, his self-sacrifice—and ends by asking White if he cannot make some reparation to the man. Her letter to Madame Collemache is less gushing, but more to the point. In it she promises to return on the morrow, implores Madame's forgiveness, and tells her all. Having written the letters she hands them to the waiter to be posted forthwith. Her letter to Madame Collemache will arrive in the morning, a few hours before the return of the unlucky criminal herself. The thought of this comforts the girl; it will pave the way for the coming interview, and make it less trying, she thinks. When it occurs to her for a moment that Madame Collemache may refuse to have any interview at all, she reflects that the lady whom Monsieur Belleisle, with an amount of delicate consideration she had certainly never given him credit for, has volunteered to introduce, will be a sufficient guarantee of her conduct, and make all right again.

Again Madeline's meditations are interrupted; this time by a carriage, which, after dashing rapidly along the street, stops suddenly before the door of the inn. Madeline runs to the window, and is just in time to see, by the flickering light of the street lamps, a figure, quietly dressed in black, descending from the *voiture* and entering the door of the inn. The arrival seems to have caused a sensation; sounds of voices come from below; steps come steadily up the stairs; then the door of the *salle à manger* opens, and the new arrivals enter the room.

One is Monsieur Belleisle, the other a lady clad in heavy widow's mourning, who leans rather heavily on his arm.

At the first glance the lady appears to be young—her step is elastic, her figure slight; but when she comes right into the room, and stands beneath the glare of the gaslight, one can see at a glance that her age must be nearly sixty.

Her hair, which is brushed very smooth beneath her widow's bonnet, is white as snow, and her whole face bears the unmistakable stamp of care. Madeline is glad; the widow's mourning, the white hair and wrinkled face, seem to shed all over her the halo of respectability. With a childish faith in the sex of the new-comer, she steps forward impulsively, holding out her hand.

Monsieur introduces the lady as his 'very good friend,

Madame de Fontenay;' then after a word or two, he takes a respectful farewell of Madeline and goes. He will not even remain in the same hotel which holds the girl that night, so careful is he of her good name—but five minutes after he has left the *salle à manger*, Madeline, who is looking from the window, sees him enter the post-chaise lately occupied by Madame de Fontenay, and drive rapidly from the door.

Madeline, stricken with remorse, has asked his plans, but he has told her nothing. When she hinted that she might wish to communicate with him, he replied that any communication for him can be sent through Madame de Fontenay.

And now, while the carriage which contains Monsieur Belleisle is rolling away through the thickening darkness, Madeline turns to discuss her tutor with her new friend. She has waxed eloquent in her praise of him, and is just in the middle of a fresh eulogium, when the waiter brings in the supper, and Madame de Fontenay retires to prepare for the meal. When she returns, divested of her bonnet and her cloak, and takes her seat at the head of the table, she says—

'When I ordered supper, ma chère Mam'selle Hazlemere,

I took the liberty of ordering it for two, for look you, ever since the days of my childhood I could never bear to eat alone. You will join me? Non? Well, you will at least break a biscuit and drink with me a glass of wine.'

Whereupon Madeline, who has turned from the supper, takes her seat at the table to crumble her biscuit and sip the wine which Madame de Fontenay has poured; but at this juncture Madeline grows thoughtful, and Madame de Fontenay, who has hitherto been rather reticent, grows very talkative indeed, sips her wine with a relish, disposes of the various courses, pausing now and again to glance with piercing eyes at the girl.

Supper being over, Madame rises and slips her hand through Madeline's arm.

'Come to the window, Mademoiselle,' she says, 'and take a breath of air while the waiter prepares the coffee. But first—see, you have not finished your wine.'

She lifts the glass, which still holds a little wine, and offers it to Madeline, but the girl, with a deprecating movement, turns away.

'I cannot take any more of that wine, Madame,' she says; 'it is very strong; I think it has made me feel quite stupid.'

Madame de Fontenay gives a little laugh, and holding her hand still tighter on her companion's arm, and leading her to a seat in the window, places herself by her side.

'Ah, my child,' she says, 'it is not the effect of the wine; it is the result of the trouble, the excitement, the fatigue, through which you have passed this day. You will get to bed, and rise in the morning refreshed for your journey back.'

Madeline assents. She sits in the window allowing the widow to stroke her feverishly burning hand; but as that strange drowsiness oppresses her more and more, she goes to bed and falls into a heavy slumber.

When she awakens it is broad day; a figure dressed in black is bending above her, holding a tray. Madeline rubs her eyes—then, looking through a mist which seems to obscure her sight, she recognises the pale, bloodless features of Madame de Fontenay; she looks round the room, everything is misted; she rises in bed, and finds she can scarcely sit up. Her temples throb, her head burns—she seems to have been seized with fever.

Then in one flash the reality of her situation comes upon her, and she gazes at the window with wild frightened eyes.

'The morning train to Rouen is gone?' she asks.

Madame de Fontenay bends above her with a kind, reassuring smile. She has placed the tray on a table which she has drawn up beside the bed; and now she presses her cold white hands to Madeline's throbbing brow. As she does so a strange light comes into her eyes, a curious smile contracts her mouth; but her voice is quite melodious when she speaks again.

'The morning train is gone—yes, that is so,' she says.

'I came and looked at you half an hour before the train started, and I did not wake you, since I saw you were not fit to travel. You are sickening for an illness, and I must remove you carefully. I have ordered a carriage to be at the door in half an hour. You will take this breakfast which I have brought to you, and dress yourself—après, we will start for Rouen.'

Madeline assents; half an hour later she is seated in a close carriage, resting her throbbing head on Madame de Fontenay's shoulder.

'How your brow burns, my dear child,' says Madame de Fontenay, drawing off one of her gloves, and laying her cool fingers on the throbbing temples of the girl; then she produces a small gold-mounted vinaigrette and offers it to the girl.

'Smell this occasionally, and it will relieve the feverish condition—above all, remain tranquil, and close your eyes.'

The latter part of this advice is quite unnecessary; although Madeline's head is burning more feverishly than ever, although her temples continue to throb, her lips feel parched and dry—she feels gradually stealing over her a strange sense of languor, which compels her to shut her eyes and lean more heavily upon her companion.

The carriage, which is drawn by two horses, proceeds quickly on its way. Madame de Fontenay thrusts her head and shoulders out of the carriage window to give some directions to the coachman. What she says Madeline does not know. She can only hear a confused murmur of voices, which seem to come to her through the vapours of a dream. She hears the murmurs, she feels the lady reseat herself, then she knows that the carriage is going even faster than before; and she again relapses into a dim state of stupor.

When next she opens her eyes the carriage has stopped, and Madame de Fontenay, with some assistance, is helping her to alight. When she stands erect in the open air her head begins to swim; she reels, and is caught in somebody's arms. She gazes vacantly about her, and as she does so she grows still more confused. She is at a railway station, and although her senses are very much dulled she possesses reason enough to know she has never been there before. She is about to speak, when Madame de Fontenay, putting an arm affectionately around her, half leads, half pushes her forward; then she is hurriedly thrust into a first-class carriage, the doors are banged to, and the train moves off. As it does so, she makes a strong effort to shake off the dreamy stupor which seems to be paralysing her whole body—she looks around the carriage. Besides herself, the only other occupant of the compartment is Madame de Fontenay, who, bending over a small wicker basket, is busily engaged in producing eatables and a little wine. There is a light burning in the carriage roof, and when Madeline looks out of the carriage window she is amazed to find that day is fast fading into night.

What a strange country they are passing through! She racks her brain, trying to remember if she has ever seen it before; but the more she tries to collect her thoughts, the more confused and clouded they become.

A light touch from her companion rouses her from her reverie; she looks round; Madame de Fontenay is offering her a sandwich—she takes it; she is growing sick and faint for want of food.

'Where are we?' asks Madeline; but it is evident that Madame de Fontenay does not hear. She sits composedly in one corner, eats some sandwiches, and sips some wine. Presently she rises, turns her back upon her companion for a moment, then approaching her, offers her a little wine. Madeline turns aside her head, and holds up her hands as if to push the glass away. She has grown to detest the wine, for whenever she sips it she seems to feel that strange drowsiness increase; but Madame de Fontenay, who is not quite so yielding as she has been heretofore, takes the girl's nerveless hands in her own, and, holding the glass to her bloodless lips, forces her to drink.

The train speeds on, the hours go by wearily and slowly, and with the passing of every hour the darkness deepens. Madeline, feeling utterly prostrated and paralysed, sits helpless in her corner of the carriage, and Madame de Fontenay sleeps. Her sleep is evidently of the lightest, for whenever the train stops she starts to her feet, rushes to the door and keeps her stand there, while sounds of feet rise and die upon the platform, and the train moves on again. Madeline tries to rise, but her strength fails her; she tries to speak—the words die upon her lips in a faint inarticulate sound—something catches her breath and parches her tongue. Thus the night passes.

Dawn breaks, and almost with the first streak of daybreak the train comes to a stand again, and Madeline is assisted out. Again she tries to speak, but her low faint murmurs are lost amidst the bustle, the confusion, the loud cries of the railway officials. She is hurried through the crowd into a carriage, and before she can collect her wandering senses to protest she is again being whirled rapidly onward. A drive of some minutes; then the carriage passes through a narrow street and stops before a door. Madeline is taken from the carriage, conducted up a flight of stone steps into a finely furnished room.

A man is standing before her. At the sight of his face her dulled senses seem suddenly to brighten. She utters two words, his name—

'Monsieur Belleisle!'

The Frenchman bows, smiles, and extends both his hands toward her.

'Madeline,' he says, 'welcome, *mon ange!*'

With a cry Madeline shrinks back, her soul sickens, her dim wandering eyes begin to dilate with fear. She presses both her hands to her throbbing temples, and stares at the Frenchman again.

'Why are *you* here, M'sieur?' she says hurriedly; 'what has been done to me—where am I?'

The Frenchman bows again.

'They have brought you to me, *mon ange,* he says. 'You are in the house of my very good friend, Madame de Fontenay.'

There is something in his face which causes Madeline to shrink back with horror; then, with, a low cry, she covers her face with her hands and falls in a swoon upon the floor.

CHAPTER XIII
MADELINE AWAKES FROM HER DREAM

That very day, either with or without her consent, Madeline Hazlemere was made Madeline Belleisle; at least, a certain form of marriage was gone through, in the presence of Madame de Fontenay and several strangers, and before a person in the habit of a priest. Madeline had now no power to resist, for the influence of some strange opiate was upon her—dulling all her senses, and making the first few days of her married life pass in a sort of dream.

They travelled for a couple of days; then paused, and lived for a week or so in some quaint little village by the sea. Where it was Madeline did not know; she had not even energy enough to inquire; unresisting, uncomplaining, she was led about like a lamb going to the slaughter. In the morning she walked along the sands by the Frenchman's side, and dreamily watched the fashionable Parisian bathers disporting themselves in the waves; then she returned home to spend the rest of the day with Madame de Fontenay (who, for some mysterious reason, had never once left the married pair), while Monsieur Belleisle betook himself to the café to spend his evenings in his own favourite way.

It could not be expected that the days would continue to glide thus smoothly along; nevertheless the peace was broken rather sooner than one would have anticipated. One morning, as Madeline rose from the breakfast table and put on her hat for a stroll along the sands, her husband laid his hand upon her arm and drew her into her seat again.

'Madeline, *mon amie!* he said in his blandest tone, 'I wish to arrange with you concerning our domestic life. I should have wished the first advance to come from you; but since that cannot be, since you take so little interest in our *menage* as to be indifferent to it, it is time for me to speak.'

The girl sat quietly where she had been placed, and fixed her eyes sadly upon the Frenchman. He had used her like a villain, but for the moment the part which he had played was partially or entirely forgotten. She thought only of the man who had first awakened romance within her. Had Monsieur Belleisle spoken kindly, had he infused into his tone and words one-half the tenderness which at one time he had at his command, she might have thrown herself into his arms, with tears of tenderness and sorrow; but his manner chilled her, and her rising tears were checked by the presence of Madame de Fontenay, who sat in the room quietly watching and waiting.

Madeline remained silent; so the Frenchman spoke again—

'How do you suppose,' said he, 'that we are to live, my dear?'

Still Madeline was dumb—what could he mean by asking her such a question?

'You will write,' continued Monsieur Belleisle—'write at once, for enough time has been wasted, to your English guardian—M'sieur White, I think you have called him—and ask him to send you two hundred pounds.'

Still Madeline stared in silence. She was not thinking of the Frenchman now. All her present surroundings faded away, and she saw only the pleasant little studio in St. John's Wood, with the dearly beloved figure of White standing amidst his brushes, canvas, and paints. But he was not looking genially about him, as she had so often seen him do; his eyes were fixed with a look of sad reproach upon the painted face of a gipsy-like girl of ten, and his voice cried out with a ring of terrible sorrow—

'Madeline—my little Madeline!'

The girl saw and heard, and in her anguish she dropped her face in her hands and burst into a passionate flood of tears.

They were the first tears she had shed since her marriage. The storm had been long in bursting; but now its violence was intense. For a time she remained utterly prostrated by her sorrow; when she raised her head she saw that the Frenchman was calmly looking on..

'Is it over?' he asked.

Madeline did not answer him; she stifled her sobs, dried her eyes, and walked over to the window. The Frenchman followed her with his eyes.

'You are longing for your morning walk, my wife,' he said; '*eh bien,* write the letter and you shall go.'

'I cannot write the letter, M'sieur Belleisle.'

'Then give me the address of M'sieur White, and I will do so for you, *mon amie.*'

'If your only object in writing is to get money,' remarked Madeline quietly, 'you may save yourself the trouble, M'sieur—I do not think Mr. White has two hundred pounds in the whole world.'

'What do you mean?'

'Just what I say, M'sieur.'

'That M'sieur White is a poor man?'

'Very, very poor— —

'And yet he sent you to the pension of Madame Collemache, and you spread the report in Millefleurs that your English guardian was a great artist and a rich man.'

'I am sure I did not spread any such report. Mr. White pinched himself to pay for my schooling, and I have repaid him by—by— —'

She paused, for Belleisle suddenly interposed with an exclamation so brutal, so coarse and savage, that she stared at him in a new terror.

The outburst over, he sank into a chair, looking positively livid. What could Madeline say or do? She did not know. She stood staring stupidly at the Frenchman until he spoke again. He rose and came towards her, hissing his words through his teeth.

'If M'sieur White has no money, if you have no money, why then did you run away from your school and marry *me?*'

'I ran away from school because I was a foolish, ungrateful, headstrong girl, M'sieur, and I married you because you used cowardly, cruel means and forced me to do so!'

The Frenchman laughed, stretching his long thin mouth from ear to ear.

'I force you to marry me, and make you a martyr, I suppose?—that is very good. But hear the truth from me, Madame—and unless you are careful, all the world shall know it too. I marry you simply out of pity. I am seduced by you to carry you off from school, and then, out of pity for you, I marry you and save you; yes, I sacrifice myself by taking a wife whose fame is gone—and then, when I look for a little help from you, you say "I give you none— —-"'

He ended with an expletive which made the girl's cheek burn with shame, and brought her trembling to her feet, with wrathful flame in her great blue eyes. For a moment he shrank before her.

'Do not try grand airs with *me.* Madame—you had better think how you are to live!— —' and, with another oath, he hurriedly left the room.

All this while Madame Fontenay had kept her seat; but though her body had been inactive, her tongue silent, her eyes had done enough for all.

During the whole of the preceding interview they had been fixed with calm, cold scrutiny on Madeline's face. She had noted every flush on her cheek, every curve of the lip, every look that was shot from the tearful eyes; finally, her cold grey orbs were fixed more steadily than ever upon the girl as she stood watching the door which had just been closed upon the enraged husband.

'Mon Dieu!' mentally exclaimed Madame de Fontenay, 'the girl is superb, is magnificent — a face like that should be fortune enough for any man!'

She rose from her seat and went over to Madeline.

'My poor child,' she said, 'this is your first quarrel, let us hope it will be your last. Emile Belleisle is a fool and a brute this morning — but he is not always so. Do not grieve, *ma chère*, or your good looks will leave you. I will reprove him for his insolence, and he — well, he shall make amends!' and she followed her accomplice, leaving Madeline alone.

For a time the girl stood, moveless, speechless, comprehending only in a dull, stupefied manner the reality of all that had passed. Her eyes were tearless, her lips firmly set together, but her hands were trembling and cold as death. She seemed to see the Frenchman's face before her, she seemed to hear his words; then again there came to her the pitiful refrain from the man whose heart she feared to have broken —

'Madeline — my little Madeline!'

Again she sank down, crying — ah, what a relief she found in those tears! When they subsided her brain began to work, and she wondered what she must do.

Up to that moment she had sometimes pitied Monsieur Belleisle, if she could not love him. But that was all over; he had slain her pity, and he had not awakened affection. She knew now why the man wooed her, carried her off from school, and by force married her — he fancied her a rich heiress, a girl who would enable him to renounce his slavery of teaching and live in luxury all his days. Had this indeed been the case, Belleisle would have made a tolerably quiet husband; the sudden darkening of his daydreams had turned him into a devil.

Again Madeline thought 'What shall I do?' but the answer would not shape itself. The idea of writing to White repelled her, for she remembered the letter which she had sent to him little more than three weeks before — a letter overflowing with eulogiums upon Monsieur Belleisle. She could not write yet — rather let White think her dead than alive to cause him further sorrow. She had made her own bed; come what may, she would lie on it alone.

So she sat, half crying, listening in a vague dreamy way to the traffic in the village street, when the room door suddenly opened, and Monsieur Belleisle returned. At his entrance she raised her head; at the sight of her tormentor she dropped it again, and coldly turned away. He did not approach her—he walked about the room for some minutes; then he sat, and there was silence. How still the room was! Madeline could hear the beating of her heart; her breath came fast and thick: her hands were growing clammily cold; anger, self-pity, resentment, were struggling in her breast, but her quivering lips would not open.

She looked round the room. There sat the Frenchman in his easy-chair, with his eyes fixed gloomily upon the empty hearth. She rose to leave the room; in a moment the man sprang forward and stood in humiliation before her.

'Madeline, my wife—will you forgive me?'

The girl looked at him in blank amazement. She could not answer him, and he continued—

'I am a passionate man—I have an uncontrollable temper, but I am not slow to say I am wrong—forgive me, my Madeline, I have wronged you.'

As he spoke he stretched forth both his hands, but she instinctively shrank away. It was well that she could not see the expression of his face as she did so. He bowed before her, and spoke again.

'Eh bien!' he said softly—so softly, so meltingly, she could hardly bring herself to believe it to be the same man who had insulted her a little before. 'Eh bien, I deserve that you should shrink from me, but now I will make amends for my brutal conduct, and you shall try to forget, chérie.'

If Madeline had been herself she might have remembered that it was in this very guise of humility that Monsieur Belleisle came to her when he had determined upon doing her the greatest wrong which she had ever received in her life; but she was a mere child, and did not remember; the agonising hours spent in the hotel at Fécamp were for the moment forgotten, and the Frenchman spoke on.

Ah, yes, his offence had been great; but he determined to make full reparation. He admitted that he was sorry to find that he had wed a penniless wife, but his sorrow was gone, his anger overcome; he declared now that his wife possessed attributes which money could not buy, and the want of money, save that it might deprive her of certain luxuries, troubled him not at all. This, then, was his purposed reparation, that Madeline should go to her room and spend the day in resting; that, subsequently, she should array herself in evening costume and accompany her Emile to a pleasant dinner, and go to a place of entertainment afterwards.

Poor Madeline looked at the man in stupefied amazement. Whether or not he was straightforward and honest she could not tell, nor did she pause to inquire; she gave a trembling consent to all his wishes, and passed alone up to her room.

How quiet it was there! What a blessed relief from the presence of her tormentor. She poured some eau de Cologne on her forehead, threw herself on the cool white bed, and closed her aching eyes. How long she lay thus she did not know; the next thing she was conscious of was a knock at the door—then a maid entered, hearing some biscuits and a glass of wine. She informed Madeline that Monsieur had sent this refreshment to Madame, as he feared that the long day's fast would make her faint for the evening; she bore also, from Monsieur, a small three-cornered note, which Madeline laid aside until the girl had quitted the room, when she proceeded to acquaint herself with the contents.

My own little wife—my beautiful Madeline [thus wrote Monsieur Belleisle, in his own language], if you wish to please me—although I am not worthy your forbearance—still, sweet one, if you can forgive me, and will try to please me, you will make yourself look tonight divinely fair. There are many fair faces in this place—many will meet us to-night, but I wish my wife to be without a rival in the loveliness which is hers! Your own

Emile.

Madeline read the letter twice, crumpled it in her hand, and threw it aside. She drank the wine which had been sent to her, and ate a biscuit; then, feeling somewhat refreshed and a good deal clearer in the head, she reviewed in her mind the exact state of affairs.

Her first impulse that morning had been to leave her husband, to travel back to England and throw herself on the compassion of Mr. White. She knew that he would forgive her, kiss her, cry over her, and, looking a little saddened perhaps, take her to his hearth, as he had once done before. But now her common sense told her that a *husband* could not be disposed of so readily. It was quite evident to her that Monsieur Belleisle, despite his violent words in the morning, did not wish to resign the bride he had taken so much trouble to win. If she were to return to her home, he might seek her out, and force her to return to him—or if she hid herself, he would be quite capable in his anger of making public such a story as would shame her for ever. The affair would be raked up for public comment, and the woman would be martyred, the man made a hero—as usual. Mrs. Grundy would hold up her hands in horror at the idea of a girl, still in her teens, forcing her music master to run away with her.

Yes, the case would always stand so, for Madeline could not even urge in palliation of her act of desertion the fact of cruelty. Belleisle had spoken harshly, to be sure, but then how many husbands often did the same, and how few of them had the good taste to make so humiliating an apology? Perhaps after all he loved her in his own peculiar fashion, and if he was willing to atone, why the best thing she could do was to meet him half way, and, if she could not be happy, to try at least and be content.

She looked at her watch; five o'clock. How quickly, and yet how wearily, the day had gone by! How white, how haggard, and old she looked! And he wanted her to eclipse the Parisian ladies who had come down to revive their beauty by the sea. She did not know that she had already done so, that during her daily walks on the seashore she had several times been pointed out as 'the beautiful Mademoiselle Anglaise,' whose sad eyes had unconsciously touched many hearts, and whose story many were guessing at, but no one knew.

At last she shook off her apathy, and tried to forget her sorrow. If she must appear in public she would not disgrace herself or her nation. She gave no thought to Monsieur Belleisle, but she rubbed her pale cheeks until the roses came, and then threw open the doors of her wardrobe to select a dress for that evening's wear.

'Select a dress!' How farcial it seemed! Belleisle had spoken truly when he said that he had wed a beggar. The only dress which was at all fit for her to wear was one which had been presented to her by himself some two days after their marriage—a dress of black silk, very youthful in cut, displaying very freely her throat, neck, shoulders, and arms, and fastening in at the waist with an amber girdle—a dress Greek in design, French in the arrangement of colours, and looking most bewitching when draped about the figure of the sad-eyed English girl; whose arms were so round and white, whose shoulders so graceful and be fair, and whose whole appearance was pretty enough to subdue the most inveterate woman-hater in the world.

Arrayed in her simple dress the child stood before the mirror well pleased with herself.

'I should like dear, kind, good Mr. White to see me now,' she said to herself. 'I should like just now to run into the dear old studio in St. John's Wood, without letting Timothy announce me, as he did once before, and throw my arms round my dear old guardian's neck.'

A knock came to the door.

'Madeline, *mon amie*, forgive me for interrupting you,' said Madame de Fontenay, advancing slowly into the room; 'I knocked twice and you did not answer me, so I thought you must be sleeping.'

Madeline bit her lip, pretended to arrange some stray locks of her hair, but said nothing.

'*Ma foi*,' continued the widow, 'but you look charming; add this diamond and your toilette will be complete.' As Madeline turned to face the widow, she started on seeing that she too wore evening dress.

Madame de Fontenay looked more motherly, more thoroughly saddened with respectability, than ever she had been before. She wore a dress of heavy widow's mourning—composed of silk, crape, and jet; a widow's cap, composed of three pretty folds, crowned her wavy masses of glittering grey hair.

'Do you go with us to-night, Madame?'

'Emile has done me the honour to ask me, and I have consented. I trust my presence will not be unpleasant to you, my child.'

For a moment Madeline did not reply. She disliked Madame de Fontenay, and yet she feared her. She knew that the widow had been instrumental in marrying her to Monsieur Belleisle, and, not content with that, had kept with them, watching as the hawk watches the dove the poor victim whom she had caught, and frequently preventing by her very presence, anything like a proper understanding between man and wife. And Madeline had a repulsion for the woman. She felt that she was the Frenchman's evil genius, ready to pander to his passions, and counteract any inclination he might have towards nobility and goodness. Still the pale widow's star was in the ascendant just then, and Madeline was powerless. She felt it would be unwise to make an open enemy of Madame; at any rate until she had won over her accomplice. So she parried the question politely, and fixed her eyes on the case which Madame held in her hand.

'Diamonds, did you say, for me, Madame? I thought Monsieur Belleisle was poor?'

'So he was a week ago, but now he gives you these—put them on, my child—and hurry down, for Emile is waiting;' and without saying more she quitted the room.

Madeline opened the case which the widow had left behind her, and looked in surprise at the contents. Three diamond stones for the hair, a ruby band for the neck, and a fragile diamond bracelet for the arm.

She put them on, and, throwing a thin lace scarf over her shoulders, ran down stairs.

She found Monsieur Belleisle waiting for her, clad also in becoming evening dress, and looking handsomer than she had ever seen him look before. He glanced at her approvingly from head to foot, kissed her, and led her to a carriage, which was waiting at the door, and which already held Madame de Fontenay. As soon as they were seated the horses moved off; whither, Madeline did not know. A drive of a few minutes brought them to the door of a brilliantly lighted building. The horses were pulled up; Monsieur Belleisle alighted, handed out Madame de Fontenay, then tenderly lifted Madeline in his arms and put her on the ground. He placed her hand upon his arm and led her forward—through a great lobby, and finally into a room where some two hundred people were seated at dinner.

The entrance of the three last guests attracted a good deal of attention. Madeline, still holding her husbands arm, and led by him down one side of the long room and up the other, began to blush and cast down her eyes in confusion, for she felt herself rapidly becoming the centre of observation.

At length places were found, and they commenced dinner. Again Madeline was confused and abashed, not by the public gaze this time, but by the assiduous attentions of her husband and Madame de Fontenay. They treated her if she were some princess, who condescended when she smiled upon them and did them honour when she spoke. The girl was more troubled than ever, but she no longer tried to solve the strange problem. She received the homage of her husband with becoming gentleness, and ate her dinner as contentedly as she could under the circumstances.

Dinner over, Monsieur Belleisle rose, offered Madeline his arm, and, with much bustle and turmoil, conducted her from the room—the pallid widow following. Again she felt herself the centre of attraction, and, feeling less abashed, she held up her head with becoming grace and confidence, and swept her bright eyes along the ranks of flushed, admiring faces.

'My dear Madeline,' said Monsieur Belleisle to her that night, 'it is not always a rich wife who brings happiness to a man. I married a treasure when I married *you, chérie.*' To the widow he said, when the two were closeted alone—

'What say you to our plan now, Madame?'

'What I said before. The girl has beauty enough to send Paris mad, if she remains in the hands of a careful master.'

CHAPTER XIV
DARKER DAYS

That one exciting evening over, Madeline's life in the place became even more monotonous than it had been before. Every morning she was taken out, either by Monsieur Belleisle or Madame de Fontenay; but her walks were made in sequestered places, not amongst the gay throng of tourists who daily dipped themselves into the sea. Her evenings were spent quietly at home. But she was always met with the promise that the dulness of her present life was transitory, that there were brighter days in store.

That some mysterious work was going on Madeline knew from the strange behaviour of her husband and the widow. Sometimes he himself would disappear for several days together, leaving his wife in the care of Madame; then the lady would disappear, and for several days Madeline would be left alone with her husband; then, just as she was congratulating herself upon the relief, the widow would return—looking more benign than ever—and adding to Madeline's wonder by endless secret interviews with Belleisle.

Had the girl's mind been occupied with this pair alone she would certainly have thought their conduct more suspicious still, but she had other things to interest and trouble her. Since that night when, dressed in diamonds and lace, she had been taken to dine in public, she had written to her guardian three times, and had waited eagerly for the reply, which, she now began to fear, would never come. The only explanation she could give of the affair was that Mr. White, on hearing of her elopement, had gone over to the school to look into the matter, and that the investigation and journey had kept him a long time from home, so that the letters written from time to time by his penitent ward were lying unopened in his studio in St. John's Wood. Madeline had arrived at this impotent conclusion, and was deriving some sad consolation from it, when her little spell of peace was brought to an end.

She was seated in the sitting-room one night, silently working at some embroidery; Belleisle reclining in an easy-chair oy the window, scanning the columns of 'Le Journal pour Rire,' when the postman arrived and letters were brought in—two for Belleisle and one for his wife. The Frenchman took his, read them, returned them to their envelopes, threw them carelessly on to a little table at his side, and again concentrated his attention on the more amusing contents of the paper, or rather he tried to do so, for by this time it did not seem so easy for him to concentrate his thoughts at all. His eyes, which had hitherto travelled from line to line, now wandered from column to column—then his hands fell slightly, lowering the paper, and his eyes looked over the top at Madeline.

She had not moved from her seat; her work lay in her lap; and her hands, now trembling violently, held the open letter, upon which her eyes were fixed. Belleisle threw the paper aside, and walked towards her.

'Madeline, what is the matter?'

The girl turned her white face towards him, gave him the letter, then burst into a violent flood of tears. He took the letter, and read as follows:—

Madame Belleisle,—When you eloped from school with your beggarly French tutor you brought disgrace upon yourself and me. Remain with your husband—be true to him, if you can—as for me, I never wish either to see or hear of you again.

M. White.

No sooner had Belleisle read the letter than he tore it into fragments and threw them into the grate.

'The man is a villain and a coward,' he exclaimed; then, as Madeline rose to protest, he threw his arms around her and kissed her tear-stained cheek.

'Forgive me, *chérie*,' he said, 'the man may say what he likes of me, but I cannot bear that he shall insult my wife. Listen, Madeline,' he continued, drawing her down upon a seat beside him, 'I will correct your bad news with good news, though I did not intend to tell you so soon; well, my wife, after all you did not marry a poor man. I have had a good sum of money left to me and a fine house in Paris—and I am going to dress you in a fashion becoming to a rich man's wife, and take you to Paris for the season. You understand me?'

For the girl was looking at him as if she comprehended nothing, and now she only said—

'Leave me a few minutes alone.'

He kissed her and led her to the door, as if his only wish in life was to bow to her will.

A few hours after, when husband and wife met again, Madeline seemed to be transformed into a different being. She walked straight up to her husband, put her hand into his, and said—

'When are we going to Paris, Monsieur?'

He smiled strangely.

'You are eager to be gone?'

'Yes, I could not bear to continue this quiet life *now*.'

'Madeline!'

'Yes.'

'You were not yourself this morning, so I did not tell you all my news. Are you composed enough to listen to me now?'

'Yes.'

'Well, then, there is a condition attached to the will which left me all the money—a condition to which I fear you will not be inclined to accede, *chérie*.'

Madeline raised her eyes to his.

'You have told me the news at a proper time then, Monsieur; I feel inclined to accede to anything to-day.'

'My wife,' said the Frenchman gravely, 'I would not ask you to accede to anything wrong. Well, the words in the will are these: "Five thousand pounds to my dear nephew, Emile Belleisle, if he is unwed. If he remain unwed for one year after my decease, the sum of three thousand pounds to be paid to him annually during his life. If he marries within the year the said three thousand pounds per annum to be paid to the State." Now when my beloved relative died I was a single man—when the news came to me I had been married two days. Perhaps it was avaricious of me; but as I was so wretchedly poor I could not bear the thought of three thousand pounds per annum being taken from me and given to the State; so I thought, "I will say nothing of being married; I will take my Madeline to the seaside, and live quietly with her until the year is expired, and then the money will be mine to pour at her feet."'

'And what has induced you to change your mind?'

'My beloved one, you shall hear. I made a confidante of my good aunt, Madame de Fontenay, and, though she loves you not as I do, her woman's heart did you more justice. She said, "Why should the child suffer because you have come into a fortune? She has a good heart and generous impulses. Tell her—throw yourself upon her mercy—and let her enjoy your good fortune to the full."'

Again he paused; and again Madeline looked at him inquiringly. What did it all mean? He was evidently afraid to speak on without some encouragement from her; and the encouragement was given.

Her curiosity being aroused, she argued within herself it could do her no possible harm just to hear what he had to propose.

'Well, M'sieur?* she cried, and Belleisle spoke on. His demand was simple in itself and easily acceded to. He would take his Madeline to Paris in a few days, he said; deck her in silks, satins, and jewels; give her a season of genuine Parisian life—if she would but consent to remove that frail band of gold from the third finger of her left hand; call her husband "Cousin," Madame de Fontenay "Maman," until the prescribed year had come to an end.

Madeline heard him without comment, and remained silent after he had ceased to speak. What could she do? Her conscience urged her not to accept. The man had deceived her infamously already, and would not scruple to do so again; but then she remembered the letter which she had received that morning, and the voice within her was hushed. After all, she said to herself, what harm could come of it; she was secure against calumny, for she was in reality Madame Belleisle—so that should the worst come, and her relationship to the man be discovered, no one could possibly blame her. And if she refused, what was the alternative? To live alone by the sea during all the long, weary winter months, with such a past to reflect on—and not a soul either to share her sorrows or her moments of calmness and peace. The prospect was so dismal that the girl shuddered, and, looking into her husband's face, said hurriedly, as if she had strange misgivings of herself—

'I consent, Monsieur, I consent—only let us get away from this place, and perhaps the excitement of the journey will take away this load from my heart.'

Just a week from that day three travellers were journeying towards the gay French capital; their names were—the Vicomte de Belleisle, for the Frenchman professed to inherit a title with his fortune; Madame and Mademoiselle de Fontenay.

CHAPTER XV
BELLEISLE SPREADS HIS NET

Madeline—I wish you to do me a favour?'

'And that is, Monsieur———?'

'To wear to-night the satin dress and the pearl ornaments which I gave to you three weeks ago.'

Belleisle was standing before his wife, buttoning the kid gloves which reached almost to her elbow; for she was ready to take her usual morning drive with Madame de Fontenay. The girl allowed him to finish his task, then she spoke.

'Why is it you wish me to wear that dress, Monsieur?'

'Because, *chérie*, we shall have a new guest.'

'Indeed?'

'A young French nobleman—whom, if we wish to stand well in society, it is our interest to fascinate.'

'To fascinate!'

The ejaculation made Belleisle look sharply into his wife's face. He was by no means pleased by what he saw there. He opened his lips to speak, but was prevented by the entrance of Madame de Fontenay.

The widow, dressed as usual in rich widow's mourning, came quickly into the room, and took Madeline's gloved hand in hers.

'A thousand apologies for having kept you waiting,' she said. 'Come, my child—Emile, be good enough to see us to the carriage, which has already waited some minutes at the door.'

Belleisle, obedient to the command, conducted the ladies down the oak staircase of the hotel, handed them into the carriage which waited to receive them, and stood bare-headed at the door to see it roll away. He smiled, waved his hand and kissed the tips of his fingers—but Madeline, to whom these blandishments were cast, had already sunk back into the carriage, and relapsed into a gloomy dream.

She had a good deal to think about—much to try and explain to herself—and she had chosen this time as the best for what she had to do.

They had been located in Paris for three months now, and during that time she had led a life which puzzled even herself. Gentle and confiding, guided wholly by her husband and his accomplice, she had carried out their wishes in every respect. She had dressed herself in the fine dresses which were brought to her—driven about in a carriage by the side of her *soidisant* mother, and behaved as she had been taught to the guests whom she met at her husband's table.

It was the behaviour of these guests which troubled her and first set her speculating as to the kind of life into which she had unwittingly been led. She was not astonished that they should court her favours, for when she announced herself single she laid herself open to the admiration of single men—what astonished her was that after these gentlemen had ceased to grace with their presence the hospitable board of the Vicomte de Belleisle, they would acknowledge with a stony stare the graceful salute of the widow if she happened to meet them during any of her daily drives about the city.

It was curious, Madeline thought, and on the impulse of the moment she mentioned the fact to her husband and Madame. They looked significantly towards each other, gave some slight explanation, and turned the conversation to other things.

But Madeline was not satisfied; she had noted the look which had passed between the pair, and it made her more curious than she had been before. What could it mean? There was some dark mystery about their life which she must discover, ere it led her into serious harm.

But how to discover it? After long pondering she resolved to pick out from the innumerable guests who frequented her husband's table some man to whom she could speak freely, and to question him.

The resolve made, she endeavoured to carry it out. Every night when, attired in clinging satin or velvet, she entered the luxurious dining-room by Madame de Fontenay's side, her eye travelled from one place to another, timidly looking for sympathy which never came. Although the guests would flatter and flirt with her, there was not one among them whom she felt she could really trust.

So the days and weeks wore on, hopelessly, sadly, despite the glitter and gaudy show. Hope died within her heart; but suddenly it was revived.

'Madeline, dearest, you did not tell me this morning whether or not you would do me the favour I asked of you?' said Belleisle again that day after her drive was over.

Madeline looked at him quietly.

'You wish me to look well to-night?'

'My charming little one, you do always look well,' retorted the polite Frenchman. 'I wish you to look second to no lady in Paris.'

'Very well, Monsieur. I will try.'

A new guest to dress for; some new flatteries to listen to. The announcement was not novel, and yet Madeline felt that night as she had never felt before. She had a pleasure in dressing, a delight in watching herself grow more beautiful under the busy hands of her maid, and, when at length her toilet was complete, she sat with beating heart and heightened colour, as if awaiting the consummation of some great event.

She entered the dining-room, as she had done hundreds of times before, by Madame de Fontenay's side. She bowed, and shook hands with all she knew, and then was introduced to the stranger.

'Monsieur le Marquis de Vaux—Mademoiselle de Fontenay.'

Madeline inclined her head for a moment, then raising her eyes she saw that she was receiving a low bow and a deep blush from the stranger.

A tall fair young fellow, of some two- or three-and-twenty, looking more like an English lad than a French Marquis. Perhaps it was this English look which touched Madeline's heart and made her feel that glow of sympathy which she had waited for so long and thought would never come.

How the dinner passed off that night Madeline never knew. She sat as one in a dream, eating little, listening to the busy hum of conversation about her, and ever conscious that a pair of feeble blue eyes were fixed upon her face.

Dinner over, Madame de Fontenay rose, and Madeline, taking the hint, followed her from the room. She did not see any of the gentlemen again that night, and the widow did not leave her until it was time to retire to rest.

Several days passed. Every day she met the Marquis at dinner, and each time she met him his manner seemed to change. Whenever he shook hands he gave her fingers a slight pressure; sometimes his eyes, after diligently trying to meet hers, would fix upon her face a look full of strange inquiry, which she, not comprehending, could not reply to. Ere long his easy freshness wore off—his manner grew nervous and changeful, his cheeks pale and haggard; he seemed to become the slave of Belleisle, and at times glanced with almost terror-stricken eyes at Madeline.

What could it all mean? Every day Madeline grew more troubled, more sick at heart.

She had resolved to elicit an explanation from the nobleman, but she soon found that to be impossible. Now that she watched for an opportunity she saw that she had none. Although apparently a free agent, she was, in reality, a prisoner—guarded and carefully watched either by her husband or Madame de Fontenay. What was to be done? Speak to him she must and would; stratagem must be employed—but how?

After long pondering and much thought, Madeline hit upon a plan which she thought might possibly succeed. Having got dressed for dinner one night, she dismissed her maid, and, before the widow could come for her, hurriedly wrote down the following lines:—

Monsieur,—I would like to see you and speak with you alone. Please meet me to-morrow night at nine o'clock in the lobby of the Hôtel Bellevue.

Madeline de Fontenay.

That evening when dinner was over and Madeline rose to follow Madame de Fontenay from the room, she deliberately shook hands with the Marquis.

'Good-night, Monsieur,' she said softly; then her hand was timidly withdrawn, and the Marquis, with a bow, let his arm drop by his side.

Madeline retired early that night; the next morning she went her usual drive with her companion.

The air was bitterly cold, for winter had set in, and Madeline, wrapped in furs, lay back in the carriage with flushed cheeks and feverishly sparkling eyes, and inhaled the chilly air with quick and feverish sigh*.

'God only knows,' she was thinking, 'what trouble this evening may bring; a few hours hence and I shall meet the Marquis, and, having met him, what can I say or do? I will throw myself upon his mercy—I will tell him the truth, and, in return, demand it of him.'

To her amazement the Marquis did not appear at dinner that night. She saw that Monsieur Belleisle was worried by his absence, and that Madame de Fontenay, too, seemed strangely ill at ease. Dinner was hurried over quickly, and the ladies retired. Having reached the drawing-room, Madeline threw herself into an easy chair and closed her eyes.

'I have a headache,' she said, in answer to Madame de Fontenay's anxious inquiries. 'I am feverish to-night, Madame, and I think I shall soon retire.' And the widow, secretly glad of the opportunity of being alone that evening, kissed the girl on both her cheeks, and soon withdrew.

Madeline was feverish. Now that the time was passing so quickly, the thought of her coming interview weighed upon her; but, having made the appointment, she was bound to keep it, or gravely compromise herself.

She drew aside her window curtain and looked out. It was a fair still night, but growing every hour still colder. She rang for her maid, and with her assistance took off her dinner dress, and clad herself in one of the plainest costumes she possessed. When she was dressed, ready to depart, she said—

'Remember, Augustine, my going out to-night is a secret both from my mother and Monsieur Belleisle. If they ask for me, say that I am still unwell, and have retired early to rest.'

Before the girl, who was doubtless in Belleisle's confidence, could reply or interfere, Madeline had hurried from the room, and was in the open street.

The place of meeting was only a few minutes distant from the hotel where she was dwelling; she reached it just as the clock struck nine. As she entered the door she saw a gentleman standing with his back towards her— the only other living being in the great vestibule.

Madeline approached him, questioningly.

'Monsieur?'

He turned with an exclamation—she recoiled. The eyes looking so steadily into hers belonged to a face which she remembered well. She was face to lace with the young Englishman whom she had met on the night of her elopement from school.

CHAPTER XVI
'WHICH DO YOU PITY?'

Dismayed at the unexpected encounter, Madeline gazed at the Englishman for a time in speechless confusion; then she turned her head and gazed helplessly around.

'Mademoiselle,' said the young man, quietly, 'I fear you are not prepared for this meeting with me. Well, let me tell you I am here on an errand of duty, not pleasure. My friend, the Marquis de Vaux, has placed this affair entirely in my hands — — — — —.'

'Oh, Monsieur!'

'Pray do not interrupt me, Mademoiselle. I have little to say, so our interview can be brief — it will be better for us both. I had the pleasure of meeting you once before — only once, when I offered you my assistance, because I feared you needed some one to pluck you from the clutches of that Frenchman, in whose company you were staying at the hotel. But when I offered you my help I thought you were some pure-minded, misguided English girl. I did not know that you were the mistress of a scoundrel, and that you were making your way to Paris to become the decoy for a gambling hell.'

'Monsieur! monsieur!'

'Pray, hear me out. 'Tis some weeks now since I discovered whither my seemingly virtuous English girl had flown. I have seen you driving in the crowded thoroughfares of Paris, smiling and bowing to the miserable wretches whom your smiles have brought to ruin. I saw you, and said nothing. Had you been discreet, I should have spared you. But since you seem to have no discretion, since you have thought it pastime to delude and cause the ruin of a friend of mine, I give you due notice I shall spare you no more. Here are the letters which from time to time you have written to my friend, and which your trusty servant has delivered for you. I give you two days to leave Paris with your protector; if, at the end of that time, you still linger here, I shall speak to the police, and let the law take its course.'

Without another word he walked away.

Madeline did not move; she stood like one turned to stone. In her hand she held a packet of letters, while the words 'decoy of a gambling hell' rang with strange echoes in her brain. How long she stood there she did not know; the sharp breath of the night air brushing her cheek, as she tottered from the hotel, recalled her to herself. She shiveringly drew her cloak around her and walked—home.

The smart French maid was amazed to see her mistress back so early.

With a wave of the hand Madeline stopped all questioning and dismissed the girl for the night. Then she sat down to think. How her head ached! How cold and shivering and wretched she felt! Days and nights seemed to have gone by since she started off on her strange errand that evening. In reality *only* a few hours had passed. How those few hours had changed her!

Presently she remembered the packet which the Englishman had given her. She took it from her pocket, burst the band which held it, and the letters were scattered on her dressing-table. She took up one, opened it, and read, in what appeared to be her own handwriting—

Be not so hasty, my dear friend. I must break the news gently to my beloved mother, who cannot bear the thought of parting with me. Our behaviour in public must not alter, but be sure I adore you. A thousand greetings from Madeline.

Again—

Be cautious in your behaviour, and above all try to please the Vicomte, my cousin. Do anything he wishes you—it will come all right in the end. He has a stupid love of play—indulge him; if he wins from you he shall be made afterwards to restore.

Madeline read the letters over and over again. She picked up several others, and found them all to be in the same tone—protestations of love for the Marquis and prayers to him not to offend Monsieur Belleisle, of whom, she avowed, she stood in the greatest fear—and the forgeries were so good as almost to deceive herself.

The past was all clear to her now—she knew what she had done and what she was; she recognised the true worth of the man she had married, and of the woman who called herself her friend.

What should she do? whither should she go? For the first time in her life she could understand the feeling which prompted wretched outcast women to stand upon the parapet of a bridge and cast their miserable bodies into the depths of the blackened river; at least their woes would be ended—their weary bodies be at rest. She felt that such a death would be acceptable to her that night. Oh, if she could only leap into the darkness, and end it all!

She gathered up the letters, which still lay upon her table, threw off her bonnet, which lay like a weight upon her head, and opened her door. It was still early enough for Belleisle to be up. She would see him, speak to him; she could not wait another hour, with that newly acquired knowledge on he mind.

With this idea she left her chamber, looked first into one room, then another—and was about to return to her own in despair, when she was arrested by the sound of voices, which she recognised as those of her husband and Madame de Fontenay. She paused and listened. The pair were closeted in Madame de Fontenay's private room, and their conversation was of an exciting nature.

Madeline soon heard her own name.

'Emile, you are a fool,' says Madame de Fontenay; 'why he stays away I know not. I only know that one little note from Madeline will bring him back again.'

'And if he comes?'

'If he comes, *mon ami*, you can win from him a few more hundreds, and then make a quarrel, refuse to give him the little one's hand, and rid yourself of him for ever.'

For a time they were silent, or spoke in undertones. Madeline was about to open the door and break up their converse, when the widow raised her voice and spoke again.

'You are a fool,' she said hotly, 'and although I advise you well, you, by your bungling, upset all my plans. Did I not advise you to provide for the future by entering a good school, and marrying, either by fair means or foul, the richest girl that the rich school contained? Yes. But you, like a fool, ran off with the poorest, and did your very best to ensure your own ruin.'

'I did not know that the girl was poor.'

'Did not know! it was your duty, my friend, to ascertain that she was rich. Well, we need not complain now. Thanks to me again, the silly girl has been useful to you, and will be so again. Listen, then——'

But Madeline, trembling outside, could bear it no longer; she turned the handle of the door, and entered the room.

She still wore her walking dress; her face was white as death, her hands trembling and cold; while her fingers closed nervously around the packet of letters which she held.

Madame de Fontenay, who believed that her dupe was quietly sleeping, gave a little scream; Belleisle started to his feet.

'Madeline, *diable!* what brings you here?' he exclaimed, thrown off his guard.

For a moment Madeline did not answer him. She stood apparently calm and collected, but with a face whiter than that of the dead, fixing her large blue eyes upon first one and then another of the faces before her.

'You are a villain!' she said at length, walking steadily up to Monsieur Belleisle; 'you have tried by cruel, cold-blooded falsehood to compass my ruin; you have nearly succeeded, but, thank God, I have found you out at last.'

Livid with rage, and completely taken off his guard, Belleisle stood with clenched fists, as if ready to strike his victim.

Madame de Fontenay stepped forward to restrain him, but Madeline stood her ground.

'Do not think to frighten me,' she said; 'those days are past, Monsieur Belleisle; though you were fifty times my husband, you shall be punished for all that you have done to me.'

'Madeline, my love, be reasonable,' said Madame de Fontenay, 'you are under some misapprehension—let me explain!'

'Let *you* explain, Madame! you did that admirably to Monsieur Belleisle before I entered the room. I know that you are the cause of all this evil; I know it is through your wicked prompting that Monsieur Belleisle has been induced to make me what I am; I know that you have plotted together to bring about the ruin of a poor girl who never did you harm. With regard to you I am powerless, but upon that man, if there is any justice in the world, I will be revenged.'

By this time Belleisle had partly recovered his composure. He walked up to the angry girl, and asked quietly—

'How will you be revenged? Tell me that!'

'I will prosecute you for forgery; you wrote these letters to the Marquis de Vaux; you forged Mr. White's writing, and sent a letter to me; he shall prosecute you too.'

Monsieur Belleisle turned whiter still.

'It would be a new sensation in court,' he said; 'a young English girl prosecuting her French paramour. It would give you notoriety doubtless, Mademoiselle.'

'What do you mean?— —'

'What I say—you are not my wife, thank God. I was by no means such a fool as you think, Mademoiselle. I went through a mock ceremony with you—thinking I would have a real one if I found your fortune was worth the sacrifice. I found it was not; therefore I have pleasure in informing you that you are free.—After all, there is not very much harm done, Mademoiselle, and it may give you pleasure to know that by gracing my table with your presence, and smiling upon my guests, you have been the means of bringing some money to me. No one but my good aunt knows that you have been my mistress—and with her I am sure your secret is safe.'

Still Madeline was silent; so, after a pause, Belleisle continued.

'Now that I have explained you will perceive, I am sure, the necessity for silence. If you dare to make a scene I shall tell the whole story, and I will bring dozens of witnesses to prove that you played very willingly into my hands. If you are silent, I too will be silent. You can go to England, marry an Englishman, and become a model English wife— —'

The Frenchman paused, for Madeline, uttering a low moan, at last sank swooning upon the floor.

CHAPTER XVII
THE BARS BROKEN

When Madeline recovered her senses she was lying upon her bed, with her maid bending anxiously above her. As she opened her eyes the girl uttered a cry.

'Oh, thank God, you have awakened, dear Mademoiselle. I feared your eyes were closed for ever.'

But, without replying, Madeline only closed her eyes and became insensible again.

What was happening nobody knew, and the servants became very alarmed. It was strange, they thought, that at such a time, when the young lady was sick to death, her mother and cousin should leave the house; and yet they had gone, and had only just left a little note for Mademoiselle. It was well for Madeline that her own maid was kindly. She kept by her mistress's side, although, one by one, the other servants fled.

Two days after the departure of Monsieur Belleisle, a strange English gentleman called at the hotel and asked for him. On being told that he was gone, and that the only occupant of the rooms now was a young lady who was supposed to be dying, he asked to be allowed to see her, and was conducted at once to Madeline's apartment.

The young man walked up the stairs with the memory of his last meeting with the girl still in his mind. He felt very bitter against her, but the moment he entered the room where she was lying his bitterness melted away. How pale and ill she looked! How wasted, wretched, and sad! He bent for a moment to sadly regard the unconscious face, he pressed the wasted hand, felt the pulse; then turned to the maid, who stood looking on in mute amazement.

When Madeline was apparently prosperous, she did not enter into his calculations at all. Once, when he thought her in need of help, he had offered it—now, when he knew her to be in need, he gave it. By a few well-applied questions he extracted from the maid such facts as, coupled with those in his own knowledge, gave him a pretty correct idea of how things stood.

He still believed Madeline to be culpable—there was nothing to convince him to the contrary; but she was a countrywoman in distress, and he was still man enough to assist her. He announced his intention of looking after her, until such time as her relations could be communicated with and she could be left in proper hands.

He provided a proper doctor, and sent a professional nurse to share the vigils of Madeline's French maid.

It was during these nights of nursing that the poor parched lips of the invalid muttered words which astonished the Englishman. For, little by little, word by word, she told him all. Sometimes she called on Belleisle for mercy, begging him to take her back to school; then she reproached him for having forced her into a marriage; then she cried and sobbed, vowing vehemently that she was his wife. She spoke again and again of the forged letters to the Marquis de Vaux; then she cried passionately, saying she could never face her guardian any more.

'Delirious people never lie,' said the young man to himself one evening, as he stood by the bed, plaintively regarding the pale, pinched face. 'If she had not been so ill I could not have extracted so much from her by days of cross-questioning. Poor, misguided, miserable child—another instance of the martyrdom of woman to the treachery of man. God help her! God help her!'

Having told this much, Madeline told more. By interrogating her during her saner moments, he learned that her guardian was a Mr. White, who lived in a studio in St. John's Wood. He risked sending a telegram, and somewhat to his amazement got a reply—

'God bless you for the information. I am starting for Paris forthwith.'

Having read the telegram, which came to his lodgings, he folded it, put it in his pocket, and walked up to the house where Madeline still lay. Good news awaited him there. The maid's face was very bright, and the cause of that brightness was that Mademoiselle had awakened, taken some nourishment, and fallen into a natural sleep. The fever had abated, and the doctor said that the crisis was now past.

'Would Monsieur like to see Mademoiselle?*

He shook his head.

'You must not mention to her that I have been here at all. But there will be an English gentleman here to-morrow, whom she will be glad to see.'

Having arranged everything to his satisfaction, he returned to his lodgings, sat down before a roaring wood fire, lit a cigar, and began to think.

His watching was at an end; his long, sad looks at Madeline were over; and, to his own surprise, he felt a sort of regret. During the last few days he had never been free from self-reproach. He had met her at a time when his help might have saved her—yet, because she repulsed him, he had quietly stood aloof and let her drift to her ruin. Yes, although his reason told him he was not to blame, in his own mind he felt culpable.

Well, it was all over now; self-accusation and recrimination would never obliterate that dark past from the girl's life—she must live and suffer—but he vowed to himself that it should be his endeavour to make that suffering easy for her to bear.

During that night he slept little, but when he did sleep he dreamed of Madeline. Now he clasped her in his arms and plunged with her into wild waters—again he drew her from some darkly surging river, or with uplifted knife stood waiting to plunge it into the heart of the grinning Frenchman. He was glad when daylight relieved him from such dreams.

His first care was to ascertain how his charge was thriving. The report was favourable again; she had passed a peaceful night, and in the morning she had lain for half an hour talking rationally to her maid. She heard with perfect equanimity of the departure and continued absence of Madame de Fontenay and Monsieur Belleisle. She opened and read the letter which Monsieur had left for her, then quietly burned it in the candle which stood beside her bed. She thanked her maid for her kindness, said she must be removed from that place, and then dropped into an exhausted sleep again.

Well satisfied with the account, the young man again returned home to await the arrival of Mr. White. In the afternoon White came. 'Twas no other, of course, than our old acquaintance, but so changed that his nearest friend would hardly know him. His cheeks were ghastly, his eyes sunken, his hair and beard unkempt, and his clothes in a deplorable condition with the long and tedious travel. Despite his disreputable appearance, however, the young man's heart went out to him at once. He gave him a cordial welcome, and tenderly told him all that he knew about his ward. In return, White gave his confidence, and then the two men walked together to the house where Madeline lay. White's hands trembled, his cheeks turned very pale, when the maid came to conduct him to Madeline's room. He went up alone.

In one of the lower salons the other awaited his return.

One hour passed, then another; he read one, read all the papers, walked restless up and down in growing excitement—till White returned to him, with cheeks more pinched and ghastly than they had been before, and pitiful tears in his eyes. He laid his tremulous hand upon the young man's shoulder.

'She has sobbed herself to sleep,' he said. 'Would you like to see her now?' The other, unable to resist, went again into the room where Madeline lay. She was quite unconscious of his presence, in a deep but troubled sleep. Her loose fair hair was scattered upon the pillow—her breath came in short quick pants, which sometimes turned to sobs. Upon one hand her cheek was resting, the other lay carelessly upon the coverlet.

The young man raised her hand gently, and pressed it to his lips.

'Farewell!' he murmured. 'God knows if we shall meet again!'

CHAPTER XVIII
IMOGEN

Behind the scenes of the Royal Parthenon Theatre, on a sultry evening in July. The first act of the play was over, and the carpenters were busy setting and preparing the scenes for the next act, while Hart, the stage manager, stood perspiring under his white hat with his back to the curtain. Figures in all kinds of costumes coming and going; female voices chattering, and male voices grumbling, made the confusion worse confounded, when Abrahams, the manager, sumptuously attired in a dress suit which might have been borrowed from a slop-shop in Hounds-ditch, came panting on to the stage.

'Well,' he asked, gazing at Hart with a bloodshot, questioning eye; 'is it a go, will she do?'

The stage manager was too old a bird to commit himself so early in the evening, but he answered off-hand, with one eye on the carpenters, the other on his employer—

'I think she will; what do they say in front?'

'Say! They're in ecstasies. Cakeford says she is the biggest thing he's seen since Desclée. Why the devil doesn't Brady act up to her? Well, it'll depend now on her legs—if her legs are all right when she comes on as the boy.'

'That's in Act III.?'

'Yes, in Act III. Hay says she's too thin, but didn't she have them in the garden scene? It was splendid. Well, I'm going to speak to her, and tell her the impression she has made. I think it's all right.'

So saying, the manager pushed his way across the stage, and, winding in and out among set pieces, wings, loose pieces of canvas, and all the flotsam and jetsam of the theatre, made his way along a dirty passage till he came to a dingy door which stood ajar. Here he knocked, and, without waiting for an invitation, entered a largish chamber, hastily fitted up as an actress's retiring room. Mirrors in various degrees of magnificent dinginess were hung on every side; a large gilded sofa, occasionally used on the stage in so-called 'banqueting' scenes, stood in a corner, chairs of divers gaudy patterns were scattered here and there, and in the centre was a white table with gilded legs.

At the further end of the room were drawn crimson curtains, communicating with the more private portion of the dressing-room.

'Hallo, White, here you are!' exclaimed the manager to a solitary figure sitting on the gilded sofa, and smoking a cigar.

The dramatic author (for it was he) rose and seized the manager's hand. His own was trembling like a leaf, and his eyes were dim with moisture very like tears.

'It's all right, then?' he said eagerly, almost pleadingly.

'If she goes on as she has begun she'll astonish the town. Ah, here she is.'

As he spoke the curtains were drawn back by the hand of a female attendant, and the heroine of the evening appeared, clad in her 'change' for the second act—an exquisite dress of white samite thinly embroidered with silver. Locks of flaxen hair fell loosely over her shoulders, and set in its midst was a face of the most dream-like and spiritual beauty, lit by two large eyes which, once seen, were never to be forgotten. In another woman perhaps those eyes might have seemed too pale, too forget-me-not like in hue, but in her they harmonised strangely with the wonderful hair and tremulous mobile lips. Tall, slight, and yet finely and even fully formed, the actress was in the prime of her womanhood, and as she advanced with eyes full of limpid light and mouth tremulously smiling, she looked supremely bright and fair.

Yet despite her loveliness and despite her air of evanescent happiness, there was something in her look, and still more in her manner, which seemed full of nameless trouble. There was too quick an attempt to seem unrestrained and gay, too strange a readiness to seize light occasions for nervous laughter, too impatient a sense of her own beauty, and of the light sparkling upon it. Her very gesture at times was at once imperious and reckless; she seemed like one who commands, yet shrinks from the obedience of, some wild animal crouching at her feet.

What was strangest of all, she seemed suddenly, in the midst of her gayest laughter, to pause with a kind of listening terror, while the light faded from her eyes, and the sickness of a nameless horror touched every feature of her face.

It is not to be supposed that these fluctuations of feeling would at once have struck any one but a very close observer. To the ordinary eye, such as that of Abrahams, hers was simply a lovely face, characterised by marvellous lights and shades of expression.

She advanced smiling into the room, and held out both her hands to White.

'Oh, Mr. White,' she said, with something of her childish manner, 'I am so glad you have come round.'

White took both her hands and held them tenderly in his own, while the manager beamed and nodded.

'How do you feel, my dear?' asked the latter. 'Nerves all right, eh? Shall I send you up some champagne?'

'No, thank you; I never drink wine.'

'And right you are,' said Abrahams. 'It's the curse of the profession, and death to a pretty face. Look at Mrs. Claudesley! She was the talk of the town for a whole season, and yet she drank herself to death. The very year she died they offered her one hundred pounds a night to star in the States, and if she had gone and kept sober she might have come back with twenty thousand pounds.'

The actress was not listening, her smile had faded, and she was gazing with strange wistfulness into White's face. She did not speak; but her look said something more significant than words, something that filled his eyes and throat with tears, and misted the glasses of his spectacles. He squeezed her little fingers in his trembling hands.

'I can't tell you how happy I am,' he said. 'More than happy; proud! This is a great night for all of us—a great night.'

'You think so?' she returned sweetly; 'then I am quite satisfied. I don't care for what the others think; I only want to please *you!*' and though her eyes were quite dry, she passed her hands lightly across them, as if brushing away a tear.

Abrahams looked at her with growing admiration.

'How about the big scene in Act III.?' he asked. 'Do you feel quite up to it, my dear? Well, that's right; and what White here says I say—this will be a great night for all of us, if you only finish as you've begun.'

Here there was a rap at the door and a shrill voice, 'Overture's finished, Miss Vére;' whereupon the three, still in conversation, moved slowly towards the stage.

The play was 'Cymbeline,' and it was 'Miss Vere's' first appearance in the character of 'Imogen.' The regular season at the Parthenon being over, and the eminent tragedian who was generally its chief ornament being away in the provinces, Abrahams had been persuaded to try the new actress in an unfamiliar Shakespearian character.

Of course, as is usual in such cases, the play was 'scamped.' All the old scenery of the theatre was called into requisition, and the costumes were a startling combination of all the early periods. This gave the critics of the daily newspapers an opportunity of saying, next morning, that 'the new and appropriate scenery was everything that could be desired, and that the strictest accuracy was observed in the minutest detail of properties and costumes.'

But the play-going public had come that night not to see the fine scenery or good costumes, not to listen to the dreary spouting of the members of the stock company, but to witness the first London appearance of a young lady of whom rumour had prophesied great things. The house was crammed with 'paper.' The critics of the big papers sat in the stalls, and the critics of the small papers were sprinkled through the dress circle. Literature, art, and the drama were well represented. Sir Tilbury Swallow, who had married the once famous actress, Miss Fawn, and who had been knighted for his literary services by the reigning family, occupied a private box with his still beautiful wife. Professional beauties, of less conspicuous virtue, shone resplendent everywhere. Deep in a stall, buried in the abyss of his own personality, and glaring thence occasionally, with saturnine cheek and lack-lustre eye, sat the great Mr. Blanco Serena, the pre-Raphaelite painter. The fact was, nearly every individual present in the better parts of the house possessed, or was supposed to possess, some sort of interest in dramatic, pictorial, or literary art.

In the centre of the stalls, however, sat a figure whose appearance was in striking contrast to that of the habitual theatre-goers surrounding him. In any gathering he would have attracted attention; in the present he was specially remarkable. He was a broad-shouldered muscular man of about thirty, with a face bronzed to a deep brown by exposure to the tropical sun. He had a high forehead, black eyes, a square, determined jaw; a thick, black moustache covered his upper lip, but his cheeks were clean shaven. Even in his well-made dress suit, with faultless linen and spotless tie, he had the appearance of a man whose true place would be leading a forlorn hope or standing alone in some position of loneliness and peril. He sat and listened, or rose and looked about him between the acts, with the air of one to whom a theatre was more or less unfamiliar, and he listened to the whole play, even to the ranting of the subordinate actors, with the approval of a man enjoying a new sensation, and quite unable or unwilling to be dissatisfied or critical.

But from the first moment the new actress appeared upon the stage this man had watched her in fascinated amazement, and as long as she remained there he had eyes for nothing else but her face. As the play proceeded, his expression changed from one of wonder and doubt to another of deep surprise and pain. His brows were knitted, his countenance strangely troubled. When the curtain fell on the first act he sat moveless, and made no attempt to join in the general applause.

Throughout the second act he remained in the same position, troubled and expectant. When it ended he rose quietly, and made his way to the saloon.

Various excited groups were congregated here. One group, consisting of several very young gentlemen, a little bald-headed man with a simpering voice, and a swarthy lean man wrapt up to the throat in a large white muffler, clearly representing the fourth estate.

The lean man in the muffler was holding forth with more zeal than eloquence on the personal appearance of the *débutante*.

'Where did she come from?' asked one of the very young gentlemen. 'Where did Abrahams pick her up?'

'I've heard that her parents lived in Paris,' answered the lean man, 'and that she used to sing once, when quite a young girl, at a *café chantant*. White knows all about her, I believe.'

'What power she showed in the cave scene!' said another very young gentleman.

'Do you think so?' the lean man said, reflectively. 'She rather disappointed me there. And I don't like her delivery of the blank verse.'

'Beastly immoral play!' drawled the man with the bald head. 'What the French call *scabreux?*'

'Why, it's Shakespeare,' gasped one of the very young gentlemen.

'Are you sure of that? And if it is? Shakespeare or no Shakespeare, the licenser would suppress it if it were submitted to him now for the first time.'

'Oh, oh!' groaned several voices.

'And what is more,' persisted the man with the bald head, 'no manager could look at such rubbish. It's very good poetry, and all that sort of thing, but it's what I call a— —bad play, though you fellows haven't the pluck to say so!'

Here there was a general laugh.

'What do you think of the Imogen?' asked the lean man.

'Pretty good,' drawled, the other. 'When I was an *attache* in Constantinople, I once saw a woman's hand waving out of a house on the Bosphorus. I jumped out of my boat, and went into the house, tripping an eunuch at the door who tried to prevent me. I ran from room to room till I came to a splendid open court with a fountain, and there I saw a veiled woman sitting in the sun. The moment I appeared she lifted up the veil, and showed the loveliest face I ever saw. I need not give you the sequel of the story. She had seen me at a distance, and been struck by my style of beauty. I afterwards found she was the favourite wife of the Grand Vizier. Well, she was the very image of the girl who is playing "Imogen" tonight. Poor little Schelsalmaigàr.'

'Was that her name?'

'Yes; old Muzid afterwards found out about my visits, and the cruel bowstring and sack business terminated the adventure. I tried to save her, but they found some of my Turkish letters (I write Turkish rather better than I write English) on her person. She kept them too long, in the hopes of getting some one to read them to her, for she couldn't read herself.'

Standing close to the group the swarthy gentleman with the moustache had listened to the close with a smile as he sipped a glass of lemonade. Suddenly he felt himself touched upon the shoulder, while a hasty voice exclaimed, 'Sutherland! is it possible!'

Turning quietly, he found himself face to face with a bright-eyed, full-bearded little man of forty, who used an eye-glass, and spoke with the greatest suspicion of a Scottish accent.

'Crieff?'

'Yes,' returned the little man. 'But is it yourself? How long have you been in England?'

'Just one month,' said Sutherland.

'When I last heard of you, you were somewhere in the wilds of North America. There was a paragraph going round that you had joined a Free-love community in the Western States. Well, of all the places in the world, the last I should expect to find you in is a theatre. Do you like the new actress?'

'I am not a very good judge of acting,' replied Sutherland, quietly; 'but if you mean do I like her personally — —'

'Well, it comes to that.'

'Then I think she is the most beautiful woman I have ever seen.'

'You don't say that!' said the little man, opening his eyes.

'Only once in my life before, and that was years ago, under extraordinary circumstances, have I seen such a face. Should it be the same—but no, that is scarcely possible. Do you know anything of Miss Vere's history?'

'Nothing.'

'Of course, it is not her first appearance on the stage.'

'I think not. She has had some years of practice in the provinces. If you are interested in the lady, come and sup with me to-night at the Harum-Scarum.'

'What's that?'

'A club of night-birds, where the small critics compare their notes and pick each other's brains for ideas. The strongest will and the loudest voice settle the matter, and what they say overnight is echoed in a dozen newspapers next morning.'

'But what has that to do with Miss Vere?' i Everything. You'll hear all that is known concerning her, for the night-birds know everything, and—but the curtain's going up. Of course you'll come?'

'Yes,' said Sutherland; and the two men returned to their places in the auditorium.

The third act was a revelation and a surprise, even to those who believed most in the new actress. In the great scene with Pisanio, when, on her way to Milford Haven, Imogen learns for the first time her husband's diabolical suspicions, the actress fairly took the house by storm, till, at the great speech ending:

> Prithee dispatch.
> The lamb entreats the butcher; where's thy knife?
> Thou art too slow to do thy master's bidding,
> When I deserve it, too!—

the whole audience rose in one surge of vehement applause. Pale as death, with her large eyes gleaming, and her delicate frame trembling like a leaf, Miss Vere trembled before the unexpected tempest, and it was some minutes before the scene could proceed. When it did so the actress seemed moved to the quick, and the pensive wail:

> Talk thy tongue weary; speak
> I have heard. I am a strumpet; and mine ear,
> Therein false struck, can make no greater wound,
> Nor tent to bottom that—

was uttered with a melancholy so infinite, pathos so despairing, that Sutherland, who had heard the excitement and enthusiasm, felt the words sink like lead into his heart. His own face was livid now, despite its tan, and a shiver ran through his veins.

A scene or two later, when Imogen is transformed into

Fidele, the actress still held her audience, but with a less mysterious fascination. In her boy's dress, which was charmingly delicate and becoming, she fully warranted the exclamation of Belarius on first beholding her:

> By Jupiter, an angel! or, if not,
> An earthly paragon! Behold divineness
> No elder than a boy.

Her acting, moreover, was pathetic in the extreme; and thenceforth, until the end of the play, her success was assured.

The curtain fell. Call after call greeted the actress, who looked completely exhausted by her efforts, and could scarcely conjure up a smile, as she accepted the bouquets which had been liberally provided for her. White sat in the dark background of a box, crying for joy.

As the audience streamed out of the theatre, Sutherland came shoulder to shoulder with little Crieff, who had invited him to sup at the Harum-Scarum.

'How glum you look!' said Crieff. 'Are you disappointed?'

'Disappointed, no!'

'You don't seem to share the general enthusiasm?'

'I do share it, but, as I told you, I am no judge of acting.'

'Well, come and hear what the night-birds say about it. Shall we walk to the club? It's only a few streets off.'

Arm-in-arm in the moonlight the two men walked away. Sutherland had lighted a cigar, and now, while the other chattered, he scarcely uttered a word.

CHAPTER XIX
THE HARUM-SCARUMS

Mr. J. Watson Crieff was assistant editor of the 'Charing Cross Chronicle,' an evening newspaper devoted to smart writing and the conservation of Church and State. He was a hard-working Scotchman, with no pretensions to literary attainments, but honourably connected with journalism in many ways. He was not a regular theatre-goer, still less a professed critic, but he sometimes, as on the present occasion, went to see a Shakespearian performance, and wrote about it afterwards honestly and well.

Passing along the Strand, he led his friend down a street running at right angles to the banks of the Thames, and soon entered the dingy building where the Harum-Scarums were accustomed to hold high festival. Proceeding upstairs, he entered a large room, at one end of which was a fire and a silver grill, presided over by a man-cook dressed in white. The room was becoming crowded by men of all degrees and ages, clean-shaven actors and hirsute journalists having the preponderance, and more than one greeted Crieff by name. He soon found a table, and ordered a plain supper for himself and friend. A loud chatter filled the air, and every one was talking of the *débutante* at the Parthenon. Among the other faces around him Sutherland at once recognised the very young gentleman and the lean man in the muffler whom he had heard discoursing at the theatre saloon.

'It's all right,' said Crieff quietly. 'The jury are bringing in an unanimous verdict of "successful." I think I shall abuse her in the "Chronicle" just to show I've a mind of my own.'

'If you do, I'll call you out!'

'There's Abrahams the manager, button-holing Day of the "Sun," and rolling his eyes in well-feigned enthusiasm. If you watch him, you'll see him take the jury seriatim, and go through the same performance with every one of them. I thought so! He's ordering champagne.'

'Who is that gentleman?' asked Sutherland, glancing towards the next table, where a little bald-headed man, surrounded by many admiring friends, was trifling with the cruet. Sutherland had recognised the individual who, in the saloon of the theatre, had introduced the little anecdote of his amours in Constantinople.

'What, don't you know him? That's Lagardère, of the "Plain Speaker."'

'Indeed! A journal, I presume?' '*The* journal of the period, based upon the new principle of extenuating nothing and setting down everything in malice. Lagardère can tell you to a nicety where La Perichole buys her false teeth, how much money Mrs. Harkaway Spangle pays her washerwoman weekly, and when any given leader of society is likely to pawn her diamonds or elope with her cook. You know Tennyson's lines—

> A lie which is all a lie can be met with and fought with outright,
> But a lie which is half a truth is a harder matter to fight!

Lagardère has achieved the complete art of so mingling truth and falsehood together that it is impossible even for himself to distinguish the one from the other. What wine will you take?'

'None. I am a water drinker.'

'Still! Well, you thrive upon the crystal draught. Hallo, what's Lagardère romancing about now?'

As he spoke the gentleman in question was leaning back in his chair, and in his peculiar drawl, to the edification of his immediate friends and admirers, speaking as follows:—

'When I was with the army in Schleswig-Holstein, the Hereditary Duke of Schlagberg-Schwangau lived in the same hotel, and there was an English girl stopping with him, disguised as a young officer. The Duke laid a wager that this girl would smoke more cigars than I could in the course of twelve hours. Bismarck, who dropped in by accident, held the stakes. We began at six p.m. and smoked on till four in the morning, when the girl gave in and had to be carried off to bed. I mention the fact because she was exactly the same height as the girl who acted to-night.'

'Impossible! Can't be the same!' said some one, feebly.

'Can't say, I'm sure. But it's the same sort of face, and the girl, when you provided her with champagne, used to recite splendidly.'

'How long was this ago, Lagardère?' asked Crieff, leaning over towards the other table.

'About twelve years. The date is fixed in my memory, because it was the year I fought the duel with the Austrian general at Vienna.'

Crieff smiled.

'And if,' he said, 'we put down Miss Vere's age at four-and-twenty (I believe she's scarcely twenty-two), she must have been, at the period you name, exactly twelve years old.'

A general laugh greeted this retort; but the journalist was not at all disconcerted.

'You see these sort of women are all so much alike,' he drawled. 'I've seen the same type of face in the harem at Stamboul, among the nautch-dancers of India, and at the Jardin Mabille.'

Sutherland, who had with difficulty kept his temper during this little scene, now turned his dusky eyes full on Lagardère.

'What do you mean by these sort of women?'

Lagardère shrugged his shoulders.

'What I meant was simply this, sir. Just as we recognise in certain faces the Jewish physiognomy; just as we see in certain religious orders the ascetic or separatist experience; just as in another way we distinguish the blood of the racehorse, or the breed of the greyhound, so we recognise in a certain type of women the type of the hetairai. The type is so uniform on the stage that if we take up a whole album of theatrical beauties, we shall find the features of a family, the characteristics of twin sisters.'

'Am I to understand,' said Sutherland, still retaining his self-possession, 'that in Miss Vere you recognise the type of woman without virtue?'

'Certainly,' drawled Lagardère. 'Observe, I am making no personal accusation. If the lady is a friend of yours——'

Sutherland rose to his feet.

'And if she is, Mr. Lagardère, since that is your name——'

'Why, then, I envy your luck, that's all.' returned Lagardère, with an ugly smile; and there was a general laugh.

Sutherland's hands came down, and they were clenched as if for a blow; but Crieff placed a warning hand upon his arm, and drew him away.

'Don't excite yourself' he said. 'It's only Lagardère.' 'The man is insufferable.'

'Everybody knows that.'

'He deserves to be horsewhipped.'

'Bless you, he has been horsewhipped over and over again; I think he rather likes it, and whenever it occurs he publishes a full account in his own journal. Come, you're no match for him, with his poisoned shafts. He'd find out the weak point in your armour at once. Come to the smoking-room, and have a cigar.'

As they crossed the room together, they heard the voice of Lagardère beginning again, with its usual drawling monotony—

'I say, Day, who's the fire-eater with Crieff? He reminds me of a man who once threatened to thrash me at St. Petersburg. It began at a card-party, where four of us were playing—the Grand Duke Nicolas, Prince Necrolowski, old Gortschenkoff, and myself.'

They heard no more. Sutherland strode on to the smoking-room, which was almost empty, and threw himself into a seat. His face was convulsed, and his frame shook with agitation.

'My dear Sutherland, you're exciting yourself for nothing. What is Miss Vere to you?'

'She is this much,' said Sutherland, 'that if I thought it would serve her I would kill that man like a dog.'

'Kill Lagardère! Ridiculous! Why, he's excellent fun.' 'Crieff, don't talk like that—it's not worthy of you. You know that man is a villain.'

'Upon my word, I don't think so.'

'What!'

'He only talks as most men do when actresses are in question, and I assure you he is a man of experience.'

'Experience!' echoed Sutherland bitterly. 'Yes, he has rolled in the shambles like the rest of us; he has polluted his body and his soul, and because he knows pollution, he dares to speak of one who is perhaps a martyr, and is, to him, an angel to a devil. Well, you are right, he only talks like the rest. Crieff, when I think of what that man is, of what most of us are, I hate my life, I wish I had never been born.'

'If you go on like this, old fellow, I shall think you are in love.'

'With my own ideal, yes. With that woman, though she almost realises it, no.'

'I'm glad to hear it,' said Crieff, earnestly. 'You're too good stuff to be wasted on an actress.5

'There again. You, too, sneer at one whose soul you cannot comprehend. Crieff, neither you nor I am worthy to tie that woman's shoestrings. Grant that her life has been evil—I'll not believe it, but assume it for the moment—what she has been society has made her. If she has fallen, it has been through the lusts of our accursed sex; and even now, her divine face, in its almost supernatural sorrow and sweetness, rebukes our lusts and puts our wicked experiences to shame. Oh, we men, we men! We who talk of purity, and seek it in our mothers and our wives! What are we? What are our lives? Sinks of foul passion, privileged by society and protected by the spirit of the law. I tell you, until a man's life is as pure as he would have the life of the woman he loves, he has no right to throw one stone at the most fallen woman in the world.'

There was silence for the space of some minutes. The two men smoked their cigars—Sutherland looking at vacancy, Crieff watching his face. The latter broke silence first.

'There's more in this than you've yet told me. Are you sure you have seen Miss Vere to-night for the first time!'

'I am not sure.'

'You know her?'

'No, but she is the ghost of a woman I once saw.'

Another pause, then Crieff spoke again.

'I tell you what, the best thing you can do is to make her acquaintance. Shall I ask Abrahams to introduce you?'

To his friend's surprise, Sutherland turned upon him a look of the uttermost consternation, and then said in a low voice—

'Not yet.'

CHAPTER XX
A PAINTER'S MODEL

While the public were busy discussing the merits and demerits of the star which had shone forth so suddenly upon the theatrical horizon, the lady herself was sitting in her dressing-room, apparently indifferent to all that passed or was likely to come. Her theatrical splendour had been cast off, and, enveloped now in a plain dark dress, she sat with dishevelled hair and pale cheeks, gazing dreamily at her own reflection in a mirror. Her maid, who was busily engaged in folding a delicate robe, was suddenly interrupted in her work by a knock at the door.

She opened it and admitted White. He walked over to the dreamy girl, put his arm round her shoulders, and kissed her fondly.

'Well, here I am,' he said quickly, with a glance at the busy, listening maid. 'Are you almost ready to come home?'

'I am quite ready,' returned Madeline, awakening from her dream.

She rose at once, coiled up her hair, put on her hat and cloak, and, after giving a few directions to her maid, took White's arm and left the room.

The house had been emptied and darkened, and the curtain raised, but confusion still prevailed upon the stage. Carpenters, scene-shifters, property men, actors and actresses, bereft of their splendour, all gathered according to their different grades around Abrahams, Hart, and the acting manager, who were holding forth like the outer world upon the merits of the heroine of the night.

Madeline, plainly dressed, thickly veiled, and clinging closely to White's arm, hoped to pass unseen through the crowd; but no sooner had she reached the centre of the stage than the keen eye of the manager fell upon her, and he advanced with outstretched hands.

'My dear Miss Vere,' he said, 'allow me to congratulate you on a big success. You've hit 'em right between the eyes, my dear. You have, by Jove!

I always said you would. Didn't I always say you would?' And turning to White, he added—

'White, old man, dine with me to-morrow at five sharp. I've a lot to talk over.'

Madeline received the homage quietly enough, and by a slight pressure of her hand upon the arm of her delighted guardian hurried him along out through the stage door.

It was a calm still night, the sky was studded with stars; not a breath of air was stirring, but the noise in the streets was deafening, the confusion bewildering. A crowd was gathered round the theatre door, cabs rattled up and down, streams of people moved hither and thither, as if in a feverish dream. Once in the open air, White paused to hail a cab, but Madeline stopped him.

'Let us walk,' she said quickly. 'I am so excited, and a breath of this cool air will do me good.'

'As you please, my dear,' returned White, and, clasping her hand more firmly upon his arm, he led her through the ever-moving crowd. What a crowd it was! Men and women, old and young, rich and poor, mingling together in one perpetual eddy; shivering, starving, half-clad children; brazen street-walkers disporting in finery even more tawdry than that which the actress had cast aside, and pale-faced outcasts glaring ghastly beneath the gaslight, clutching at their rags, and forcing their parched heated lips to offer up a curse to Him who had made them what they were.

Still veiled, still clinging closely to White's arms, Madeline passed slowly on, watching the crowd surging up and down beside her, seeing the faces pale, haggard, gaunt, and famine-stricken, flashing like phantoms. Now and then, as some weary woman passed beneath the glare of the gaslight, Madeline would pause and instinctively stretch forth her hand, as if to offer succour; but White, tightening his hold upon her, soothed the strange agitation which he knew to be rising, and firmly urged her on. Thus they left the trouble and the turmoil behind them, and passing into a sequestered square, with green trees around them, and the starlit heaven above, paused for a moment.

Madeline raised her veil, and looked upward.

'To think,' she said, 'that such a bright sky should shine upon so much wickedness and sorrow! I wonder if any people are ever happy until they die?'

'Happy! Of course they are. But come, we are lingering too long. I mean to drink a bottle of champagne to-night to celebrate your success, my dear.'

Madeline said no more, but quietly suffered him to lead her home.

It was certainly not such a home as one would picture as the abode of the queen of the night; for White, whose circumstances had never been affluent, had been brought lower than ever of late through the demands made upon him by Madeline, whom it had been necessary to fit out superbly before she could be presented to the gaze of the world. Still, poor as they were, the rooms were dear to Madeline, and as she entered them she felt stealing over her a sense of security and peace which she had not experienced all that evening before.

The good news had sped quickly, and the welcome given to the young actress was in keeping with all the rest. The table was spread for supper, the solitary bottle of champagne stood at the head, and poor Madame de Berny, now very worn and much aged, stood upon the narrow, dimly lighted stairs, with outstretched hands and quivering voice.

'Ah, my dear,' she said, as she drew Madeline into the bedroom, and assisted her to remove her hat and cloak, 'to think that only a few years ago you stood at my poor dear Marie's knee, and listened, with open eyes and mouth, to the stories she used to tell about the theatre. Now, you are a leading lady, and she—oh! my poor girl!'

'Don't cry, Madame,' said Madeline gently. 'I think Marie is happy.'

'Ah, Miss Madeline, how can I help grieving when I think of all my child has lost? To think that when she was rising so rapidly she could throw herself away upon a man who only betrayed her; that she should cause her father to die of a broken heart, and bring me to this!' As Madeline listened she sank into a chair, and let her weary head rest upon her hands. Her face was paler than it had been before, and Madame de Berny looking at her saw that a look of terrible sadness, which she had often noticed before, was creeping again into her eyes.

'Madeline, my dear,' she said, '*you* at least ought to be happy.'

The girl raised her head and smiled, and the smile was even more pitiful to behold than the look of sadness had been.

'Yes, you are right, Madame de Berny,' she said, 'I ought to be happy, so I will try to be from this night forth;' and as if to avoid further conversation she passed out into the sitting-room, where she found White awaiting her with a look of contented happiness in his face.

Puzzled and thoughtful, the old lady saw her go. What was the matter with the girl? She could not tell. Some few months before that day, when, in answer to an appeal from her, White had offered her a home, with himself and ward, she had come full of her own troubles, expecting to find a bright-eyed vivacious beautiful girl to soothe and cheer her. But instead of being the comforted she became the comforter. The first sight of the girl rent her heartstrings. Could this be Madeline Hazelmere? Could this be the lissome blue-eyed child, who had been the very impersonation of happy impulse and joy? This woman with the pale cheeks and strange, sad eyes? Madame de Berny paused before her shattered vision, gave one prolonged look, and burst into tears.

'Do not cry, dear Madame,' Madeline had said, kindly taking her old friend affectionately in her arms; 'the poor chevalier has gone from a world in which it is more terrible to live than to leave. I hope he has no memory of it—that at least he is at peace.'

Strange words, to come from a girl scarcely twenty years of age. They affected the Frenchwoman curiously at the time, and set her pondering afterwards.

The longer she remained with White the more she became impressed with the painful change that had taken place in Madeline. It was not that the child had become a woman, and had learnt to subdue her spirits to a sadder, more womanly tone; her soul was haunted by a memory which poisoned every pleasure which was lifted to her lips, and converted the world into a tomb. What the memory was, Madame could not understand, but she knew, whenever the girl's prospects seemed brightest, it haunted her the most, and that on that night when she had shone forth upon the world, and made hundreds envy her, it seemed to loom before her eyes more terribly than ever.

For several days after that night when she had achieved her great theatrical triumph, Madeline was too much occupied with business to give much thought to herself. She seemed to be lifted on a whirlwind, and carried along in tumult—forgetting the past, thinking nothing of the future, and scarcely conscious even of the bewildering present.

On the third morning, however, a note arrived which dispelled the dream that enveloped her, and brought her to herself again. The note had been placed among many others upon the breakfast table. She looked twice or thrice at the handwriting, then opened the envelope, and read as follows—

My dear Ophelia,—For the last few days I have been looking every hour, nay, every minute, for a visit from you. Am I to be again honoured by a visit from you in my studio, or may I take the liberty of waiting upon you? I have been putting one or two finishing touches to my work, but without the presence of the original I cannot bring it to completion.

Accept my friendly homage, which must be to you like a drop of water to the ocean.

Blanco Serena.

Having perused the note, Madeline laid it down again upon the table and looked round the room. How poverty-stricken it looked; how opposed to everything in the house of the successful painter who wrote that letter! She turned to White, who sat near her with his head buried in the folds of the 'Times.'

'Mr. Serena thinks that success has turned my head,' she said quietly. 'I must undeceive him by giving him my last sitting for "Ophelia" to-day.'

Accordingly, as soon as the breakfast was over, White retired to his studio, and Madeline went on her way.

On arriving at the house of Mr. Blanco Serena, she was made to feel her new greatness more than ever she had done before. The servant in livery looked at her with unusual respect, as he led her solemnly through long corridors to the studio, and ushered her into the presence of the great man himself.

Mr. Blanco Serena sat among his pictures. He wore an Eastern dressing-gown, and smoked a fantastically twisted meerschaum pipe. His eyes were fixed with rapt attention on the walls where his own handiwork was displayed; but when Madeline came in, he withdrew his gaze, collected his thoughts, and gave her a kindly welcome. To all his congratulations Madeline listened quietly, then she took her place before the painter, and, as he painted, her thoughts wandered to the past.

'Ah, those eyes, those eyes,' thought Serena to himself as he painted rapidly. 'I cannot put them on canvas. The critics will rave about my "Ophelia," but their praise will never satisfy me. If I could only paint the expression of that face I should think myself the genius they call me, not the poor impostor I know myself to be.'

Nevertheless, he tried and tried again, while Madeline sat patiently. Presently the studio door was opened, and with much ceremony, but no announcement, a stranger was shown in.

CHAPTER XXI
A WALK ACROSS HYDE PARK

The new-comer was a tall, robust-looking man in the prime of life, who was dressed with the utmost neatness and exactness, in the plain frock coat and grey-coloured trousers so much in favour among so-called business men Despite the ceremony with which he was introduced, and which showed that he was an individual of no small importance, his manner was modest and retiring in the extreme, and he looked around him on the splendid temple of modern painting, and at its famous owner, with smiling and good-humoured homage.

Serena put down his brush at once, and warmly shook hands. Then, seeing Madeline, the new-comer made a movement as if to retire.

'I am afraid I interrupt you,' he exclaimed.

But before he could say more, Madeline came forward gently, and offered her hand.

'Miss Hazelmere!' he exclaimed, recognising her; 'or shall I rather call you by the name you've already made so famous?'

'You know each other?' interrupted Serena, with some surprise.

'Oh yes,' cried Madeline, smiling. 'Mr. Forster and I are old, old friends.'

At this statement even the new-comer himself evinced some surprise; but Madeline continued —

'When I was only a very little girl, Mr. Forster, I remember how you came to see my guardian one day when he was sick, and how, when you went away, he cried and told me how good you were. You came often after that, and we used to talk of you together. And the other night at the theatre, when I saw your face in the box, I felt so glad, and I said to myself, "I won't be afraid now, for there are at least two kind faces in front—one my dear guardian's, the other the face of the best friend he ever had in the world."'

Under this simple praise Forster looked a little uncomfortable.

'How is White?' he inquired nervously, as if for want of something better to say.

Madeline did not immediately reply, so Serena answered for her.

'At the present moment, my dear Forster, our friend White is the happiest fellow in all the world, or shall I rather say, in all Bohemia. A hundred successful original plays, a thousand successful adaptations, could not have given him half the pleasure that he feels at the triumph of his charming ward. And well may he be proud. He has hatched at his lonely hearth a phoenix, who rises out of the ashes of our drama, to glorify the stage.'

'Ah, but you spoil me,' said Madeline, well pleased, nevertheless. 'It is so easy to act; and, besides, who but my dear guardian has taught me the little I know?'

'For you it is easy,' returned Serena, gallantly; 'ah yes—and it is easy for a flower to look beautiful or for a lark to sing a splendid song. That is all the difference between genius and talent. All you have to do is to be natural, to be your charming self, and the art comes of itself, like the perfume from a rose.'

Madeline looked at Forster and laughed.

'Mr. Serena would not say that,' she said, 'if he knew what a goose I was when I first began. It was in that little theatre at Ryde, in the Isle of Wight, and when I went on the people could not hear a word, and I did not know what to do with my hands and feet. The manager said I was the greatest idiot who ever stept upon his stage, and he was right.'

Serena was not to be dismayed.

'Another proof of genius,' he cried. 'Mere talent would have caught all the tricks of the stage, and by means of its affectations and insincerities gained cheap applause at the outset. I have often heard my friend Eugene Aram say that when he began he was so great a stick that no manager would keep him in his theatre. The people laughed at his legs, mimicked his voice. Critics compared him to the Knight of the Rueful Visage. He was invertebrate, inchoate, inarticulate. Look at him now. The people adore his legs and consider his voice music itself. That's genius, my dear, depend upon it.'

'One touch of genius makes amends for much,' observed Forster quietly. 'I don't think Aram is a good actor even now, but he is interesting and intelligent, and his eccentricities have a fascination.' He added, turning to the picture in the easel, 'May I ask, is that picture a commission?'

Serena shook his head.

'If I could afford it,' he answered, 'I should say "Yes," and make a present of it—to the original. But it's not worthy of her; upon my word it's not worthy. I'm ashamed of my art when I compare my miserable attempt to the reality.'

'It is very like,' said Forster thoughtfully, studying before the canvas; 'but too sorrowful; too sorrowful! I should not like to see Miss Hazelmere look like that.'

'You see, it's an "Ophelia,"' observed Serena apologetically.

'I would rather you had painted her as smiling and happy. So young a face should not reveal such depths of suffering. There is no hope here, and in Miss Hazelmere's face all should be hope and happiness.'

Turning to glance at Madeline, he was startled and surprised. She was gazing now at the picture with the very expression depicted in it; all life, all pleasure seemed to have faded out of her face, leaving nothing but blankness there, and the shadow of a painful dream. Her thoughts seemed to have wandered far away, and have left her unconscious of the presence in which she stood.

But while he gazed the look faded, and the light came back to her eyes. Meeting his gaze she smiled, and held out her hand.

'I must go now,' she said; 'my sitting is over, and I am already past my time.'

'Do you ride or walk?' asked Forster.

'I am going to walk across the park, and then, at the Marble Arch, I shall take a cab.'

'May I offer myself as an escort?' he said, after a moment's hesitation. 'I am going that way, and—and———'

He paused, smiling benignly and blushing boyishly, but Madeline at once put her hand upon his arm and accepted his escort with a happy smile. Serena saw them to the door, and watched them as they walked chatting up the street.

'I think I know the signs,' muttered the painter to himself, 'and if Forster is not fascinated, Eros Athanatos is no true god. Well, so be it. It will be none the worse for my pictures, and a splendid thing for the girl.'

Left alone with Madeline, Forster felt constrained and a little uneasy, but her perfect simplicity and frankness soon put him entirely at his ease. She was indeed happy beyond measure in his accidental companionship. Since her early childhood his name had been familiar to her as that of one whom

White emphatically pronounced to be 'the best man he had ever known or hoped to know,' and his perfect gentleness and kindliness, which impressed even the most casual observer of his countenance, won the open-hearted girl at once. Leaning lightly on his arm, she chatted away frankly and fearlessly, as she might have done to White himself. Frank without boldness, fearless without forwardness, in every word and gesture free and *spirituelle* without affectation, she fairly won her way to his heart of hearts. Talking with her was like talking with a child; she was so unconscious of herself, so un reserved; and this, seeing her wonderful physical beauty, constituted at once her peril and her charm.

Passing in at Albert Gate, they crossed Rotten Row, and strolled quietly across the park. It was a bright golden day, and Madeline, always the creature of physical and external impressions, seemed to kindle into new gladness. She looked at the fair horsewomen, of whom there was a fair sprinkling already, though it was early in the afternoon, and laughed for pleasure.

'Do you like riding?' she asked. 'I have never ridden; but I think if I were on a horse's back, I could ride—and ride—and ride—and never stop.'

'You would find it duller than you think,' said Forster. 'I ride here often, and do not think it very amusing.'

To his astonishment Madeline asked, quietly—

'Does Mrs. Forster ride?'

'Mrs. Forster?' he repeated.

'I mean your wife.'

'My wife,' he echoed, in still greater astonishment. 'I am not married!'

'How strange!' exclaimed Madeline, with raised eyebrows. 'Not married?'

'Why is it so strange?' asked Forster, with a laugh.

'You do not look like an old bachelor—no, I don't mean that; but there is something in your manner which makes one think of a kind wife, and little children, and home. You are not old, and yet I feel as if I could speak to you so freely, and could tell you anything, as I do my dear guardian. Do you understand?'

'I think I do—partly,' answered Forster, not without a certain uneasiness.

'And that lady whom I saw you with at the theatre on the first night of "Cymbeline"—I thought *she* was Mrs. Forster.'

'That was my sister.'

They walked on for a little in silence. Forster was the first to speak.

'It is curious, after all, that you should class me among the married people, for the fact is, I am a widower. My poor wife died many years ago, and left me one child, a boy. My sister keeps my house; but when you talk of home, and home ties, I cannot help telling you that I am a very lonely man—quite an old bachelor, indeed, in my way. When, after a long day in the City, I return to my house, and get among my books and pictures, I am still lonely, but sometimes very happy after all.'

A girl less naïve and unsuspicious than Madeline might have been astonished at this fragment of autobiography, coming from such a man, and might have questioned her own fascinations as to the origin of such candour. But Madeline thought it quite natural, as between friend and friend.

'But let us speak of other things,* continued Forster, after a pause, 'of yourself. I sometimes think, if you will forgive me for saying so, that you must be rather lonely too.'

'No,' she replied readily; adding with her brightest smile, 'not while I have Mr. White.'

'Ah, he is a good fellow—but you have neither father nor mother.'

Madeline shook her head.

'They died long ago. I do not remember them.'

'Your other relations?'

'I have none.'

'None?'

'When my father died I was left with poor people, who brought me up. Then trouble came, and Uncle Mark died, and I was brought to Mr. White. Uncle Luke brought me. After he went away he used to write me, but at last all letters ceased. Mr. White made inquiries, but he had disappeared, and no one knew where he had gone. Dear Uncle Luke!'

Her voice was broken, and her eyes were full of tears.

'What made you think of going upon the stage?'

'I used to go to the theatre with Mademoiselle de Berny, and she used to make me hear her go through her parts. I always loved acting, Mr. Forster, and at Mr. White's there were so many professional people. Afterwards, when I was older, I tried to think how I could repay my dear guardian for all his kindness, and then I thought if I could act—only a little—it would be some help. When he first heard me recite he was pleased, and I told him I would like to become an actress and act in *his* plays. So he sent me down into the country to try. That was how it began.'

'And you like acting?'

'Better than anything in the world; best of all, Mr. Forster, because it makes my dear guardian happy.'

'You will make a great name/

'I don't care for that—yes, I do care; for a great name would mean a great deal of money, and I want *that?*

'Indeed! Why?'

'Because Mr. White is poor, and I want to make him rich—as rich as he deserves to be, for all his goodness to me. I love him so much. I should like to put him in a palace and surround him with splendour, like a king in a fairy tale.'

Forster laughed merrily.

'I don't think White would care for a palace, and he's too Bohemian for a king.'

'What do you mean by Bohemian?' asked Madeline, with her characteristic frankness. 'I often hear the word, and I don't understand it.'

'I'm not sure that I do either,' he answered at once, 'unless it means unconventionality, carelessness of appearances, contempt for Mrs. Grundy. In White's case, though, it means far more—honesty, lightness of heart, patience under disappointment, all combined in one of the best fellows in the world.'

'If you knew all about him, Mr. Forster, you would say even more than that. If you knew—if you knew—but nō one will ever know but God! Oh, I should die if he even thought me ungrateful—he is so good. I have no other friend in all the world!'

'Do not cry; you have one other.'

'No.'

'While I live, I hope you will not doubt it.'

She paused, and, looking at him through her tears, held out both her hands.

'It is so kind of you to say so,' she cried. 'Yes, you are good also; but no one in the world can be to me what Mr. White has been.'

'It is right that you should be grateful,' said Forster, gently, 'and I think more highly of you for that holy feeling. But here we are at the Marble Arch. Must I call a cab?'

'If you please, unless you will drive home with me, and see Mr. White. I know he is at home, for he is very busy on his new play.'

The offer was accepted as frankly as it was made, and Forster's face shone with pleasure.

'Shall it be a hansom or a four-wheeler?' he said, smiling.

'A hansom, please; I cannot bear these slow old things, and I love hansoms. I used to think when I was a little girl that I would like to have one all to myself, and drive about in it for ever.'

A hansom was called, and the pair entered it; they drove swiftly away to St. John's Wood. Very little more was said on either side, but Forster felt very happy.

They turned into the old familiar street, and reined up before the old familiar 'studio,' which Madeline knew and loved so well. They found the dramatist *en déshabille* and very busy, not on the new play, as Madeline had stated, but on a picture—which, on their entry, he hastily covered up.

'My dear Forster,' he exclaimed, with real delight. 'How glad I am! But, upon my life, you puzzle me. How does it happen that——'

He paused and looked questioningly at Madeline, who laughed and explained.

'I met Mr. Forster when I was sitting for my portrait, and he brought me home.'

'Very good of him.'

'Was it not? But what are you doing? Painting something! You told me the other day that you did not intend to paint any more.'

'It's nothing,' returned the dramatist, 'nothing at all. Only a kind of sketch—a little thing of memory. No, no,' he added, as Madeline approached the canvas, 'you mustn't look at it. It's a secret. It's—it's a—portrait—of—a—young—lady—I—admire.'

Quietly laughing, he endeavoured to prevent Madeline from inspecting the picture, but she was too quick for him, and had already uncovered the easel.

'Why, it's *me!*' she cried, and continued merrily, with a theatrical gesture, 'I mean "it is I"!—which is the same thing, and more grammatical.'

'Grammar was never your strong point, my dear,' observed White, gently. 'Well, what do you think of it?'

It was Madeline indeed, but Madeline the child, as she first appeared, with wild, wistful eyes, in that lonely studio. The colours were crude, the drawing incorrect, but for all that the expression was there, and the whole thing was instinct with life.

With smiling face and clasped hands, Madeline stood gazing at the likeness; then, as if moved by a sudden impulse, she threw her arms round White's neck and kissed him, first on one cheek then on the other, while Forster looked on in amused sympathy.

'You like it, my dear? It was—ahem!—a sort of a kind of an inspiration. It came upon me when I was looking at the play, and, by Jove, I had to do it.'

'It is really capital,' said Forster. 'I should have recognised the likeness anywhere.'

'Of course, it's only a daub,' returned White, humbly. 'I might have painted decently if I had stuck to it, instead of dangling after Jew managers and doing potboilers for Eugene Aram. But you're fresh from seeing Serena's picture, and that gives my thing no chance.'

'I don't care for Mr. Serena's picture,' cried Madeline. 'I do not like to tell him so, but I am sure I am not so lovely as he makes me, and I know my eyes are not *green*. I like your picture ever so much the best—and, oh! it was so kind of you to do it, Mr. White. It is just like me as I was—a nasty, little, pale thing, with shock hair!'

And she stood contemplating the likeness in an ecstasy of honest reminiscence.

'My dear, you were never nasty,' said White, good humouredly. 'Shock haired, if you like, but charming as you are now.'

'Always charming, I'm sure,' suggested Forster, mildly 'Do you know, I should like to buy this picture?'

White opened his eyes.

'Take it, my dear fellow, it's of no pecuniary value. Stop, though! I can make a composition of it by putting in some flowers and a bit of background, and calling it "Primroses—a Study," or something of that sort.'

'You'll allow *me* to fix the price?' said Forster.

But there Madeline interfered.

'No, Mr. White, you must not sell it; that is, you will sell it to no one but the original. How much must I give you for it? A thousand guineas? Two thousand? Tell me, and I'll begin to save at once.'

She paused with sparkling eyes, looking into her guardian's face.

'Miss Hazelmere is right,' said Forster; 'she must keep the sketch as a souvenir of her childhood. No other person in the world has a right to possess it.'

No more was said on the subject, and White soon led the way into the adjoining house, there to dispense the hospitalities to his friend, who, however, soon took his leave, and departed by omnibus towards his home in South Kensington.

The night afterwards, however, Madeline saw his hearty face looking from a box in the theatre, and between the acts he came round to speak to her. He said little, but what he did say set her wits working, and the next morning she told White, as they sat at breakfast, that Mr. Forster had witnessed the performance on the previous evening.

'Oh, indeed,' said the dramatist with a pleased smile. 'Did he come round?'

'Yes, for a few minutes.'

'It's rather odd, and I think you may take it as a compliment. Forster doesn't care for the drama as a rule.'

'Indeed!'

'Fact, my dear. Why, though we're such capital friends, he has seldom come even to see *my* plays.'

'Do you know his sister?'

'Who told you he had a sister?' asked White, slyly.

'He did.'

'Indeed. Well, the fact is, I don't know her. She's a sort of amiable Ogre; pious, you know, and all that sort of thing. Whenever I have dined at the house, she has been invisible; but we've generally met at his club.'

'And his little boy?'

'Eh? Who told you he had a little boy? The same informant. Why, he's been giving you his autobiography!'

'He only told me he was a widower.'

'And that's more than he ever told to me, though of course I was aware of it. You see, our friendship has been a sort of club friendship, and, besides, all the favour has been on his side. A rich man like Forster and a poor devil like myself can't meet on equal terms.'

'He is rich, then?'

'Very. One of the oldest firms in the city. His house in Cromwell Road is like a palace, and the pictures in it alone would realise a fortune.'

Madeline looked thoughtful, then she said—'I'm sorry he's so rich.'

'God bless me! why?'

'I don't like rich people, and—and he's so nice!' 'If you were a poor poet, or a struggling painter, or a musician with a craze, you wouldn't blame the dear fellow for his good fortune. He's so generous, so good-hearted—not only to me, but to every fellow-creature who needs his help. Then look how modest and unaffected he is. His own flunkeys are lords to him, and when he asks for a cup in his own house he's like a humble City clerk asking deferentially for refreshment in a large hotel.'

Having thus begun, White did not pause till he had sounded the praises of his patron over and over again; told of his goodness and generosity to himself personally; of his countless good deeds to others, who would otherwise have sunk long ago in the dark waters of Bohemia. The theme brought honest tears, as White concluded that 'if ever there was an angel in a frock-coat and grey trousers, it was James Forster.'

Unsuspicious as Madeline herself, White at first saw nothing remarkable in the close interest with which Forster followed the fortunes of his ward. Nor, when some days afterwards the merchant again put in an appearance, bringing with him a bouquet of choice flowers, did the simple soul awake to much suspicion of the truth.

One afternoon, however, as White sat at work on the scenario of a new play, which he was about to submit to the distinguished Mr. Aram, Madeline entered in great agitation.

'Are you busy? May I speak to you?' she exclaimed.

'Certainly, my dear; my time is yours. But what's the matter?'

'Something terrible has happened.'

'Indeed!'

The dramatist pushed his papers aside, and arose trembling to his feet.

'Mr. Forster——'

There she paused.

'Not ill, I hope?'

'Oh, no, no. But I have just left him. He was at Mr. Serena's, and he came part of the way home.'

'Yes. Pray go on.'

'Oh, I was afraid of it!' cried Madeline, with a sob. 'I should have avoided him!—and yet, at first, I could not believe it possible.'

'Do explain!' cried White, in hopeless perplexity.

Madeline sank into a chair, crying, and hid her face in her hands.

'He has asked me to become his wife.'

CHAPTER XXII
BLANCO SERENA

Mr. Blanco Serena, the prophet of a new school of painting, the object of which was more closely to reconcile and blend the kindred arts of painting, poetry, and music, occupied a large detached house in South Kensington, whither his worshippers flocked every Sunday, as to the shrine of some patron saint. The walls were embellished with designs from his own pencil, or those of his own friends; the furniture was his own invention, in form as well as colour; the ceilings were cerulean, like the heavens, and like the heavens were studded with golden stars; so that when the rapt creature looked up in contemplation or in inspiration, his vision was rewarded by celestial glimpses. There were no carpets on the floors, but here and there costly rugs were strewn. The house formed a quadrangle, in the centre of which was an open court with a playing fountain, and by the fountain, in fine weather, the prophet and the faithful would lie upon tiger and lion skins, smoking pipes and calumets of strange device.

Serena himself was a middle-aged man, with a high, bald forehead, long apostolic beard, and large brown dreamy eyes. He was a good soul, with the kindest disposition, and the affectations of his profession did not extend to his personal character. The fault lay more in his stars than himself that he had become an eccentric painter. He began merrily, in Bohemian fashion, with a clay pipe in his mouth, painting real landscapes from nature and human beings from the life, and producing compositions noteworthy for fine colour and honest effect. But he discovered early, as many another prophet has discovered, that it did not pay. In an angry moment, one day, disgusted with a picture which he had just completed, he took up his brush and deliberately reversed all the colours of his composition. Where water was blue, he made it vermilion; where boughs were green and golden, he made them purple and cerulean; a white human figure standing by water became an Ethiop, through excess of shadow; and finally, out of sheer devilry, he covered the daffodil sky with layers of pea-green cloud. He had just completed his work, and was scowling at it grimly, when there entered Ponto, the new art critic from Camford. No sooner did Ponto see the mutilated picture than he clasped his hands and raised his eyes rapturously to heaven.

'At last!' he cried, and wrung Serena by the hand. 'Only paint like this, and your fame is sure.' The 'Megatherium' of the following Saturday contained an article by Ponto, entitled, 'Mr. Blanco Serena's new painting—a Reverie in Vermilion and Pea-green,' in which article it was clearly demonstrated, not merely that the painting was one of the masterpieces of the world, but that the painter was the first 'modern man' who had dared 'to give prominence on canvas to evanescent cosmic moods.' From that day forth the epithets cosmic, august, titanic, supersensuous, sublime, and other adjectives of equal meaning were the especial property of Serena and his imitators; for that imitators came soon goes perhaps without saying, seeing that imitation is so easy. 'Reveries' on canvas became the rage; to be non-natural was the fashion. Artists who had once in their innocence strained every nerve to study great models and to copy nature, now tortured ingenuity to represent 'evanescent cosmic moods'—out of colour, out of drawing, and out of all harmony with anything but the diseased invention of bad painters and the bad critics who urged them on.

Serena, as we have said, was a good fellow, and took his success sensibly. Only to one man in the world did he secretly confess the facts of the case. 'I know I am a humbug,' he said to Forster, 'and that those who praise me are humbugs. I know that I paint worse than I did at twenty, and that, when I die, and my school dies with me, posterity will find me out. This is why, now and then, I follow the true lights of my soul, and paint a true picture; just to keep my work from utterly perishing in Limbo, just to enable some poor soul in the far future to say, "After all, Blanco Serena might, had he chosen, have escaped from being the æsthetic Prig of his period." But what I am the scribblers and the public have made me. If another man painted a bony woman in yellow gauze, with red hair and pale green eyes, and impossible arms and legs, he would be found out directly: but only let me paint such a figure, and call it "Persephone musing by the waters of Lethe," or "Memory kneeling by the grave of Hope," or "Fading away: a Sonata in Sunset tints," and I am sure at least of Ponto's praise and the public approval. Well, of all humbugs Art humbug is the worst, though, after all, worse saints have been canonised than Blanco Serena.'

To the studio of Serena, a few days after Madeline's visit, came Ponto, the art critic, bringing with him a thin, middle-aged. Frenchman, with a coarse mouth and a sinister expression of countenance. The painter, with deft and careless hand, was adding a few touches to the picture of Ophelia.

'Serena,' cried Ponto, 'let me introduce you to M. Auguste de Gavrolles, from Paris—the friend and pupil of the supreme and impeccable Gautier. He is a poet, an ardent worshipper of your genius, and in all matters of art completely sane a cosmic.'

Serena smiled and held out his hand, which the Frenchman took rapturously, and raised it to his lips.

'Ah, Monsieur,' he exclaimed, 'this is the proudest moment of my life!'

Ponto threw himself into a chair, and looked around him with a smile of feline insipidity.

'What's that you have there, my dear Serena?' he asked, blinking at the picture. 'Ah, I see, another superbly musical meditation in the minor key of flake white!'

'It is a portrait,' said Serena, quietly.

'An ideal portrait—quite so. How wonderfully in that floating drapery you have conveyed the serene insouciance of trances of languor crescending into aberration of supersensual dream!'

'It is neither more nor less than a careful likeness of the original,' returned Serena, modestly. 'In the arrangement of the colours I wish to convey— —'

'The spirituality of a superb and life-consuming dream, fired with the arid flame of incipient passion—ethereal, almost epicene—conscious of throbbing vistas of asexual retrospection and chromatic wastes of fruitless future fantasy, interspersed with forlorn gulfs of irremediable darkness and despair. Added to this, and seen in the pose of the limp hand and the melancholy texture of the flesh tints, is the Lethean consciousness of a drowned and devastated ideal, unlightened by one star of promise and irredeemed by one flower of celestial ruth. Am I right? Do I take your meaning?'

'Just so,' said Serena, dryly, and turned to look at the Frenchman.

The latter, with shoulders elevated, and *pince-nez* in position, was gazing eagerly at the portrait. He now turned with a bow to Serena.

'A portrait, did you say, Monsieur?'

'Yes.'

'May I ask of whom?'

'Of the new actress, Miss Diana Vere.'

'It is curious,' said Gavrolles; 'but pardon, the face seems familiar to me. I have seen it somewhere before.'

'Indeed! Well, such a face, once seen, is not likely to be forgotten.'

'Is it not beautiful!' cried the Frenchman, with elevated shoulders and extended hands; 'and seen upon your canvas, how sublime! How shall I express to you—to you, great artist, great genius, what at this moment I feel? But tell me, Monsieur, this—is she a friend of yours? No? Yes?'

'I know her slightly, that is all.'

'What would I not give to see her, to have the honour of her acquaintance!'

'If you wish to see her,' said Serena, 'you have only to go to the Parthenon Theatre, where she appears nightly.'

'I will go; but stay, I return this night to Paris—but I shall return, and then, perhaps, you will introduce me?' Serena shook his head.

'I'm afraid not,' he answered. 'The lady sees no one, and is quite a recluse. What is still more peculiar is the fact that she has a particular aversion to gentlemen of your nation—to France and to Frenchmen without exception.'

'You amaze me, Monsieur! Ah, this insular prejudice, how bête! But perhaps she has reason—perhaps she has lived in my country.'

'Can't say,' returned Serena, as if tired of the subject; and he commenced again to work at the picture.

Ponto looked over his shoulder as he worked with admiring eyes.

'You must know Gavrolles better,' he observed; 'I like him; we all like him. He is a man of ideas.'

Gavrolles placed his hand upon his heart and bowed.

'I have learned of my master, the immortal Théophile, to worship what is beautiful, to adore what is superb.'

'In France, at the present moment,' continued Ponto, patronisingly, 'Gavrolles represents the school of supersensuous personal yearning. In his last book of poems, "Parfums de la Chair," and particularly in that superb fragment, "Cameo Satanique," he has supplied the connecting link between the celestial appetite of Gautier and the divine nausea of Baudelaire. Till Gavrolles came, the calendar of imperial passion was incomplete. What Smith, Jones, and Keats are to our august poetry, that is he to the poetry of modern France.'

'Ah, Monsieur, forbear!' cried the Frenchman. 'You overwhelm me with shame. Such praise—before the master!'

'I will go further,' cried Ponto, recklessly, 'and I will fearlessly assert, that in the golden roll of the fearless and fecund Parisian Parnassus, there is no more affluent name than that of my friend Gavrolles. His "Chant Aromatique" to the Venus of Dahomey would alone entitle him to a place in that Pantheon where the names of Victor Hugo and Achille de Ganville shine effulgent, while his masterly management of the Sestina, in his great address to myself, is only to be compared with the Titanic sculpture cf Michael Angelo, or the colossal imagery of Potts.'

Serena smiled gloomily. He was familiar with that sort of praise, as addressed to himself, but, with all his cynicism, he scarcely approved of its lavish application to an obscure Frenchman. The fact was, that the whole speech formed part and parcel of an eulogistic article, in Ponto's best manner, then in type for the 'Megatherium,' a widely circulated literary journal in which nepotism and malignity formed equal parts.

'By the way,' observed Serena, still quietly at work, 'I see that MacAlpine has been falling foul of our friend Potts in the "North British."'

MacAlpine was a cantankerous critic, hailing from beyond the Border, and with a Highland disregard of consequences in the expression of his literary opinions. Ponto turned livid.

'MacAlpine,' he exclaims, 'bears to the immortal Potts the relation that a leper does to Paian Apollo. It is well known that MacAlpine has been guilty of murder, bigamy, rapine, incest, and larceny, but all these are nothing compared to his fiendish and futile statement that Potts is not the most stupendous, wonderful, awe-inspiring, celestial, and cosmic creature existing on this planet. Mac Alpine, it is notorious, left his grandmother to starve in the workhouse, and kicked his little brother to death, but these crimes are venial by the side of his hateful and hellish assertion that your divine and spirit-compelling picture of "Psyche watching the Sleep of Eros" is out of proportion.'

Serena sighed, then smiled.

'Do you know, my dear Ponto, I sometimes think that a little hostile criticism is refreshing. I really find it so, when it comes in my way.'

Ponto shuddered.

'The only true attitude of criticism is that of worship,' he exclaimed. 'The man who, in contemplating your consummate masterpiece, could be conscious of any feeling save of the surging forces of cosmic yearning, flowering into the form of perfect idealisation, and shining with the reflected light of coruscating eternities of sterile pain—such a man, I say, is capable of any social crime, and incapable of any aesthetic perception.'

'Pardon me,' returned Serena. 'What you say is doubtless very flattering, but if criticism is pure worship, how do you account for your own attacks on the literary productions of the enemies of the aesthetic school?'

'All modern schools but one are execrable,' returned Ponto, with a grinding of the teeth and a waving of the hand. 'It is enough for us to pronounce that they are not—Art! In approaching them we do not criticise—we simply obliterate; we crush, as we crush a reptile or an unclean thing. The man who denies absolute perfection to Potts, or universal mastery to Blanco Serena, at once proclaims, not merely his incompetence to speak on any artistic subject whatever, but by inference his moral degradation as a human being. We wave him from our vision—we wipe him out. He is a loathsome Philistine, an outcast, physically and intellectually abominable. Such a man once said, in my hearing, that "Mademoiselle de Maupin" was not the purest, wholesomest, most supremely sane and salutary book produced since the Divine Comedy, and that, on the whole, he preferred Wordsworth to Gautier as a moral teacher. My whole soul revolted. I shrank from that man with a shudder, and I am convinced that the wretch is ethically lost and intellectually paralytic.'

The Frenchman shook his head dolefully, as over some sad chronicle of human wickedness or sorrow. Serena laughed and turned with twinkling eyes to the excited critic.

'Confess between ourselves that "Mademoiselle de Maupin" is not virile. For my own part, I never read it without feeling as if I had been slobbered over by a dirty baby.'

'For God's sake, Serena,' cried Ponto, 'don't talk like that. I know you don't mean it, but the very expression is worthy that infernal scoundrel MacAlpine. Not virile? Certainly not, and Heaven forbid! Virility, dear master, is coarseness, ugliness, rudeness, and hideousness. Is a rose-leaf virile? Are sweet shawms, exquisite scents, forlorn pulsations, and cadences of sexless and impotent desire, are these virile? The book of which we speak has been exquisitely called by a contemporary the Golden Book of spirit and sense; nay more, "The Holy Writ of Beauty!" In every page of it we feel the swooning consciousness, the stinging and slaying scourge, of fruitless and rootless passion, and the divine dew of incommunicable and luminous lust watering the spent fibres of a parched and palpitating aesthetic dream. We feel more! We feel that in realising this swoon of sensuous yet despairing pain, sharp as tears, bitter as brine, and sinuous as the serpent, and in falling back like a fountain to the ground from the heaven of eternally unsatisfied longing and delight, we penetrate to the central mystery of life, and see the white heart of the great rose of being pulsating with one melodious throb of self-satiating and non-virile bliss!'

Serena yawned, for he had heard all this before, and he was not particularly interested. As for the Frenchman, he listened and applauded, with many shrugs and smiles, but there was a lurking expression in his cat-like eye which showed that he was not altogether blind to the absurdity of the fatuous Ponto.

It is not our intention further to place on record the lucubrations of this typical critic of the period. The reader is doubtless familiar with the kind of criticism of which he and such as he are the mouthpieces. It has, perhaps, one redeeming merit—that of earnestness and thoroughness—and even its characteristic nepotism should not blind us to the fact that it reveals the existence of a real aspiration.

Arm-in-arm, Ponto and Gavrolles presently sallied forth, leaving Serena to enjoy his quiet meerschaum alone. As they went, the Frenchman was loud in praise of the painter, of his mighty genius and unassuming ways.

'But this "Ophelia" whom he has painted,' he cried presently, 'is she so fair as that?'

Ponto confessed that he seldom went to the theatre, and he had not seen the original.

'Ah, I am interested much,' cried the other. 'I must see her, I must know her, when I return to London.'

They hailed a hansom and got into it together. As they drove along the crowded streets in eager conversation, a young man, passing along on foot, glanced at their faces, started, and gazed eagerly at Gavrolles. The gaze only occupied a moment, then the vehicle was gone.

The young man was Edgar Sutherland, strolling along to his club.

'That face!' he muttered to himself, standing and looking after the hansom. 'Where have I seen it before? Is it possible? Good heavens, now I remember! Can it be indeed the same?'

Lost in thought, with set lips and knitted brow, he walked on to his destination.

CHAPTER XXIII
AT THE CLUB

James Forster, of the great City firm of Forster and Forster, found himself at the early age of thirty-five a rich and prosperous man, with plenty of leisure and a simple taste for imaginative literature and the fine arts. He was a widower, his wife having died ten years previously in the first year of their marriage, leaving him an only son; and his fine mansion in Cromwell Road, South Kensington, was presided over by his spinster sister Margaret, his elder by some five years.

The cares of business sat lightly on this good man's shoulders, and he could at any moment have retired with a large independence; but early habits and inclination kept him to the office, long after his daily presence there was unnecessary, and he wished to remain there until his son was old enough to take his place. His office hours, however, were very short, and when they were over he assiduously cultivated the society of painters and men of letters. Many a struggling artist had cause to bless his liberality. The walls of his house were decorated with some of the finest paintings of the period; and he loved nothing better than to add to his collection by discovering genius, and paying liberally for its works, long before the trumpet of fame had given those works a price in the market.

Although himself a strict man of business, he loved Bohemian society and Bohemian ways, always holding good-humouredly that it was the prerogative of artists and authors to play pranks denied to plain men like himself. His admiration for genius was quite simple and boy-like. In certain departments of literature, particularly in that of early English poetry, he had an almost special knowledge, gained in the course of his acquisition of a fine old-fashioned library; and nothing delighted him more than to communicate informally to the 'Megatherium' or to 'Notes and Queries' occasional notes and correspondence on the pet subjects of his study.

He had known White for years, and been his staunchest helper and benefactor. Poor White, the best and kindliest fellow in the world, had neither the art of making money nor the knack of keeping it when it came; so that he was generally neck deep in difficulties, and would have sunk often in the quagmire of bankruptcy had no helping hand been near. As a painter he was not a genius; yet Forster bought his pictures, very often commissioning and paying for them long before they had taken shape on the easel. So that the gentle Bohemian had been heard more than once to exclaim that, in the course of his long heavenward pilgrimage, he had encountered only one guardian angel, and that angel was James Forster.

The day after the interview described in a recent chapter, White and Forster sat alone dining at a quiet table in the Junior Athenæum Club, of which the merchant was a member.

'I am glad she has told you,' said Forster quietly. 'Yes, I have asked her to become my wife.'

White did not speak for some minutes, and his expression was very sad and scared.

'I am very sorry,' he murmured at last. 'I can't tell how sorry I am. I—I don't know what to say, upon my soul. It is such an honour—such a surprise too—and you, God knows you are the best man in the world. But it can't be. You had it from her own lips. She will never marry.'

White's eyes were full of tears, and he gulped down a glass of wine in extreme emotion.

'After all,' he added eagerly, not meeting the other's eyes, 'she's only a poor girl, and it wouldn't be right for a man in your position to marry an actress.'

'I never loved a woman before,' returned the merchant, 'and I know I shall never love again. My first marriage was not altogether a happy one, and I was driven more than led into it; but, thank God, I did my duty, and I have my boy. But I'm a lonely man—you don't know how lonely, and I thought—I thought this might have been.'

'I wish to God it could, I do with all my soul.'

'I am sure of that.'

'And oh, my dear Forster,' cried White, almost sobbing, 'don't fancy that my dear girl doesn't value you at your worth. She knows how good you are. She knows what a friend you have been to us all, but—but——'

'But she does not love me. Well, I could hardly dare to expect it.'

'It's not that. I swear it's not that. As I'm a living man I believe she worships the very ground you tread on. "Dear Guardian," she said to me last night, "I never was so happy and proud, and yet I never was so sad.

Tell him how grateful I am, how gladly I would die to serve him—but as for marriage, you know it can never be."'

'Do you know that?' asked Forster, looking keenly at his companion.

White's face was pale as death.

'I do know it.'

'She will never marry?'

'Never.'

I think I understand,' said Forster, with a sigh of relief. 'She has made up her mind to devote herself to her noble profession, and she believes, perhaps wisely, that a great artist should be free of all domestic ties. But do you think I am one of those idiots, those miserable moneybags, who account the profession of an actress a degradation? She should never leave the stage, unless of her own wish and will. She should be encouraged, helped as far as a plain fellow like myself could help her—in all the aspirations of her art. I should glory in her success, and triumph in her triumph—I should indeed.'

White looked at the bright open face of Forster, and fairly wrung his hands in despair.

'I wish it were possible,' he groaned. 'For her sake, even more than yours.'

Forster leant over the table, and continued in rapid, eager tones.

'If she loves another man, tell me, and I shall be satisfied. I don't want to know his name, but if he is poor let me make him rich. More than anything in the world, even more than my own happiness, I seek her welfare. I love her, White, and mine is not a selfish love.'

'You are wrong, dear friend. She loves no one else. Poor child! She has never known what love is, and she never will know it.'

Something in White's manner at last awoke the other's suspicion and wonder. The face of the poor fellow was so utterly forlorn, his words and gestures so extraordinary, that Forster began to share his agitation.

'There is some mystery. Cannot I know it?' 'Impossible. But you are right.'

'Does it concern Madeline herself?'

'Yes.'

'Her friends and relations?'

'No.'

'For God's sake, tell me—that is, if it can be told.'

White fell back in his chair, and let his hands drop heedlessly by his side, 'It cannot be told. My poor darling! It is something in her past life.'

There he paused in despair. But Forster, himself trembling violently, touched him on the arm.

'Her past life? What is that to me? I know nothing of it, and I seek to know nothing. If there is any page in her life she wishes me not to read, let her close the book; I will never ask her to open it. I love her too absolutely not to be content with what she is, the sweetest and purest woman I have ever known.'

'You think her pure? So she is, God knows.'

'I think she is worthy to be a queen. I think I am not worthy to tie her shoe-strings. But this does not prevent me loving her; it only makes my love something like idolatry. Don't think that it is mere infatuation. I know my own mind well, and I shall never change.'

More followed in the same strain, but Forster did not succeed in eliciting any further explanation.

So White remained the very picture of misery, and, with his eyes full of tears, wrung the merchant's hand again and again, uttering wild professions of personal attachment.

Some hours later they parted. White, with somewhat unsteady steps, for he had drunk liberally, made his way to his favourite club. Forster walked rapidly to Piccadilly, and, entering an omnibus, rode in sad reverie to South Kensington.

A footman in gorgeous livery admitted the plain man into his princely home; and along a lobby hung with choice pictures, up a staircase ornamented with some of the most perfect specimens of modern sculpture, he found his way to the drawing-room, where his sister Margaret was sitting in solitary state.

Margaret Forster was fresh and wholesome-looking like her brother, but her forehead was lower, her lips thinner and tighter, her whole expression colder, harder, and more respectable, and she wore much more gorgeous apparel She adored her brother and his child, with the quiet adoration of a frosty and impeccable well-dressed virgin. In matters of religion she was very High Church, a staunch follower of the Rev. Father Seraphin, of the Kensington Oratory, and there was scarcely a day in the year on which she did not hear morning and evening mass.

'You are late, James,' she said as he entered. 'I suppose you have dined?'

'Yes, at the club. I have just time to dress for the theatre. Will you come and bring James? I have a box.'

'What theatre, James?'

'The Parthenon.'

'What are they playing?'

'Shakespeare's "Cymbeline."'

'Why, James, you have seen that performance twice already to my knowledge,' said Margaret, lifting her eyebrows. 'Is it so very good?'

'So much so that I want you to see it again, and—and I want James to see it. The new actress is charming. But there is no time to lose, and the carriage will be at the door in half an hour.'

Margaret rose, smiling, well pleased at the attention of her brother, and passed upstairs to prepare her little nephew. Left alone in the drawing-room, Forster paced up and down in a somewhat gloomy brown study, muttering again and again to himself, and pausing from time to time to gaze into one of the great mirrors; he was not, however, gazing at his own reflection, though he seemed to be doing so—he was contemplating a visionary figure far away.

Later on in the evening, Forster, with his sister and his son, occupied a box in the Parthenon. They arrived late, and when they entered 'Imogen' was in the middle of her first parting with 'Posthumus,' but as she left the stage she glanced up and met Forster's eyes. Margaret Forster saw that look, and in a moment her suspicions were awakened. For the rest of the evening she was busily engaged, not following the play, but jealously watching her brother. As she did so, her face hardened and her eyes grew cold as steel; for she had discovered his secret.

The play ended, the curtain descended, and in answer to the enthusiastic applause of the audience Imogen came before the curtain. Then Margaret Forster saw the actress glance up again with a smile of recognition.

They drove home and supped together in the great dining-room. Forster was generally a water-drinker, but on this occasion he ordered champagne, and pressed his sister to partake of it with him. The wise virgin, who saw that something was coming, was not to be persuaded.

Presently Forster dismissed the footman in waiting; then, looking to Margaret with a bright but somewhat nervous smile he asked—

'Well, how did you like her?'

'Miss Vere? I think she is rather pretty and acts intelligently.'

'Intelligently! She is a genius. Do take some champagne.'

Margaret shook her head. She saw that her brother was excited, and determined to keep cool. To try him, she changed the subject.

'How pretty the Princess looked. I suppose the greyheaded gentleman with her was her father, the King of Denmark?'

'Yes—but Miss Vere! How beautifully she spoke those lines at the mouth of the cave!'

'I liked her best in the earlier portions of the play,' returned Margaret quietly. 'I have a prejudice against seeing women dressed up in male attire. I suppose she is a modest woman, but—by the way, James, she seemed to recognise you? Do you know her?'

'Yes.'

'You cannot have met her in society?'

'I was introduced to her by her guardian, White, the dramatic author. We have been acquainted for some time.'

'Indeed!' said Margaret, more coldly than ever.

She drew back her chair, and rose to go. 'I am very tired. I think I will say good-night.' 'Don't go yet,' exclaimed Forster. 'I—I want to talk to you.'

'Yes?'

'About Miss Vere.' Then he continued, nervously and hurriedly, 'I have not only a great respect for her, Margaret, but a stronger feeling. I should have spoken to you concerning her before, but I had certain reasons for keeping silence. Now I think you ought to know everything. I have asked her to marry me.'

Margaret Forster gazed at her brother in horror. Her face went ghastly pale, and she felt as if a sharp knife had stabbed her to the heart.

'You cannot be serious!' she cried.

'Quite serious!'

'My dear James, you are joking with me. I will never believe you capable of such folly.'

'You think it is folly to marry again?'

'That is for you to determine, James; but whenever you marry, you will at least marry a lady.'

Forster's face darkened. 'He knew his sister's strong prepossessions on certain subjects, but he hardly expected so decided an opposition, 'Listen to me, Margaret,' he said firmly; 'and before we go further let me beseech you, for my sake, to refrain from saying anything offensive concerning Miss Vere. Understand me clearly. I love her—deeply, passionately; and with a man at my age, love means the highest sort of respect. She is as far my superior in every gift of nature as I, perhaps, am hers in worldly position.'

He paused, but Margaret made no sign. She kept her cold eyes fixed upon his face, as if fascinated by the horror of a degrading confession; but her pulses temperately kept time, and her self-control was perfect.

Then he continued:—

'I repeat, that I ought possibly to have consulted you earlier on this subject, and I am not at all astonished at your surprise. I never thought to have married a second time. My first experience, as you know, was not encouraging, and since her death you have made my home very happy. My dear Margaret, forgive me if I have seemed unkind, but setting aside the reasons to which I have alluded, I thought it better not to speak of this until I had spoken to Miss Vere. Well, I have spoken, and I thought you ought to know the result. That is why I took you to the theatre. That is why I have spoken.'

He paused again. This time his sister replied—

'Of course, James, you are your own master. I have no right to object.'

'That is not the question,' he cried impatiently. 'I should certainly take no important step in life without consulting you. I am to understand, then, that you object?'

'Most certainly.'

'To my marrying?'

'No, James. To your marrying a person in Miss Vere's position.'

Forster rose to his feet with an angry exclamation.

'Her position is as good as mine. I am a clod, she is a genius.'

'She is not a lady,' returned Margaret, compressing her lips firmly.

'Good heavens, what do you mean? There is not a whisper against her, she is divinely gifted, all the world is raving about her. Not a lady! she is a queen!'

Margaret smiled—a cold sickly smile of supreme feminine pity. Irritated by the smile, and driven out of his usual reticence by the wine he had taken at supper, Forster took a rapid turn round the room, and then, turning back to his sister, cried in a voice broken with agitation—

II thought you above these shameful prejudices. The profession of an actress is one of the noblest under the sun. The same insane bigotry which still pursues theatrical performers persecuted until lately all the arts, literature and painting more particularly. At the bottom of it all is the Church—the Church which denied Adrienne Lecouvreur Christian burial, and which from the beginning of time has been the enemy of light, freedom, knowledge.'

He was going on in the same strain when his sister quietly interfered—

'My dear James, how absurd! I am very fond of the theatre, as you know.'

'But you despise those who act.'

'Nothing of the kind. I only desire to see them in their proper place in society.'

'Where is that, pray?'

'Among themselves—in their own artistic world. In point of fact, they are much happier there.'

'Stop a moment, Margaret,' said Forster, with a short, excited laugh. 'You speak of their world. What is mine? To what sphere do I belong?'

'You? My dear James, you are a merchant and a gentleman.'

'I am a *tradesman*, Margaret, received in certain circles because I have so much money, rejected in others because I have neither the birth nor the breeding of an aristocrat. The same measure you mete to Miss Vere is meted to me—to you also—by those who affect to be our social superiors. What nonsense it all is! What d—d nonsense!'

Margaret Forster shuddered. She had never before in her life heard her brother swear, and his use of even so mild an oath showed the situation to be desperate. She went up to him gently, and put her cheek for his goodnight salute.

'I think I had better go now,' she said. 'We are both tired, and if you are really in earnest, we can talk it over to-morrow. Good-night, James.'

'Good-night,' returned Forster, just touching her cheek with his lips. 'But don't go till you have heard me out, I have told you that I love Miss Vere, and that I have proposed to her, but there is something more.'

'Yes?'

'She has refused me—that is all.'

CHAPTER XXIV
WHITE BIDS A LAST FAREWELL TO BOHEMIA

All this time Madeline was dwelling with White in a familiar corner of Bohemia—a quarter of the world which is fast disappearing before the brand-new dwellings of artistic gentility—and which, when it finally disappears (as seems inevitable), will take something with it that even respectability can never quite replace.

The dwellers in Bohemia, now rapidly disappearing like the dear old quarter itself, had many faults and not a few vices, but these were all forgotten in the presence of natural charm and irresistible *bonhomie*. They wore great beards, drank beer, and smoked great pipes; their clothes were seedy and eccentric, their manners rough and merry, their tastes the very reverse of refined; they had very little money, but that little they freely shared among one another; they loved late hours, wild talk, song-singing, and the social glass; they still regarded the theatre as an educational institution, and talked with pagan enthusiasm of the old gods of the stage. They were neither very clever nor very wise, and they have left no literary monuments to keep their memories fresh; but they enjoyed life, and in their own rough way respected the literary craft to which they belonged. For them Bohemia was a pleasant place.

Here Marmaduke White was born, and bred, and was, in due season, to die. All attempts to coax him to cleaner and cosier quarters were unavailing. Although one by one his fellow-Bohemians fell away, corrupted by the heresy of respectability and clean linen; although those who were born in the same quarter with him listened to the new commercial culte and became prosperous men of business; although Jones the novelist drove his brougham and frequented genteel parties, while Brown the painter wore fine raiment, sold his pictures for splendid prices, and put up at a fashionable club, White still remained as he had been—impecunious, irresponsible, generally out-at-elbow. It was his constant complaint that the old landmarks were fast changing. 'If I live long enough,' he said, 'I shall stand on the ruins of the last chop-house and see the last night-house turned into a temperance hotel. The downfall of Bohemia dates from the day when Thackeray became famous, smoked cigars, and built that nice house at Kensington. It is the apotheosis of the Snob. Even at the Garrick, where one used to meet all the talent, the Snob is rampant. There is not a *foyer* of the old kind in all London. The literary man has become a commercial gent the artist is a spiritualised bagman—even the actor wears fine clothes and goes to swell garden-parties. *Sic transit gloria Bohemio!* I begin to feel like a man who has endured beyond his due time; a sort of Wandering Jew, the old clothes-man of an extinct existence and a perished creed. I should not so much care if people were much better for the change—but they are not. Fellows are valued now, not for what they are, but for what they earn. The very journals are grown brazen-fronted and rave of Mammon. A great book is a book that makes a great deal of money; a great artist is one who earns a great sum. At my time of life I can't, set up as a swell, I like my glass of good beer, and my pipe, and my shirt sleeves. When I die my epitaph will be "Et ille in Bohemia fuit" —and I suppose I shall be the last of the race.'

Now the good man, though he had the perennial heart of a boy, was not young. Time, which had dealt gently with his disposition, had thinned his once flowing hair, made his limbs feeble, and set many a crowsfoot under his kindly eyes. Nor where the habits of the Bohemia he still inhabited favourable to longevity. The small hours always found him up, at work or play, and he saw little of the early sunshine. He was always behindhand with his work, always working against time; feeding irregularly, and at unreasonable hours; drinking, alas! more than was good for him, and even consuming that nicotine which would destroy even a Promethean liver. He had saved nothing, so that rest was denied him; and indeed he could not have rested, for he loved labour, in the old, reckless, perfunctory, Bohemian way. His old friends had gradually drifted away from him, died and been buried, or passed up to those shining social heights where dress suits and white linen are provided for aspiring pilgrims. Even managers of theatres, grown genteel too, pitied him. 'Poor White,' they would say; 'he is such a Bohemian!' So that his occupation partly failed him Good old blank-verse plays were no longer in demand. Brand-new adaptors, fresh from picking the pockets of French authors in Parisian forays, splashed him with the wheels of their triumphal chariots; gorgeous Jew *entrepreneurs* shook their heads at him. 'Vat ve vant now, my boy, is realism; plenty of swell clothes, and upholstery, and last cackle; the public don't vant poetry, and as for blank verse, it ventilates de theatre. They'll stand Shakespeare now and then, especially when Eugene Aram does it, because it's genteel; but all de rest of de drama comsh from France.' In his anxiety to suit the market he too tried pocket-picking, but he lacked the deft rapidity and supreme impudence of the dramatic thief by profession. He took too much trouble with work of this kind, and the public found it old-fashioned.

So it came to pass that from one reason and another, whether because he was physically tired out or intellectually weary of a race in which he was unevenly handicapped, White began to show signs of failing health. Once or twice he took to his bed with some trifling ailment, and on each occasion so weak were his bodily powers that he found it hard work to get up again. He himself attached no importance to those indications of weakness; he was as cheerful to outward seeming, as sanguine, and as full of magnificent 'subjects,' as ever. He still sketched out tragedies which no one would produce on such pert subjects as 'Semiramis,' 'Julian the Apostate,' and 'Boadicea,' and infinitely laboured comedies full of the spirit of the Restoration. His style was still that of the last decadence, when Lalor Shiel was a genius and Sheridan Knowles a prophet. He still clung to the superstition which placed Bulwer Lytton in the pantheon of tinsel divinities. But the game was all over. *Et ille in Bohemia fuit*, that was all.

One night, or rather early one morning, he came home to the old studio in St. John's Wood, evidently under the influence of violent fever. He had caught cold, he thought, at the wings of the Duchess's Theatre, and, though he had tried the panacea of hot whisky and water, applied in allopathic doses, it had only seemed to make him worse. He went to bed, and the next day he was unable to rise.

When Madeline went to his bedside she was shocked at his appearance. He looked haggard and old, the great veins on his temple were blue and swollen, and he gasped like one who could hardly get his breath. The ghost of his old smile came to his face as he reached out his trembling hands, which were hot as fire.

'Don't be alarmed, my dear,' he said cheerily, but in a strange, faint voice. 'I'm not quite myself, but I shall be all right presently. I think it's the effect of Burnard's jokes. He was at the "Harum-Scarum" last night, so I'm afraid I partook too freely of pun-salad, which is worse than the nightmare-producing lobster.'

He tried to laugh, but the laugh died away into a moan, and he sank back upon his pillow.

Later on in the day the symptoms became so alarming that a physician was sent for. He made light of the patient's condition, but wrote him a prescription, and ordered him to be kept as quiet as possible.

Within the next twenty-four hours the symptoms became manifestly those of low or gastric fever. Madeline wrote a hurried line for Forster, who came almost immediately, accompanied by the celebrated Dr. Tain, well known for his kindness to literary men. The good doctor looked somewhat grave, but expressed his opinion that the case would yield to treatment.

From that time forward Madeline scarcely left her guardian's bedside, ministering to him with infinite tenderness and care. The fever ran its course for fourteen days, during several of which White was more or less insensible. On the morning of the fourteenth day he opened his eyes, saw Madeline seated by his bedside, and smiled brightly.

'Are you there, my dear?' he asked. 'I was dreaming about you. I thought you were a little girl again, and I—dear me, how weak I feel! Have I been very ill?'

'Very ill,' answered Madeline. 'But do not talk; the doctor says you must not. Let me bring your beef-tea.'

The doctor had ordered him to have beef-tea in liberal portions every hour: it was the only way, he said, to combat the fever.

'I think I shall soon be all right,' said White, presently. 'I must take more care of myself for the future, though. I'm getting quite an old fellow, and must go to bed at ten.'

When Dr. Tain entered, White looked up and nodded cheerfully.

'Here I am, you see! *Pallida Mors* won't have me this time, after all, and I was thinking that I could eat a mutton chop, well peppered.'

The doctor replied cheerfully, and patted White gently on the shoulder; but Madeline, catching the expression of his face as he turned away, was somewhat troubled.

'Keep him quiet,' he whispered to her at the door.

'I'll look in again in the afternoon.'

From this intimation it became clear that the doctor was uneasy. Scarcely had he gone when the patient exhibited great restlessness and difficulty of breathing; and when the doctor returned in the afternoon he found him rambling incoherently.

Leaving the sick room, he went into the studio, where Forster, whose attentions had been unremitting, was impatiently waiting.

'My fears are realised,' said the physician, gravely.

'Peritonitis has supervened.'

Before long it became manifest that White was sinking; as the hours progressed he grew weaker and weaker, until the end seemed likely to come in stupor. With despairing love and pity, but almost with dry eyes, Madeline sat by the bedside; and as she gazed upon the wild, worn face, watched the thin, white hand laying outside the coverlet, and heard the quiet, monotonous breathing, she already seemed to feel the shadow of death upon her life. As one standing safe on some dark river's shore watches the struggles of an almost spent drowning man, and forgets everything in the intense dread and horror of the contemplation, so she watched the sick bed; unable to weep, unable to pray (for, indeed, her hopes and fears seldom at any time took the shape of prayer), but feeling always as if with the slow ebb of her guardian's life her life was ebbing too. For White, she felt, was her only friend in this hard world, the only being who knew the full extent of her own sorrow, the only kind soul for whom she cared to live. In all her gentle theatrical ambition her thought had been of him; how she could bring comfort to his heart, see the pride and pleasure kindle on his face, make his old age pleasant, and walk by his side the dark descent to the grave. And now, if he left her, what remained?

In these hours of sorrow the frequent presence of Forster was a secret source of irritation to the troubled girl. His very devotion troubled her, for she seemed to read in it, not merely friendly kindness and affection, but an ever-encroaching assumption of a higher sympathy. He was a good man, a true friend, she knew, but she would have loved him far better if he had loved her less, and her mind was quite made up—if her dear guardian died, no living man, friend or husband, should ever take his place.

The shadow came nearer, and it became clear at last that White was drifting away beyond all human hope. He suffered little or no pain, but momentarily grew weaker. At last one morning he seemed to rally a little, and spoke clearly and collectedly on his approaching end.

'I am going to leave you, my dear,' he said softly, while she held his hand fondly in her own. 'I wanted to live a little longer, just to see a dear girl at the top of the tree, but I suppose it is all for the best. Well, I want you to promise me one thing before I go.'

'Do not talk so,' cried Madeline, kissing the hot hand and sobbing wildly. 'You will get well! We will be so happy together.'

'Don't cry, Madeline! I'm not afraid to die, and after all I'm an old fogey, and the world has left me far behind. I used to think I should live to regenerate the drama. Ah, well! that dream is over. I shan't even finish "Semiramis," the best thing I ever wrote; but you'll give the first two acts and the scenario to Eugene Aram when I am gone.'

He paused, and Madeline cried between her sobs—

'If you die, I shall die too! You are my only friend.'

'You mustn't talk like that, my dear. You have a great future before you, and perhaps—who knows?—I shall be able to see it from afar off. If the dead can watch over those they love, I shall still take care of you—ah, yes!—and if there's a heaven as the preachers say, I shall meet poor Fred your father there, and we shall both look down and bless you.'

'I have no father but you! You are all the world to me! You will not die!'

But White continued quietly, as if pursuing his own thoughts—

'And while dear Forster lives you will not be without a friend; many a time has he lightened my load, and I wish you'd let him help you to carry yours. If you would promise me to become his wife, I should be very happy.'

'I cannot! You know I cannot!'

As she uttered the words, he became conscious of a movement in the room, and looking round saw Forster standing at the foot of the bed.

'Is that you, Forster?' asked White, faintly. 'Come here, I wish to speak to you;' and he added when Forster had passed round and stood looking down sadly upon him.

'You'll be kind to Madeline, old fellow, after——'

And he turned his face on the pillow to hide his tears. Forster did not reply in words, but with tears glistening on his own cheeks laid his hand softly on the sick man's shoulder. Presently White looked round, and, fixing his great dim eyes on Madeline's face, whispered—

'My dear! Will you go—only a little while? I wish to speak to Forster.'

She bent over the bed and kissed him tenderly on the forehead; then with a sob as if her heart was breaking she left the room.

She went into the next chamber, a small room overlooking the garden, and, sitting at the window, looked out through streaming tears. Many minutes passed, and at last, anxious and impatient, she rose to return to her post. As she did so, Forster appeared at the door and beckoned.

'Will you come now?' he whispered. 'He is asking for you.'

She stepped softly in, and approached the bedside. With a smile of ineffable love and tenderness the dying man turned his face up to hers and, reaching out his tremulous hands, gave one to her, the other to Forster; then he said in a voice so indistinct that they had to stoop their heads to catch the word—

'I have spoken to Forster... he will take care of of you, my dear... a good fellow... always my best friend, God bless him... now I can go in peace.'

Then feebly but firmly he drew the two hands together and joined them; that of Madeline lay in that of Forster, with the fingers of the dying man encircling both; and she did not draw hers away for fear of disturbing her dear guardian's last moments. In this position he closed his eyes, and seemed to doze. A little while after the breath fluttered, the feeble frame trembled, and the gentle spirit was gone for ever.

What followed was to Madeline a dark and painful dream. Ever wild and impressionable in her grief as well as her joyful impulses, she yielded to such a storm of grief as threatened for a time to overthrow her reason. During this time of sorrow Madame de Berny watched her with maternal tenderness, and the touch of her tender ministration brought a certain comfort.

But when the first wild shock was over, the brave disposition of the girl asserted itself, and, hushing the tumult of her pain, she went with Madame de Berny to see the place which Forster had chosen for his friend's last resting-place, It was a pretty spot, in a green corner of the cemetery at Hampstead, with green boughs all round, flowers on every side, and the spires of the great city in the distance; and standing here, near the place chosen for the grave, Madeline could hear the chimes of London sounding faint and far away.

When the day of the funeral came, she went as chief mourner, for her soul revolted at the cruel custom which keeps our womankind from following the dead. She stood by the side of the grave, heard the solemn words of blessing, and saw the coffin lowered to its place; and she raised her weeping face to the bright skies, praying and believing that her guardian's spirit had gone *there*.

Near her that day stood a motley crowd of artistic Bohemians, bearded men for the most part, shabby of apparel, but full of honest grief; some of them, with true tears in their eyes, came softly up to speak a few words of sympathy to the mourning girl; and she loved the rough fellows for their resemblance to him who had passed away.

Then Madeline went back to the home that was home no longer, and thought day and night of the beloved dead.

It was many weeks after these sad events that Forster came one day to St. John's Wood, and found Madeline still sitting in the shadow of her great grief; but she had found one sweet comfort in looking over her guardian's papers and placing them in order with her loving hand, for she remembered one lifelong dream of the poor Bohemian—to see his beloved plays arranged together and published in book form; and she thought to herself that the world should know what a beautiful genius it had lost, when it saw the creatures of his imagination gathered together for the first time.

When Forster came they talked for some time of the proposed publication. An old friend of White, eminent as a critic and a dramatic poet, was to revise the work, and prepare it with a short biography, and at the end of the book were to be printed a few last memorials, and some obituary verses by members of the Bohemian Club, to which White had belonged.

Presently, however, Forster changed the subject, and spoke of the wish which was still nearest his heart. Then, when Madeline turned away as if shocked and pained, he took her hand and said earnestly—

'It was *his* wish, do not forget that. He knew I loved you, and he joined our hands together.'

'No, no!' said Madeline. 'Do not speak of it—he knew it was impossible—he could not wish it.'

'Madeline, he *did* wish it, with all his heart. Listen to me, my darling! That day before he joined our hands together he asked to speak to me alone—do you remember?

'Yes.'

'Do you know what he wished to say?'

Madeline shook her head sadly.

'He wished to tell me something concerning yourself. "Forster," he said, "I tell you these things because I trust you before God, because I think that it is best that you should know, and because I feel you will never love my darling less." Then, Madeline, he told me why you refused to marry me, why you had said you would never marry any living man.'

Pale as death, Madeline turned her face away.

'He told you that!' she murmured, shivering as if chilled.

'He told me everything, my darling; and now, knowing everything, knowing your great sorrow, and knowing and loving you a thousandfold, I ask you again to become my wife.'

CHAPTER XXV
MADELINE CHANGES HER NAME

Afew months later the following announcement appeared amongst the 'Births, Deaths, and Marriages,' on the first page of the 'Times':—

On the 23rd, at Christ Church, Hampstead, James Forster, of Hampden House, Cromwell Road, South Kensington, to Madeline, only daughter of the late Fred. Hazelmere, Esq., of the Inner Temple.

Only a few of those who read this announcement were aware that the lady in question was the young actress known under another name to the audiences of the Theatre Royal Parthenon.

It was a very quiet marriage. After the ceremony the newly married couple drove to the cemetery, in the immediate neighbourhood, and Madeline placed a fresh garland on White's grave; then with a heavy heart she returned to a quiet wedding breakfast, to which only a few very intimate friends were invited, and in the afternoon departed with her husband to Switzerland.

Long before that wedding day Madeline had discovered, by secret inquisition of her own heart, that the tender respect she felt lor James Forster was not yet love—not such love, at least, as blends the lives of man and woman in perfect sympathy and joy; and she would have given the world, therefore, if he had been content to remain what he had been—her friend, her brother, her benefactor. But seeing clearly that his happiness depended on the formation of a closer relationship, she, by slow degrees, was reconciled to the possibility. What weighed with her more than any other consideration was the thought of poor White's last injunction. He had wished this union—had, indeed, enjoined it upon her—so that to shrink from fulfilling his fond request seemed selfish and ungrateful, and the more so as she remembered so vividly the noble and unselfish devotion of Forster during all the last years of poor White's earthly struggle.

So she consented, not without many secret tears and forebodings, for the shadow of her first cruel experience was still upon her, and she could not stifle the secret sense of shame.

Before finally yielding her hand, however, she questioned Forster again, and more explicitly, concerning his secret interview with White, just before the latter's death.

'You wish me to be your wife,' she said, 'but are you sure that you know what you are asking? I feel quite an old woman, and I am not good enough to be your wife. Sometimes, even now, the old restless fit is on me, the old wicked wilfulness. I shall never bring happiness to any one, I am sure.'

'You are unjust to yourself. Dear Madeline, trust me. I will try to deserve your trust.'

Do you know that there are some things, some thoughts and acts, which seem to pollute the very air we breathe; to make the bright world hateful; to chill the very heart within us, like the touch of death? I feel like a girl who has been shrouded for the grave and who still exists, but who will never have the wholesome, happy life of good people. Do not ask me to marry. Choose some innocent girl, and give your love to her.'

'We cannot love as we will,' said Forster, earnestly, 'but as God wills; and I have given my love to you. Dearest, it is just because you have been unhappy that I yearn to bring you happiness; just because you have been wronged that I long to make amends. You must leave these sorrowful thoughts behind you; you must rise from the tomb of your dead grief, and live anew.'

'I cannot; it is too late.'

'Yet you are so young, so beautiful; and I love you so much.'

'I do not deserve such love.'

'You deserve far more than I can bring you.'

'Did Mr. White tell you what I had been? Do not turn away, but look me in the face—you see I am not afraid. What did he say to you? Tell me everything.'

'He told me that you had been deceived by a villain, who afterwards abandoned you. Dearest, he did you full justice—he knew that you were innocent, an angel deluded by a devil.'

'I was not innocent,' returned Madeline, sadly. 'I was to blame, and ah! I was so ungrateful. If I had been innocent, do you think I should ever have placed myself in that man's power?'

'You were very young, and it is an evil world. Do not speak of it again. Bury the past, and become my honoured wife.'

'You say that now; but some day, years hence, perhaps, the past would rise like a ghost, and your life would be darkened by regret and shame.'

'Never by shame! never!'

'I am not fit to make connections, I am not fit to have friends; it is better for such women as I to be alone in the world, and then, if shame comes, it falls only on the one who has the most right to suffer. It is this thought that reconciles me to the death of my dear guardian. I am alone in the world now, and can bring harm to no one.'

To a man like Forster it was terrible to hear her talk so. He was willing to forget the past, and he saw no dark cloud looming in the future. He had set his heart on making Madeline his wife, and he would never rest until his object had been attained. 'She hesitates to take the plunge,' he said to himself, 'but once she has taken it all will be well.' So he pleaded and pleaded, until at length Madeline was brought to consent.

It was a short honeymoon, but to Madeline, at least, it was a tolerably happy one. She had refused to take a maid with her, and he had consented to dispense with the services of a valet, so they spent their days in happy unconcern, roaming about among the Swiss mountains, travelling from one picturesque village to another, and living in little quaint rustic inns, whose primitive accommodation would have made Miss Forster turn cold with dismay.

It was just the kind of life which Madeline loved. After all, the unnatural atmosphere of town smoke and footlights had not left much taint upon her; she felt once more the little girl who, with tangled hair and disordered dress, had raced like a young untrained colt about the marshes of Grayfleet.

But the pleasures of the honeymoon were not destined to continue. Forster, though a rich man, could never be spared long from the office—so at the end of a month he told his young wife that the two must turn their faces towards home. 'That's the penalty of marrying a City man,' he said; 'things always seem to go wrong when I'm away; and though I grumble about the office a good deal, I think, after all, I like it.'

'I'm sure you do.'

'I shall have to leave you a good deal alone, my darling.'

'Never mind that. While you are away I'll be thinking what I can do to make you comfortable when you come home again.'

'You'll do no such thing, my dear. I'll not have my Madeline made a drudge. You'll enjoy yourself as you do now, and my sister is quite willing to look after things a bit. She's used to it, and doesn't mind.'

'Miss Forster?'

'Yes, Margaret.'

'Is she going to live with us?'

'Well, yes, I suppose so. You see she has lived with me for years, and it never occurred to me that you would wish her to go. She will be very useful to you, Madeline; besides, she'll be company for you while I'm away.'

To this Madeline said nothing. She felt she had no right to object to this arrangement, but she was sorry it had been made. However, for her husband's sake she resolved to make the best of it, and to look upon Miss Forster henceforth as an affectionate sister and friend.

One afternoon, about a month after the wedding-day, a carriage and pair drove up to the door of Forster's town house, the large handsomely furnished mansion in South Kensington, and Forster, alighting, handed out his bride.

'Welcome home, my darling,' he said, giving her hand a tender pressure.

Madeline's heart bounded at the touch, and, with flushed cheek and sparkling eyes, she ran up the steps to the open door. On the threshold stood Miss Forster, with a distant smile and a cordial 'how do you do?' Madeline held forth both her hands, but the lady's stately figure became more stately as she coldly placed her fingers in one of the palms, and graciously led the way into the house. Somewhat chilled at so cold a greeting, Madeline followed her through a stately hall into a handsomely furnished room. Madeline sat down, and Miss Forster paused before her.

'If you will be so good as to give me your keys,' she said politely, 'your maid shall unpack your things. James asked me to engage one for you, and I hope she will give satisfaction.'

With a nod and a smile Madeline handed over the keys, and Miss Forster retired.

Madeline sighed, leaned back in her chair, and looked around her. She was in the drawing-room of Hampden House, a spacious apartment, elegantly furnished in the most costly style. Her eyes, carelessly scanning the costly pictures which covered the walls, became suddenly fixed upon one. She leapt up from her seat, ran over to it, stood for a moment regarding it with tear-dimmed gaze. Then, raising herself on tiptoe, she pressed upon it her warm, ripe, trembling lips. It was a pretty little landscape, looking insignificant enough in its golden setting, but trebly dear to Madeline, for it was almost the last picture which poor White had painted. Saddened a little at the memory it brought her, she stood looking at it in a dream; she felt the tears roll slowly down her cheeks, the sobs contract her throat—she was growing almost hysterical, when a voice recalled her to herself.

'Shall I show you to your rooms?'

She started, turned, and found herself face to face with her husband's sister. Unable to hide her tears, she said, turning faintly—

'Thank you, I think I should like to be alone. I feel rather tired and depressed to-day.'

Miss Forster said nothing, but quietly led the way out of the room.

Two of the best rooms in the house had been fitted up for Madeline's special use, and as she walked into them she felt for the first time that day that she had really come home. Here, as elsewhere, there were splendid upholstery, splendid pictures, tastefully designed ceilings, and dim rose-coloured curtains to moderate the light; but besides all this Madeline saw some of the crude but well-loved pictures which brought to her the fond memory of her guardian; there was a little bookcase, containing his favourite volumes; and, above all, there were his favourite plays. She saw all this, but she saw more. Passing on through the sitting-room she looked into the dressing-room adjoining it. She found her dresses laid out, and a smart maid kneeling before a box which was half unpacked. The girl rose and asked which dress her mistress would wear for dinner, but Madeline said—

'I don't know; any one; will you leave me alone, please: and when I want you I will ring.'

The maid retired, and Madeline, left to herself, returned to the sitting-room. She took off her bonnet and cloak, and sat down in an easy chair close to a gipsy table on which stood a silver tray and some tea. She poured out a cup, and, while sipping it, looked with dubious eyes around her.

'I ought to be happy,' she said. 'So I am; so I will be. He is so good and kind! I trust to God he will never be made to repent. If his sister knew—if the world knew—but why should they?—I cannot undo the past, but I can guide the future. Yes, I will bury my dead, as he said, and try to forget.'

A light tap upon the door. Madeline started up, but before she could speak the door opened and a tiny figure came in—a little bright-eyed boy, who ran forward with outstretched hands, and sprang with a joyful cry into her lap. She clasped him fondly in her arms, and kissed him eagerly.

'My darling, you have come to bid me welcome home?'

'Yes, mamma.'

'Who sent you?'

'Papa. Kiss me again, please. Papa says if I am good you are sure to love me.'

He held up his rosy lips and she kissed them again and again; then she caught him up in her arms and carried him to her dressing-room. She turned over the things in her unpacked boxes and produced some toys— these she gave to the child, embracing him the while.

'Do you know why I brought these, dear?'

'No, mamma, unless because, as papa says, you are so good.'

'No,' she said quietly, 'it is because I love you, and I want you to love me.'

Late that night Madeline came quietly down from her room and entered the library. Forster was still there; he was smoking a cigar, and looking through a batch of letters which had accumulated during his absence.

'Why, Madeline, can't you sleep?' he asked, as she came forward.

'No, James, not till I have thanked you for all your goodness to me. Tell me, how can I repay you?'

'By being happy in your home.'

Good advice, and for a time at least Madeline followed it. She was happy. Her husband was a good deal away, but she had always his boy to comfort her, and upon the child she lavished all the affection of her impulsive heart. There was one thing only in the house which chilled and repelled her; it was the presence of her husband's sister.

Madeline had not been long in the house before she found that the cold eyes of Margaret Forster watched her continually in suspicious distrust, as if trying in vain to penetrate the mystery which shrouded the young girl's life. But this Madeline soon forgot. Why should she fear Miss Forster? The past was buried; and as yet she had no idea that the future had its hidden mystery to disclose.

CHAPTER XXVI
THE PUPIL OF THE IMPECCABLE

Within the charmed circle to which he was introduced by Ponto, Gavrolles was popular in the extreme. He possessed all the enthusiasm of the aesthetics, combined with an impudence and a knowledge of the world — especially of the gay world of Paris — which were exquisitely charming. He knew all the wits and poets of the Empire, and his acquaintance with *scabreux* literature was profound; yet he had sat at the feet of Victor Hugo, and was a Republican by profession. His own verses had been praised by the impeccable Gautier. He could talk glibly of Art for Art's sake, of the heresy of instruction, of Villon and Bohemia, and of the Renaissance. He wore his hair long, had a willowy droop of the shoulders, and adored the *culte* of the lily. He had a shrill style, a shrill voice, a shrill disposition. Inspired young ladies found him charming, feeble young gentlemen paid him the homage of imitation.

On his return to London, Gavrolles took rooms in one of the bye-streets near Portland Place. They were rather high up, but he had them furnished in the best æsthetic style, with a few risky pictures and a small collection of books. 'Come and see me,' he would say; 'I am only a poor artiste, but I have my books, and in these I live.' On the whole they were not nice books — a Philistine might have even called them nasty; but many of them bore the autographs of the writers, and were priceless accordingly.

About this time the name of Gavrolles began to be a good deal talked about, as that of a young Frenchman with Communist views who had written some delightfully wicked volumes of verse. The 'Megatherium,' inspired by Ponto, had a good deal to say about him, classing him in the great bagnio of Art somewhere by the side of Gautier and Baudelaire; and taking occasion at the same time to express its horror of realists like Zola, who called a spade a spade, and reduced the fair features of vice to a *caput mortuum*.

One night, Crieff, who knew everybody, took Sutherland to the lodgings of Gavrolles, and introduced him. Quite a little symposium was there, including Ponto the fatuous; Cassius Gass, a lean and limp critic from

Cambridge; Blanco Serena, and several other painters; young Botticelli Jones, and one or two more callow poets, not to speak of Wallace MacNeill, the editor of the 'Megatherium.'

Sutherland sat very silent. After the first, quick look at Gavrolles, and a second shock of recognition, he remained quiescent, but quietly observant.

The talk was of 'Lily and Rue,' an anonymous poem which had just appeared, and which Ponto had just criticised with admiration.

'I wonder who is the writer?' said Botticelli Jones. 'There are passages in it which are worthy of Byron.'

'Byron was a Philistine,' cried Ponto; 'he could never have written a piece of this kind. Look at the technique of his verse! It would disgrace a schoolboy! No, this is a cameo cut by an artist.'

'Shall I confess it!' observed Gavrolles, smiling languidly. 'I am of Henri Taine's opinion, and prefer to your Byron our Alfred de Musset.'

Here Crieff, who was puffing carelessly at a briar-root pipe, threw himself back in his chair and laughed loudly.

'I say! Is it possible you don't know?'

'What?' cried several voices.

'That MacAlpine——'

A shudder ran through the assemblage at the mention of the hated name.

'That MacAlpine has acknowledged the authorship of this poem.'

'What poem?' demanded Ponto, trembling and turning pale.

'Why, of "Lily and Eue." Go and buy the third edition—you'll find his name on the title-page.'

A terrible silence followed. The men looked in horror at one another. One man rose, livid and ghastly, put his hand to his head and left without a word. It was the editor of the 'Megatherium.'

'Poor MacNeill,' cried Crieff, with another laugh. 'This is the second trick of the kind that MacAlpine has played him; this is the second time that he has devoted columns of praise to an author whom he would gladly see handed over, like the old heretics, to the secular arm. It only shows what humbug criticism is!'

'Excuse me,' said Gass the critic, hysterically, 'criticism is not humbug. It would be easy to show, on a profounder examination of this disagreeable work, that it is the work of a Philistine. The over-accentuation of the sensuous passages (which, by the way, are not sensuous, but prurient and ponderous), the want of finish in the trochaic couplets, the crudeness of the poetic terminology—'

'Would all have been evident enough,' interrupted Crieff, dryly, 'if MacAlpine's name had been on the title-page. Without that, even superhuman insight, like yours, could not detect them.'

And he laughed again; but no one joined in the laugh except Blanco Serena, who was not a little amused. There was a general feeling of discomfort, to relieve which Gavrolles went to his bookcase, and took down several new importations from France. Passed from hand to hand, these works were freely and generally discussed; but when they reached Crieff, that rude person again shocked the sensibilities of his companions.

'The literature of the Lollipop,' he said with a grin. 'Somehow I never touch any of it without feeling nasty; "sticky" all over, as it were.'

'To the mind of a Philistine,' observed the critic Gass, severely, 'such things do not appeal. I regret to see that a certain person, who shall be nameless, is drifting more and more into moral Philistinism. Well, he will at least be able to say, "Et ego in Arcadia fui," when it is too late to return.'

Crieff laughed good-humouredly.

'I dare say it is my early training,' he said, 'and the fact that I was taught to respect all women in the person of my mother. But here is my friend Sutherland, who is a Philistine of Philistines, for he actually believes, with St. Benedict, that the law of purity is binding upon both sexes alike, and in his benighted eyes your Gautier, your Baudelaire, and "hoc genus omne" are simply dirty descendants of Sir Pandarus of Troy.'

'I sincerely hope you are libelling your friend,' observed the critic, glancing at Sutherland. 'Personal purity, as you call it, is simply a reminiscence of asceticism, and one of the many fallacies we owe to the mediaeval perversions of Christianity.'

'Bosh,' returned Crieff, bluntly.

Sutherland, who throughout the conversation had scarcely taken his eyes off Gavrolles, now spoke.

'I am neither an ascetic nor a Puritan, but I must frankly confess that the literature you are discussing excites my strongest abhorrence. Whatever is unfit for a pure woman to read is unfit to be read by a pure man. Would you give these books to your wives and sisters—that is the question?'

'Certainly,' cried Ponto from the other side of the room. 'Provided their aesthetic education had been complete, they would find nothing but pleasure from the perusal. Why in Heaven's name should Woman remain for ever the slave of Virtue? I would make her the archpriestess of the Beautiful, ministering to mortals in all the passionate nudity of Art.'

'And you, monsieur?' said Sutherland, turning suddenly to Gavrolles. 'What is your opinion?'

'Oh, I am an artiste,' answered the Frenchman, with a shrug of the shoulders and an unpleasant smile. 'I, too, would make woman the priestess of Beauty. Ah, yes, with the greatest of possible pleasure!'

The words were of little meaning, but the tone was significant, and a titter went round the room. Sutherland's face darkened.

'I presume that your experience of the sex is large?' he asked in a low voice. 'Gentlemen of your nation are generally fortunate — —'

'I am no exception to the rule,' answered Gavrolles. 'My whole life has been *une bonne fortune!* But look you, as I say, I am an artiste — in affairs of gallantry as in all others. I do not suffer these things to cloud the equanimity of my artiste's soul. When I have plucked a rose — observe! I smell it; I wear it a little while; then I take it from my button-hole and throw it away. You understand?'

'I think so,' said Sutherland, rising to his feet. 'Pray does it ever occur to you what becomes of the rose afterwards! If it is trampled underfoot, who is responsible?'

'Pardon me, that is the rose's affair, not mine. *Au reste*, roses must bloom and fade; Art, Art — for which I live — is imperishable and divine.'

It was hard to say whether he was jesting or in earnest, for his manner was peculiar, a combination of mock-enthusiasm and flippant audacity. But despite his appearance of *sang-froid*, something in the face and manner of Sutherland thrilled him, and reminded him of an unpleasant meeting many years before.

He bowed profoundly as Sutherland prepared to go, and held out his hand — which the other did not seem to notice.

'*Au revoir!*' he said gaily; 'and *au revoir*, Monsieur Crieff. My friend Ponto will convert you presently; ah, yes!'

In another minute Crieff and Sutherland were in the street. The latter was very pale, and trembled violently.

'My dear Sutherland, what is the matter?'

'Nothing; only that man's face and his talk have upset me. I could have strangled him.'

'What an excitable fellow you are!' said Crieff, taking his arm. 'Upon my life, you take these things far too seriously. The other day you were seriously angry with Lagardère, and here you are actually distressing yourself over the prattle of a child like Gavrolles.'

'You do not understand. I know the man, and have reason to remember him.'

'That alters the case. Where did you meet?'

'In France—some years ago.'

Crieff listened for further explanations, but none came. Pressed to say more, Sutherland shook his head, and relapsed into silence; so the little journalist proceeded to give his muscular friend a lesson in social philosophy.

'You are too thoroughly in earnest, and in company your earnestness makes other people uncomfortable. Life would be impossible if every bit of idle chit-chat or *ad captandum* argument were taken *au sérieux*. Looked at in the proper light, Gavrolles is charming—a droll creature with a touch of genius. To you he is merely a dissolute young man, who reads improper books.'

'To me,' returned Sutherland, fiercely, 'he is a thorough scoundrel, whom I should like to choke.'

Crieff soon perceived that remonstrance was useless, and, mentally determining not to introduce his companion to any more choice spirits, he changed the subject. The pair soon parted, Crieff to stroll down to the gallery of the House of Commons, Sutherland to pace the solitary streets, full of the troubled recollections awakened by that chance encounter.

Later on that evening Gavrolles sat alone in his lodgings. He now recollected Sutherland perfectly, and roundly cursed the unlucky chance which had occasioned a second meeting. On reflection, however, he felt confident that the Englishman could do him no serious damage in the eyes of his new acquaintances, even if he attempted to do so, which was doubtful.

When the clock struck eight he lit a cigar and strolled out into the streets. As he walked along, his attention was attracted by a theatre bill in one of the shop windows. One of the names struck him immediately as that of the young actress whose portrait he had seen in the studio of Blanco Serena. He looked at the name of the theatre; it was the Theatre Royal Parthenon. He strolled away in the direction of that building.

On arriving at the theatre, however, he found the doors closed, and discovered that the theatrical season had ended on the previous Saturday.

Strolling carelessly along, he entered one of the smaller theatres in the Strand, a house devoted to opera bouffe. He paid his money and got a seat in the back row of the pit. There, perspiring and half-suffocated, he was listening to the hideous din and watching the insane performance upon the stage, when his attention was attracted by a movement in a box above him, and glancing up he beheld a face he knew.

The face of a woman, young and very beautiful, though trifle pale and sad. She was plainly clad in black satin, with an opera cloak of snowy white, with fringe of down encircling her white neck. No ornaments in her hair, no jewels on her person, and surely she needed neither, for her simple pathetic beauty was better unadorned.

With her was a gentleman, not young, but with the fresh face and manners of a boy. He looked very happy and proud, and gazed less at the stage than at his companion, as, indeed, was natural.

These two were our heroine and her husband, James Forster.

A child might have gathered, from the man's looks of pleasure and admiration, that Forster loved the beautiful creature by his side. His eyes scarcely left her, he was eager to respond to her slightest look or word. When she talked, he hung upon her speech; and when she was silent he waited for her to speak again.

Gavrolles comprehended the situation directly—almost as rapidly as he recognised Madeline. For the rest of the evening he occupied himself in looking up, with a keen and cat-like gaze. How beautiful she seemed! How much fairer and riper than when he had seen her last, in her wild girlish *gaucherie! Pardieu*, she was a child then; but *now!*

As he gazed his thoughts went back to the days when he had seen her first, a giddy schoolgirl, a very will-o'-the-wisp among the decorous young French damsels of the ladies' seminary. He remembered her wild ways, her odd sayings in schoolgirl's French, her pretty fits of petulance, her innocent entanglement with him, the ever-seductive Gavrolles—or Belleisle, as he then called himself. He thought of the mad elopement, and the strange days that followed, when the fluttering bird was in his power.

'After all,' he reflected, 'I was a fool to let her go.'

And the man with her, who seemed so greatly to adore her, who was he? Surely her lover; perhaps her husband—but no, that was scarcely possible. A rich man, certainly; yes, with all the style and manner of a rich man. She, too, with her popular fame, her great artistic position, was no longer poor. Perhaps, after all, it was for the best that he had let her go, since fortune had been kind to her, and what was lost could be easily regained.

Gavrolles smiled. Once, when the audience was busy applauding the actors, his exhilaration was so great that he impulsively kissed his hand in the direction of the box. The action was unnoticed, of course, but it seemed to place him *en rapport* with his old love.

'Courage, Gavrolles!' he said to himself. 'You are Fortune's favourite, after all. Just when you were in despair, just when your purse was empty and your great soul in despair, the cards befriend you, and a good angel appears in the distance. Madeline, *mon ange*, I greet you. You will be my guardian spirit after all.'

When the opera was over, Gavrolles stood in the corner of the box lobby, and watched Madeline go past on Forster's arm. He kept his face well averted, for he did not wish to be recognised, just yet. Then, following the pair to the theatre door, he saw a brougham draw up, smiled upon the pair as they entered and gaily lit a cigar as they drove away.

CHAPTER XXVII
ADELE LAMBERT

Cigar in mouth, Gavrolles strolled leisurely along the streets in the direction of Regent Circus. Arrived in Waterloo Place he found the pavement thronged with those painted faces,

"Which only smile by night beneath the gas,

and saw what, to a man with any pity in his soul, is the saddest sight beneath the sun.

Bright jets of gas were flaming over the Criterion Restaurant, the night houses on every side were opening their foul jaws, and from the darkness of every street and lane were fluttering forth the moths of night. Painted and bedizened creatures, fluttering gladly in the gaslight; some faint and feeble, as if already scorched with the destroying flame; others splendidly merry, with the new flush of the infernal brightness upon them; many beautiful beyond measure, with faces as pure and sweet as those of little children that know not sin.

With the smile and swagger of one who knew his company, Gavrolles made his way from group to group, accosted from time to time by some passing figure, and more than once plucked softly by the sleeve. Once, as he paused under a lamplight, a slight form, clad in the thinnest of silk, paused before him, and a baby face leered hideously up into his; but he pushed the shape softly aside, and swaggered on. To him, as to many of his class, the sight was quite proper and pleasant; his fine nerves were not shocked, his noble soul was not sadly stirred; indeed, such a man might walk confidently by the side of the very flames of Hell, and be conscious of nothing but the picturesque lights and shadows of the dreadful place. Yes, for as Swedenborg has sublimely guessed, Hell is Heaven to the devilish nature, and the penalty of the morally damned is not to *know* that it is Hell.

Not far away, that very night, walked another man, one of nobler fibre, with the shuddering sense of infinite pity and despair. He, too, was familiar with the sight of moral leprosy and spiritual disease, and as he gazed on those painted things, all and each of whom were infected with the *goitre* of incurable infamy, he felt weary of the world. 'So long as this is possible,' thought Edgar Sutherland, 'how can the dead Christ rise?'

Crossing the street at the Quadrant, Sutherland saw, standing in the lamplight of the corner, two figures, one an elderly woman with a face swollen and deformed by drink, the other a wild-looking girl, poorly clad, coughing violently as if in sharp physical pain. As he was passing he heard them speak to each other in French; he paused and listened.

'You are a fool, Adèle,' said the elder woman. 'Come and have some brandy—you will be all right then.'

The girl laughed hoarsely and uttered a coarse oath, then the cough seized her again with a paroxysm so violent that her whole frame shook like a leaf.

'Devil take the cough,' she said. 'I shall have to go into the hospital after all.'

A few more words passed, and then the elder woman, impatient to reach the bar of some neighbouring public-house, ran across the street. The young girl was feebly following, when Sutherland stepped forward, lifting his hat.

'Good evening, mademoiselle,' he said, speaking in her own language. 'I am afraid you are ill?'

Something in the tone startled her, and the gentle voice, the respectful gesture, acted like a charm. She replied courteously, with a polite inclination of the head, 'I am not very well, monsieur; I have been ill for some time.'

'I am very sorry. If you will take my advice you will go home—you are not fit to be in the streets.'

She gazed at him strangely, and then said—

'Pardon, monsieur, but you are not a Frenchman?'

'No.'

'I think I have seen your face before? You have been abroad,—in Brussels?'

As she spoke, something in her form and face seemed familiar; with an exclamation he took her by the arm, and drew her close under the light of the lamp.

'Is it possible?' he cried. 'Adèle Lambert? Do you remember me?'

That she did so was now clear; for with a hysterical cry she shrank from him and hid her face in her hands. Two years before, in Brussels, he had found this poor creature, then a pretty girl, in the power of infamous people, who had decoyed her to ruin; with infinite trouble and great pecuniary expense he had released her and restored her to her friends; and when he had last heard of her she seemed on the threshold of a new and purer life. And now, this was the sequel! He shuddered in horror, as he looked upon her spectral face.

'My poor girl,' he said gently, 'what brought you to England?'

Then she told him, with many tears; for the sight of him and the remembrance of his former charity touched the deep springs of sorrow in her poor outcast soul. She had indeed gone home, but not to stay. Soon after her return her mother had died, and her father had taken another wife; her life was not happy, and the taint of her shame still clung to her; and at last, in despair, she had drifted back to Brussels, finding all ways of life closed to her but one.

'And since then, monsieur. I have suffered so much. I was never strong, and now I am—as you see. A year ago they took me to the hospital in my own country—would to God I had died there! but I came out, and after that I went from bad to worse. Two months ago I came with that woman to England. I thought no one would know me here, and now—is it not strange?—I meet with *you*.'

As she spoke, another figure came sauntering up in the full light of the lamp. It was Gavrolles, indifferent and happy, smoking his cigar. The moment the girl's eyes fell upon him, her manner changed; and, to Sutherland's astonishment, she uttered a cry, and rushed up to the newcomer.

'Let me look at your face,' she cried. 'Quick! It is he!' And she clung with strange fury to Gavrolles, who in vain attempted to shake her off.

'Let me go,' he said in English The woman is drunk. I will call the police.'

With a fierce shriek she raised her hand and struck at his face with her clenched fist.

'You devil! You devil!' she cried in French. 'I have been waiting so long to see you, and now at last we meet. If I had a knife I would stab you. It is I Adèle.' 'I do not know you!'

'It is false. You are a liar and a devil.'

And she struck him in the face with both hands. Livid and trembling, Gavrolles threw her off; she fell back screaming, and would have fallen had not Sutherland caught her in his arms. While he held her she struggled madly, hysterical with an overmastering passion. A crowd of outcast women and well-dressed men already surrounded them, and a policeman, pushing his way into the circle, roughly demanded the cause of the disturbance.

Gavrolles forced a laugh.

'It is nothing,' he said. 'Only a drunken woman, as you see.'

The policeman approached the girl and touched her on the shoulder.

'Come now, just you move on, or I'll have to run you in,' he said; and as she spoke rapidly in her own language, he shook his sagacious head and continued, 'We don't want none of your parleyvoo. Leave the gentleman alone, d'ye hear, and move on.'

'The woman is not drunk,' said Sutherland. 'She is ill, and—look, she has fainted!'

Overmastered by her excitement, she had indeed fallen into a sort of faint or fit. Sutherland supported her gently, while the crowd, with cries and murmurs, pressed close! round them. In the commotion which ensued Gavrolles slipped away, stepped into a hansom, and was driven off.

'Keep back—give her air!' cried Sutherland. 'Does any one know where she lives?'

At this moment the woman whom he had first seen in her company stepped forward.

'Yes, monsieur, we lodge together. Look up, Adèle! What ails you?'

'Help me to take her home,' said Sutherland, in a low voice.

The policeman called a cab, and Sutherland raised the girl in his arms and placed her in it; then he stepped in himself, followed by the other woman.

They drove to a wretched lodging-house in Gerrard Street, Soho, a dismal fetid den, presided over by a hideous old Frenchwoman, who at first refused to take her in.

'You'd better drive her to the hospital,' said this person, blocking the doorway. 'She owes me two weeks' rent already, and I can't take care of her.'

The sight of Sutherland's purse, however, worked wonders; and with many protestations of sympathy the hag suffered the girl to be carried to a room upstairs. The fainting fit had by this time passed away, to be followed by an attack of hysterical weeping and coughing. Sutherland shuddered, for as she coughed, and spat he saw on her lips a thin tinge of crimson blood.

He had her well cared for that night, and the next day he called with a physician, and found her in bed, wild and ghastly, as if she had not got long to live.

'Ah! monsieur, forgive me!' she cried, with a sad smile, reaching out her wasted hand. 'I was *méchante* last night, but to see that man made me mad. I think I should have killed him had I been able. I was good and *gentille* when he first knew me, and he coaxed me away from my friends and took me to that evil place where you found me. But for him I might have been a good woman—you comprehend.'

'Do not speak of it now. This gentleman is a doctor, I have brought him to see you.'

'All, monsieur, how good you are!' sobbed the girl, with a look of ineffable gratitude; and she raised his hand to her feverish lips and kissed it.

Edgar Sutherland was not the man to do any good deed by halves. Thanks to his generosity, Adèle Lambert was removed to a better lodging, and comfortably nursed; the doctor's opinion being that the disease, though certainly mortal, would progress slowly, and that much might be done to alleviate her distressing condition. Not content with assisting her with money, the young man visited her almost daily, and did his best to lighten her miserable lot; talked to her cheerfully, read to her; and without obtruding any moral or religious sentiment, contrived to turn her bewildered and despairing thoughts in the direction of some heavenly compassion.

In the course of these kindly visits he learned the whole story of the unfortunate girl's connection with the French adventurer, whom he had again recognised. That story cannot be told here; it would be too shocking for a society that hushes up revolting truths, and bases its moral security on the existence of an evil which philosophers contemplate with tranquillity, and men of the world with pleasant cynicism. Not even in the pages of a fiction with a purpose can an English writer print the record of what is at the best an accursed human sacrifice, a trade to which the slave trade was venial; a social abomination which destroys the body and too often obliterates the germinating soul.

I know well how, in discussing this question, philosophy and sentimentalism are at issue; how statistics have been twisted to show that actual seduction is rare, and rarest upon the man's side; how the majority of the lost live happily, healthily, and long; how their existence is a necessity of civilisation, the security of virtue, the protection of the household, the safeguard of the morals of the State. Well, I say with Sutherland, God help our civilisation if this be so! So long as such a canker exists, so long as the moral holocaust continues, there is no hope for any living woman, and the Kingdom of Heaven upon earth, which poets have dreamed of, is whole eternities away.

CHAPTER XXVIII
AT THE COUNTESS AURELIA'S

Once or twice during the season it was the custom of the Countess Aurelia Van Homrigh to give a literary party. This party had at first been but a small social gathering, invitations being issued only to a few of the most select of the lady's literary and scientific friends, but every year the invitations had grown more numerous, until the yearly reunions became quite the mode, and each one was an event to which the world of art, science, and letters looked forward with delight.

The Countess was a pretty little Englishwoman, married to a foreign adventurer, who had made an enormous fortune in certain obscure branches of trade. While yet a maiden Miss Aurelia Blackeston was well known in aesthetic circles as the writer of many charming volumes of verse, and as the favoured lady to whom a certain great and titled poet addressed the lines commencing

'Aurelia, pretty one, brightest of blues!'

As a wife and a lady of title the same lady doubled her social charms. Her husband, standing quietly in her shadow, watched her with morose adoration, whilst she dispensed hospitality to all the lions of the land.

For Aurelia loved a lion, just as some people love a lord. On each occasion there were new ones to be sought out, secured and made much of, before the party could be complete. In difficulties of this sort she generally appealed to her old friend and admirer Serena, who, being full-manned and leonine himself, was a good judge of the noble animal in demand. Serena, we may remark *en passant*, had painted the Countess in every attitude and from every conceivable point of view; as a Pythoness, as a 'Psyche by the Waters of Love's Wanness,' as 'A Study in Rose Pink,' as 'Vivien the Enchantress,' in which doleful composition the painter himself appeared as Merlin; and most of these portraits adorned the walls of the cerulean house at Barnes, on the banks of the Thames.

One morning, early in the season, Madeline, sitting at breakfast with her husband, received the Countess's invitation; accompanying it was a little note from Serena. 'I hope you will come; indeed, you must come,' wrote the great man, 'since on this occasion the fair Aurelia's rooms will be graced by the presence of a gentleman whom I wish particularly to make known to you, a charming creature whose soul is redolent of music and divine song. He comes to my rooms, he contemplates your picture by the hour—he vows that so divine a creature cannot exist. I wish to show him that she does exist, and that, in trying to place it upon canvas, my poor hand has signally failed.'

Madeline read the letter with a smile, then she handed it to her husband.

'The Countess is not content with mere lions this year,' she said. 'She evidently intends to make a lioness of *me*. Shall we go?'

'Yes, we had better go, my dear,' returned Forster quietly. 'Beneath all her humbug the Countess is an excellent person; she would be really pained if we stayed away.'

So without more ado—without more thought—the step was taken which was to become the great turning point in Madeline's life.

Breakfast over, Forster went to the City, while Madeline wrote a little note accepting the lady's invitation; then put the whole matter from her mind, ordered her carriage, and an hour later was driving down Regent Street, with the little boy who was now her constant companion.

The life into which Madeline had entered on her marriage had proved so far to be a happy one. James Forster, always kind and considerate, was devoted to his young wife; while Madeline tried to repay some of his kindness to her by lavishing her affection on his child. 'He shall never repent marrying me,' she said to herself a hundred times a day. 'He alone knows I did not bring him honour, but I will bring him happiness.' And she tried to keep her word.

Meantime, the days flew past, and at length the momentous one arrived on which Mr. and Mrs. Forster were to appear at the Countess's house at Barnes. Forster went to the City as usual, but promised to return early; he was detained, however, so that when he reached home he found his wife already arrayed for the night. He looked at her, then gently kissed her.

'Madeline, my dear,' he said, 'I never saw you look more lovely': then he added quietly—'Should you mind very much, my love, if I stayed at home to-night?'

'Stayed at home?'

'Yes, I have had one of my nervous headaches all day, and I don't feel equal to facing the Countess's crowded rooms.'

'Then you shall remain at home, and I will remain with you.'

'Not so, my love: you must go, and Margaret shall accompany you.'

'But I would rather stay.'

'Nonsense, Madeline. If you talk like that I shall go, and punish you for your perversity by being more than usually disagreeable.'

So it was settled, the carriage was ordered, and Madeline drove down to Barnes with Miss Forster by her side.

The gathering, as we have said, was always numerous, but this time it seemed of greater importance than ever. The street on the river side was so blocked with carriages that some time elapsed before Forster's brougham could pull up at the door, and when at length it did, and the ladies passed over the carpeted pavement into the hall, they found themselves in so dense a throng that it was with difficulty they made their way along at all. At length, however, they reached the top of the crowded staircase, at the door of a crowded room. Here Madeline paused; her eyes, lately accustomed to the darkness, were dazzled by the brilliant glare of light which met them, so that at first she could find out nothing very distinctly; in a moment, however, the feeling of confusion passed away, and with one swift glance she took in the scene.

In a suite of lofty rooms running from one to another, like a picture gallery, and almost as thickly covered with works of art, were ladies and gentlemen of all shapes and ages, the majority of the ladies clad in what is now known as the aesthetic, or high-waisted, style, and the greater number of the gentlemen resembling one another in a certain limp and flaccid self-consciousness of attitude. Scattered here and there, as a sort of leaven, were swarthy artists, with beards, spectacled *savants* and scientists, stout literary ladies, and acidulous lady members of the London School Board. It was, indeed, a scene too familiar to need much describing. The chatter was deafening, reminding an irreverent spectator of the noise in the monkey-house at the Zoological Gardens.

While Madeline and Miss Forster stood hesitating within the threshold of the room, they were espied from a distance by Serena, who immediately made his way over to them, and forthwith, in the manner of one having authority, led them to the lady of the house.

The Countess, who was shining resplendent in a dress composed entirely of Indian shawls folded tight round her lissome figure, welcomed Madeline with effusion, and gave the tip of her fingers to Miss Forster; then after a little desultory prattle, she introduced Madeline to a limp gentleman standing near, and floated away to another part of the room.

'A charming creature the Countess,' said the limp gentleman. 'So far above the vulgar prejudices of our too crowded civilisation, with no creed but Beauty, and no God but Art.'

'Yes,' murmured Madeline, scarcely attending, as she gazed rather vacantly round the room.

'Have you seen Botticelli Jones's picture of her ladyship as "A Lily of Languor in the Garden of Proserpine"? No? Well, Ponto says it is the most superbly sane and cosmic thing— —'

He was interrupted by a cry from Madeline, who, leaving his side without a word of apology, crossed the room rapidly, and approached a grim-looking person with a light beard, clad in a very shabby dress suit and rather disreputable boots.

This was no other person than Jack Bingham, an artist by profession, of the old 'pipe and beer' school, and a bosom friend of Marmaduke White.

'What, Jack!' she cried, holding out both her hands.

Everybody called him Jack.

As she spoke the grim face relaxed into a smile.

'What, is it you?' returned Jack, with a delighted laugh.

'Yes, and I am so glad to see you. But who would have thought of meeting you here, of all the places in the world? Dear, dear Jack, the very sight of you calls up old times.'

And tears stood in her eyes as she gazed upon his homely face. Jack was affected too in his rough way, so he made a diversion.

'Beastly slow, isn't it?' he said. 'There doesn't seem to be a smoke room, and none of the fellows are my sort.'

'Why haven't you come to see me?' asked Madeline, nodding.

'Since your marriage?'

'Yes.'

'Well, I don't know—you didn't ask me—and your husband's a swell.'

'He's nothing of the sort, Jack, and as to not being asked, you ought to have known my house was open to every friend of my dear guardian. You might smoke in the drawing-room if you liked, and no one would object.'

Jack laughed.

'I'm not quite such a beast as that; but there, I'll come since you wish it, and have a talk about old times.'

At this point they were interrupted by Blanco Serena.

'Mrs. Forster,' said he, 'permit me; I wish to make two clever people known to each other.'

Madeline placed her hand on Serena's proffered arm, and with a smile and a nod to Bingham moved a few steps away. Presently she paused and looked up into her companion's face.

'Mr. Serena,' she said, 'who is the person? Nobody very clever, I hope; I am so afraid of very clever people.'

'I am going, my dear Imogen, to introduce you to one who, if the "Megatherium" is to be trusted, is one of the greatest minds of the age. A man who is all spirit, whose soul is a combination of music and song, whose——'

'Dear me,' broke in Madeline, 'he must be a dreadful person. Suppose you point him out to me before we meet him, in case I get quite overcome.'

Serena gazed round the room. The crowd was so great he could not at first find the individual he sought, and with Madeline's hand still upon his arm he moved a few more steps forward. Suddenly he paused again, gazed across the room, and Madeline, following the gaze with her eyes, beheld a form the first sight of which chilled her to the soul.

The room was long and vast, and the further end of it curved off into a kind of alcove, which at this moment was filled with an admiring group, such as Du Maurier loves to draw—aesthetic ladies, for the most part tall and limp, and lean gentlemen, crowded together, who stood gazing in rapt admiration upon a figure who stood in their midst. It was upon this figure that Madeline's eyes had fallen. In this wonderful creature, this new lion of the night, she recognised, with a sickening shock of surprise, none other than her old friend and tormentor, Belleisle!

For a moment all power of speech deserted her, the room, the crowds, melted away—she stood as if alone, gazing upon the figure of a man in overwhelming fear—all the blood had deserted her cheeks, the hand which lay upon her companion's arm was cold and death-like.

She was recalled to herself by the sound of Serena's voice.

'Mrs. Forster,' he said, 'will you come on now—may I be permitted the honour of presenting you to my friend Gavrolles?'

But Madeline neither moved nor spoke. Her companion turned towards her, and noticed the ghastly hue of her face.

'Good heavens!' he exclaimed. 'What has happened? My dear Mrs. Forster, let me trust you are not ill?'

Madeline clutched nervously at his arm.

'Hush, not so loud,' she whispered; then forcing a faint smile to her bloodless lips, she murmured, 'I am not feeling well, Mr. Serena, but indeed there is no cause for alarm. The rooms are hot, you see, and I have grown a little faint. Pray let me sit for a moment, but take no further notice of this, I beseech you.'

Utterly bewildered as to what it all meant, but feeling instinctively that something wrong had happened, Serena did as he was requested. He led Madeline to an ottoman; she sank down on it with a sigh.

'Now let me fetch you a glass of wine, or something to take away the faintness,' he said anxiously; and Madeline bowed her head in silent acquiescence.

The moment he had gone she turned her weary, bewildered eyes upon the gay crowd surrounding her, and gazed again with a sickening sense of shrinking fear towards the spot where the man had stood.

Had her eyes deceived her, had it been some hideous vision conjured up to cast a black shadow upon the happiness which was hers at last? Madeline turned her eyes, hoping, half believing this might be so; but one look gave the death-blow to all her hopes, and made her terror more terrible than it had been before.

Yes, there he stood, the man who had blighted her young life, who had dragged her into the mud, from which, in spite of him, she had arisen. He was changed, certainly, but what changes could disguise him? His hair, once short, was now long and luxuriant, he was clothed in garments of the newest cut, he was talking rapidly, twisting his body into various contortions, for the benefit of the small crowd about him. There was no mistaking those pitiless eyes, that cruel mouth. Yes, it was Belleisle, the man who had cheated her into becoming his mistress, who had made her the decoy of a gambling hell, who had dragged her into the very depths of dishonour and pollution.

She sat for a time concealing her face with her fan, but gazing upon him in a wild fascination; then a terror seized her that the dreadful figure might approach and she would be recognised. The mere possibility sent a cold thrill through all her frame, and she realised for the first time all the evil which one word from the man's lips could bring upon her head. Serena returned with a glass of wine and a biscuit. She sipped the wine, but put the biscuit from her. Then she turned her white face towards Serena, and whispered eagerly—

'Mr. Serena, I must go home!'

'Go home! My dear Mrs. Forster, the evening has hardly begun. We cannot lose one of our brightest ornaments—besides, I have yet to introduce you to——'

'Hush,' interrupted Madeline, eagerly, 'do, pray, let me go. Take me downstairs, I can bear this place no longer. I will wait in the hall for the carriage, and you can bring Miss Forster to me.'

So saying, and without giving Serena time to reply, she rose, took his arm, and drew him out of the crowded room, down the stairs. Once clear of the room she seemed to breathe more freely, but her cheek still retained its ashen grey hue, and the hand which rested upon his arm trembled violently. He led her to the hall, wrapped her cloak about her, and ordered her carriage; then, at her request, he returned to the room to fetch Miss Forster.

It was yet early, carriages continued to drive up to the door, and new streams of people made their way into the dwelling, but in the confusion no one noticed Madeline. She had withdrawn into the shadow, and stood now tremulous with excitement and eager to be gone, and inwardly thanking God that she had escaped the Frenchman's eye.

Suddenly she felt herself lightly touched upon the arm. She turned quickly, and found herself face to face with the very man she feared!

Instantly she shrank away, and a quick cry of pain escaped her lips. She put her hand to her head in a wild bewildered fear, and stared stupidly at her foe.

The Frenchman was by no means disconcerted. He bowed politely before her, asked in an audible voice if he could be of any service to her, but whispered low——

'I must see you alone to-morrow. Name a place where we shall meet!'

Madeline did not utter a cry this time, but she shrank farther and farther away. Then she raised her head and looked straight into the Frenchman's eyes. For a moment she had been seized with a mad idea to disown any knowledge of him—that one look into his eyes convinced her that the device was hopeless.

'Name a time and place,' he repeated. Madeline knew that to refuse was impossible—so she said hurriedly—'Albert Memorial to-morrow morning at 11.' Then she gazed like a frightened child about her, and saw with dismay that Miss Forster stood close at hand. Had she heard or seen? Madeline could not tell, for the lady's face betrayed nothing. She came quickly forward, and said, in her cold, unsympathetic voice—

'What is the matter, Madeline?'

Madeline's face, which had lately been so pale, suddenly became crimson.

She stammered out that nothing was the matter.

'Mr. Serena told me that you had been ill.'

'I did not feel well,' returned Madeline, regaining some of her self-command, 'and I should like to go home—but, dear Miss Forster, if you will permit me I will go alone. It seems a pity to take you away so soon.'

The lady replied, coldly—

'I have no wish to stay. I came because my brother wished me to come; that was all.'

By this time Serena, who had been busy hurrying up the carriage, came to announce that it was ready, to offer his arm to the ladies, and once more to express his deep grief at Madeline's untimely departure. Madeline took his arm in silence. As she moved away, she turned and gazed uneasily around her.

The Frenchman was nowhere to be seen.

The drive home was made in profound silence. Miss Forster sat in stately reticence and gazed from the carriage window at the flashing lamps of the street, while Madeline threw herself into her corner, closed her weary eyes, and tried to persuade herself that the event of the last hour had been but a dream. She was a little bewildered as yet, and unable to realise all that the man's presence might mean. To her as yet he had only recalled the horror of her past-life; he had cast no actual shadow over her home.

When the carriage was pulled up at the door and she stepped out, she felt herself shivering from head to foot, though in reality her hands and lips were burning. When she pleaded illness as the cause of her early return, Forster readily believed her, and while folding her in his arms he blamed his own folly for allowing her to go forth at all that night. Was it his fancy, or did Madeline really shrink from his embrace; yes, shrink from it, as she had never done before? He turned anxiously towards her, he noticed that her cheek was flushed, and that a strange light shone in her eyes; but he saw no mystery there.

Having satisfactorily explained her return, Madeline went at once to her room, where she found her maid awaiting her. The girl assisted her mistress to remove her dress; to take down her hair, and put on her dressing gown; then she was summarily dismissed for the night, and Madeline, after locking her door, sat down to think what it would be best for her to do.

What had she done? Nothing as yet. She had let the man see that she feared him, certainly, but then he needed no sign from her to assure him of that. She had, moreover, in her desperation and fear of exposure, made an assignation with him. But then that assignation need never be kept. There was one way open to her—one open, honest course; but she shrank from it appalled. Her heart counselled thus—'Go to your husband, tell him all, and throw yourself upon his sympathy;' but her courage failed her, she shrank back like a contaminated guilty thing.

'Go to him, look in his eyes, and say to him—"I have seen to-night the man who made me his mistress; with one word he can bring disgrace upon me, and *you*" — — — —-'

No, she could not do it. Whatever her husband had heard of her past she hoped by this time he had forgotten. In Forster's sight, at least, she would not be degraded; come what might, she would fight her battle alone.

CHAPTER XXIX
GAVROLLES

When Madeline came down to breakfast next morning she looked very ill. There was a wild light in her eyes and a feverish flush upon her face. Quite unsuspicious of the real cause of the change in her, Forster attributed it to the indisposition of the night before, and began to wonder if the sudden change in her habits was going to tell upon her health.

It certainly was a great change to be transported from the wild excitement of public life to the monotonous existence of a quiet house like his; but when he had asked her to give up the stage, he had thought he was lifting from her shoulders a load of which she would gladly be free. He had wished his wife to take her ease and enjoy her days, not to toil wearily as if for her daily bread. But now he began to think that he had been totally wrong. While he had been working away with unconscious happiness in the City, his beautiful wild bird had been beating her breast against the bars of her gilded cage, and pining for that freedom which to all gifted beings is so dear. These thoughts and many more of the same strain passed through Forster's mind, while he made his way to the City. Long before he reached his office he had decided how to act.

'I will speak to Madeline to-night,' he said to himself, and hear her views. Something must be done to make her contented.'

Meanwhile Madeline, left with Miss Forster, walked about the room in new restlessness. She looked out of the window; it was a damp, dark day; she looked at her watch, it was past ten o'clock. In an hour she had promised to meet the man, and by this time she had settled in her mind that she must go.

What he could want with her she could not tell, and she had not paused to inquire. That he meant her no good she knew, but it was useless to anticipate the evil, till she knew its nature.

She went upstairs with a heavy heart, and returned, greatly to Miss Forster's surprise, in walking costume.

The little boy, confident of his reception, came bounding in and clung affectionately to her skirts. She kissed him fondly, but told him he could not go with her that morning.

'Not at all? May I not go a little way, mamma?'

'Not even a little way, darling; I must go alone to-day.'

There was such a strange ring in her voice that Miss Forster looked up in some amazement, while the child clung closer to Madeline, and ardently kissed the cold, pale cheek.

'Mamma is going to see a doctor,' he said; 'is it not so, mamma?'

"No, dear.'

'Then where are you going alone, on such a cold wet day?'

Madeline flushed uneasily, and impatiently put the child from her.

'You should not ask so many questions,' she said; 'it is rude!' Then, noting the little crestfallen face, she hurriedly caught him up again and kissed him, while her own eyes filled with tears.

'Hush, do not mind, I was wrong; but I did not mean to pain you, darling—no, no—not *you!*'

During the enacting of this scene Miss Forster had still remained in the room. Up to this moment she had said nothing; but her eyes had followed all her sister-in-law's movements, and watched her face with peculiar interest. When Madeline had put down the boy, and was about to leave the room, she spoke.

'The carriage has not come round,' she said.

Madeline started, and turned. She had ignored the presence of her sister-in-law; and that lady noticed that the sudden recollection of it brought another uncomfortable flush to the pale cheek, and caused another anxious look about the room.

'I—I have not ordered the carriage,' she said.

'Indeed?'

No question had been asked, therefore Madeline was not bound to reply; but feeling that she must say something, she stammered rather awkwardly—

'I am going to walk. I prefer it to-day, as my head is bad, but I shall not be long away.' Then, as if in dread of further questioning, she hurried from the room.

It was certainly a most inclement morning, but Madeline, being suitably clad, did not heed the weather. After walking a short distance, she hailed a passing hansom and drove to the park gate, close to the Albert Memorial; here she alighted, and crossing to the footpath sank wearily upon one of the seats to watch for the Frenchman's arrival.

She had not sat long when she saw him.

Previous to her coming, Gavrolles, as we must continue to call him, had been parading theatrically round the memorial for a quarter of an hour, to the great admiration of several idle nursemaids. He did not at first see Madeline. He was smoking a cigar, glancing with careless interest at the somewhat tawdry designs, and keeping a cat-like eye on the figures which were moving about the park.

Another turn round the monument; then his eye fell upon Madeline, who still retained her seat close by. In a moment the whole man seemed to change. He smiled, tossed away his cigar, and advanced gallantly towards her. He raised his hat, then cordially extended his right hand.

'Good morning,' he exclaimed in French; 'charmed to see you abroad so early! May I so far presume upon your friendship as to walk with you a very little way around the park?'

Madeline rose in silence, took no notice of his extended hand, and walked along by his side. She looked cold, haughty, and defiant; but in truth her heart was sinking terribly. As for Gavrolles, if he was a little disconcerted at first, he quickly regained his composure. As he drew back his rejected hand he smiled, and the smile seemed to say: 'It is your turn now, Madame! *Eh bien*, enjoy your pride to the full; my time is at hand, and I mean to take advantage of it.'

'*Parbleu!* he exclaimed, 'how the place is deserted; and yet to my mind the morning is the pleasantest time of the day. See how fresh the flowers and the grass!—and the breeze is still sweet and cool with last night's dew! It seems to bring new life to a man. Ah, yes; it is charming!'

He expanded his chest, he raised his hat to let the breeze play with his flowing locks of hair, then he gave a sidelong glance at Madeline, and met her eyes. She paused, and for the first time that day addressed him—

'I cannot stay,' she said quietly. 'Why have you forced me to meet you here to-day?'

He shrugged his shoulders, he raised his hand in polite protestation.

'Forced you!' he exclaimed. 'Ah, but you use hard words, my dear Madeline. I employ force to no one; certainly not to one so esteemed. If your memory is good, you must know that I merely asked an interview. You were gracious enough not only to grant it, but to name also our place of meeting.'

She looked him steadily in the face, and her lip curled contemptuously.

'Will you oblige me by answering my question?' Again he smiled, but while he did so his face was by no means pleasant to see.

'I will make my best endeavours, madame.'

'First, tell me this: when you went to that house last night were you certain of meeting me there?'

'I most certainly hoped to have the pleasure of meeting you. I have lived in this strange world long enough to know that nothing is certain.'

'Did you know that I had married an honourable man?'

'I knew that; yes.'

'And yet you made up your mind to thrust yourself upon me?'

He bowed profoundly. 'My dear Madeline, your penetration is wonderful. I perceive you are one of the few beings in this stupid world fully capable of understanding me.'

'Unfortunately for myself,' Madeline continued, 'I understand you sufficiently to know that you would not plan this meeting if there was no purpose to be obtained by it. What new injury do you wish to do me *now?*'

He gazed at her flushed face and muttered, '*Ma foi*, but she is charming!' Then he added, aloud—

'I merely wished to tell you, Madeline, something that you do not know.'

'And that is——'

'Only this—that although you have married an honourable man, as you say, you are nevertheless still my wife.'

CHAPTER XXX
IN THE TOILS

He spoke quietly enough, but she recoiled as if he had struck her.

'Your wife!' she exclaimed. '*Your wife*, monsieur!'

A dark look passed over the Frenchman's face. He bowed profoundly.

'It is an honour which has been coveted by many, madame,' he returned, 'to be the wife of your humble *serviteur*; but I am proud to say it has been reserved for one who is truly worthy of it. Yes, Madeline, I will own it— at one time I thought the position too elevated for you; but when I saw you nobly rising to fame, I said to myself, "After all, I was wrong. She is a splendid creature; she will adorn our world of Art; at the right moment I will reveal the truth, and claim her"—and so, my dear Madeline, I claim you *now!*'

He smiled, he held forth his hand; but Madeline recoiled again.

'Do not touch me,' she cried wildly.

He shrugged his shoulders.

'*Eh bien*—I have no wish to touch you, *chère amie*—but if you play the tragedy queen in the park you will gather a crowd about you, and that would not be pleasant for *you*.

He spoke with quiet malignity; nevertheless Madeline knew that he spoke truly. She was utterly in his power, and for her own sake she dared not make a scene; whatever she said must be said quietly for fear of attracting attention. She cast a fearful glance around her, then, pale and trembling with disgust and shame, she turned again to the Frenchman.

'This is another of your falsehoods. Why have you chosen to tell me it to-day?'

'*Mon Dieu!* what a question! I do not choose to tell you a story. I came to claim my wife.'

'It is false. I am not your wife.'

'No? Then this little writing lies.'

As he spoke he drew forth a paper and waved it carelessly in the air.

'Ah, my dear Madeline, there was once a time when you would joyfully have received the news I bring you to-day. You did not always scorn the thought of being madame my lady!'

'You are right, monsieur,' answered Madeline. 'There was once a time when the news which you bring me today would have been welcome to me, but thank God that time has gone, and I am changed!'

'Yes,' he returned quietly, 'you are changed, as you say; so also am I. At that period of my career to which you allude I was not perfect, and, pardon me for saying so, Madeline, neither were you. I confess with all humility that I told lies, and we both showed temper, but—*nous avons changé tout cela!* I come to-day to tell you the truth, and to offer you your rightful home.'

Again he moved as if to approach her. Again she shrank away.

'It is not the truth,' she returned vehemently; 'I refuse to believe you! You told me the truth once, but you are lying to me to-day!'

Again his face darkened, but when he spoke his voice was as sweet as it had been before.

'Your judgment is harsh, *chérie*, but I have without doubt deserved it— that being so, I bear it with patience. I say to you that I lied to you before; therefore I must not expect you to believe me now. Before I could not prove the truth of my statement, but that is all changed at last!'

Again he produced his slip of paper; this time he held it out before Madeline's eyes. In a dazed, troubled way she looked at it. She saw at a glance that it was the certificate, real or forged, of the marriage between Auguste Belleisle and Madeline Hazel mere. Therefore she completely lost her self control, and did what, under the circumstances, it was most injudicious that she should do—she allowed the Frenchman to see that she was afraid.

'I will not—I cannot—believe it,' she cried. 'If it is so, why did you tell me that wicked falsehood, when I did not know you well enough to doubt your word?'

'I will tell you, dearest. When I induced you to fly with me from the school I was poor—miserably poor, and I believed I was eloping with a lady who would become possessed of a fortune when she was of age. Ah! forgive me, but I was wicked, corrupt! Then I said to myself, "She is a charming girl; she will become the victim of fortune-hunters; she evidently adores me, and

I care for her; the fortune must be mine!" Afterwards you repented of your mad folly. I knew you did so too late—in spite of your wishes I married you. Shortly after our marriage you yourself informed me, *chérie*, that you were poor. I felt that I had been befooled, and I grew enraged. Still, as I could not easily rid myself of my wife, I resolved to make her useful. I did so. You fell into my plans until you discovered them; then you showed temper, and threatened to become dangerous. I wondered for a second time what I should do with you. I determined to try a bold stroke, and succeed or fail. I succeeded. I told you a lie, *mon ange*, and in your charming innocence you believed it to be the truth. You asked for no proofs, which was lucky for me, since I could produce none. You believed that you had been my mistress. I knew that you were bound to me by a nearer and a dearer tie.'

He paused and looked at her. Her face was ghastly, her eyes wildly fixed; she shivered through all her frame.

'Madame, you are not well.'

Again she shrank away. He smiled and nodded.

'*Mon ange*, I know I have done wrong, but you must forget and forgive. I came to make amends. Since those days of which I have spoken I also have changed. I am no longer a penniless, nameless Frenchman. I have risen to a position which henceforth I hope to adorn. The divine Muse has entered into my soul. Art is now my adored mistress; the great men and women of the land are pleased, so to speak, to prostrate themselves before me. I offer you a position which thousands would give their lives to fill. *Bien!* I care nothing for them. I accept their adulation, but I am willing to place you beside me and say to the world, "This charming creature is my wife!"'

What wonderful self-sacrifice!—what condescension!

He stood as if expecting her to fall in ecstasy at his feet. She simply stared at him in dumb amazement, till, disgusted at her silence, Gavrolles, who had all his wits about him, spoke again.

'*Mon Dieu*, but am I not generous!' he said. 'I say to you, "Come to me, my wife;" while you think, "Alas! it is too late. I have taken to myself another husband." Well, that shall make no difference to me. I take the blame of that, since it was I who deceived you. Yes, *mon ange*, I forgive you from my soul! *

She looked at him in deepening horror, while she said in a hollow voice—

'What of my husband, monsieur?'

'*Parbleu*, I had no thought of him. What is he?—a common tradesman, I believe; a dull creature, incapable of comprehending the splendours of a nature like mine; there is no poetry in his soul. He adds up his accounts now; he will add them up when you are gone—that is all!'

Madeline's face grew even whiter, but her eyes flashed fire.

'Take care,' she cried, 'take care. Say what you like of me, do what you can to me, but don't dare to put a slight on *him*.'

It was now the Frenchman's turn to be astonished. For a moment the lackadaisical look of condescension passed completely from his eyes.

'What do you mean?' he asked sharply.

'Only this, monsieur, that the gentleman whom you are pleased to denounce as commonplace is as far above you as the sun is above the earth. That after you had tried to destroy me it was he who nobly put out his hand to save me. That sooner than let you bring disgrace and sorrow to him I will make a sacrifice of myself, perhaps of you!'

'*Parbleu*, but you are heroic,' sneered the Frenchman.

'What I am,' continued Madeline, 'I am; thanks to you, and you only. I have been dragged as low almost as the women who nightly walk the streets. Now you come to me and ask me to return to shame and degradation. Your wife I may be, as you say, but sooner than return to you and live with you— in honourable wedlock, as the world would call it—I would destroy myself. I expect no mercy from you. Well, you may do you worst—what that may be I neither know nor care.'

And before the Frenchman could utter a word she turned from him and walked swiftly away.

He did not attempt to follow her. This sudden and unexpected onslaught of his victim had found him quite unprepared, and he gazed after her with eyes full of perplexity and amazement. Then he, too, turned and walked away. He strolled slowly through the park in the direction of the Serpentine; having reached it, he paused on one of the bridges, leant over the parapet, and watched the swans. He felt in his pocket, threw them some broken biscuits, and watched them eat.

While so watching, he soliloquised. 'As I suspected,' he murmured, 'she still possesses a spirit and a temper—*eh bien*, it is for me to manage both. If this little piece of paper (touching the certificate) were genuine, if that spirited creature were indeed my wife, I should find my work easy. The law would give her to me, and there would be an end to the whole matter. I would place her again upon the stage; she would make me a rich man, while I could pursue my dream, mount rapidly up the ladder of fame, become the idol of mankind, and make my name immortal. But, alas! that cannot be. The charming creature detests me, and means to resist me. I dare not appeal to the law, for it would require more proofs of my sagacity than my charming Madeline does. *Parbleu!* what must I do *now?*'

He ran his thin fingers through his long hair; he gazed again meditatively at the water; he threw some more biscuits to the swans. Suddenly the perplexed look passed away from his face, which lit up into positive ecstasy.

'The husband! 5 he cried. *'Mon Dieu!* but she adores the husband even more cordially than she detests me. Let me think of him; let my plans involve him, and my success is tolerably sure.'

CHAPTER XXXI
IN THE ROW

While Gavrolles, in a grotesque attitude, was soliloquising and feeding the swans, Madeline was walking along the pavement of the principal street in Knightsbridge. Her eyes rested upon the gaily decked shop windows and the busy crowd about her, but her thoughts were still with the man whom she had just left. Already she repented of her madness in having defied him. Once or twice she paused with the intention of returning to him and asking for pity, but her resolutions were no sooner made than conquered; to expect mercy from that man was like looking for water to flow from a stone.

She paused and looked blankly in at a shop window; as she did so she felt herself touched lightly and timidly on the arm; and on looking down she found that she had been accosted by a flower girl; a pale, little creature, clad in miserable rags, with a face pinched and pallid from starvation, who timidly held forth a bunch of half-withered violets. Madeline looked down, and her eyes filled with tears; not with sorrow for the child—they were tears of self-pity—for as she pressed some silver into the child's hand, she thought, 'What would I give to change places with you to-day?'

Thus recalled to herself, she looked at her watch. It was one o'clock; at two she knew that Miss Forster would expect her to preside at the luncheon table. She determined to hurry home, in order to have a few minutes to compose herself before she was compelled to meet her sister-in-law. She called a hansom, and ordered the man to drive to her house. She stopped him at the street corner, however, and finished her journey on foot.

To her intense relief she was able to gain her room without encountering the lady whose presence seemed to inspire her with so much dread. Having reached the room she shut herself in, sank down on an ottoman, and stared despairingly before her.

'His wife!' Could it be that he had spoken truly, that she was really bound by the sacred tie to the man who had done his best to ruin her? Could it be that she had brought shame and disgrace on the man who had been noble enough to shut out the past and to cleanse and purify her with his unstained name? 'My God,' she murmured, I think I am accursed. I am like a leper—a vile, unclean thing which contaminates all it touches. I did sin, in a wild, impulsive, girlish way, but why should that sin for ever drag me down? I have repented—I have tried to atone—but for me there seems no mercy.' Then came the question, What must she do? Return to Monsieur Belleisle, whom the world would doubtless call her lawful husband? Live with him in degradation as great as any she had yet been made to bear?

'No!' she cried. 'I would sooner, as I said to him, destroy my miserable life!'

A gentle tap at the door aroused her. She opened it and admitted her little step-son. It was a custom of the child to call at Madeline's room, and if he found her go down with her to lunch. He bounded in in his usual light-hearted way, but on seeing her face his hilarity received a check. He took her hand and kissed it, he looked up wistfully into her eyes—

'Mamma's headache is no better,' he said quietly, 'Why do you think that, darling?'

'Why?—because you are so white—and because your eyes are all wet. Why have you been crying, mamma; what is there to make you cry?'

'Ah, what indeed?' echoed Madeline, seizing up the child and clasping him passionately in her arms. 'But, remember, my pet, I spoke roughly to you this morning—I have been away from you for hours; perhaps I thought you would not be glad to see me back again.'

'Ah, no! you would not think that,' he said, pressing his rosy cheek against her cold, pale face. 'What would papa do? What should we all do if mamma went away?'

She shuddered, but held the child closely to her as she descended to the dining-room.

The meal was got through in oppressive silence. To be sure, the presence of the servants acted as a barrier to anything like conversation; but every one felt on this occasion that there was something more. Even the child and the very servants seemed oppressed by that indescribable gloom which all felt but none could understand. The luncheon over, Madeline rose with a sigh of infinite relief, and ordered the carriage.

The rain had ceased to fall, but the sky still looked threatening, and the drive did not prove to be a pleasant one. Still it seemed to Madeline that anything would be better than sitting in the house all the afternoon tormented by her own wretched thoughts. Presently, however, as she was putting on her hat, the thought occurred to her that it might be well for her to seek another interview with Belleisle. When, therefore, she descended the stairs she merely kissed the child, who was standing half expecting to be invited to go, and entered the carriage alone.

She drove straight to Regent Street, made one or two trifling purchases, then she ordered her coachman to take a few turns round the park.

The season was rapidly drawing to a close; many families had already betaken themselves to the country, and most of those who lingered were busily preparing to go. Still, in spite of this, there were still enough people left to make a tolerable show in the Row, and Madeline had not been ten minutes in the drive before she was greeted with many gracious smiles and bows.

Suddenly, however, her heart gave a great throb, then seemed to stand still, for her eyes rested upon the very form she sought. Could it be possible? Yes, there he was on horseback, on a sorry hack sicklied o'er with the shade of the livery stable, and accompanied by two young ladies in green riding-habits and hats composed of peacocks' feathers. The three horses were walking, and the three riders seemed heedless of everything but each other.

The great and cosmic creature was holding forth, while the two girls were gazing upon him in rapt devotion.

Madeline felt her cheek grow crimson, for it seemed to her as if every soul about her suddenly read her secret.

She bent forward to speak to her coachman, and met the Frenchman's eye; his face became suddenly irradiated, he politely lifted his hat as the carriage passed him; but she felt herself utterly unable to make any sign in return.

That day had passed wearily enough to James Forster. From the moment he had entered the office he had been able to think of nothing but his wife; so great was his anxiety and his eagerness to see her that he left business two hours before his usual time, and hurried home. It was not fair to her, he thought, that he should spend so many hours of the day away from her side. He pictured her at home, sitting disconsolately beside his lonely hearth. When he reached the house, however, he was disenchanted. He went up to the drawing-room and found his sister prim and neat as usual, working at some simple embroider work, and keeping an eye upon the child, who played at her feet. She looked surprised to see her brother at such an early hour.

'Has anything happened, James?' she said.

He laughed a little impatiently.

'Why, Margaret, have I grown such a methodical old fellow that you must imagine something has happened merely because I come home a couple of hours before dinner time? No, nothing has happened. I hurried home because I wanted to have a talk with Madeline. Where is she?'

'Madeline is out.'

'Out?'

'Yes, she has been out all day.'

'Why, where has she gone to?'

'Really, James, I am not Madeline's keeper. Since she didn't choose to tell me I thought it was not my duty to ask. I only know that she went out walking all the morning, and that immediately after lunch she went out driving. I have not seen her since.'

'Why, I thought when she went out she generally took the boy?'

'She has always taken him before, but she did not want him to-day. She said it was necessary for her to go alone.'

Miss Forster concluded with a significant 'Hem!' which spoke volumes. Forster made no reply; he turned away, went to his study, and sat there to await his wife's return.

One hour, two hours passed. She did not come. The first dinner bell rang—he rose to go to his room, and as he was crossing the hall he heard his wife's knock at the door.

'So late!' he murmured. 'Where can she have been at this hour?'

Then he thought of his sister's peculiar manner when she had spoken to him, and instead of waiting to see his wife come in he went straight up to his room.

When he went down to dinner he found Madeline already at the table. Her face was paler than it had been on the preceding night, and there was the same strange, wild light in her eyes. Was it his fancy again, or did she really shrink from him when he put his arms around her and kissed her cold cheek? Why did she flush and look uneasily about the room when he asked her innocently enough what interesting appointment she could possibly have to keep her out all day? There was certainly something the matter which he was faintly conscious of, but which he could not possibly understand.

The dinner over, Forster rose and asked his wife to go with him to his study. The request was a simple one, but Madeline started, her face grew paler than before, and a sickening sense of dread seized her heart. She filled a glass of water and drank off its contents; then with a courage born only of despair she went with him.

CHAPTER XXXII
HUSBAND AND WIFE

Forster's study was the smallest room in the mansion, furnished very plainly but cosily, and shut off by two baize doors from the rest of the house. It contained, besides the ordinary furniture, a few favourite pictures in water-colour, and a small number of books, selected from the shelves of the library. Here Forster spent many a pleasant evening, following those studies in early English poetry and literature which were his chief recreation.

The couple entered and seated themselves. Madeline had her eyes fixed thoughtfully on the fire, but she was fully conscious that her husband, leaning back in his writing chair, had his eyes intently upon her face. What could it mean? What was coming? She waited and trembled.

'My dear Madeline,' he said at last, 'I have been thinking about you all day long. That, of course, is nothing unusual, for I need not tell you that you are ever uppermost in my thoughts; but to-day I have been much troubled on your account.'

She started and looked at him. What did he mean? His face was curiously grave, and in his eyes there was the shadow of a great and wistful pain.

'I am sorry you have been troubled,' she said in a low sad voice, 'and that I have been the cause.'

'Nay, my dear, it is no fault of yours; but the truth is I am very anxious. Sometimes of late—not always, but sometimes—I have thought that you are a little disappointed, a little weary. All my wish, all the dream of my life, is to see you happy; and yet— —'

He paused, and passed his hand across his eyes; for tears were there.

'Do not think I am unhappy,' she replied. 'I am not. I am happier than I deserve.'

'This is a dull house, I know,' continued Forster, as if pursuing his own thoughts, 'and Margaret, I am afraid, a somewhat dull companion. It is not at all the life which you have been accustomed to, and I do not wonder that you find it dull. Well, how shall we brighten it?' Here his face was lit by a loving smile. 'How shall I make my darling happy? I think I have discovered the way. Indeed, if I had not been a commonplace fool, I might have discovered it long before.'

Still more puzzled than ever, she kept her eyes fixed upon his face; then seeing him smile so brightly, so kindly, she drew near to him and kissed him.

'Don't cry, my darling!'

'I can't help it—you are so good to me!'

'Not half so good as you deserve. Now listen—I have settled it. You shall return to the stage.'

She started in amazement.

'No, no!'

'But yes! Your divine gift shall not perish from want of use; you shall go back to the Art which you so love, and I—I shall be by, to rejoice in your happiness and your success.'

Instead of receiving the proposal with joy, as he had anticipated, Madeline rose, trembling and very pale.

'Do not decide hastily,' said Forster, gently, 'but think it well over.'

'It is quite unnecessary—I shall never act again; never! never!'

'Madeline!'

'I have disgraced you enough already.'

'Disgraced me—God forbid! Madeline, you are my pride, my treasure— only honour can come to me through you. Don't think I am such a Philistine as to underrate your gifts, or the art you delight to follow. When I persuaded you to adopt this quiet life, I thought it might be better for your peace of mind, for your health. I see that I was wrong. Genius like yours cannot be contented with the mere humdrum of an English home. I was selfish, dear. You shall be my Imogen again, and, as I said, I will share your happy triumphs.'

'It is impossible,' cried Madeline, impetuously. 'I hate the stage. Rather than return to it I would die.'

It was now Forster's turn to be amazed.

'Hate the stage!' he echoed. 'Ah, you do not mean what you say.'

'But I do mean it. When I first acted it was for my guardian's sake—to make him happy, and, perhaps, rich. But I never loved the life, and now—I sicken at it. Oh, James!' she continued, in deepening agitation, 'do not think me foolish or ungrateful. I am quite, quite happy here with you. Yes, when we are alone together, when we are away from the world and all its feverish tumult, I am more than happy—I am at peace. Don't think otherwise. You ask me to go back into the world; it is the world that makes me miserable. If we should go away together—far from London, far from the wicked city—to some green country place, where none could know us, none could care for us, then, I think, I should be at peace indeed.' As she spoke, she threw herself into his arms, for he had risen as if to implore her to be calm, and laid her head upon his breast.

'Then you are not unhappy?'

'I don't know—I cannot tell!' she sobbed. 'I think it is my disposition—never quite contented, never restful. When I was a child, I was a trouble to those who loved me; and afterwards—afterwards everything seemed to go wrong with me. But oh! do not think that I am ungrateful—that I do not love you as you deserve. I do! I do! I do!'

And as she clung to him sobbing, she repeated her protestations again and again. He too was strongly moved, and tried in vain to calm her.

'It is like you to reproach yourself,' he said tenderly. 'My loving, unselfish darling!'

'But I am selfish,' she said. 'I am not good, like you, James. It would have been better, far better, if we had never met.'

'Don't say that, Madeline!'

'I must say it. I bring sorrow to all that love me.'

'You have never brought sorrow to me. Only happiness, my dear!'

'If I could believe that! But where another woman would have been contented, I have been ill at ease. I hate myself for it! I hate my life! But oh! I love you! You do not doubt it, dear?'

'If I doubted it I should be a miserable man.'

'Whatever happened, you would still believe it.'

'Till my dying day. You have proved it,'

'Have I, James?'

'God knows you have. You are not like common women—you are greater and better, and it is your very affection which makes you reproach yourself. But let us speak again—calmly, seriously—of what I proposed. You want occupation—you want play for your noble powers; here, darling, you are like a bird in a golden cage. Let me persuade you to try your wings again, to end this dreary existence. I can easily arrange everything for your return to the profession.'

She shook her head sadly. 'Never! never!'

'But why?'

'Have I not told you? Because I prefer to remain alone with *you*.'

He pressed her still, suspecting that her determination was caused by solicitude on his account, or some secret fear of compromising him; but when he saw that she was firm he was pleased. In the secresy of his own mind he rather dreaded the step that he proposed; lest that step, if taken, might draw them further asunder, and in more than one way lead to misconstruction. He was far too little of a Philistine to despise the theatre, to undervalue a beautiful and much-neglected art; but he knew its decadence, and understood its baser ambitions. He preferred to keep the woman he loved to himself, to screen her from the contamination of mercenary speculators and the coarse admiration of the dregs of the public which unhappily fill our theatres. The excitements of the stage, he thought, were not beneficial to a nature so overwrought as that of his wife; its *morale* was not edifying, its literature not spiritually ennobling, its successes were evanescent, its rewards too often achieved by ignoble means. All this he thought, yet did not say, for he honestly set his wife's personal happiness above all considerations of prejudice; but when he heard her emphatic determination, a weight was taken from his mind.

So the interview ended, bringing the husband and wife more closely and tenderly together, but still leaving on the woman's heart the sense of a nameless dread, which she dared not utter, and which he, of course, did not understand.

CHAPTER XXXIII
OLD JOURNALISM—AND NEW

Calling at Sutherland's rooms one morning, Crieff found him surrounded by a number of unwieldy volumes, dirty and dingy enough to have been picked up, as indeed they had been, in the uncleanest shop in Holywell Street. One of these volumes he was examining with considerable impatience when Crieff entered.

'What have you got there?' asked the journalist, peeping over his shoulder. 'As I live, an old volume of the "Satyrnine Review."'

'Yes. I saw the rubbish ticketed up very cheap, and bought it. It is not a complete set, but sufficiently so for my purpose.'

And he threw the volume down among its fellows.

'You'll find some spicy writing there,' said Crieff. 'A little out of date now, of course, for the new society journals have killed the "Satyrnine," but it used to be deucedly clever.'

'Clever!' echoed Sutherland. 'During the whole of last evening, and for hours this morning, I have been searching these volumes in vain for one spark of insight, for a ray of pure talent. They are simply trash, and spiteful trash, which is the worst of all.'

'Perhaps you expect too much, old fellow. The "Satyrnine" only professes to be smart.'

'I hate that word, though it expresses well enough the journalism we speak of—the journalism of the "Satyr," who now wears fine clothes and calls himself a gentleman, but is at the best a production of literature's slimy deposits—a Faun, earth-grubbing, ugliness-loving, screeching at the mysteries of artistic sunlight and moonlight. Even your friend Lagardère's style is better—it makes no hideous pretences.'

'Come, I'm glad you see some merit in Lagardère, after all!'

'But this rubbish'—here he touched the volume contemptuously with his foot—'this rubbish, in its horrible baseness and unintelligence, has not even the redeeming quality of honesty. The writers are ignorant, but they are also vicious; uninstructed, but at the same time pertinacious. Who are these men? Does any one know them? I should be curious, for example, to see the goatfooted animal who wrote this article on Thackeray.'

'Well, you see,' answered Crieff, reflectively, 'they rather make a point of working in the dark, keeping up a mystery, so to speak; but nowadays, when the journal has gone downhill, and spicier papers like the "Plain Speaker" have practically killed it, the "Satyrnines" are better known than they used to be.'

'Are they persons of reputation?'

'Well, no; of course not.'

'Gentlemen?'

'Some of them, perhaps,' said Crieff, with a smile; 'but for the most part just like the rest of us—a mixed breed. There's our friend Gass, whom you met at Gavrolles'; *he's* one. He has his finger in most journalistic pies, and writes on all sides to turn an honest penny.'

'Humph!' muttered Sutherland. 'I once had a "Satyrnine Reviewer" pointed out to me at a party. He looked like a creature fresh from some large drapery establishment; dressed within an inch of his life, with *pince-nez* on nose, but goat-eared and goat-footed for all that—I am sure the animal couldn't even spell. But turning from the men to the matter, what I have been most struck by in reading these wretched volumes is their utter want of the positively human qualities—veracity, reverence, generous aspiration. There is not a single public man of any nobility, either in politics or literature, who is not persistently gibbered at and reviled. Our present Liberal statesmen are insulted by the grossest personalities. Our great literary men are for the most part decried—when they are praised the reason is not far to seek. Thackeray, inspected by the Satyr, is "no gentleman." * Dickens is an ignoramus. Browning is a dunce, ignorant even of grammar. Worse than this is the vicious determination to ignore any kind of modest merit. In the course of the long years over which these files extend, many men, now distinguished, have arisen. In no single instance has this representative journal been able to recognise the coming genius, or willing to help the struggling aspirant. The method has been to ignore new men as long as possible; then when ignorance could not be pleaded, to interpose every possible impertinence of interpretation between the men and the public; and finally, when they have been crowned, to insult them with a monkey's gibbering interposition. For fatuousness, ignorance, ami dwarfish spitefulness—in a word, for all the old ear tidiness of the cloven foot—commend me to this "Satyrnine Review."'

'Never mind,' says the practised Crieff, cheerily. 'Nemesis has come—the "Satyrnine" is done for. The curse of dulness is upon it. It once sold 20,000. The other day, when it was in the market, it could hardly find a purchaser. It lingers on with a country subscription among retrograde old rectors and blue-buskin'd village spinsters, but by-and-by the acidulous short paragraph system will conquer even *them*.'

Thereupon Crieff, whose life was one of hard work and bustling visits, was about to take his departure, when at Sutherland's entreaty he promised to return for lunch; for Sutherland liked the little man, and found a curious fascination in his tittle-tattle concerning the world of art and letters.

Later in the day the two lunched together. For a wonder, it was an idle day with Crieff, and, once comfortably seated in an arm-chair, with a good cigar in his mouth, he seemed determined to enjoy himself. The two chatted pleasantly for some time; that is to say, the journalist, who was garrulous by nature and habit, chatted, and the other smoked, listened, and occasionally interpolated a remark.

Presently Crieff's face darkened, and, after looking keenly at his companion for a minute, he said, with a certain indignation—

'I'm afraid I shall have to give up Lagardère, after all. He's been at it again.'

'What do you mean?'

'I'm almost afraid to tell you, old fellow, for fear of arousing the slumbering lion. Yet I think it's only fair, as I fancy you take an interest in the lady.'

'The lady?'

'Yes. You remember the young actress who appeared at the Parthenon this summer? Ah, I see you do. Well, of course you know that she retired into private life—married Forster, the merchant, a rich man and a thoroughly good fellow.'

'Yes, I heard of it, and—I was glad.'

'And so was I. She was too good for the stage. Well, now, I'm afraid there's something unpleasant brewing. Just read this!'

As he spoke Crieff drew from his pocket several newspapers, and handed one, with a certain page turned down to indicate a paragraph, to Sutherland.

The paper was the 'Plain Speaker,' edited by Lagardère. The paragraph was as follows:—

'Does a talented young actress, who recently left the stage, and, in the words of the immortal "Vilikens and his Dinah" (why not, on this occasion, read "Diana"?), married a rich merchant who in London did dwell, recollect a certain boarding school somewhere in France, an infatuated male teacher, and an elopement? It is said that Luna was once caught tripping, to the great amusement of Pan and the Satyrs. Luna was another name for Diana. *Verb. sap.*'

As he read, the lace of Sutherland grew black as night, his fist clenched, and he uttered an angry exclamation.

'Do you understand the reference?' asked Crieff. 'I don't, but I think there is no doubt as to whom it points. But Lagardère is fond of reiteration. Read a little lower down.'

Further down, after a number of jaunty and not too grammatical paragraphs on various topics of the day, came the following—

'When I was last in Paris, and the guest of Gambetta (it is a curious fact, by the way, that Gambetta has an exceedingly foul breath, and seldom or never changes his woollen shirt or washes his large feet), our talk turned on a volume which had just appeared, "Parfums de la Chair." The title having a strong attraction for the not too clean Republican, he had bought the book. He admired it exceedingly. The affair is brought to my memory by the fact that the author is now in London. The other night, when we met at the house of a mutual friend, I asked him if he had ever been at Brussels, and visited professionally at a certain boarding school, and, if so, whether he had acquired there sufficient classical attainments to tell me if the goddess Diana had ever eloped with her music master, or appeared upon the public stage?'

Sutherland rose to his feet, crushing the paper between his clenched hands.

'It is simply devilish,' he cried. 'O that I had the ruffian by the throat! I would choke him like a dog!'

'I grant you it is horrible,' said Crieff, 'but what does it mean?'

'Cannot you see? It is an infernal plot to ruin an unhappy woman.'

'There is no doubt as to whom it points?'

'None.'

'Diana Vere was her stage name, you see? But is there any truth — — — —'

'Truth? Do you expect it from these vermin? Their end is calumny, torture their delight. If I were only her brother—even her friend!'

'Eh, what would you do?'

'Thrash this devil within an inch of his life!'

'And if you did, he would only thank you for an excellent advertisement. That's the worst of it; he *lives* on recriminations. I'm really very sorry; for Lagardère, I have always held, has his good points. He has really a kind heart, as has been repeatedly shown by his generosity to the sick and suffering. He got up that idea of supplying old toys to the sick children in the hospitals, and I know for a fact that he kept Potts Peters, the dramatist, from starvation. I don't think he realises the mischief he does. He calls it "plain speaking," another name for calumny.'

'Damn him!' said Sutherland between his set teeth.

'With all my heart, but I'll pity him too; for one act of true kindness atones for many sins of judgment. But I haven't shown you all. The wasps are all at it. Look at this in the "Whirligig."'

He handed another journal to Sutherland, who took it with trembling hands, and, glancing down a number of paragraphs similar to those in the 'Plain Speaker,' came upon the following:—

'My dear Hubert, why will you pretend to omniscience? You are all very well when you are telling us of your escapades in Russia, and your sad experiences of theatrical mismanagement in St. Mary Axe, but you should really try to be correct in your classical gossip. Diana never bolted with a music master, and she was never at Brussels. The affair to which you allude took place at Rouen, and the gentleman was a teacher of languages. Try again, Hubert.'

After a few general paragraphs, one of which accused a certain royal personage of having a *liaison* with his cook, came another piece of mysterious gossip:—

'If it is to become a *cause célèbre*, no one will regret it more than myself; though I shall rejoice, too, if it brings the peccant fair one back to the stage. I am sorry for the husband, but it is really his own fault. A person so well known as an Art connoisseur ought to have seen at a glance that the picture was damaged—*before he bought it.*'

The italics were the writer's.

Livid with horror and indignation, Sutherland held the newspaper to Crieff.

'Who—who wrote this?' he cried.

'Yahoo, I suspect—the editor of the "Whirligig."'

'Who and what is he?'

'Edgar Yahoo, the last descendant of the race of the Yahoos, for the history of which see Swift's "Gulliver"; the only difference being that this Yahoo no longer waits upon the nobler animal, but delights in airing himself upon its back.'

'Explain!'

'Yahoo lays claim to be the founder of the new system of journalism. From childhood upward he has aspired to be the social *chiffonnier* of his age. He rakes for garbage in the filth of the street and in the sewers. Don't you remember the verses MacAlpine wrote about him?

> Who prances on through Rotten Row
> Upon his golden-footed hay?
> Who prances, ambles, to and fro,
> Always gay?
> Who canters back along Mayfair,
> Spreading foul odours on the air,
> While all draw back to cry 'Beware!
> The Scavenger of Society!'

But, for Heaven's sake, my dear Sutherland, don't take this affair too seriously. It is very offensive, but no worse than they write of everybody, from the Queen downwards; and I dare say it will do the lady in question no real harm.'

Sutherland was pacing up and down the room, a prey to the most violent agitation. He wheeled round suddenly, and faced his companion.

'Even while we speak, perhaps the poisoned arrows have shot home. I can see the poor child—for she is still a child—sickening under the shameless attack. I picture to myself a broken heart, a ruined home, and then——'

'But suppose the insinuations are false?'

'They may be false in essence, while having a certain foundation in fact. Remember the lines you yourself quoted to me when Lagardère was our theme on a former occasion—I mean the lines about "A lie which is half a truth." Oh, it is horrible! horrible! I would rather live among the foulest of savages than among your literary Yahoos, your so-called human beings.'

Sutherland's fears were right. When the poisoned arrows of slander and calumny are in the air, it is not long ere they reach their victim; and even as he spoke the cowardly work was complete.

That afternoon Madeline drove down to the Grosvenor Library, of which she was a member, to change some books. When she had made her choice of some new literature, and handed it to her footman to place in her carriage, she went upstairs to the ladies' reading-room on the second floor.

The room was quite empty, and she strolled from table to table, turning over the new magazines, glancing at the journals. Presently she sat down, and began reading one of the theatrical papers, full of current gossip; for the old interest in histrionic affairs still clung to her, though she had abandoned all thoughts of returning to the stage.

Placing the theatrical paper aside after a few minutes, she took the next journal which came to her hand. It was the 'Whirligig.'

Idly and listlessly she began glancing over its imbecile tittle-tattle. Suddenly her gaze was riveted. She had come upon the paragraph beginning 'My dear Hubert.'

There was no mistaking the innuendo. That it referred to herself she could not doubt. Trembling like a leaf, she held the abominable journal in her hand, and almost by accident came upon the second paragraph.

She read on in horror, stung to the quick—

'A person so well known as an Art connoisseur ought to have seen at a glance that the picture was damaged, before he bought it.'

It was real, then; all her horrible fear was justified. Her enemy had not threatened in vain.

The room swam round her as she sank back, half swooning in her chair. Fortunately there was no one to observe her, for her face was pale as marble, and she seemed like one about to die.

Presently, summoning all her strength, she looked round the room, and her eye fell upon the last number ol the 'Plain Speaker.' She remembered the paragraph beginning 'My dear Hubert and knowing enough of the amenities of personal journalism to be aware that the reference was to a paragraph in Lagardère's paper, she took that paper up and searched it for the poison.

She had not far to search. She came without delay on the allusions to Luna, Diana, Pan, and the Satyrs, and on the mysterious matter concerning a boarding school and a music master.

The paper fell from her hands, and a low moan broke from her lips. She felt that she was lost indeed.

More than an hour elapsed before Madeline descended to her carriage. Her first impulse had been to fly, to destroy herself, to put herself beyond the power of calumny and cruelty. But at last, conquering her first fear, she determined to return home, and face her fate.

CHAPTER XXXIV
A SELF-CONSTITUTED CHAMPION

Gavrolles was an *artiste,* and, with an *artiste's* eye, he saw at a glance that the tactics of the newest thing in journalism furnished an admirable means of carrying out his designs. The affair was soon arranged. A few whispers at the Club, a few significant looks and intonations, a few anonymous lines to the editors of the society journals, and the thing was complete. It was a neck-to-neck race between Lagardère and the Yahoo as to which should use the poison first.

Gavrolles bought the 'Plain Speaker,' and grinned diabolically. He bought the 'Whirligig,' and positively beamed with malignant delight.

'Ah, madame!' he murmured to himself, 'what will you say for yourself *now?*'

In the aesthetic circle of which he was so brilliant an ornament, and where the scandal was soon the topic of passing conversation, Gavrolles assumed an aspect of lofty indignation, and affected to deplore the public taste which could find pleasure in journalism so *brutale.* Pressed by his intimates for an explanation of the innuendoes, he would smile sadly, pass his thin fingers through his hair, and profess his determination to 'compromise no one.' There were subjects, he said, in which a woman's honour was concerned, and which he could not discuss; there were secrets which it was a man's duty to lock firmly in his breast, lest the happiness of another should suffer—ah, yes! And the lean young gentlemen and limp young ladies looked at their plaster of Paris idol with increased adoration.

About this time, it should be noted, Gavrolles was sincerely inspired by the Divine Muse. He wrote a great many verses, which he would read aloud to himself, with much gesticulation, in the privacy of his lodging. Sometimes he even entertained his aesthetic admirers with a selection from these splendid inspirations. Ponto was spellbound, sent a little article to the 'Megatherium' as a sort of puff preliminary, expressing a hope that these new 'adumbrations of an august poesy' would soon be published in post octavo, on rough paper with blunt type, like the divine 'Parfums de la Chair.' As a specimen of the new work (which, he took occasion to say, posterity would remember when Racine, Molière, and Lamartine were all forgotten, and only Gautier, Baudelaire, and Gavrolles remembered) he quoted at full length the priceless pearl of loveliness, the 'ballade' entitled 'Diane: Chute d'un Ange.'

One morning, as this great cosmic creature was sipping his coffee and turning over the leaves of a new book by Zola (not without much superfine disgust, for he held that eccentric writer in very genuine dislike), a gentleman was announced, and before Gavrolles could utter a word the gentleman entered. One glance at his face sufficed. The Frenchman had seen it already once or twice before, and hated it cordially.

'My name is Sutherland,' said the new comer, quietly closing the door behind him. 'Possibly you remember me?'

Gavrolles rose smiling, though his cheek was a little pale, his mouth a little venomous. 'Ah! yes,' he remembered well Monsieur Sutherland, who had been introduced to him by that 'drôle' of a Crieff. He was delighted to make his acquaintance. If he could serve him in any way, he would be enraptured.

'Your rapture will diminish, perhaps,' said Sutherland, paying no attention to the hand which waved him to a chair, 'when I tell you what brings me here.'

'Indeed!' exclaimed Gavrolles, rather nervously, for his visitor's manner was not encouraging.

'You have alluded to our second meeting. Pray do you remember our first?'

'Our *first*, Monsieur?'

He did remember, only too well for his mental comfort, and even as he spoke the dreary *salle à manger* in the little French town arose before him, and he faced again the powerful figure with the stern eyes and the firm square jaw.

'It was a few years ago, in France. You had then in your company a young lady whom you called your wife, and to whom, suspecting the nature of your connection with her, I offered my assistance. I afterwards saw you again, when this lady was still in your power, and you were using her as the decoy of a gambling hell.'

Gavrolles was now livid. He saw that his visitor meant mischief, and with an execration he sprang up as if to move to the door. But Sutherland blocked the way with an ominous scowl.

'Keep your seat! I have not yet done with you!'

'Monsieur, this outrage— —'

'Bah! do not trouble yourself to seem indignant. You shall hear me out.5

'I shall do nothing of the kind!'

'If you attempt to leave this room,' said Sutherland calmly, 'I shall thrash you within an inch of your life!'

As he spoke he held in the air a riding-whip, which he appeared to have provided for the purpose.

'Robber! assassin!' cried Gavrolles, and he put the table between himself and his visitor.

'I am neither,' said Sutherland. 'I am simply the friend of a lady whom it seems your determination to persecute and destroy. Nor is she the only one of your victims with whom I am acquainted. Have you forgotten Adèle Lambert?'

'I know no such person.'

'You are a liar!' returned Sutherland dryly. 'You know her—you betrayed her—only a few nights ago she struck you in the face.'

'Leave my apartment—scoundrel!'

'It is you who are the scoundrel. I have come to call you to an account.'

Gavrolles threw his arms in the air in savage desperation.

'I don't know you or your degraded companions. If we were not living in a country where the code of honour is unknown, you should answer with your life for this outrage. But there! You are a coward, and trade upon the immunity given by your absurd laws. You know that we cannot in England meet as gentlemen—that is why you venture so far.'

'You are mistaken,' returned Sutherland, still with the same *sang-froid*. 'It would give me the greatest pleasure to rid the world of so consummate a reptile, but that is neither here nor there. To come to my business. You must give me forthwith y our promise to abandon your persecution of Mrs. Forster, and to leave England with out delay.'

'I do not understand.'

'Oh yes, you do!'

'Who is the lady?' asked Gavrolles, with a sneer. 'Pray be explicit. I know no person of the name you mention.'

'I mean the wife of Mr. James Forster, of Kensington. Do not assume ignorance. I know the nature of your relations together.'

'Pardon me, but in your capacity of bully, of *bandit*, monsieur, you overrate my intelligence. I know the gentleman to whom you allude. I have not the pleasure of knowing his wife.'

'Read those paragraphs.'

Sutherland drew from his breast pocket, and handed across the table, copies of the 'Whirligig' and the 'Plain Speaker,' with the passages concerning Madeline marked in pencil. Gavrolles glanced at them, and smiled curiously—then tossed them back across the table.

'You understand those references?'

'Completely,' answered Gavrolles, with a mock bow. He was rapidly regaining his composure, and making ready to strike his strongest blow.

'Yet you have the assurance to tell me that you are unacquainted with the lady whose name I have mentioned?' Gavrolles bowed again.

'Is she not the same with whom I saw you in company over there in France?'

'And if she is?'

'If she is, you are a liar on your own showing. You professed not to know her.'

'I professed nothing of the kind. I said I did not know *Mrs. Forster.*'

'She is the same person.'

'Pardon me, that is impossible. She may be living under that gentleman's roof, she may even be bearing his name—but she is not *his wife!*'

It was now Sutherland's turn to look astonished. Something in the man's supercilious smile, in his growing audacity and self-possession, disconcerted him.

'What!—do you actually insinuate——'

'Nothing whatever, monsieur. I merely state a fact. But before we continue the conversation, may I ask you a question? Has the lady herself sent you here?'

'No,' returned Sutherland, with a heightened colour; 'I came on my own responsibility.'

'Oh!—a self-constituted champion, I presume?'

'If you put it in that way, yes.'

'You are a friend of hers, of course?'

'I am so far her friend that I will not see her victimised by a scoundrel.'

'Referring to me, monsieur?' asked Gavrolles, with venomous politeness.

Gavrolles, now completely master of himself, leant over the table and looked straight into Sutherland's eyes.

'You are very impetuous, monsieur, and not too choice in your use of— what you call—Beelingsgate; but I should wish very much to give you a little piece of advice. Before you proceed any further in this affair I should recommend you to consult the lady herself.'

'Why?'

'It would be better—for the lady.'

There was no mistaking the threatening significance of the Frenchman's tone; but, as he spoke, he took a cigarette from a box upon the table, lit it, and looked keenly through the smoke at Sutherland.

Seeing that he did not immediately reply, but seemed dubious and perplexed, Gavrolles airily continued—

'I am content, you see, to take the lady's opinion on the subject. If she sends you here as her accredited agent and defender, I will speak to you, as one gentleman to another. Even then, look you, I should be condescending, amiable. It is not every man who would permit a complete stranger to dictate to him on a matter concerning only himself and madame his wife.'

'What do you mean?' cried Sutherland, now thoroughly startled. 'You cannot mean that——'

'If you will permit me,' said Gavrolles, now thoroughly master of the situation, 'I will explain; but bear in mind, monsieur, you have forced this avowal upon me by your brutal English violence. Otherwise, I should never have spoken. You have been good enough, Monsieur Sutherland, to say that I am a liar. *Au contraire*, I do not lie. When we first met, I said the young lady in my company was my wife. It was the truth. A little while ago, I said there was no such person as Mrs. Forster. It was the truth. Why? do you ask. Because a lady cannot bear the name of a second husband, when her first husband is alive.'

There was no mistaking the supreme assurance of the man; he spoke with the strength of a settled conviction. Sutherland looked at him in amaze, as the full horror of the situation dawned upon his bewildered mind.

'You thought me a commonplace seducer,' continued the Frenchman, loftily; 'on the contrary, I am an *artiste* and a man of honour. I took that lady in honourable marriage. Afterwards, a cruel series of events drew us asunder, that was all.'

'You deserted her,' cried Sutherland. 'You left her to starve or die!'

'Unfortunately, we did not agree; she was violent, and I—I will confess it—I was violent too. *Eh bien*! At the time of which I speak I was heavily in debt, and had to escape my creditors. I asked her to accompany me, and she refused. A brief separation was necessary. Alas! Little did I dream that in so short a space of time she would forget her lawful husband, and contract a bigamous union with another man.'

He paused a moment, then he concluded—

'Now, monsieur, the champion of madame, I hope you are satisfied. In any case, there is the door.'

As he spoke he sat down in his chair beside the fire as if intimating that the interview had come to an end.

Sutherland stood perplexed, and watched him for some moments in silence. Then putting on his hat, he said in a low voice—

'Your tale is plausible, but I do not believe it. In any case you proclaim yourself a scoundrel. If it were not for your victim's sake, for the fear of creating a scandal, I think I should carry out my promise, and thrash you. However, I shall postpone your punishment for the present. But remember, if the lady we have been discussing comes to grief through your malignity, if these calumnies grow, and any evil happens to her through them or you, you will have to settle accounts with *me!*'

So saying he left the room, and rapidly descended the stairs into the street.

No sooner had he gone than Gavrolles, who with assumed *sang-froid* had with difficulty concealed a savage ferocity, sprang wildly up, crossed the room, and took from a sideboard an oblong mahogany box, which he opened with a small key. Inside was a set of delicately finished duelling pistols, with cartridges to match.

And now, with eyes flashing, mouth foaming, all his body working in epileptiform rage, Gavrolles took up one of the weapons, and evoked an imaginary opponent in the air.

'You would thrash me, you would profane me with a blow!' he hissed aloud. 'Ah, ruffian! bandit! devil! dog of an Englishman! if I had you before me—thus!—in my own country, I would put a bullet through your heart. Come again, with your bulldog face, and I shall be prepared!'

With these words the cosmic creature put the pistol back in its case, and proceeded to dress himself for his usual morning promenade.

Meanwhile Sutherland was pursuing his way along the streets, in a brown study—or shall we rather say a black one—as expressed in a face of the blackest gloom. So! His ideal heroine, the idol he had set up in his heart as a type of all-patient and suffering woman, was a guilty creature, one who, to entrap an honourable man, had represented herself as single, whereas she knew that her husband lived! It was scarcely credible, yet the tale, as he had said, seemed plausible enough, and the Frenchman seemed to have the courage of conviction.

A man less satisfied in his own mind of the superiority of the weaker sex over the stronger would doubtless have withdrawn from all interference in an affair so suspicious; but Sutherland, perhaps because he was a bachelor with very little practical experience of female baseness, took an optimistic view of womankind. He could scarcely conceive the idea of an utterly impure and wicked woman, though he had the strongest possible belief in the impurity and wickedness of men. He was thoroughly inexperienced, impartial, and ideal. Having decided in his own mind that women are the victims of a social conspiracy (a terrible social truth, although one which he lacked the worldly philosophy to formulate truly), he never hesitated for a moment to battle upon their side, with all the deep enthusiasm and moral pugnacity of his nature. So there is little occasion for wonder in the fact that the more he thought over the matter the deeper grew his conviction that Madeline was a martyr and Gavrolles an even blacker scoundrel than he had at first believed.

CHAPTER XXXV
MADELINE PREPARES FOR FLIGHT

Pale as marble, like a woman to whom worldly phenomena can bring neither thought nor care, because she is doomed to an ignominious and cruel death, Madeline returned home. Entering the house, she fled up to her own room, and there, heartbroken and alone, remained face to face with her despair.

She did not weep—or pray. The sense of an arid and heart-burning oppression kept her eyes dry, and turned her heart, that might have been the fountain of pure prayer, to stone. She hated herself, the world, all that she had seen and known. God Himself seemed against her, for she knew her own innocence. Ah, yes! How she had tried, and tried, to be good, to be at peace; and it was all in vain. At every turn of her young life the evil shadow rose, pushing her down to some desolate abyss of shame.

As she sat thinking it all over, she seemed covered from head to foot with some horrible pollution. Though her spirit was pure, impurity was upon her, choking and stifling her with its abomination. She shuddered and moaned, praying for one thing only—that death might quickly come.

What should she say or do, when she saw the kind eyes harden into indignation, the kind lace darken with this last shame? Sooner or later, her husband must know the truth, if he did not know it already, if the malignant voices in the air had not already whispered it to him. She shrank in horror, thinking of how she could meet his gaze.

One thing now seemed certain to her—that the roof which covered her was no longer hers, that to remain with James Forster as his lawful wife was to live on in open adultery, which was not marriage. He himself> she knew, would be the first to recognise the infamy of that union; and then, even if *he* pitied her, as was faintly possible, how should she bear the scrutiny of the world, the worldly scorn of his sister's cruel eyes?

As she sat despairing there came a soft knock at the door, which she had locked on entering; and the voice of her little step-son cried—

'Mamma! mamma!'

She could not answer, she seemed choking; and now for the first time her eyes were dim and blind. The cry was repeated—

'Mamma! mamma! open the door!'

Without stirring she at last found strength to speak.

'Who is there?'

'It is I, mamma! Let me in!'

'Go away, dear; I am dressing.'

'Papa has sent me for you. He has just come home, and is waiting to see you.'

Waiting to see her? She shuddered as if stabbed, and unconsciously made a gesture of supplication. Could he have heard the truth, or a whisper of the truth?

'Mamma, do you hear? Will you not come?'

She forced herself to answer—

'Yes, I am coming. Go away now, dear! I will be down directly.'

Then she heard the little feet pattering away. She rose and wearily paced up and down the room. Her heart felt dead within her, her whole life frozen in her veins. She looked in the glass, and was startled at her face; it was so ghastly in its set look of pain.

What could she do? She knew that if she did not go down Forster would be certain to come to seek her. At last she resolved in very desperation to answer his summons. She cared not what happened now; if the worst came, it must come sooner or later. Perhaps she might summon up courage to tell him the truth with her own lips.

She went slowly downstairs. In the lobby she saw the child, who ran to her and took her hand.

'Papa is in the study. Come.'

And he tried to draw her along with him. She stooped and kissed him on the brow.

'Wait for me in the drawing-room,' she 'said. 'Is Aunt Margaret there?'

'Yes,' said the boy. 'You will bring papa?'

He bounded from her, and she walked slowly towards the study. The door was closed, and for a moment she paused, faltering, before she opened it; then she passed in, and saw her husband sitting reading by the fire.

He had a newspaper in his hand. At a glance she recognised Lagardère's journal, the 'Plain Speaker.' The room swam round her; she felt as if she was about to faint.

But Forster looked up with a bright smile, and tossed down the journal.

'Ah, my dear Madeline,' he said. 'You see I am home early again; I'm afraid I'm losing all my business habits. But good heavens!' he continued, noticing her face, 'how pale you look! Is anything the matter?'

'Nothing; only—I have a bad headache.'

'I am sorry for that. Not so bad, I hope, as to prevent you going out this evening? Serena, who can't go, has sent me a box for the first night of "A Trip to Scarborough," at the Parthenon. Talking of Serena, there is a most amusing "Verbal Phototype" of him in the "Plain Speaker."'

It was clear that he knew nothing, that he had heard nothing, read nothing—though the very journal which contained the poison had just left his hand. Madeline breathed again. There was at least to be a little respite.

'But you do not look at all yourself,' he continued, 'and as the night is damp, you are perhaps better at home.'

'Yes; I cannot go.'

'I am so sorry, as Aram's first nights are generally amusing, and you would have enjoyed yourself. What shall we do with the box? It is too late, I fear, to send it to any of your friends.'

'*You* will go, of course,' said Madeline eagerly. 'Miss Forster will go with you.*

'*No*; I shall remain with you.'

'You *must* go!'

The tone was so strange, so full of entreaty, that Forster was startled. He gazed at his wife again with deep solicitude, and drew her gently to his side.

'I should not think of going out and leaving you alone. My darling, you are far from well. You must see Dr. Quin to-morrow, and see if his advice is any use.'

As he spoke, he drew her down as if to kiss her fondly; but with a nervous shudder she disengaged herself from his arms.

'No, no!' she cried. 'It is only a headache, and will pass away. You must go to the theatre with your sister; I shall be better—when you return.'

'I would much rather remain with you.'

'But I wish you to go—I—I should be wretched if you remained on my account.'

'And I should be wretched there without you. I really will not go.'

'Not if I *wish* it, James?'

'Why should you wish it?'

She looked at him sadly, and turned away; for her heart was bursting at sight of his kind face, so gentle and so unsuspecting.

'Why should you wish it? You know, dearest, I have no pleasure in anything of this kind unless you are with me. I would rather have a quiet evening at home in your company than go out alone to any entertainment, however amusing.'

'I know that,' she said in a low voice, 'but to-night—I would rather be alone. When you are gone, and all is quiet, I shall lie down, and when you come back I shall be quite well. So go, for my sake—I wish you to be there.' Seeing her so persistent, and thinking her wish was a mere whim which it would be unkind not to gratify, Forster at last assented, though with a very unwilling mind. He was really alarmed at his wife's look and manner, and setting it down, in his loving solicitude, to some growing illness, he determined in his own mind to consult the family physician without delay.

Having extracted his promise, Madeline prepared to go. Before retiring, however, she took up the 'Plain Speaker,' and said—

'May I take this with me? I may be able to read a little, and—and—I should like to read about Mr. Serena.'

Her hands shook like a leaf as she clutched the paper, her faced assumed an even ghastlier pallor. She moved tremulously to the door.

'I shall not come down to dinner,' she said.

'No? Then let me send you something to your room.'

'I could not touch a morsel, while my headache lasts. Don't mind me, but go to the theatre and enjoy yourself. Good—good-bye!'

Not 'good-night,' but 'good-bye.' He did not notice the words then, but they recurred to him long afterwards, with an ominous and piteous sound. As she uttered them, she yielded to an irresistible impulse, and, quickly returning to his side, stooped over him and kissed him. As she did so, he felt a hot tear fall upon his cheek.

'Madeline, my darling!' he cried in astonishment, and stretched out his arms to embrace her, but before he could do so she was gone.

She fled back to her lonely room, and there, locked in and alone, she threw herself upon the bed and sobbed wildly. By the bedside lay the fatal journal, which she had carried with her, and which had now fallen from her lax and feeble hand.

An hour and a half passed away. At last she heard a knock at the bedroom door, and then Forster's voice—

'Madeline, are you asleep? May I come in?'

She waited, trembling, for a little time before she replied. Then she answered, not rising from the bed—

'I am trying to rest. I thought that you had gone to the theatre.'

'The carriage is at the dcor. How is your headache?'

'A little better.'

'Try to sleep, my darling. I shall come back very early.'

She heard him pass downstairs; then, rising from her bed, she listened eagerly. Presently she heard the front door open and close, and the carriage drive away. Her whole manner now changed, and she moved about her room, lifting one thing and another as if with a set determination.

She had resolved to leave James Forster's house that night.

CHAPTER XXXVI
'GOOD-BYE!'

To remain under that roof another night, when she knew the horrible truth, was profanation. For some days she had hoped and prayed that her enemy had lied when he claimed her as his lawful wife; and so, doubting and fearing, avoiding Forster's society on the plea of indisposition, she had delayed and waited. Now, however, delay was impossible. That her enemy meant mischief was proved by the fact that he had already breathed these slanders into the air. She could not stay to face the anger of the man she loved, or, worst of all, his sorrow. She would go at once, without another hour's delay.

Her resolve once made, its very intensity sustained her. She dried her eyes, and quietly prepared to go forth on foot. At first she thought of taking with her a portion of her wardrobe, and a few simple ornaments which Forster had given her; but this thought was soon abandoned. Keeping on the dress she wore, a plain robe of dark material, she drew on a dark bonnet, and threw round her shoulders a shawl, the commonest thing of the kind she possessed, but costly nevertheless. In her impulsive haste she forgot the bracelets upon her hands.

She listened till all was still. Then she stole softly downstairs.

In the hall she hesitated. Should she leave him no message; no intimation of her resolve? If she disappeared without a word of explanation there would be a scandal, a hue and cry. Besides, it would be so cruel. No; she could not go away without leaving a few written words.

She passed along the lobby into the little study, and sitting down in Forster's chair tried to scribble some hurried lines. As she did so her tears began to fall. She was sitting thus, in deep agitation, when a footman entered to attend to the fire, and, after standing amazed for a moment at the sight of his mistress, retired with a murmur of apology.

This intrusion brought her back to herself. After writing and destroying several wild effusions, she wrote the following:—

'*I am going away. Do not follow me or try to find me; by the time you receive this I shall perhaps have done with this world for ever. Try to forgive me. Indeed, indeed, I am grateful to you for all your goodness, but when you learn the truth you will see that I could not stay. Kiss your little boy for me. God bless him and you!* '*Madeline.*'

The paper was wet with tears, but she folded it up and inclosed it in an envelope, which she addressed and left upon the study table.

Then, shuddering, she rose and left the room, drawing down her thick veil over her face. In the lobby she met the same servant who had surprised her in the study.

'I am going out,' she said, in reply to his amazed stare. 'If your master returns— —'

'Beg pardon, ma'am,' exclaimed the man, 'but you can't think of it. It's pouring wet.'

'I cannot help that. It is very important.'

Aghast at her persistence, the man opened the front door, and she saw the gleam of the gas in the wet street and on the falling shafts of rain. He was about to interfere once more, when she slipped by him, and disappeared in the darkness.

'And without an umbrella, too!' he afterwards explained to his fellow-servants. 'She's off her head, I think. I see the tears quite plain in her eyes as she sat writing in master's room. There's something wrong, I'm sure; but, after all, it's no business ot mine.'

About half-past eleven o'clock Forster and his sister returned from the theatre. On entering the house, Forster at once hurried upstairs to Madeline's boudoir, and found it empty, as well as the adjoining bedroom. Then he hastened downstairs, thinking to find his wife there.

At the foot of the stairs he found Miss Forster, in low conversation with one of the men-servants. Without noticing their agitated appearance and demeanour, he inquired if Mrs. Forster was in the drawing-room.

The servant did not reply, but Margaret Forster, very pale, placed her hand upon her brother's arm.

'Madeline is not there,' she said, adding, with an emotion unusual to her, while her eyes filled with tears, 'Oh, James! my poor brother.'

Forster stood terrified.

'Something has happened!' he cried. 'Madeline is ill? Where is she? For God's sake tell me!'

Then he turned to the servant.

'Speak, you! Are you dumb? Where is your mistress?'

The man was about to make some blundering reply, when Miss Forster interposed.

'Madeline is not at home.'

'Not at home!' echoed Forster wildly.

'Oh, James, keep calm! Perhaps she will soon come back; but she went out two hours ago on foot quite alone, and has not yet returned.'

Gone out? And at such an hour, and on such a night. The thing seemed utterly inconceivable, and Forster could not trust his ears. But the servant on being pressed gave so circumstantial an account of what had occurred, that doubt was no longer possible. He reserved his most important piece of information till the last.

'And please, sir, I think she left a letter for you, sir; leastways she was writing one, and I see it lying afterwards on the study table.'

Without waiting to hear more, Forster rushed toward the study, while his sister still remained questioning the servant. A few minutes afterwards Miss Forster heard a cry and a fall, and on entering the study found Forster lying on the hearth, insensible, with Madeline's letter open in his hand.

CHAPTER XXXVII
THE SEARCH

It was the first great shock that Forster had ever felt during a life of quiet activity, marked from time to time by small and frequently ignoble troubles; and it struck him like a thunderbolt—to use the familiar but terribly expressive simile. When he came to himself, he was like a man mentally stupefied and physically decrepit. He read the letter over and over again, and wept over it; and the more he read it, the less he understood its true meaning. Only one thing was clear—that Madeline had left his house of her own freewill, with no intention of returning, and with no hint of any reason for her flight.

Despite his sister's entreaties, he himself left the house in search of the fugitive. It was now long past midnight, and the rain was still falling heavily; but he buttoned his greatcoat round him, and rushed out into the street.

His first inquiries were of the policemen in the neighbourhood, but they could tell him nothing. He hastened then to the nearest cabstand, thinking that possibly Madeline might have hired a vehicle there; but he gained no information. Then he stood helpless under the dark sky, in the midst of the great city, uncertain which way to turn.

For he had not the slightest clue to guide him in his search. Madeline had no friends in the city to whom she might fly; none, certainly to his knowledge, and White himself had told him that she was a friendless orphan. The thought of White, however, brought up the recollection of Madame de Berny, who had been keeping house for White when he died, and who was still, thanks to Forster's assistance, in possession of the old quarters, which she let in lodgings. It was just possible Madeline might have gone there.

The thought was enough. He hailed a hansom, and was driven rapidly to St. John's Wood.

He was doomed to disappointment. When he had aroused the sleeping house, and scared Madame de Berny out of her wits by the sight of his haggard, spectral face, he found that the poor soul knew nothing. He hurried away with scarcely a word of explanation.

All that night he haunted the streets, seeking for a trace of any kind. Of course, it was in vain.

Long after daybreak he returned to his lonely house and found his sister awaiting him in deep anxiety.

She saw by one glance at his face that he had been unsuccessful. He walked into the study, threw himself into a chair; she followed him, and touched him softly on the shoulder. He looked up wildly, like a man whose wits are going.

'You have heard nothing?' she asked.

He shook his head in despair.

'I feared you would not,' she continued. 'My dear James, you must have courage—you must look this terrible event in the face. May I speak to you? Do you think you can bear to talk of it, of her?'

'What have you to say?'

His tone was irritable, almost querulous.

'Only this, James—that you must not torture yourself unnecessarily. Remember there are others who love you—myself—your darling boy. If Madeline has left you, it is of her own freewill. I am not surprised that you have not found her; she doubtless provided well against that. She wished to leave you! Don't forget that!'

'Why should she wish it?' he groaned.

'Why do other wives leave their husbands? They *do* leave them, every day.'

There was something in her tone so significant, so ominous, that he could not misconceive her. He sprang up as if stung and faced her.

'What do you mean?'

'I never thought Madeline quite happy in this house. I never thought she loved you as you deserved. If she is unworthy to bear your name— —'

'She is not unworthy! I will never believe it. I will not hear one word against her, even from you. Do you hear? not one word! I know you never cared for her, never treated her like a sister, and now you would poison my soul against her. I tell you I will not listen to you—never, never!'

Margaret Forster felt not a little indignant; her brow darkened, and the sympathetic dimness passed away from her cold grey eyes; but being truly mistress of the situation, she could afford to be, and was, magnanimous.

'You are very unjust to me,' she said, 'but I shall think it is your trouble that speaks, and not yourself I have never been unkind to Madeline; on the contrary, I have treated her with the greatest affection and respect. If I have sometimes thought that she was scarcely conscious of the duties of a lady in her position, I have always silenced myself with the reflection that she was your choice. Yes, James, always No matter what I have feared, what I have seen, I have been silent for your sake.'

'In the name of God,' said Forster, impatiently, 'cease to torture me. If you know anything to relieve my suspense, speak out. If not, leave me, leave me!'

As he spoke he sank again into his chair, hiding his face in his hands. She watched him for some moments in silence, sighing heavily and occasionally wiping her eyes, for she was genuinely affected; but with the firmness of a skilled surgeon, who sympathises with the patient whom it is impossible to spare, since a cruel operation is imperative, she at length spoke again.

'You will hear sad truths sooner or later, James; it is better that you should hear them first from me. I want you to understand, once for all, that it is useless to waste your strength, to break your heart, over what is irrecoverable.'

'Do you mean Madeline? I tell you I will find her. If I search the whole world I will find her.'

'And if you do, what then?'

'I will pray to her on my knees to return.'

'Whether she is worthy or unworthy?'

'Margaret, take care! I won't hear one whisper against her.'

Margaret's lips tightened, and her surgical manner increased.

'If you will not listen to me,' she said, 'at least attend to what the world says. These papers were sent, under cover, to *me*, this morning. It is my duty, James, to bring them to your attention.'

So saying, she handed to him copies of the 'Plain Speaker' and the 'Whirligig'; they had indeed been sent to her by an anonymous correspondent, who had taken the trouble to mark the obnoxious paragraphs very carefully in red ink.

Forster looked at them, and seemed to read them in a dazed, stupefied sort of way; and as he did so shudder after shudder ran through his frame. But he evinced less surprise than his sister had anticipated.

'Of course, James, you understand these allusions? Do they refer in any way to your wife? In any case, can you explain them?'

'*Yes!* he answered, looking up into her eyes.

'They refer to Madeline?9

'I believe so,' he answered, rising; 'and now—oh,

God!—I begin to see what has driven my darling away. She feared some infamous persecution; she dreaded these infernal slanders; she read these very words. But I will follow her. I will tell her——'

'James, dear James, listen to me!'

'Well, well!'

'Are these insinuations *true?* Is there any foundation for the statement that—that when you married Madeline there was something dreadful, of which you knew nothing, in her past life?'

'It is a lie!' cried Forster, with strange energy. 'She never deceived me— she is incapable of deceit—she is a martyr! Do you think that *I* doubt her? If you dream so, you little know either of us. She deceived me in nothing.'

'But there *was* some scandal, and you heard of it?'

'Whatever there was, *I knew,* answered Forster, firmly; 'but I will not discuss it—it is sacrilege!'

He made a movement as if to leave the room, but Margaret, who had not yet applied the knife to her own satisfaction, again restrained him.

'Are you sure you knew everything?' she demanded sadly. 'Everything, I mean, before your marriage—and after?'

He turned eagerly and looked at her, for he saw, by her tone and by the expression of her face, that her words meant more than met the ear.

'After our marriage?' he repeated.

'Yes, James. Did Madeline inform you that recently, on two separate occasions, she had meetings with a French gentleman—with the very man, I believe, referred to in these paragraphs?'

'She had not! No, it is impossible!'

'Then she did not tell you?'

'No!'

'But it is the truth!'

'It is not the truth—I will never believe it.'

'I repeat that it is my duty to make you do so,' said Margaret Forster. 'Dear James, you must believe it—better now than later on. There is no smoke without fire—no slander without some foundation in fact. May I tell you all I heard?'

She saw that he was at her mercy; and forthwith, in her zeal to protect him against any further machinations of an unworthy woman, she informed him that she had herself witnessed the meeting with Gavrolles at the Countess Aurelia's, and had seen enough to shock and terrify her exceedingly. Then with a certain amount of nervousness, but no compunction, she admitted that, in duty to her brother, she had afterwards played the spy, and had watched from a distance, next day, the secret meeting at the Albert Memorial in Hyde Park.

Forster heard her out with a strange sickness of heart; and when she had finished he looked at her with a face so wistful, so sorrowful, that she could no longer restrain her tears.

'Oh, James!' she cried, 'forget her! She was never worthy of your love. Think of those who do love you—and of your child!'

He answered her in a voice hollow but determined—

'My first thought must be of *her*. What you have told me confirms me in my opinion that she is sinless. Until I find her and ask her forgiveness, I shall not rest. O Madeline! my love! my wife!'

He rushed weeping from the room. Miss Forster remained spell-bound. 'Find her, and ask her forgiveness?' She could scarcely believe the evidence of her ears; the idea was so utterly preposterous.

Owing to the circumstances of the case, it was impossible to advertise for the fugitive in the public journals, in any such way as would lead to her discovery and discomfiture. She had gone away of her own freewill, and any mystery attached to her disappearance was of her own making. To awaken the hue and cry for her by name would have been to set all the bells of slander pealing, and Forster was determined to spare both himself and the woman he loved so utter a humiliation.

Nevertheless, he inserted in the 'agony' column of the 'Times' a brief appeal, signed 'F.,' and headed 'Queen's Gate,' which the initiated only understood. Then he went to the head of a private inquiry office, conducted by a firm of ex-detectives, and secured his co-operation.

'If she's in London, we'll find her, sir,' said the chief, a jaunty, military-looking man, with a bald head and French moustache and imperial. 'We'll set to work at once. You say she'd no friends handy?'

'None, that I am aware of.'

'Equally sure, I suppose, that there ain't a gentleman in the case? Excuse me. All in the way of business, you know.'

'I am quite certain she is alone.'

'Very good, sir. I'll let you know the moment we hear anything of importance.'

Forster was going to leave the office, when he suddenly recollected, with a shudder, his sister's insinuations as to the mysterious meetings with the Frenchman. With a deep sense of shame, while strongly expressing his own faith in his wife's purity, he explained to the officer what had taken place. That functionary immediately pricked up his ears, for he saw a clue. Could Forster supply him with the Frenchman's name? Forster could not, in the spur of the moment, but that afternoon he procured it from his sister (who had noted it carefully down for future use when at the Countess's), and sent it on to the inquiry office.

A few days afterwards he was informed, quasi-officially, that the French gentleman in question, M. Gavrolles, was living quietly at his London lodgings, and, though watched day and night, appeared quite innocent of any knowledge of the fugitive's whereabouts.

This, we may remark in parenthesis, was literally true. The news of Madeline's flight, which had, of course, been bruited abroad despite all Forster's precautions, had taken Gavrolles utterly by surprise. The cosmic creature felt himself circumvented, bewildered. His victim had escaped him for the time being, that was clear, and until she reappeared upon the scene he could do nothing whatever in the matter.

One morning, as the chief of the private inquiry office sat waiting for business, there was shown in a gentleman, who, after a brief conversation, proved to have come on the very same business already entrusted to the firm by Forster. He wished the strictest inquiry to be made concerning the whereabouts of the missing lady, until she was traced and discovered, when he was at once to receive intimation.

'You'll excuse me, sir,' said the chief, looking very mysterious, 'but may I ask, are you any relation to the lady?'

'None whatever.'

'A friend, perhaps?'

'Scarcely that. I am interested deeply in her fate, however, and if you find out what has become of her I will pay you handsomely.'

The chief seemed to reflect deeply.

'I don't think you mean any harm, sir,' he said presently, 'and I can see you're a real gentleman, but you see we have to be careful. Is Mr. Forster a friend of yours?'

'No; I don't think I ever saw him in my life.'

'Then, of course, sir, you can't owe him any grudge?'

'Certainly not. All the harm I wish him is that he may recover his wife, and that they may be happily reconciled.'

The chief smiled.

'Then I don't mind telling you, sir,' he said, 'that we're instructed already—by the husband. You can't serve two masters, as the saying is, but if we can oblige you in any way, without breaking faith to our first employer, we'll do it.'

'You can keep me informed of your progress, and if you are successful— —'

'Let you know? Well, I think we can promise that. I'll take down your name, if you please, sir.'

'Edgar Sutherland,' replied the gentleman, adding the address of his club.

'Ah, sir,' said the officer, 'I'm sorry you're not a friend of the poor gentleman's. He really *wants* a friend. To see him coming here day after day, as white as a ghost, and his eyes all wild with crying, almost turned me over, old hand as I am; and the rummest thing of all is, he won't hear a word, not as much as a whisper, against the lady—though it looks black about her, it really does. Good-morning, sir! We'll be sure to let you know.'

Had Sutherland been asked why he occupied himself so closely with the fate of a woman almost a stranger to him, he could hardly have replied. His first chivalrous interest had grown into a sentimental fancy, that was all; and being a man of very determined prepossessions, especially where his great hobby concerning Womanhood was concerned, he had been led on and on, from one phase of feeling to another, till his interest in Madeline became very like a strong ideal passion. Like all the world, he had heard of her disappearance, and, learning her connection with Gavrolles, he had a pretty shrewd guess at its cause. So he had yielded to his overmastering interest and curiosity, and determined to make the matter a subject for private, but thorough, inquiry.

Before many days had passed he received a summons which caused him no little agitation. The chief wanted to see him at once. Madeline had been discovered, but under circumstances so dreadful that he scarcely dared to communicate them at all to her distracted husband.

CHAPTER XXXVIII
'ONE MORE UNFORTUNATE'

On arriving at the inquiry office, Sutherland was at once shown in to the chief of the establishment, who looked truly concerned and anxious.

'Glad you've come, sir,' he said at once; 'for perhaps you can help me out of my quandary. You got my little note? Well, the fact is, I think—I'm almost sure, in fact—that we've discovered the lady.'

'So you wrote; but how? Where? 9 'Well, it's a sad case!' murmured the chief with a shake of the head. 'How we're to break it to the husband, who is half mad with grief and anxiety, is a puzzler. My great fear is that the news may get to him before we've time to break it.'

'Explain!' cried Sutherland impatiently.

The chief opened his desk, and took out a large handbill, which he unfolded.

'Just look at this, sir,' he said, while the young man read it with a shudder. 'This is only a copy of the bill which the police will have all over London to-morrow, and perhaps in some of the papers. I've already been down to Chelsea to make an inspection, and I don't think there's any mistake about it. What makes it quite clear is the bracelets. Her Christian name—Madeline—is graven inside.—But you're not well, sir. I don't wonder it has turned you sick. Shall I give you a drop of brandy? I have it handy.'

Sutherland, who had turned faint and deadly pale, recovered himself with an effort.

'Never mind me. Think of him, her husband. You say you haven't communicated with him?'

'No, sir. It was only found early this morning, and the moment I heard of the discovery I sent straight to you.' 'But the police——'

'I've squared that. They won't send to him to-night without communicating with me.'

'The shock will be frightful—enough to kill him.'

'No doubt of that, but there's no help for it—he must know.'

'The first thing to do is to make certain of the identity. The description may be misleading. I suppose I can see her?'

'Yes, sir, returned the chief with alacrity. 'If you like I'll go down with you at once.'

A few minutes later Sutherland and the inquiry officer were rattling down towards Putney in a hansom cab. It was a dark and dismal afternoon in autumn, and as they rapidly passed the gates of Hyde Park the leafless trees looked desolate through a thin mist of rain. To the eye of Edgar Sutherland everything was sombre and dreadful, dark with tragic shadows of sin and death.

They drove through Knightsbridge to Hammersmith, then crossing Hammersmith Bridge, beneath which the river rolled black and sinister, came into the gloomy purlieus of a desolate waterside suburb. It was now growing dark, and the street lamps, which were few and far between, flashed dismally on cheerless brand-new villas, for the most part untenanted and faced with boards 'To Let,' gloomy gardens, dark brickfields, and spaces of damp meadow stretching down to the river side. Here and there a tavern opened its bloodshot eyes, and attracted one or two dreary moths to its dingy gleam.

After passing through a mile or more of this gloomy neighbourhood, the cab turned down a narrow street running at right angles to the river banks, and pulled up before a desolate stone building with the inscription—'Police Station.'

The officer alighted and led the way into a whitewashed room, lit by a solitary gas jet, and occupied by a policeman in uniform, who stood at a desk writing. Wafered on the wall, close to the desk, was a placard similar to that which Sutherland had already seen, headed in bold capitals—

FOUND DROWNED!

and giving the description of the body of a female found that morning by a waterman in the near neighbourhood of Putney Bridge.

After a few hurried words with the inquiry officer, the police sergeant turned to Sutherland.

'You wish to identify, sir? I'm afraid you'll find it a difficult job. As far as I can make out, it's been a long time in the water.'

Sutherland shuddered as the sergeant, in the most business-like way possible, took down a key from a nail and led the way to the back of the building, across a damp yard, and up to a low wooden door: this he opened leisurely with his key, and revealed a sort of rude mortuary, lit by a gas jet turned so low down as to leave the place almost in darkness. They entered, and when the sergeant had leisurely turned up the gas, saw, stretched out upon a wooden slab, what had once been a living woman.

She lay exactly as she had been found, with clenched hands and shoeless feet, clad in a plain dress of serge, partly torn and eaten away. Round her shoulders were the remains of a valuable shawl, firmly secured by a large common shawl pin. Her head was bare, and the loose, fair hair, tangled and twisted in moist knots, hung around the disfigured lineaments of a skeletonian face. So horrible was this face, so unrecognisable in its lost humanity, that Sutherland almost swooned as he looked upon it. Alas, what likeness of living flesh and blood could he discover there?

'She must have been drifting up and down for weeks,' said the sergeant with professional stolidity; 'and I suppose last night's high tide brought her up this way, and carried her into the shallows. There isn't much remaining of the poor creature except clothes, sir; and her own father could scarcely know her. Seems to have been a fine woman, and quite young, though it's hard to tell even that.'

There's a ring on her finger,' cried Sutherland—'a wedding-ring?'

'Yes,' returned the sergeant, 'and I understand the missing lady was married. But I shouldn't go too much by that, sir. Most of the unfortunates who make a hole in the water wear wedding-rings. But these bracelets now, there's no mistaking *them*. Just look, sir.'

As he spoke, the sergeant took from a slab at the corpse's side one or two elegant bracelets, greatly tarnished by the water, but of solid gold.

'We took them off and had them cleaned for identification; they were in a shocking state, sir, and had worked right into the bone.'

Sutherland took the bracelet, and uttered a horrified exclamation, as he deciphered, cut clearly on the solid surface, these words—

To Dear Madeline.

A birthday gift from her sister,

—Margaret Forster.

At that very moment, as Sutherland stood looking at the bracelets and feeling his heart turn sick within him, a figure flitted in through the open door, and, pushing the two other men aside, gazed on the corpse with a face almost as terrible, almost as ghastly, as its own. The inquiry officer recognised James Forster in a moment, and made a movement as if to intercept his view of the dead woman, but in an instant he was on his knees, gazing wildly into the cold disfigured face, and stretching out his arms in horrified entreaty and recognition. 'Madeline! My darling!'

The wild cry rang out in the desolate place, with a tone of infinite agony and woe.

CHAPTER XXXIX
DUST TO DUST

Let us draw a veil over the horrors and sorrows of that night. It is enough to say that the distracted husband, when he had recovered from the first paralysing shock of the spectacle, recognised without hesitation in the distorted and disfigured mass the remains of his beloved wife. But, indeed, there was no room for doubt. The form and complexion were the same, and the bracelets with their inscription placed the identity beyond question. Not without difficulty did Sutherland and the police officials persuade Forster to leave the corpse's side. He would fain have remained by it, watching and praying, till daybreak; but at last they prevailed, and Sutherland helped him home. His grief was, indeed, piteous to behold. After the first wild ebullition, he scarcely wept; his face was like a stone, set in horror and despair; only from to time he uttered a wild, heart-rending moan, and shivered through all his frame like a man struck by ague. So he was led home to his lonely house, to the care of his sister, who was stirred to the depths for his sake, and watched him with infinite tenderness.

Early the next morning Sutherland called, and Miss Forster rejoiced to see him and accepted with eagerness his offer of personal assistance. All night long her brother had remained like one physically crushed and broken, always conscious and uttering intermittent cries of pain. At daybreak he would have flown down to Putney, but they restrained him almost by main force, yet with less difficulty than might have been anticipated, for his strong will seemed shattered and all his spirit clouded as by a frightful dream.

Of course, under the circumstances, a public inquest was unavoidable. At the inquest, evidence of identity was given. Forster claimed the remains as those of his wife, and a sympathetic jury returned a verdict of 'Accidentally drowned.' Society was for some days slightly agitated on the subject, the general impression being that the unfortunate lady, for some unexplained reason, had committed suicide. For a marvel, the so-called society journals preserved a decent silence; the fact being that Sutherland, in his capacity of self-constituted champion, had interviewed both Lagardère and Yahoo, and extracted from them, jointly and severally, a promise to abstain from any immediate allusions to the case. How he effected this object has never been disclosed; but he was, as we know, a determined man, and possibly the gentlemen perceived that publication would make a corporal chastisement inevitable. They were the more willing to forego their usual carrion as they were greatly exercising their readers at that time in speculations as to whether a certain Italian *prima donna* who shall be nameless was or was not the daughter of an itinerant pieman in the Seven Dials, and as to what were the precise relations between the Prince of Scotland and Mademoiselle Schwangau, the charming topical singer of the Parisian *cafés chantants*.

So it came to pass that the poor remains, in a sealed coffin, were taken to Queen's Gate, and remained there until the day fixed for a quiet funeral. Most of the necessary arrangements were superintended by Sutherland, who had, as if almost by right, quietly established himself as a friend of the family. The brother and sister accepted his services gratefully, and almost without a word of explanation.

The funeral took place at Kensal Green. The only followers were Forster and his new acquaintance. At the grave the former utterly broke down, his wild tears flowing for the first time.

The two men returned to Forster's house together.

'I shall never forget your kindness,' said Forster, during an interval of comparative calmness. 'May God bless you for it! I am a broken man now, and have nothing left to live for; but while I live let us be friends.'

And he wrung the young man's hands.

'You have nothing to thank me for,' replied Sutherland. 'What I have done for you, I would, of course, do for any fellow-man in distress. But I had a deep respect, a profound sympathy, for your wife.'

'Though, as I understand, you scarcely knew her,' said Forster, not without a certain wistful curiosity.

'I could not be said to know her at all. We met twice or thrice, almost as strangers, and then I saw her performances at the Parthenon.'

'We were so happy,' cried Forster, with a sudden access of passionate emotion; 'and she was so good! All goodness—all goodness! God knows under what misconceptions she left my roof. But I know she had an enemy, and perhaps——'

'Can you bear to speak of that!' interrupted Sutherland. 'Hitherto I have forborne from touching on the subject, but with your permission I should like to say a few words now.'

'Do so—I will try to attend.'

'You are aware that Mrs. Forster was acquainted with a Frenchman, named Gavrolles, now in London?'

'Yes.'

'Do you know—forgive me if I pain you—the nature of her relations with him?'

'I think I do,' returned Forster. 'Before my darling's guardian died, he confided to me that, when quite a child, she had been betrayed into a mock marriage with a foreigner, who almost immediately abandoned her. I knew this when I married her. I have no doubt that this Gavrolles is the same man; that he again thrust himself in her way; that, in order to avoid him, and dreading some misunderstanding on my part, she yielded to a wild impulse and—and——'

But here Forster broke down sobbing, and hid his face in his hands. Deeply moved, Sutherland touched him gently on the shoulder, as he said:—

'I think it has all been as you say. With regard to Mrs. Forster's first acquaintance with this man, I can myself tell you something which will, I think, convince you of her innocence in the matter.' Sutherland thereupon briefly recounted his first meeting with Madeline in the hotel at Fecamp, his suspicions of her companions, his offers of assistance; and explained also briefly the part he had taken afterwards, when they met again in Paris— saying nothing, however, of his own temporary misconception of Madeline's true character, but describing the manner in which, on her abandonment by her pseudo-husband, he had restored her into the hands of her guardian.

'That is all I know,' he said in conclusion, 'and I think it is enough to justify you in your noble faith in Mrs. Forster's honour. From first to last, when a mere child, she was this man's victim, and so sure as there is a God above us, her death lies at his door.'

Trembling with agitation, Forster rose to his feet.

'Where is he? Let me see him! Yes, you are right—he has killed her. Tell me where he is, that I may find him out, and——'

At this moment a servant entered, bearing a card. A gentleman, he said, was waiting below desirous of seeing Mr. Forster on most important business. Almost mechanically Forster took the card and glanced at it. As he read the inscription upon it, he uttered a sharp cry and turned deathly pale.

Graven on the card, in fantastic letters, with many characteristic flourishes, was the name—

M. Auguste de Gavrolles.

The first shock of surprise over, Forster glanced up and found that Sutherland's eyes were bent inquiringly upon his. He handed him the card.

'My wish has been answered,' he said with ominous calmness. 'The very man I most wished to see is here, only I had rather the meeting had taken place beneath any roof but mine;' then turning to the servant, he added, 'Show the person into the drawing-room, and say I will come to him.'

The servant retired, and once more Sutherland and Forster were left alone. Sutherland stood as if transfixed, with the elegant piece of pasteboard bearing the Frenchman's name held still before his eyes; while Forster, bereft now of all his calmness, paced excitedly up and down the room. The sight of the Frenchman's name at such a time almost transformed him into a madman. Trembling from head to foot, yet pale as death, he at last rushed to the door, when Sutherland laid his hand upon his shoulder to detain him.

'I see you have made up your mind to meet the man.' 'I have.'

'Well, so far I think you have done well, but before you meet him will you listen to some advice from me?'

'What do you want me to do?'

'Nothing against your own interest or *hers*. I know that if you had descended the stairs two minutes ago you would either have strangled this Frenchman or thrashed him within an inch of his life. Your conduct would have been justifiable, but not wise. You yourself would have regretted it before the morning. Be sure retribution shall come to him, though it may not come to-night. Now, I want you to forget for a time that this scoundrel ever intended the slightest harm to your dead wife.'

'My God!'

'I know the task will be a hard one, but remember it is for *her* sake. So far he has played his cards well. He knows even now that his person is sacred, because, if in your grief and anger you were tempted to assault him, you would only be the means of scandalising the name of the departed.'

'Mr. Sutherland, what does all this mean?'

'Only this. I want you to do me a favour. Will, you? Yes or no?'

'Yes, certainly, if I can.'

'Let *me* still be the champion of your wife?'

'What!'

'It is for *her* sake, remember. She shall be avenged but she must not be scandalised. This Frenchman has some deep motive in coming here. It would be well for both our sakes that I should learn what this motive is. Will you interview him in this room, and conceal me in some place where I can hear your conversation?'

At first Forster protested. To meet the Frenchman in a seemingly amiable spirit seemed beyond him, but Sutherland was so urgent in his pleading that at length his point was won. Forster yielded for Madeline's sake.

There was a small lavatory adjoining the study—into this Sutherland retired, leaving the door ajar. Forster by a tremendous effort controlled his agitation, and, ringing the bell, ordered the Frenchman to be shown in to him.

Gavrolles entered the room.

He was neatly clad in black, and on his white face there was a grave look of sorrow. As the door closed behind him, he stepped daintily forward to where Forster sat, and as he did so a sickly perfume seemed to penetrate the whole atmosphere. Forster raised his head, looked at the Frenchman's outstretched hand, but did not move.

'Ah, monsieur,' exclamed Gavrolles, 'how shall I thank you for this interview? I know, monsieur, I must be *de trop* at such a time as this, but I am as it were a mere machine. I follow not my own inclinations, but the force of circumstances; they have brought me here.'

'Is this what you have come to say to me?' asked Forster coldly.

'Not all, by no means all,' returned the Frenchman eagerly; 'but before we proceed to business I must express to you, monsieur, my deep condolence in a great affliction which has befallen you!'

Forster's face grew livid, he half rose from his chair; then remembering his promise to Sutherland he sank back again with a groan.

'Be careful,' he said sternly. 'If you come here on business, pray state it without further preamble; at all events be good enough not to allude again to my domestic affairs.'

The Frenchman shrugged his shoulders and turned upon Forster a pair of eyes lit with a sickly sinister light.

'Pardon, monsieur,' he returned blandly. 'I am sorry if I have pained you—but in this world it is not the fortune of any one that his path should be all sunshine. Though it is much against my inclination, it is of your affairs that I must speak. Listen, monsieur. A little bird has already whispered abroad that Auguste de Gavrolles and Madame Forster were acquainted. Having learned so much, the curious are naturally anxious to hear more. They love romances. Here is one ready made, they say, but there is only one man who can tell it truly; and that man is Gavrolles. Accordingly Gavrolles is besieged. Well, he does not wish to speak, for though he has been maligned he is a man of honour and an *artiste*. He is on the horns of a dilemma. The only course for him to take would be to travel far away, but he is a poor man, and without money one can do nothing—absolutely nothing. Do you understand, monsieur?'

Forster shook his head.

'I confess I do not.'

'Then I must speak more plainly. Would it not be well, if you said to me, "Monsieur Gavrolles, since I am a rich man, it shall not be for the want of a little filthy lucre that my wife's name is unpleasantly discussed. You shall not want the means to move away."'

He paused, and for a moment there was silence. The Frenchman's face went very pale, his smile became even more baleful, as he saw Forster rise slowly from his seat and point to the door.

'That is enough,' he exclaimed; 'leave my house. If we stood face to face beneath any other roof but mine, I'd kill you like a dog.'

'Monsieur, you do not understand.'

'Not understand! You villain, I understand too well. I know what you have done. I know what you would do. You made my wife's life a hell; you tortured her into her grave; and now instead of feeling any pity for your victim, you come to me and ask me to pay you money to keep you from slandering her name. Leave my house, or as sure as there is a God above us I'll have you whipped like a cur into the street!'

Forster was trembling from head to foot with rage. The Frenchman, who was still cool, turned to speak, but one look in the other's face silenced him. He made two steps towards the door; there he paused. He felt in his pocket, drew forth a card, wrote rapidly upon it, then turned to Forster again.

'Monsieur,' he said quietly, 'that is my address for three days at least. I leave it, in case you may wish to write to me.'

So saying, and with a profound bow, he took his leave. Scarcely had the door closed upon the Frenchman when Sutherland burst excitedly into the room.

'Mr. Forster,' he said, 'once more will you do me a favour for your wife's sake?'

But Forster seemed deaf to his words. He sank into his chair, murmuring, in heart-broken tones—

'Madeline! my poor murdered wife 1'

'Pray, listen to me. Send the scoundrel the money—let him have his price—conditionally!'

'You advise me to do this?'

'I do.'

He bent down and whispered in Forster's ear—Forster started—the two men looked at each other.

After some hesitation Forster spoke.

'He shall have the money!' he said.

'And you will make those conditions?'

'Certainly.'

Forster sat down at once, and wrote a note to Gavrolles. In it he said that he (Gavrolles) should be supplied with a certain sum, if he would pledge himself to return at once to France.

CHAPTER XL
'RESURGAM.'

On a sombre autumn afternoon, the solitary figure of a woman stood looking backward and westward, towards the round red ball of the sun, which was sinking slowly into the very heart, as it were, of the great far-away cloud which she knew was London.

All around her, on every side, stretched desolate marshes, silent save for the hoarse cry of a heron dapping slowly towards his crimson fishing pools, or for the faint forlorn whistle of a distant curlew. No other human figure was in sight, not even a human habitation; but over the trees of a lonely plantation, skirting the marshes to the southward, the spire of Grayfleet Church glittered back the rays of the setting sun.

The woman, though pale and haggard, was young and beautiful; and as she watched the far-off sunset its dim ray touched her cheeks with a faint tinge of red. She stood like one in a dream, shading her eyes and gazing on the dusky pageant—cloud, smoke, and mist irradiated into gloomy splendour, and assuming, as the fancy willed, strange forms of crumbling buildings, fiery streets, columns, roofs, arches, spires, and turrets, all duskily aflame.

It did not seem real; no more real than the city she had left behind her, than the grave from which she had risen into some dimmer and sadder life. Yet her eyes dimmed with tears as she thought of one solitary figure waiting lonely and despairing yonder, listening for a foot that came not, praying for a love cast away and lost.

Nothing seemed real; not the cloudy pageant, or the darkening sun, or the desolate earth; not the life that she had lived, or the life that she had voluntarily left behind; not the long years of a confused and broken experience, chiefly of helplessness and sorrow; nothing but the clinging, contaminating sense of some great sin and shame. As a creature half choked and drowned, just dragged living out of some watery ooze, with all the foul moisture and the slimy filth clinging to her garments, this woman seemed and felt. The consciousness of a complete moral contamination, from which she had barely emerged, still remained with her, and not all the perfumes of Arabia could have cleansed it away.

She had been wandering in that dreary district for days, sleeping at night in lonely farmhouses and squalid inns, and ever creeping out in the early dawn to follow some aimless pilgrimage she scarcely knew whither. Yet all that afternoon she had been hanging around Grayfleet, looking in vain for some face that she might know and remember. She had stood gazing sadly at the little row of white-washed cottages where Mark and Luke Peartree once had dwelt; but strange folk now lived there, and the name of Peartree was quite forgotten. She had looked at the shining river, and she had seen, in a dream, the boat rowing in with its maimed and broken burden, while Uncle Luke stood in the bow wringing his hands. She had wandered into the old churchyard and looked in upon the very tombs where a troop of merry girls were playing, one happy Sabbath, so many years ago. Ah, that sweet, that far-off, half-forgotten life—was it all a dream too?

Tramps and wanderers of all kinds were common in those parts, and few had paid any attention to the pale worn woman, plainly and poorly clad, who haunted the old village that afternoon. Now and then she had received a country greeting, and quietly replied. She had entered the Ferry Inn, and bought some bread and cheese, and while making her poor meal she had tried to question the landlord, a rough waterside character, about people she remembered. But he was a stranger where all seemed strangers. Then her feet had strayed again to the old churchyard, and this time she had strolled through the gate and searched among the graves. But she found no headstone or memorial to show her where Mark Peartree was lying, or where slept the kindly dame who had followed him so soon.

So the day passed, and in the afternoon she had come out again upon the lonely marshes, where she now stood watching the smoky sun.

Ah, yes, it must all have been a dream. Wandering out of the great city, fearful of pursuit, with no definite aim or hopes save that of forgetting and of being forgot, she had strayed half unconsciously towards the old landmarks—towards the only spot in the world where she had known a happy and peaceful time. What impulse had brought her thither she could scarcely divine; it was an instinct that sometimes brings the bird to its deserted nest, the hare to its long-abandoned form. She herself quite knew that it was hopeless. She knew that the little household at Grayfleet had been desolate for years; and that the only surviving member of it, if indeed he still survived, was Luke Peartree, after whose whereabouts unavailing inquiries had been made again and again. After Madeline Hazelmere was sent to France she had heard nothing of her uncle; then her great trouble had come, and in its shadow, while it lasted, all else was forgotten; but once more, after her return to England, she had tried to discover poor Uncle Luke's whereabouts—always in vain.

Turning her back at last on the sullen sunset, the woman wandered slowly along the narrow road which wound and wound for miles and miles, seaward, through the marshes. In the near distance on her right hand moved great sails, tall masts, smoking funnels, going and coming with a strange silentness; for the river was there, sunk so low down in its muddy bed that the traffic moving upon it had this curious appearance, as of ghostly objects moving to and fro, in silhouette, upon the solid earth.

She walked on and on still as if in a dream, and still with the sense of a suffocating taint. The sun sank into the sombre cloud of the distant city; darkness descended upon and rose from the marshes, save where here and there a roadside pool flashed duskily; and still she walked on.

The moon rose large and yellow out of the far-off sea, and the air became full of a visible and delicate dimness. So dense was the stillness, so sad the darkening prospect all around, that now, more than ever, the woman seemed walking in a dead world, a world of weariful dreams.

At last she reached another village, lying close down by the riverside. It was a small place, strongly saturated with brackish moisture, and much frequented by forlorn seagulls of a ragged species, too lazy and disreputable to earn a decent living out at sea. Here, in a peasant woman's house, she procured a bed, or rather a 'shake-down' before the kitchen fire. The woman, a childless widow, stolid with ill fortune, dazed with a life of wretchedness, asked no questions, and seemed to note little difference between this delicate-skinned white-handed wanderer and tramps of the common sort.

Early next morning she was away again, in broken aimless flight.

But it was at last evident that the physical frame of this woman was unable to bear the strain put upon it by her impatient and apparently indomitable spirit. Her walk was weary and unsure, and very often she paused to rest; her breath came and went heavily; and in a word, her trembling frame and aching limbs betokened that her strength was failing fast.

About midday a country fellow, driving a light farm cart, passed her, looked back, paused, drove on again, paused once more, and finally waited till she came up; then, after looking at her curiously from head to foot, accosted her as follows:—

'Missis! Be you a-going to Seachester?'

She did not know the name, but scarcely knowing what she did she answered in the affirmative.

'Ah!—Do you know, missis, how far it be?'

She shook her head.

'From London, I s'pose?'

She did not answer, and he continued:—

'Well, it be seven miles, missis, to Seachester, and sure enough you seem dead beat. Telee what, missis! I'll give you a lift along.'

Weary and overpowered, she accepted his offer, and with his assistance she climbed into they cart. They jogged along slowly, for the roads were heavy and clogged with mud. From time to time the man looked at her, surveying her quietly from head to foot, noting with no little surprise her delicate form, her small hands, her beautiful face. More than once he seemed about to question her, but refrained. To avoid meeting his inquisitive gaze, she closed her eyes, and presently, through sheer fatigue, she fell into a heavy doze.

She was wakened by a hoarse voice in her ear:—

'Now, then, missis, here we be!'

She stirred, opened her eyes, and saw that they were standing near to a very small village, not far from a great water, the river or the sea. Shivering, and dazed, she alighted from the cart, and taking out a small purse offered the man a piece of silver.

'Noa, keep your money, missis,' he said, with a stern shake of his head. 'Look, now, this be Seachester, and up there be the house where you're a-going.'

He pointed as he spoke to a small cottage, like a lodge, standing surrounded by trees, at the gate of a kind of avenue.

'The house?' she echoed. 'Do you mean where they will give me a night's lodging?'

He looked at her with a curious expression, indicative of rural suspicion.

'You're like the rest on 'em, missis! You know well enough where you're a-coming, but you won't let on to know. Never mind, you ain't the fust by many as has had a lift in my old cart. There, go up right through that gate, missis, and they'll give you a night's lodgings, never fear!'

So saying, with a grim nod, the countryman drove away, leaving the woman perplexed and even alarmed.

What could he mean? Could he have any suspicion that she was a fugitive? She was too dazed and weak quite ta understand, or even heed his mysterious allusions. A sickening weight was on her heart, and though her hands and feet were stony cold, her frame was on fire. She stood tottering, as if about to faint.

It was again afternoon, and the red sunlight fell on the little lodge and on the long avenue beyond, overshadowed with sere and yellow trees. The place seemed still and peaceful. She crept nearer, and presently stood with her face against the iron gate, looking in.

As she stood thus, there came on her ear the sound of female voices; and she saw approaching down the avenue, a troop of about thirty women walking in couples, talking and laughing as they came along. They were plainly dressed, for the most part in plain stuff dresses and dark shawls, and each wore a tight-fitting bonnet of the same description. On they came, chattering like children. Most of them, even in their not too becoming costume, showed the signs of personal comeliness, and a few were really pretty.

Suddenly they turned into a side path and disappeared. The sound of their voices died quietly away among the trees.

Trembling and wondering, the woman opened the iron gate and approached the door of the lodge. She knocked feebly, but in a moment the door was opened, and a goodlooking country dame, very clean and bright, stood on the threshold.

'Can I—can I—'—the wanderer began feebly, but breath failed her, and she stood trembling.

'Come in, my dear,' said the woman compassionately, leading her to a chair in a cosy little kitchen. 'Come in, and welcome. Lord, how pale you be! Have you come far?'

'Yes. I want——'

'Never mind about that, *now*—wait till I get thee a nice drink of warm milk, and then you can go on the Home.'

But even as she spoke the wanderer fainted away.

The good dame uttered an exclamation.

'Poor dear, she's fainted. How wet and draggled she be! Why, she must have tramped it all the way. Here, Johnnie—Johnnie!'

A flaxen-haired boy of about twelve appeared on the threshold.

'Run up to the house, quick, and ask Sister Ursula, with mother's compliments, to step down here at once. Poor unfortunate,' she continued, chafing the woman's fingers, 'what pretty white hands she has! She looks like a lady born!'

CHAPTER XLI
THE SISTERS OF MOUNT EDEN

A considerable interval of time must have passed from the moment when the woman recovered consciousness; for on opening her eyes she found herself lying in bed, in a large, dimly lighted room. The bed was white and clean, with snowy hangings, and the chamber contained four other beds of the same description. The curtains of the window were closely drawn, and on the hearth there burnt a cheerful fire.

Seated close to the bedside was a young girl, dressed like a nurse, in clean white cap, white apron and cotton gown, and reading a book.

For some minutes the wanderer lay silent, not stirring, but looking vacantly around her; on the cleanly papered walls, cosily lit by the firelight: on the engraving of the Crucifixion, hanging over the mantelpiece on the snowy beds, at the head of each of which hung a picture of the Madonna — each different, but all copies from the works of Raphael; and finally, on the quiet, thoughtful-looking girl, who sat intent upon her book.

At last, thoroughly awakened, she uttered an exclamation. The girl looked up, and their eyes met.

'Where am I? What place is this? Why am I lying here?'

The girl smiled, and, without answering, touched a handbell standing on a small table at her side. Scarcely had she done so when a tall, slight figure, also wearing a white cap, entered the room. Her hair was quite white, but her face seemed fresh and young; and her eyes had a cold virginal steadfastness which harmonised well with the lines of a mouth firm almost to hardness. No sooner, however, did her gaze fall upon the occupant of the bed than her face was lit by a smile of strange brightness and sweetness; the coldness passed from her eyes, the lines of her mouth grew soft and tender; and her whole expression was transformed into one of winning kindness and beauty.

The girl rose and curtsied as the newcomer advanced to the bedside.

'You are better now?'

The wanderer looked up wildly, scrutinising the kind thoughtful face which was bending over her.

'Where am I?' she cried again. 'What place is this?'

'You are among friends,' was the quiet reply.

'In the hospital? Have I been ill?'

'You were faint and weak when they brought you in, and afterwards you fell into a sleep.'

'Yes, I remember—but this place, and you? I do not know you.'

'I am Sister Ursula. Perhaps you have heard my name?'

'No.'

'Nor the name of this place—Mount Eden? 5

'No! no!5 cried the wanderer, in surprise.

'You are welcome all the same; but, before we talk any more, let Barbara'—here Barbara, as the young girl was called, curtsied—'bring you some warm soup, or some tea and toast. I am sure you are weak from want of food.'

At first the invalid, confused and to some extent alarmed by her position, refused to take any sustenance, but Sister Ursula, with gentle firmness, at last persuaded her to drink some warm tea and eat a little dry toast. When she had done so, and Barbara, at a signal from her superior, had retired, Sister Ursula sat quietly down by the bedside.

'And now, may I ask you a few questions about yourself? Do not think I speak from mere curiosity, and do not answer anything unless you please. In the first place, am I right in guessing that you are in trouble?'

'Yes.'

As she answered, almost under her breath, the wanderer kept her large, wistful, watchful eyes fixed, with strange intensity, on the Sister's face.

'Next, may I ask your name?'

There was a long pause, but at last, in the same low tone, the answer came—

'Jane Peartree.'

'Well, Jane (may I call you Jane? it is our habit in this place to call each other by the Christian name), I do not wish to inquire into your history, until you choose to tell me it, or any portion of it. What I wish you to do is to regard me and all here as friends and sufferers like yourself, sisters in sorrow and in heavenly hope. You will rest here, certain of help and sympathy, until such a time as you feel strong enough to face the world again. By-the-bye, are you a Londoner?'

'No; I was born in the country.'

'And you have lived—-'

'Do not ask me! I cannot tell!'

And as she spoke, she turned her face upon the pillow, crying.

'You shall tell me nothing,' said the lady softly, 'until you wish it of your own freewill. I can see that you have had sorrow, great sorrow; and that, unlike so many who come here, your speech is gentle, and your manner that of a lady. Take courage! Whatever your offence has been, whatever pain you have undergone, you are as safe now as a little child on its mother's breast—no one can tempt you, no one can harm you, here.'

The wanderer turned her face again, and looked long and wistfully at the Sister; then she sighed deeply, while her tears still fell.

'You have not told me what place this is, but I suppose it is some religious home. Well, I am not religious; I scarcely know what religion is. All I ask is a night's shelter, and then—I will pay you for it, and go away.'

Sister Ursula's face looked very grave.

'We never accept payment from those who take shelter here; and you are mistaken—this is not a religious house in the sense you mean. True, we believe in one God and one Redeemer, and our experience teaches us that, for the truly sorrowful and penitent, knowledge of Christ the Saviour is the only preservation.'

The wanderer sighed drearily.

'You are Roman Catholics, I suppose?' she said, with a curious indifference. 'I have heard they are good people.'

'We are of all religions,' returned Sister Ursula, smiling; 'that is to say, the unfortunate are welcome here, whatever their creed. I myself am a member of the Church of England, but some of our inmates are Catholics, others Dissenters, many, like yourself, of no particular persuasion. We do not insist on these things. Our love and sympathy are for all the world.'

'And the house is—not a religious house? What then?'

'A refuge for sisters who have fallen, and who repent.'

The wanderer shuddered, for she had read of such places; then, after a moment, she gave a low, faint, bitter laugh.

'How stupid I was not to understand! And you think I am one of those — those women?'

'I think, Jane, that you have a great trouble, whatever it has been; but do not think I am judging you, or wishing to proclaim your fault. Whatever you are, I am no better than yourself. Twenty years ago I left a good husband, and lived in wickedness and shame with another man, who afterwards abandoned me. I have suffered a great deal, though no more than I deserve.'

Raising herself upon her elbow, the woman calling herself Jane Pear tree gazed in amazement at the calm grey sister, who, without a tremor in her voice, coldly proclaimed her own sin to a stranger.

'I am no better than the worst here,' said Sister Ursula; 'but my own experience has helped me to be of service to those who, like myself, have sinned and suffered. Many here are infinitely my superiors insomuch as they have suffered, and been dragged into pollution, through no fault of their own.'

As she spoke, a bell sounded in the distance, and a sound of footsteps was heard upon the staircase beyond the chamber. The door stood open, and Jane Peartree saw numerous female figures, all clad in white caps and aprons, pass quickly by. Several looked in, smiling at Sister Ursula, and cried, 'Good-night.' Then four young women, clad like the others, entered that chamber, curtseying and looking curiously at the stranger.

'It is ten o'clock,' said Sister Ursula, rising, 'and bedtime. We breakfast early, at half-past seven, but you are weak and must not attempt to get up. Good-night, Jane.'

Stooping gently, the lady kissed Jane Peartree on the forehead, and then, with a bright good-night to the others, left the room, closing the door behind her.

Jane lay still, and looked at her companions, who were slowly undressing by the light of a small lamp. The eldest was about eight-and-twenty, the youngest not much over eighteen; and, with one exception, they showed no refinement either of appearance or of manner, and clearly belonged to that portion of the lower orders from which society recruits its domestic servants. The exception was a pale, slender girl, obviously in delicate health, who exchanged but few remarks with her companions, and spoke, when she did speak, with a strong French accent. She sat on the side of the bed, slowly removing her outer garments, and breathing heavily, while the others chattered in low tones to each other and occasionally gave vent to a vacant giggling laugh.

Presently her eyes met those of Jane Peartree, and after a moment's hesitation she walked across the room and stood by the bedside.

'Pardon, mademoiselle,' she said gently, 'but you are not well, and you are a stranger. Can I get you anything?'

Jane shook her head; then, seeing the other hesitate, and being attracted by her foreign grace, she asked, in her own tongue—

'Are you French?'

The girl's face brightened strangely at the sound of her native language.

'No, mademoiselle; I am Belgian. I came from near Brussels.'

'What's your name?'

'Adèle, mademoiselle.'

'Have you been long here—in this house, I mean?'

'Not long—a few weeks. I was sick, and in need of country air, and a kind friend (ah, the kindest in the world) had me sent down here. It is very pleasant all around, and reminds me of my home, and Sister Ursula is so good, but there are many here whom you would detest. You, mademoiselle, are different; I saw that at a glance; for abroad we can tell a lady always from one of these *canaille!*'

The girl spoke rapidly in her own language, while her companions, attracted by the foreign speech, listened without understanding a word, whispered, and made signs to each other.

'You mistake——, I am no lady,' cried Jane Peartree, eagerly.

Without contradicting her in speech, the French girl smiled sceptically and shook her head. She then began to prattle on, with the fluency of her race, until the new comer, sometimes listening and sometimes questioning, was furnished at last with a tolerably complete account of the house into which she had accidentally been brought, and of the individuals by whom she was surrounded.

The house, as she had already been informed, was called Mount Eden, and it formed the centre of a small estate, consisting of woods, arable and grazing fields, farm buildings, and outlying cottages. Originally an old country manor, it had about ten years before come into the market, and had been purchased by the lady named Sister Ursula (partly out of a large inheritance of her own, and partly by means of voluntary subscription) for the purpose of founding in it a home for penitent and fallen women. The scheme on which the establishment was based was unusually wide and broad in its provisions. In the first place there were no religious barriers, and in the second place there was no attempt made to imitate the severe ethics of the penitentiary. The place was, in the truest sense, a Home. All the inmates, if in good health, were required to work in some way—generally in the way to which they had been best accustomed; some performing the higher or lower household duties; others working in the laundry; others, again, doing dairy and field work on the home farm—all in fact being occupied pleasantly and profitably, with a goodly share of interest in the result of their own labours. No attempt was made at any irritating supervision of the morals of the inmates; once admitted it was taken for granted that they were tired of evil doing, at any rate for the time being, and that it was unnecessary to preach to them, six days out of seven, on the wickedness of their ways. At the same time they were daily brought into contact with sound, sweet, and beautiful associations.

A special feature of the establishment, copied from some of the Magdalen institutions in France, was the reception—particularly in the summer season—of sick and delicate children, many of them babes in arms, from the neighbouring city. These children were distributed among the poor sisters, and it was wonderful to see with what eagerness they were received, with what tenderness they were guarded, by these kind foster-mothers. Many a helplessly degraded woman, on whom all their holy influences had been unavailing, was saved and consecrated by the necessity of tending a child; many an evil creature felt for the first time, with tiny arms clinging round her neck, the instincts of a pure maternity and the inspiration of a heavenly hope.

Another rule, to which indeed the foregoing was a pendant, gave to an inmate, if a mother, the privilege of bringing her own offspring with her, and of rearing it in the house. No attempt was made to separate mother and child. No penitentiary laws were in existence, based upon the assumption that the former was an alien, and the latter a 'child of sin.'

Sister Ursula herself was the younger daughter of a peer of the realm. In her girlhood she had made a marriage, unfortunate in a worldly point of view, and had completed her folly by afterwards forming an attachment for an officer, with whom she eloped. Few, however, would have traced in that calm, cold face the record of strong passions and improprieties, if the lady herself had not, with a curious persistency, insisted on making no secret of her own sin; her theory being that one who had herself been a sinner, and sadly acquainted with the world's sorrows and temptations, was better qualified to deal with fellow-sinners than the most irreproachable of female saints.

During the night the wanderer snatched a troubled sleep, starting up at times to listen to the wind which shook the windows, and to gaze wildly round the dark room; but towards morning she slept quite soundly. She was awakened by the loud ringing of a bell in the hall below; and, opening her eyes, she saw the four companions of her chamber busy dressing.

No sooner had she awakened than Adèle, who had been watching her, came over and said gently, in French:—

'I am glad you have slept, mademoiselle.'

Jane Peartree thanked her, and, rising on her elbow, looked round her, as if preparing to rise also.

'Ah! but you must not rise,' continued the other. 'It is very early, and Sister Ursula says you are to keep your bed. Shall I fetch you a cup of tea?'

Jane Peartree did not reply. She was looking around her in a vain search for the clothes she had worn the previous day, and of these there was no sign.

'I must get up,' she said impatiently. 'Call the lady—tell her I wish to go. I have a long journey before me, and I cannot remain any longer in this place.'

But even as she spoke her head swam round, and she sank shivering back upon her pillow. On her cheeks there were two hectic spots, her eyes seemed wild and wandering, and the left pupil of one was widely dilated.

A minute afterwards Sister Ursula entered the room, and, after a quiet good morning to the other women, bent over the occupant of the bed.

'Good-morning, Jane,' she said, smiling.

Jane Peartree looked up; as she did so her face flushed and her teeth chattered in her head.

'Please let me have my things,' she cried. 'I wish to go away.'

'So soon?'

'Yes. They are following me. It will kill me if they find me. I am quite well. Quick! Let me go, for God's sake!'

Sister Ursula did not reply, but stooping over the bed took the girl's hand and placed her fingers upon the pulse, which she found bounding with all the force of violent fever.

'Take my advice,' she said gravely, 'and stay with us to-day; to-morrow, perhaps, you will be strong enough to go.'

'I am quite strong. I must go now. You have no right to detain me!' cried the wanderer; and as she spoke she sat up, looking wildly and even angrily at her protectress. But it was only for a moment. Her head swam again, and she sank back shuddering.

'O, madame!' cried Adèle, 'I am afraid she is very ill.'

'Hush!' said Sister Ursula. 'Go down, and leave us alone together.'

The girls, accustomed to obey, left the room in a body, and Sister Ursula sat down by the bedside.

Jane Peartree lay moaning, and it was soon evident that her mind was wandering. She made no more attempts to rise, but murmured wildly to herself. Presently, when Sister Ursula bent over to speak to her again, she remained with half-closed eyes and made no articulate reply.

'Poor child,' thought the lady. 'How pretty she looks, and different to most of those who come to this roof for shelter. And she has a secret, which weighs upon her mind.'

She added, still to herself—

'"Jane Peartree." That was the name she gave me. Yet the initials upon her linen are "M. F." Who can she be?'

CHAPTER XLII
EXIT GAVROLLES

Several weeks after the wandering woman, who called herself 'Jane Peartree,' became an inmate of Mount Eden, that cosmic creature, Auguste de Gavrolles, author of the immortal 'Parfums de la Chair,' was entertained at a little supper in the house of Ponto, the art-critic. The occasion was an interesting one, originating in the fact that London was about to lose, for a time at least, the light of the French poet's presence. Urgent private affairs, no less than the home-sickness of a great man for the scene of his struggles and his triumphs, were the reason of his departure. Frankly, as he confessed to his admirers, London was insufferably *bête* after the true centre of the universe, Paris. It contained many choice spirits, notably those who had nourished their sublime youth with the fiery fleshliness of the Impeccable Master, but even these could not compensate for the fine atmosphere of Parisian *salons*, the soul-satisfying sunlight of Parisian streets. In a word, both duty and pleasure beckoned the cosmic creature back to his Cosmos, and he was compelled, though with a certain reluctance, to say farewell.

The gathering was a very quiet one Ponto's house, situated in the dismally aesthetic region of Chiswick, was a small but elegant artistic villa, furnished in the superbest spirit of enlightened chilliness and elegant squalor. There, in a tiny reception room with golden-spotted walls and a cerulean ceiling, some dozen gentlemen and about half a dozen ladies assembled; among the company being the young aesthetic poets, Botticelli Jones and Omar Milde; Lady Milde, mother of the bard, known in her girlhood as the fair 'Lachryma' of the albums; Gass and Barbius, Ponto's brother-critics; the editor of the 'Megatherium'; Clothilde Max, daughter of the Teutonic patriot, Hermann Max; and a few others. The affair was affecting, if not festive. There were gay spongecakes and nondescript confectionery on a sideboard, together with the finest Marsala wine, for those who sought refreshment. When, in a few well-chosen words, Ponto wished Godspeed to the guest of the evening, several persons present were dismally affected. Gavrolles, more than usually jubilant, replied, thanking perfidious Albion, in the person of its noblest representatives, for their cordial treatment of him, a stranger, an exile. He had come to them on his merits, a poor *artiste*, a lover of the beautiful, a pupil of Gautier, and they had received him as a brother. He should bear back to his beloved Paris the memory of their kindness. He should inform his countrymen that France and England were thenceforth bound together by a tie stronger than all commercial treaties— the tie of sympathy in poetic aspirations, in divine Art. He should tell his compatriots that even in England, despite its Philistinism, despite its climate, there were singers as sweet and critics as profound as even those who possessed the inestimable advantages of a Parisian education. Need he mention, as a sample of all that was superb in song, his friend, Botticelli Jones? Need he cite, as an example of all that was subtle in perception and perfect in expression, the name of his friend and host—nay, might he not say, his brother?—Ponto, prince of critics?

The lank and limp ladies clung around him, with every expression of sympathy and affection, until the hour of parting came. Then Gavrolles, with tears in his eyes, read aloud, with considerable emphasis, a French sonnet which he had composed for the occasion, and in which the names of many present were touchingly introduced. This effusion was afterwards passed from hand to hand until it reached the editor of the 'Megatherium,' who claimed the privilege of publishing it in the forthcoming number of his journal, along with a reply (in the same language) from Young Botticelli Jones. Finally, the party separated, and Gavrolles, triumphant, drove home to his lodgings in a hansom cab.

The next evening, bearing with him in a small portmanteau and a morocco hand-bag all his worldly goods, Gavrolles left Charing Cross by the night mail, *en route* for Boulogne.

It was a wild wintry night, pitch dark, with gusts of rain and sleet; even the station looked dreary and forlorn, despite the pale brilliance of the electric light. Wrapt in a large travelling cloak, profusely trimmed with fur, and wearing an artistic felt hat, the broad brim of which was drawn down over his face, Gavrolles strolled up and down the platform with a theatrical swagger, taking care to clutch always his little handbag of black morocco. When the ticket office opened he approached the aperture, and, opening a purse full of bright new sovereigns, took a first-class ticket to Boulogne. He looked at nobody, heeded nobody, he seemed too obviously wrapt up in his own happy thoughts. His air, his walk, the feverishly delighted laugh in which he indulged from time to time, all seemed to betoken some special good fortune; and what wonder, seeing he had that very day cashed a large open cheque—payable to 'Bearer'—at a London bank, and afterwards, at a neighbouring money-changer's, converted the greater portion of the amount into glittering coin of the French realm.

Perhaps, had he been less jubilant and self-involved, he might have taken some little notice of his fellow-passengers—particularly of two individuals who, closely wrapped up and muffled almost to the eyes, observed him from a distance, listened in the shadow when, in a loud voice, he demanded his ticket, and then, after he had withdrawn, took two tickets, also for Boulogne, but second-class.

The express left London and plunged into the darkness. Gavrolles found himself alone—for there were few passengers that night—in the smoking compartment of a first-class carriage. While the rain hissed upon the window pane, and the noise of the train drowned even the roaring of the wind, he opened his little handbag, and eagerly recounted his treasure. His eye glittered with delight as he fingered the glittering gold pieces, and found them all safe. Then he wrapt his cloak around him, and resigned himself to a doze.

At Folkestone the weather looked ugly in the extreme; the wind roared, and the sea flashed in the darkness, while the packet rocked and throbbed with an uneasy motion. At first Gavrolles hesitated, but his horror of sea-sickness yielded to his intense longing to be again among certain choice spirits on his native soil, and with a few shivering compatriots he crept on board. Among those who followed him were the two men who had watched him so curiously at Charing Cross.

The passage was a miserable one. Gavrolles, to whom expense was no consideration when he was in funds, occupied the deck cabin, and suffered agonies through seasickness. In the grey of a wintry morning, he alighted, a piteous spectacle, ghastly, dishevelled, hideous, on the quay at Boulogne.

Among the groups assembled to see the voyagers alight was a white-haired woman, respectably but plainly dressed in black. She watched the passengers alighting one by one, until her eye fell upon a sinister-looking individual smoking, with serene defiance of the elements, a clay pipe. She at once greeted him by name, and, leading him aside, accosted him in French.

'What! do you come alone? Where are those in your charge?'

'Calm yourself, madame,' said the man with gruff politeness. 'I shall fulfil my contract. They would not cross in such weather.'

'But they remain?'

'Safe in the charge of my wife, at Folkestone. You will find two of them charming; the third not so good-looking, but *très gentille*. As I wrote you, one is a domestic servant, another a tradesman's runaway daughter, the third a figurante of the theatre. They all seek situations, which I have promised them, as you are aware.' 'But do they understand? With the last there was a scandal, and I want no more trouble.'

'Trust my wife, madame; there will be no difficulty. As usual, when they find themselves under your kind care, they will behave discreetly.'

At this juncture Gavrolles crawled up the gangway, the picture of misery and collapse. No sooner did the woman espy him than she uttered an exclamation.

'I see another friend!' she exclaimed to her companion. 'Go on to my house, and await me there.'

Gavrolles, followed by a porter carrying his portmanteau, elbowed his way along the pier. Suddenly he felt a touch upon his arm, and, turning sharply, saw the woman.

'Well met, Belleisle!' she said with a grim smile and a not too amiable compression of the lips.

So worn and washed out was the cosmic creature that at the first glance he failed to recognise his old companion, Madame de Fontenay.

'What!' she exclaimed. 'Do you forget me?'

At last, his glazed and fish-like countenance expressed a dim and irritated recognition.

'Is it you, Madame Louise?'

'Yes; it is I!—And you? It is many a long day since we met, though I have often inquired after you in vain. You are a sly rascal, Belleisle; you forget old friends, old services, old debts. Ah! but *I* remember.'

'I have been in England,' replied Gavrolles, surveying her with strong dislike.

'Ah, yes, so I heard. Have you been fortunate there, *mon ami?*'

'On the contrary. But you? You live here?'

'Yes,' said the woman.

'You follow the old trade, madame?'

The woman nodded, and the two passed on in conversation. Gavrolles did not look back, or he would have seen, still watching him with curiosity, the two men who had followed him from Charing Cross.

Gavrolles slept that night in the Hôtel de Rouen, a chilly place, half-hotel, half-prison, in a back street of Boulogne. Here he had the pleasure of meeting two or three gentlemen of his acquaintance, who earned their money at the card table and in the billiard room, and spent it in dingy dissipation, like cavaliers of pleasure.

With one of these individuals, an elderly man in a seedy military undress, and with the face and manners of a fire-eater, Gavrolles strolled out next morning, cigar in mouth. Roaming along by the sea, he came face to face, in a quiet spot, with two Englishmen—James Forster and Edgar Sutherland.

Gavrolles started and turned livid, clinging to his companion's arm, as Sutherland accosted him.

'I salute you, Monsieur Gavrolles. A word with you, if you please.'

'What do you seek with me?' cried Gavrolles, shrilly, 'I see you are not alone. If *monsieur le mari* yonder wishes to recede from his bargain, it is too late. As for you, monsieur, I once warned you; and, as we are no longer in England, beware!'

Sutherland smiled. Forster, who looked pale as death, was about to interpose, when the younger man continued: 'Monsieur Gavrolles, it is precisely because we are no longer in England that I accost you. Once, in London, you did me the honour to express a hope that we might meet on French soil. It was simply to realise that hope that my friend supplied you with money. You came—*we* followed—you understand?'

Gavrolles shrank back from the powerful figure, and eyed the determined face with baleful hate.

'I have no quarrel with you. I—I do not know you.' Before Sutherland could say another word Forster interfered.

'The man is right. As I said to you from the first—his quarrel is with me. Listen to me, man!' he continued, facing Gavrolles. 'I am not a duellist, I know nothing of your weapons, but unless you consent to fight me I shall have you arrested as an extortioner and a thief.

You are still wanted in London, and if you refuse— —'

Gavrolles, who had been watching the speaker keenly, and had paid particular attention to his words, answered with a scowl:—

'With you it is another affair, monsieur. I am at your service.'

'When?'

'As soon as you please. I am sorry that we could not end our little disagreement amicably, but since you are determined— —'

And Gavrolles shrugged his shoulders.

Sutherland pulled Forster aside, while Gavrolles, with an ugly smile, turned and volubly explained matters to his companion.

'You are mad!' Sutherland cried. 'You should have left this affair to me. He is an expert duellist, and may kill you.'

'And if he does, so much the better.'

'You are determined?'

'Yes. For God's sake settle the matter as soon as possible.'

Here Gavrolles' companion with pompous dignity approached Sutherland.

'Monsieur, that is my card. I am the Chevalier de Beauvoisin, and I represent my friend. Where and when can I see you and arrange the preliminaries?'

'Now, on this spot.'

The two men walked aside, and remained for some minutes in conversation. Then Sutherland returned to Forster, took his arm, and led him away.

'It is arranged for to-morrow at daybreak,' he said, 'on the sands yonder, two miles from Boulogne. As you are the challenger, they had the choice of weapons. They have chosen pistols.'

'Very well.'

'Have you ever practised at a mark?'

Forster-shook his head.

'I have never fired a pistol in my life.'

'Then it is an ugly affair. Let me entreat you, accept me as your substitute—I will force them to consent——' ＿

'No,' answered Forster with determination. 'It is my place, not yours. I shall either avenge my poor martyred wife or follow her to the grave.'

CHAPTER XLIII
ON BOULOGNE SANDS

In the early grey of the next morning, Forster and Sutherland stood waiting at the place appointed, a solitary spot just above high water mark. Far as the eye could see nothing was visible but the cold sea on the one hand, and the long, flat stretch of a great marsh, blackened here and there by leafless tree, upon the other.

'They are late,' said Forster impatiently. 'If he should take flight after all.'

'I think he will come. But you are shaking like a leaf.'

'Do you think I am afraid?' asked Forster with a strange smile.

Sutherland knew better, and shook his head sadly. But Forster's agitation, caused mainly by the mental strain of the last few days, filled him with deep concern.

A few minutes later three figures emerged on the open space of sand. These were Gavrolles, the Chevalier, his second, carrying a case of duelling pistols, and a little baldheaded man, carrying another case filled with surgical instruments.

The Chevalier led Sutherland apart.

'These are the weapons. Do they meet with your approbation?'

Sutherland examined the pistols, and nodded.

'Will you load them, monsieur, or shall I?' asked the Chevalier, still politely.

Sutherland undertook the operation, while the Chevalier watched him keenly. The pistols loaded, Gavrolles took one, Forster the other, and they moved to their places. It was arranged that the Chevalier and Sutherland should simultaneously count ten, and then utter the word "Fire," which should be the signal for the duellists to discharge their weapons.

Sutherland placed his man in position. So little did Forster know of how to protect himself, so clumsy was his exposure of his vital parts, that the surgeon in attendance uttered an exclamation.

'Mon Dieu!' he cried. 'It is not like a duel—but an assassination!'

Trembling with fear for Forster, who seemed quite helpless, Sutherland made one last appeal for him to withdraw, but the appeal was altogether useless.

'Well, then, since it must be, cover your man well, and aim low. The moment the word is given, raise your aim and fire; don't lose an instant, or he will anticipate you. You understand?'

'Yes.'

The seconds moved away, while Gavrolles and Forster faced each other. On the face of the Frenchman there was a curious blending of self-confidence, malignity, and nervous anticipation.

The sun rose coldly over the damp sands, but the air was still dank and cold, and the seconds, in slow monotonous voices, began simultaneously to count.

One—two—three—four—five—six—seven—eight—nine—ten—'fire!'

Before the last word was half pronounced, Gavrolles had raised his weapon, covered his opponent with lightning rapidity, and fired.

At the very moment he was about to raise his pistol in the air, Forster felt his arm suddenly grow powerless, while the weapon dropped from his hand.

Sutherland and the little surgeon simultaneously uttered an exclamation. The former reached his friend just in time to catch him in his arms.

'He is wounded!' he cried. 'I call you all to witness, it is a murder, not a duel.'

Swift as thought, the surgeon placed Forster on the ground, stripped off his coat, and cutting away a portion of his shirt, which was saturated with blood, disclosed an ugly wound in the shoulder. Forster, who had scarcely lost consciousness, opened his eyes with a twinge of pain, as the surgeon began to probe the wound for the bullet. It was the work of a moment; for the lead, after striking and partially fracturing the bone, had embedded itself in the fleshy part of the arm.

'It is not so bad as I feared,' said the surgeon; 'but it was not fairly done.'

'It was most foully done,' cried Sutherland, springing up and facing Gavrolles, who had approached and stood very pale, looking on. 'Monsieur Gavrolles, it is now my turn. You shall fight *me!*'

'I shall do nothing of the kind,' returned the Frenchman, turning on his heel.

'But you *shall!*' Sutherland exclaimed, seizing him by the arm and whirling him savagely round. 'If you do not, I will shoot you like a dog.'

As he spoke he stooped and picked up Forster's undischarged pistol, and covered Gavrolles, who cowered and shook like a leaf.

'I repeat, my friend has fallen by foul play. You fired too soon—ah I I know the old device of scoundrels like yourself. I demand satisfaction.'

Here the Chevalier thought it time to interfere.

'If that is so, *I* am at your service.'

'All in good time, but my business is first with the assassin. I appeal to you as his second and a man of honour. Was it a fair duel?'

The Chevalier scowled and looked uneasily from one to another.

'It was a mistake, doubtless,' he said; 'your principal was so slow.'

'It was no mistake; it was a *ruse*. He shall fight me—by God he shall!'

The Chevalier turned to Gavrolles.

'What do you say?'

Gavrolles shrugged his shoulders.

'The man is mad—I have no quarrel with him—nevertheless, if he wishes to be served like his companion— —'

'No, it is impossible,' said the Chevalier. 'An affair of honour must be conducted according to the code. Even if my friend consented to this preposterous arrangement, you would have to be properly represented, and, there being no second present, I decline, on my friend's account.'

But here the little surgeon, who had carefully drest Forster's wound, and placed him carefully and comfortably in a sitting posture against a large fragment of stone, leapt up in excitement.

'Pardon, monsieur! I am here, and I will act as the English monsieur's second.'

'You?' exclaimed the Chevalier.

'Yes, Beauvoisin, I! I saw it all, and I repeat—it was not a duel, but an assassination.'

'Monsieur, take care!'

'Do you take care, Beauvoisin!' screamed the little man fiercely. 'I refuse to be a party to a cheat, either with pistols or cards.'

More high words ensued, and the two combatants seemed likely to fly at each other's throats, when Gavrolles, who saw Sutherland still ready to fire upon him if he attempted to leave the ground, seized his second angrily by the arm.

'It is enough—I will fight the scoundrel. If he falls he will have himself to blame.'

So at last it was arranged. Gavrolles' pistol was reloaded, while Sutherland still retained the weapon undischarged by Forster. The ground was measured; the men took their places, and the seconds stood aside, ready to give the signal.

It was arranged this time that 'three' only should be counted, and the moment the last number was given the men were to fire.

Sutherland stood cold and collected; Gavrolles, this time, shook violently, and seemed to lose his self-possession.

'Stop!' he cried, just as the second prepared to count.

'No! It is infamous! I will not fight again.'

And he threw down his pistol.

'A coward,' said Sutherland; 'I thought so!'

But the fire-eating Chevalier now walked over, lifted the weapon, and handed it back to his principal.

'On the contrary, you *must* fight now,' he said grimly. 'If not, I shall proclaim you to be what the Englishman calls you, a coward.'

With one fierce glare into his friend's face, Gavrolles snatched the pistol, uttered an execration, and again took his stand facing Sutherland.

The Chevalier walked back to his place.

'One—two—three!'

Before the last number was uttered, Gavrolles had raised his pistol; but Sutherland, who had watched him keenly, was as quick as he. The weapons were discharged simultaneously, and one sharp report rang out in the air.

Sutherland stood unscathed, though the bullet had almost grazed his brow. Gavrolles, with a stifled scream, threw up his arms, and fell forward on his face—shot through the heart.

CHAPTER XLIV
'JANE PEARTREE.'

The stream of my narrative, instead of lingering round that group of excited duellists on the French coast, turns again back to England, and to that place of refuge which the wandering woman, 'Jane Peartree,' found in the extremity of her distress.

After her first night under the roof of Mount Eden, and after her first wild impulse to rise and fly on and on, she subsided into a kind of restless slumber, accompanied with violent shivering and nausea, and before twenty-four hours had passed violent fever had set in. Over the details of this illness, which lasted many weeks, I have no intention to linger. We pass on to the period when the invalid, sufficiently convalescent to sit up in the smaller chamber to which she had been conveyed, began thoroughly to realise the fiery ordeal through which her life had passed.

It was a room overlooking the lawn and shrubberies, which, at that season, were carpeted and draped with snow; and she sat one morning, looking out—on the white ground, on the shrouded trees, on the red sun beyond, hanging like a pink balloon close to the cold and foggy marshes, through which flowed the sullen Thames.

By her side stood the French girl Adèle, who, throughout the sickness, had been her voluntary nurse, and had watched her with extraordinary tenderness and care.

'You are stronger to-day than ever, mademoiselle,' she was saying in French; 'you will soon be able to leave this room.'

The invalid sat silent, her eyes on the dreary, winter landscape, her pale beautiful face set like a mask of utter forlornness and despair; then slowly, convulsively, her bosom shook, her eyes filled, and large tears coursed silently over her cheek.

'O mademoiselle, do not weep! It breaks my heart to see you. Courage! Are you not nearly well? Ah, yes! and there will be happy days in store for you, after so great trouble.'

The invalid smiled sadly, and shook her head; then reaching out a wasted hand, she took one of the French girl's.

'Adèle!'

'Yes?'

'Did you ever care for any one very, very much? I don't mean foolishly, like young girls who think they love; but passionately, religiously, with your whole heart and soul? I do not speak of women, but of men, Adèle; though there are good women too.'

With a curiously beautiful shame Adèle turned her face away, while a faint flush crept over her face. After a moment she replied evasively:—

'There are few good men, mademoiselle.'

'But have you known none?'

'Yes, one—one only,' replied Adèle with sudden warmth, 'and I think there is no other like him in the world. Ah, mademoiselle, it is so strange that you should ask me, since he is coming here to see me this very day.'

'Tell me about him, Adèle,' said the invalid gently.

'To tell you truly all he is, mademoiselle, I should have to tell you all I have been, and then, you might hate me! But no, you are too good. I know you have never been *there*—-where he found me—in the life which is worse than hell. If you have been unfortunate, you have not-been to blame; but I—I have been a devil, tempted by a devil! Ah, yes!'

As she proceeded, the girl seemed to yield more and more to the hysterical excitement of her temperament and race. Her face went ghastly pale, her eyes swam with tears, her hands opened and shut convulsively.

'Do not speak of it,' said the other, taking her hand again gently—'since it gives you such pain.'

'No, mademoiselle, let me speak,' returned Adèle struggling with her agitation, 'but I will not speak of *that*, but of him who raised me from it and saved my life for God. Twice, mademoiselle, he came like the angel he is; the first time it was too soon; the second time I thought it was the Lord Himself, standing—ah, so beautiful!—at my bedside.'

She ceased, and, pressing her hands upon her bosom, gazed out through the window, as if indeed she saw before her the heavenly vision of which she spoke. Then, after a little time, the invalid broke the silence, saying:—

'I think I understand you. I, too, have known such a man as you describe—all goodness, all kindness—so different to the rest. But I brought great misery to him, and sometimes I think his heart must be quite broken. That is what fills me with despair.'

'Truly, mademoiselle?'

'Yes. If I could be certain that he was happy, that he had forgotten me, I should not mind.'

'Was he your lover, mademoiselle?' asked Adèle, suddenly looking into her companion's eye.

'He was my husband,' was the reply.

Adèle uttered an exclamation.

'Ah, that is different!' she cried in wonder. 'And—and—you left him, *madame?*'

'Yes, Adèle.'

'Although you loved him so much!'

'Because I loved him.'

'And does he live, *madame?*'

Again the softly summoned word 'madame,' so significant of a new curiosity and a new respect.

'Yes, he lives, unless he has died of sorrow. I brought disgrace upon him; it was unhappy for him that we ever met; and so—I left him.'

'Does he know you are *here*, madame?'

Jane Peartree started nervously; then, smiling sadly at her own terror, shook her head.

'God forbid!'

'And you are really *his wife*, madame?'

'Yes.'

Adèle walked to the window thoughtfully, and stood there continuing the conversation.

'It must be so dreadful,' she said, 'for husband and wife to part. I was never married, madame, but I understand. A little time ago I was reading in an English newspaper, of an English merchant, a rich man, whose wife left him suddenly, and no one knew why. She had been an actress in the theatre, and he had fallen in love with her upon the stage. Then, owing to some disagreement, she ran away.'

Fortunately, Adèle was not looking at her companion; otherwise she would have been startled by the change that had come over her. Leaning back in her invalid chair, with the last trace of colour faded from her cheek, and her form trembling violently, she murmured, in a voice of forced composure—

'Yes;—and did she return?'

'Ah, no, madame. The lady drowned herself that very night, and the body was afterwards found in the *Morgue*, at the police station, and identified by her husband. It was the account of the inquest which I read in the journals. Though the body had been long in the water, and was quite disfigured, the husband recognised it at once.'

'But how?'

'Easily. By the clothes upon it, and by a pair of bracelets which the gentleman's sister had given to the lady, as a birthday gift.'

The invalid uttered a low moan, and Adèle, approaching her, saw with surprise that she had fainted in her chair.

Reproaching herself for having wearied out her charge, the French girl knelt by her side, chafed her hands, and gradually drew her back to consciousness. At last opening her eyes, she shuddered violently, and shrank away as if possessed by some unaccountable terror.

'Jane! Madame! Calm yourself. It is I, Adèle. Forgive me for tiring you with my foolish chatter, since you are so weak. I will fetch you your beef-tea, and then you will be better.'

Gradually the invalid became more composed, and partook of the nourishment which the kind nurse brought to her; but she still, from time to time, seemed to fix her eyes on some sight of horror, and to tremble with secret agitation.

A little later in the day, as she sat leaning back in her chair and gazing in the fire, she heard the sound of wheels on the gravel outside. Adèle, who was at the window, uttered a joyful cry.

'Madame! it is he! it is my friend!'

A few minutes later came a message from Sister Ursula saying that Adèle was wanted below, and that during her absence the messenger, a young country girl of seventeen, was to remain in the sick room.

Adèle, with sparkling eyes and heightened colour, kissed the invalid, and departed.

A long time elapsed. Jane Peartree, with her eyes on the fire, fell into a light sleep, broken by feverish flashes of dream. She was awakened by the sound of voices at her door. Then Adèle, smiling brightly, entered, accompanied by Sister Ursula.

'I have brought my friend,' she cried, 'to speak to you before he goes. Come in, Mr. Sutherland.'

Before Jane Peartree could reply, a gentleman, hat in hand, entered the room. The invalid looked up as if startled, sat erect in her chair, and the full light of the wintry afternoon fell upon her beautiful face.

She did not recognise the gentleman, but at the first glance he, to her horror and alarm, seemed to recognise her. Turning ghastly pale, and uttering a wild exclamation, he stood and gazed upon her, as upon a spirit risen from the dead.

'What is the matter?' cried Sister Ursula, in astonishment, while Adèle Lambert stood by trembling, and Jane Peartree, startled and terrified, shrank back in her chair.

But directly the first shock of surprise was over Sutherland mastered his agitation, and quietly advanced into the room.

'It is nothing,' he said to Sister Ursula. 'Pray forgive my stupidity, but for the moment I was startled out of my self-possession by a somewhat singular resemblance.'

He added, looking steadily at Jane Peartree:—

'They tell me you have been very ill. I trust you are now almost well.'

He waited for a reply, but none came. Jane Peartree still shrank back in terror or aversion, and endeavoured to turn away her face.

'You spoke of a resemblance,' said Sister Ursula. 'What did you mean?'

Sutherland still kept his eyes upon the averted form of Jane Peartree, and saw that it trembled violently, as he replied:—

'It is scarcely worth mentioning further, for such resemblances are common; but at the first glance, this lady seemed very like a person I once knew.'

To his intense surprise, Jane Peartree now turned her eyes and looked steadily up at him. Her face was white as death, but firm and resolved. Again the peculiar likeness struck him, and he gazed in wonder; but she bore his gaze steadily, as she asked, in a low deep tone, very unlike that of her usual voice—

'Who is the person of whom you speak?'

'A lady—a married lady.'

'A friend of yours, sir?'

'Scarcely that; one whom I met on several occasions, and whose character I greatly admired.'

'Is she still living, sir?'

'No, she is dead,' answered Sutherland.

Jane Peartree turned her eyes away, and sighed heavily, while Adèle stepped to the side of the chair, and adjusted the pillows behind her head.

'Her life was unhappy,' Sutherland, continued, 'and her death was very pitiful. She had just this lady's eyes, her hair, even something of her voice. If a human being could rise from the grave, I should say this lady was the same; that I know is impossible. Ah! if she only lived—if I could only see her again—if I could only tell her of what has passed since she died!'

As he spoke, he quietly watched the invalid, and saw that she was still greatly agitated. Eager to spare her pain, though still strangely curious and suspicious, he changed the conversation, and talked lightly for some minutes to Adèle and Sister Ursula. Finally he glanced towards the door, and held out his hand to the invalid.

'Good-night,' he said.

'Good-night, sir,' said Jane Peartree, not turning her face again.

'Good-night, Adèle,' he said, smiling.

'Good-night, monsieur,' answered Adèle, looking at him with bright, almost worshipping eyes; then, lifting his hand to her lips, she kissed it gently.

Accompanied by Sister Ursula, Sutherland descended to the lower part of the house, and entered a small sitting-room, or office, reserved for the superior's private use.

'Tell me something more of your invalid,' he said quickly. 'I feel rather interested in her. What did you say was her name?'

'Jane Peartree.'

'Jane Peartree?'

'Yes; but it may be assumed. I have noticed one thing which I may tell you in confidence. The initials on the clothes she wore when she came here are quite different.'

'Indeed.'

'Not "J. P."—but "M. F."'

Sutherland started in new surprise.

'Impossible!' he exclaimed.

'Yes, "M. F." Do you know any person with those initials? Who was the person to whom you referred upstairs?'

Sutherland's reply was singular.

'I cannot tell you; not, at least, to-night. Promise me, however, before I go, that this lady—she is a lady, that is clear, and very different to the usual inmates of the Home—shall not go away from Mount Eden until you hear from me again. In the meantime assure her, should she question you, that I have *not* recognised her.'

'That you have not recognised her?' echoed Sister Ursula, puzzled and anxious.

'Just so. It is important that you should not alarm her; it is equally important that she should not be lost sight of, if what I suspect is possible.'

'But can you not explain?'

'Do not ask me to-night. As soon as I can I will write—or come to you. Pray trust me in this matter; it is a sort of miracle, not quite comprehended even by myself.'

'As you please,' returned Sister Ursula, smiling, 'since you are determined to be inscrutable.'

CHAPTER XLV
AN OLD PICTURE

And now before I go,' said Sutherland, changing his manner, 'I have something for you: I think it will be a surprise. Look there!'

So speaking, he took out a pocket-book and drew from it a cheque for fifty pounds, payable to 'bearer.'

'I see,' said Sister Ursula; 'another contribution to Mount Eden. Ah! you are indefatigable.'

'I assure you this is quite a windfall; I did not even shake the tree. Look at the signature. Do you know it? 5 '"Hubert Lagardère." No!' 'Lagardère, the editor of the "Plain Speaker."' Sister Ursula raised her eyebrows and lifted her hands.

'That man! Why, I thought— —'

'And so did I,' cried Sutherland, laughing. 'So thorough a worldling did I think him, that I have been twice on the point of horsewhipping him. Well, I was sitting yesterday morning in my rooms when he was shown in. It turned out afterwards that he had seen my name connected in some way with this institution. He entered mysteriously, carefully closed the door, and before I could address him he handed me that cheque, with the intimation that it was to be paid over to you. "It seems to me rather a good sort of idea," he said in his drawling way; "so I have brought you a trifle I won from Banbri Pasha last night at nap."

"Really, Mr. Lagardère," I said, "I didn't give you credit for so much sympathy with misfortune." I added: "I shall have much pleasure in making public acknowledgment of your liberality." As I spoke the words he trembled violently and clutched me by the arm.' 'How singular!' said Sister Ursula.

'"For God's sake," he cried, "do nothing of the kind."

"Excuse me," I said, "it is only just. To be frank, I, in common with many others, have held your style of journalism in the utmost detestation. In one case, at least, I know you have helped to wreck a human life; it is only fair to proclaim that you are perhaps penitent, and— —"

He interrupted me with an expletive. "Nothing of the sort," he exclaimed; "I don't profess to be a saint, and I won't have my character taken away. Damme, sir, what would the readers of the 'Plain Speaker' think, if they thought I had any commonplace compunctions? They'd all go back to the 'Whirligig,' vote me a molly-coddle, and, as a journalist, I should be ruined." So I took the cheque, on the condition that I should not disturb the public in its happy confidence in the moral perversity of the donor.'

Sister Ursula joined heartily in Sutherland's laughter.

'Well,' she said, 'you have certainly discovered a phenomenon. Most men, even some good men, like to have their charities written large for the world to read; whereas Mr. Lagardère is actually ashamed of a good action.'

'After all,' answered Sutherland, as they shook hands, 'he is what the world has made him. In a society which sets success above goodness, and despises any kind of sentiment, he poses as a Cockney Mephistopheles. For the future I shall never think of him without calling up the lines of Burns:—

> Then fare-thee-weel, auld Nickie-Ben,
> Ah, wad you tak' a thoucht, and men'!
> You aiblins might—I dinna ken—
> Still hae a stake!
> I'm wae to think upon yon den,
> E'en for *your* sake!

For "den" substitute "journal," and the allusion—though not the rhyme—would be perfect. I, for one, am "wae to think" of the diabolic journalism of the period, even for the sake of—Lagardère!'

As Sutherland hurried away through the night, driving to catch a late train at a lonely railway station seven miles from Mount Eden, his thoughts were not of Lagardère and the newest thing in journalism, but of her whom that man and that system had helped to destroy. A wild suspicion, deepening almost to certainty, and based upon the extraordinary resemblance between Madeline Forster and the woman calling herself Jane Peartree, had complete possession of his mind. Strange and impossible as it seemed, he could not shake away the belief that Jane Peartree was, in flesh or spirit, the living image of the woman whose death he had avenged on the body of Gavrolles.

It may be *a propos*, at this point, to allay the reader's curiosity as to what took place at Boulogne after Gavrolles fell by Sutherland's hand. Of course there was an inquiry and a great scandal—duels with fatal terminations being very unusual in these days. Forster lay at the hotel slowly recovering from his wound, under surveillance. Sutherland was under arrest for some hours, and was only released on giving substantial pledges to appear when called upon. For a time it seemed likely that a prosecution of a serious nature would ensue; but money and influence were brought to bear on the authorities, and the two Englishmen were eventually suffered, whilst the police pretended to 'look another way,' to cross the Channel.

After the death of Gavrolles, Forster seemed to resign himself more and more to melancholic prostration; and more than once when his wound was slowly healing, he avowed his regret that it was not to have a fatal termination. He would sit for days in a sort of mental stupor, scarcely looking up when spoken to, seldom or never uttering a word. On his return to England, instead of again occupying his house at Kensington, he took chambers near Bond Street for himself and his little son, and had the family mansion closed. His sister Margaret wished to remain with him, but at his strong desire she went away to dwell with some relations in the country. To tell the truth, he had not quite forgiven her the want of sympathy she had shown for the lost idol of his life.

The morning after his return from Mount Eden, Sutherland found Forster, sad, despairing, but convalescent, in his lonely chambers. The two had by this time become great friends, or more than friends; and Sutherland was welcomed with as bright a smile as the weary face could wear.

'I have been looking over some old photographs,' said Forster presently. 'Strange! how they one and all fail to represent her I have lost. Here is one of "Imogen." The features are there, but the soul is altogether wanting.'

Sutherland glanced over the pictures, which were lying on a small writing-table at Forster's side; then he said quietly—

'Do you think it wise to open up old wounds in this way? Can you not try to forget?'

'Never, never!' returned Forster, while his eyes filled with tears. 'My only comfort, *now*, is to think of my darling—to wait and pray until, with God's blessing, we meet again.'

'Can you bear to speak of her, *now*?'

'Yes.'

'Could you bear to think it possible that, after all, you might yet meet— not up yonder in the heaven of the preacher, but here, on solid earth, in broad day?'

'What do you mean!' cried Forster, trembling violently. 'Alas, she is dead! dead!'

'The dead have once risen. Might they not rise again?'

CHAPTER XLVI
HOW MADELINE ROSE AGAIN

A few days after Edgar Sutherland's visit to Mount Eden, Jane Peartree walked out for the first time after her illness into the sun. She wore the plain cap and gown of the other inmates of the Home, and even in that simple costume (or rather, perhaps, because of it) she looked strangely beautiful. Leaning on the arm of Adèle Lambert, she passed feebly across the green lawn in front of the house, and gained a garden seat in a quiet walk leading to the home farm.

The day was very mild for winter tide, the sun was shining gently, and here and there from the dark earth a snowdrop was peeping. The air, moreover, was full of that cool, balmy sweetness which so often in our chill climate precedes the resurrection of the spring.

But Jane Peartree was ill at ease. Ever since her encounter with Sutherland she had been strangely fretful and uneasy, and had not her strength failed she would certainly have taken her departure before that day.

As they sat together on the window-seat, her cry was still for speedy flight.

'I must go to-morrow!—yes, Adèle, to-morrow! I have already stayed too long!'

'But, madame, you are still so weak. Why should you go so soon?'

'I cannot stay! I have so far to go,—and—and I shall go mad, I think, if I remain. You are all kind—kinder than I deserve—but it is not that! No, no!' 'But *where* will you go, madame? Have you not told me you have no home—no friends?'

'I have none—I want none,' returned Jane Peartree; 'but all the same, I must leave this place. Here, I feel like a dead woman in her shroud, dead and cold, but being forced back to life, just when I would be left alone to rest for ever. I do not feel at peace. In the night I cannot sleep, and in the day I am afraid. Why should I be sitting here in the sunshine, when by rights I should be lying in my grave?'

Adèle looked at her companion in deep sorrow and pain, and wondered, indeed, if her wits were going, since her words were so incomprehensible and strange. Just then, as they sat side by side, there passed across the lawn, some hundred yards away, the figure of a man, at the sight of whom Adèle brightened, and said, forcing a smile:—

'Sister Ursula tells me your name is uncommon, even in England; yet you have a namesake yonder, madame.'

'A namesake?' repeated Jane Peartree.

'Yes; one of the gardeners upon the estate. That is he crossing to the shrubberies.'

Jane Peartree turned her weary eyes towards the man, and in a moment her heart leapt up in wondering recognition, her pale face flushed, and she uttered a low cry. Who that had once seen it could fail to remember the little, quaint, old-fashioned figure, the curious gait, of Luke Peartree? Yes, it was Uncle Luke, greyer and older than when, long years before, he led little Madeline home from Grayfleet Churchyard, but still living—'to brighten the sunshine.'

'Quick! call him! I must speak to him!' cried the invalid, rising faintly to her feet.

Adèle ran off instantly after the man, who had disappeared into the shrubberies. Presently she reappeared, the little gnome-like figure trotting by her side. As he came up, clad in homespun and leather gaiters, and carrying a pruning-hook, his wrinkled face expanded into the vacant wondering smile that was so familiar.

What was his surprise to see a strange woman, tall and pale, standing with extended arms, gazing upon him through streaming tears?

'Uncle Luke! don't you know me?'

Uncle Luke stood and scratched his head, smiling, more amicably than ever, the smile of honest stupefaction. Before he could utter a word, which, indeed, he was in no hurry to do, the strange woman had flung her arms around his neck, and, sobbing and crying, was kissing him upon the cheek.

'Uncle Luke! it is I—Madeline!'

The little man staggered as if under a blow, and went quite pale.

'Madlin!' he cried. 'Not little Madlin as I brung to London! Why, lor', so it be!'

And at a loss for any other means of expressing his utter bewilderment and delight, he grinned from ear to ear.

Very pretty it was, as well as pitiful, to see Madeline (whom we shall call by her assumed name no longer) lead the little man to the garden seat, sit by his side, hold his hand, and look fondly in his eyes, as she questioned him, lifting his rough hand to kiss it from time to time. The weight of years, the burden of sorrow, had rolled away from her in a moment, and she was a child again, while the heaven that 'bends above us in our infancy' was opening over her—bright, tranquil, peaceful, and divine.

Meantime, poor Uncle Luke seemed too stupefied to understand completely what was taking place. He sat blushing and grinning, scarcely able to recognise, in the beautiful, full-grown woman fondling him, the little Madlin of his remembrance; and indeed that remembrance was sadly clouded, like the rest of his feeble mind, by the mists of years. When she told him how diligently and how often she had sought to trace him, when she questioned him as to the reasons which had prevented him from seeking her out, he had little or no reply to give. She gathered, however, that he had been for years in the service of a distant kinsman, who was a head gardener on the estate.

It was destined to be a day of strange surprises. As Madeline sat by Uncle Luke, her face wet with happy tears, two gentlemen approached along the garden wall behind her. Adèle saw them first, and was about to utter a delighted cry, when the younger of the two placed his finger to his lips to enjoin silence. Thus it happened that, before Madeline knew or suspected the truth, she saw her husband standing before her, gazing upon her with wistful, wondering eyes; and before she could stir or speak she beheld him kneeling beside her, sobbing wildly, touching her with his outstretched hand.

'Madeline! My darling!'

She rose wildly to her feet, looking this way and that, as if in act to fly. Uncle Luke rose too, completely puzzled, till Adèle beckoned him away. So it came to pass that the other three walked aside, and the husband and wife were left alone.

'Madeline! speak to me; my Madeline, my own dear wife!'

She shuddered at the last word, and made a feeble attempt to withdraw from his embrace; but at last, sobbing hysterically, she yielded, and suffered him, with tenderest kisses, to place her head upon his breast.

EPILOGUE

In that manner, and in no other, Madeline rose from the grave.

When the first shock of meeting was over, and calmer speech was possible, Forster told his wife of the duel on Boulogne sands and the death of her persecutor at the hands of Edgar Sutherland; thus assuring her that, whether the marriage with Gavrolles was real or a delusion, she was then a free woman. She listened sadly, and seemed little comforted, until Forster assured her of his intention, with her consent, to quit England, and seek some country where the story of their sorrows was unknown, and where the viperous journal of the period has not yet begun to crawl. Then she again laid her head upon his breast, and promised to go with him, anywhere out of the old world of scandal, cruelty, and shame.

So she lived, who had died. By her own lips the mystery of her resurrection was explained. She told him how, while flying in despair, she had encountered the poor waif of the streets, and in some wild impulse of dread, fearing pursuit, and wishing to destroy all traces of identity, she had taken the shawl from her shoulders, bracelets from her wrists, and given them to her outcast sister. The rest was clear. Mad with drink and misery, the outcast must have yielded to death's fascination, and cast herself away into the river—whence, long afterwards, her disfigured body was taken to be identified by Forster and buried, as the reader is aware.

Madeline lived again. She still lives, but far away from the scene of her martyrdom. Sometimes in the course of his wanderings (for he is still a wanderer and unmarried) Edgar Sutherland visits a pleasant home on the bank of a great American river, where a happy wife and husband are growing old together among their children. There he is ever an honoured guest, certain of having attentive auditors while he discourses, more garrulously as years creep on, on his pet theme—the purification of manhood and the regeneration of womankind.

Uncle Luke is yonder, too. At Madeline's strong entreaty, he accompanied her from England; and now, very old and feeble, but still bright and simple as ever, he goes hand in hand through the woods and fields, with another 'little Madlin,' the very image of the little girl he used to love so well. For a long time he hardly seemed to recognise in the gentle woman who took him to her home the pretty Madeline of other years; but when the child came, he, a child himself, found his happiness in her, and recognised the vision of his old playmate, re-risen to delight his declining days.

And now, what remains to be told? The human shadows that have arisen throughout our story fade one by one away. Of only one of these, Adèle Lambert, will the reader care to hear a last record. She died in the springtime at Mount Eden, passing away, in perfect peace and faith: her spirit purified; her hand in that of the man who had pointed her upward to a holier life, her eyes on the face she had learned to regard as that of an angel, sent to succour sinners in this dark world.

This world remains as most men find it; a tomb, save for those superb spirits who come to bless the wretcheder dwellers in it, with deeds of beautiful self-sacrifice and words of divine love. In the depth of its darker recesses, still the snake-like seducer slimes his victim, and the slanderer spits his venom, and the literature of the Liar still festers like a feverish sore, spreading moral sickness and contamination all around. Thence, and thence only, comes the voice which would fain proclaim to the unhappy that there is no God, and but one gospel—'Eat and drink, for tomorrow you die.' But God is, as sure as Love is, or Hope, or heavenly Purity and Light. Therefore let no man despair, though now, as ever, 'the Light shineth in Darkness, and the Darkness comprehendeth it not.'